At a very early age, Morgan Leone had a deep fascination and love for story-telling; by six, Morgan would tell everyone that one day she would be an author. Growing up in London, Ontario, Morgan completed her master's in arts, focusing her interests on the Southern United States and the sublime and the beautiful, and was accepted into the doctorate program in English at the University of Western Ontario. Embracing the south in all of its glory and shame, it became inevitable that Morgan's first novel would have the characters in her book live and breathe the southern life.

Morgan Leone

SINCE WE ALL HAVE YESTERDAYS

AUSTIN MACAULEY PUBLISHERS™

LONDON * CAMBRIDGE * NEW YORK * SHARJAH

Ordering Information
Quantity sales: Special discounts are available on quantity purchases by corporations, associations, and others. For details, contact the publisher at the address below.

Publisher's Cataloging-in-Publication data
Leone, Morgan
Since We All Have Yesterdays

ISBN 9798891550414 (Paperback)
ISBN 9798891550421 (Hardback)
ISBN 9798891550438 (ePub e-book)

Library of Congress Control Number: 2023918112

www.austinmacauley.com/us

First Published 2024
Austin Macauley Publishers LLC
40 Wall Street, 33rd Floor, Suite 3302
New York, NY 10005
USA

mail-usa@austinmacauley.com
+1 (646) 5125767

I want to acknowledge Vivien Leigh, whose presence in my life has been felt since the day I was born. I love her, and without her, this book would never have come into fruition. She will always be a special person to me as a fellow human being, and as a writer.

Part 1

Chapter 1

October 5th 1965

The cry traveled urgently through the house like a storm siren, echoing off the walls as though the structure itself was refusing responsibility for any role it might have played in causing the pain which drove the sound. When it reached my room, I shut the door quietly, keeping the handle twisted so there would be no click as the latch bolt met the frame.

My heart pounded thick and deafening as I moved toward the block of sunlight that stained my pale carpet in late afternoons. Declining to blink, my eyes resisted the abrasive bright, and rolled backward in retreat under my heavily lashed lids. I forced them forward, welcoming the pain of my pupils shrinking, for I desired to be disoriented in a way that I, myself, had deliberately invoked.

Unfortunately, however, the sun's assault functioned only to exacerbate the panic I was willfully intending to displace. In turn, a high-pitched ringing was added to the drumline of my heartbeat, and the nausea attacking my core stole the blood from my hands and feet, rendering me helpless and immobile. All at once, the function of breathing transformed into a conscious and demanding exercise—the mechanisms of which became more slippery, foreign, and impossible by the second.

I was familiar with this struggle for air and had I not been so caught up in the shift of my reality, I might have appreciated the irony of my dilemma. Overthinking the act of breath is a luxury. When you are being crushed or choked, your panic cannot afford to work against you. It opens your airways. It squeezes oxygen into your lungs past barriers of debilitating weight on your chest or stifling vomit in your throat.

When you are surviving, breath is your only thought and it is never over thought. It simply can't be. You can only overthink the act of breathing when you are free. And in that moment, I was.

Chapter 2

October 8ᵗʰ 1965

Though I couldn't understand why my mother wasn't driving any faster, I knew better than to speak out. Surely there was a reason, likely an obvious one, and I have always hated nothing more than making a show of my own ignorance. That night was different, quite different however, being full of circumstances which might be worth being chided for thinking like the 14-year-old that I was.

Perhaps my mother was plainly too distracted to recognize that she was driving no more quickly than if we were headed home from church? I wondered if Gen knew why. Oh, surely, she must, or she would say something. She was the one who said something to begin with. No, I don't mean about driving. But it's why the three of us were in a strange car, on our way to a strange place, with only one suitcase each and no goodbyes.

I pressed my forehead against the cool window as I realized my contemplations sounded bitter. They weren't bitter though. They couldn't be bitter if I wasn't angry. Truthfully, I was grateful my sister had put an end to it, even if normally my pride would have been injured by the fact that I had not been consulted beforehand. It wasn't just her secret to tell after all, it was mine too.

Regardless, I knew Gen had not gone behind me in spite, and most of me was thankful not to have been called upon to participate in the revelation. Looking back on it, I still can't tell you if I saw it coming, but when I heard Mama cry out like a poor wounded animal, I had known what Gen's muffled condolences were for.

Chapter 3

October 6ᵗʰ 1965

It was not until the following evening that my mother acknowledged to me that she knew. She was home, uncharacteristically, when we got off the bus from school, having told my father that due to a headache Mary-Beth had insisted the sew-shop could do without her for the afternoon. When I was younger the fact that my mother worked at all had been a constant source of tension between my parents.

For the longest time, my father felt that my mother having a job made it look like he didn't provide sufficiently for the family and his threatened masculinity made him volatile. Whenever there was nothing else for him to be angry at, he would start into her about how she was bringing shame on the family for not knowing that 'a woman's place was in the home.'

This was one of the many reasons he used as an excuse to strike her—a cross she bore with a silent type of dignity I still cannot fathom. When I was small, I would howl for her, confused at why she showed no sign of pain which the marks would reflect. Gen would coax or drag me away, explaining best as a child could that crying from anyone only made him angrier.

She was only two years older than me, but I regarded her with the degree of respect generally reserved for those in authority. He never hit us, and Mama was satisfied to bear the brunt of his constant discontent at the expense of herself. He was 'father' to both of us but 'daddy' only to me.

What I mean is, Gen didn't remember her real daddy at all, and even if she wanted to know him, Mama wouldn't let her. He had hurt Gen when she was just a baby, and it must have been something awful because she left that man and never looked back.

She explained to Gen that he wasn't a bad man, but that the war had changed him in a way where the person that she'd fallen in love with as a girl was gone forever. She mourned the loss of him like a widow, never expecting to fall in love again. She must have liked my father though, or at least trusted him, because she married him—something she never got around to doing with Gen's daddy.

Charles Mair was a Virginia man, fifteen years my mother's senior with a steady job and a nice house. He had accepted Gen like she was his own, and if he hadn't, my mother's interest in him would have waned before she had a ring on her finger, and I had the chance to be born. Everyone thought my mama looked like Scarlett O'Hara, and she was not out of touch with her superior appearance.

Being from Maryland, she carried within her the social conscientiousness of the Northeast and the stubborn fiery disposition of the South. Though she didn't necessarily want a man, nor to belong to one, she was acutely aware that the world around her believed she and her child required one. My mother was far prettier than my father was handsome, and he knew this. He was conflicted inside about the admiration he received for marrying a woman with a face and figure like hers.

Some days he would revel in the compliments and stares he received with her on his arm, others, he would grow resentful. When his insecurities got the best of him, he would always remind Mama of the roof over her head and clothes on her back and how nobody else would have wanted her, having had Gen. I think these degrading speeches were among the many reasons why she stopped liking him.

Working at the sew-shop made her feel like she could survive on her own if she wanted to, though most of the money she made went to paying Henrietta, our Negro housekeeper. This drove my father crazy; it made no sense to him to pay someone for the job he married my mother to do. There was nothing in it for him, Mama working, not for the longest time that is, and for a man who viewed life as a game of win and lose this was intolerable.

When I was eleven and Gen was thirteen, my father announced at dinner that he was letting Henrietta go. Naturally, my mother protested, suspecting behind his decision was a tactic to make her submit to the role of housewife she had rejected since shortly after my birth. This was not his rationale however, as he further explained that Gen and I were 'young women now' and old enough to take up the chores previously expected of Henrietta.

My face became hot with sadness at the thought of losing her. She had been our maid for as far back as my memory went. It was she who had nursed me back from fevers, taught me how to lace my shoes and all about the rhythm and blues music I had integrated into my soul. Like Gen always warned, tears were a source of great agitation for my father, and he accused me of crying out of laziness rather than recognizing the grief from which my tears were born.

I looked to my mother to support my heartfelt qualms, but since it had dawned upon her that this change did not entail her quitting the sew-shop, her dissent had faded and alone I stood in my stance of refute. I knew Gen felt the same way as I did, and that Henrietta was just as much family to her as she was to me, but my sister's manners counted her out on such occasions.

Occasions, that is, when outwardly challenging my father's assertations were necessary. My mother always told me to 'pick my battles' when it came to him, and oh how I wished *she* would pick that one. But she didn't and everything changed. Truly everything. That moment in time is one of those that sticks with you for all your life, and when you call it forward, it dances forth with the vividness of yesterday, no matter how many years have built up between then and now.

So many questions are attached to that particular incident for me. Was it a plan? Did he let her go to open the door for his actions, or did the door open and then the opportunity inspire him? If my mother had picked that battle as I so desired her to, would it have all been different? I guess the better question is, would I choose it to be? I suppose most people ask themselves this when they stand before God, sorting their experiences into stockpiles of blessings and curses.

It's then that you notice how you can't untangle them, no matter how hard you try; if you take a curse away a blessing often goes too. You also see how blessings are worth so much more than the curses in the end, even if they are outnumbered. That's what makes life so complicated, and the question of whether I would change my past impossible to answer. The chain reaction that creates destiny is certainly a fickle weave, and who would I be to make that call?

Chapter 4

Midnight, October 8th 1965

"If I drive too fast it could draw attention to us," my mother said as if she had heard the exact question I had been anxiously pondering. I was caught off guard by her intuitive commentary and momentarily afraid I had spoken aloud my concern.

"The last thing we need is to be pulled over by a patrol officer—you know how they are when they have nothing better to do. Even being noticed could ruin everything."

She struggled to maintain a steady tone and wrung the wheel under the tight grip of both her hands, white knuckled.

"Your father will start looking as soon as it comes to his attention, and when he sends out his inquiries, I want no one to be able to call to mind this car with the three of us in it. I pray we have until the morning when his shift is over; by then we should be in Andrews."

She paused for a moment and drew a breath that shook as it exhaled through her lips pursed with equal part fright and determination.

"He is going to think we're headed north across the river to Nana's. I want to keep it that way. I will keep it that way. I know it seems counter intuitive to drive so leisurely, but it's the way it must be. You know what they say, slow and steady wins the race."

My mother always used extravagant words like 'counter intuitive' they rolled off her tongue casually making her seem exotic and untouchable. I used to assume that when I grew up, my vocabulary would be as expansive, and that this linguistic sophistication came part and parcel with maturity. As a means to solidify the inevitability of this, I made a habit of parroting the words back to her in perfunctory rhetorical responses that I felt mirrored her cleverness.

"Oh no Mama. It doesn't seem counter intuitive. Not at all. I understand. How about I lay down back here so if someone does spot us, they only see you

14

and Gen. That way they won't know it was us since they'd be expecting a car with three in it not just two."

A satisfaction rose up in me at the thought of my idea, which I felt to be rather revolutionary; but it was quickly sabotaged by Gen who let out a short laugh from the front.

"I don't think that will make that much of a difference," she retorted, glancing briefly over her shoulder in dismissive amusement.

I despised how she never took me seriously and would oftentimes console myself by reasoning that she was jealous of my forward thinking. In this case however, I was unsure, and for that my heart sank a little. I felt all the more inclined to defend my suggestion, but my mother took it up before I had the chance.

"You know what, Kim? I think that's a fine idea. Are you sure you would be comfortable? We don't want to put you out or for you to start feeling unwell. I suspect we have another five hours to go."

My cheeks flushed with my mother's validation, though five hours did seem like a rather long time not to be able to look outside.

"It's really no trouble at all. I'll sit up once we are across state lines. Don't worry about me Mama." I spoke confidently as to conceal my dismay at the length of drive we still had ahead and pulled off my sweater to use behind my head as a makeshift pillow.

The upholstery was smooth on my bare arms, and as I shifted my weight, I disturbed the scent of cigarette smoke embedded in the gray vinyl seat. Both of my parents smoked, but it was a rule of my father's that neither he nor my mother were to smoke in the family car. He wanted it to smell new forever and would trade it in at the first olfactory sign of deterioration.

Whoever owned this car before my mama got it for us must not have cared about such things. Now, I had the chance to realize I didn't either.

Chapter 5

October 6th 1965

It was that time late in the day when trees look like charcoal etches carved into the canvas of the dimming sky when I was alerted to Mama's presence by her sigh outside my bedroom door. It had been slightly more than twenty-four hours since her cry had risen up from the kitchen and I had spent the time wrapped in anxiety distantly ruminating.

I did so while actively avoiding any direct meditation on the feelings or reaction I might be faced with when she finally did. This was an unconscious strategy I had gainfully employed over the past three years. Not once during that time had I let my mind wander to what my mother might think. Only to that she must not know.

Because of this, I never got close enough to recognizing the feasibility of her gaining awareness, or close enough to imagine what would or could happen if she did. There was no 'if' to me, for telling her was no more of an option than going to the moon. What I mean is, you don't wake up in the morning and consider going to the moon instead of to school.

Perhaps if you are feeling both weary and daring enough you might consider sticking the thermometer under a lamp and claiming a fever, but you don't ever mull over going to the moon instead of boarding the school bus. Indeed, telling my mother had no more occurred to me than the idea of ditching school for space travel. It was not that I chose to not tell her, there was no choice involved because there was, in my perception, no possibility.

You know as well as I that a person can spend a lifetime looking at the moon and not once contemplate visiting it.

Possibility, of course, precedes choice, and the neatly compartmentalized landscape of my eleven-to-fourteen-year-old mind had provided no fertile ground within its developing and uncompromising organization for the possibility of telling my mother to take root. Still, I had known the reason for her cry when I had heard it, I had known instinctively without thought.

The answer existed before I had the time to ask the question to myself. How could it be that I knew the source of her anguish having never entertained the possibility of her finding out? Yet there I was, with my legs swung over the side of my bed's pink comforter, so out of my element that I might have been on the aforementioned rock in the sky, knowing what was to come about.

It set in quickly that not only had I adequately failed to anticipate and prepare for my mother's thoughts, feelings, and reaction, but that ultimately, despite my ruminations, I had neglected to take into account the true depth of my own confused and long tempered emotions as raw variables of the scene.

Two spheres of my life, intended by the creator of their separateness to forever rotate each other without contact were colliding before me and within me all at once. Like the seasons bleed together, so did I.

As my mother crossed the threshold into my room, I initially set my gaze upon the carpet, and in doing so, became abruptly conscious of my size, noticing how my feet grazed its plush surface without me stretching my toes. In light of this, I made the bold choice to look at her earnestly when she sat down next to me, and my searching eyes found that she had not yet registered how my legs were nearly as long as hers.

Over time, I have wondered whether it was because, in that moment, I sensed how my mother viewed me as a child that I became acutely aware of perceiving myself as a woman, or whether it was because I perceived myself as a woman that I was able to discern my mother's view of me as a girl?

Regardless, I was humbled and comforted by the lens through which I intuited she was seeing, understanding, and loving me as a child; and no matter how skewed I feared it to be I did not wish to change it. A desire to alter what I felt to be my unworthiness was added to the shroud of shame that already hung over the pantomime of us like heavy musty curtains that suspend night indefinitely.

"Oh Kim," she began, her voice filled with pity and regret, that although uncomfortable to receive, indicated she did not feel betrayed by me.

Only with the allocation of this relief was my fear that she would blame me able to be internally articulated. The feeling had been so paralyzing, its translation into thought had been stunted as to preserve myself—my psyche and my heart.

Tipping her chin toward the ceiling, Mama closed her eyes in a fleeting beatified stance conducive to spontaneous prayer. With a sigh as deep as the one which had signaled her arrival outside my door, she shifted her body toward me, and put her hand on the slippery comforter between us, as if to smooth its already unwrinkled fabric.

"I got a car for us this afternoon. It's nothing special of course, but it's a car for you, me and Gen. I'm taking you girls and we are leaving Virginia. I don't know where yet, but I will tonight. I'm going to fix this, and it will all be in the past. Do you trust that your Mama's going to make it better?"

I had been skating along the surface of her words; hearing them but not absorbing them. I was too anxious and planned to revisit them when I was alone. Though I could repeat verbatim, what she had said, I had not internalized them, and therefore my response to her question reflected merely my desire to please her, to atone her guilt, and protect her feelings.

I managed to utter, "Of course, I trust you, Mama."

Afterwards, when I played back her words in my mind, I realized there was in fact no one, not one single person I could think of in the world, that I trusted to 'make it better'. It was part of why she never was to know. Why no one was.

My father had told me how he could kill us all and no one would suspect him. He was above the law. Hell, he was the law, and we were below it. He knew it and he figured Gen knew too, I guess. Did my mother understand the danger?

If she did, then reminding her of it would make matters no easier. She knew his job. If she didn't comprehend the full extent of the danger, would she change her mind when she did? Was it my place to reinforce the idea to her?

I quickly went over the first part of what she had said: "I'm taking you girls and we're leaving Virginia."

I wanted to go. I wanted out, to get away from him, from all of it. I couldn't tell her. What if she changed her mind? I could not let that happen. I had never contemplated freedom, I had never looked at the possibilities outside of my circumstance, and now that I had—beginning with that mournful cry through the house and now confirmed with her words—no other option would do.

Thankfully, fate favored my inclinations, for by the time I had processed the overtures of my predicament, Mama had already hugged me long hard and without breath. She had already exited into the hallway from which her sigh had been released, made her way through the kitchen from where her cry had risen up, and was on her way to seek crucial counsel from the one whose absence had started it all. Henrietta.

No, I did not believe Mama could make it better. Like I said, I did not believe anybody could. With, however, that specific type of curiosity void of all frivolous connotations I involuntarily imagined how leaving could stop it all from getting worse and this threadbare hope was instinctively enough for me to wager my trust, what I perceived to be my life, and the lives of those I loved the most. This time, saying nothing could help set me free. So, I hung tight to my silence.

October 8th 1965

My father's shift started at nine o'clock pm and my mother wasted no time, as there was none, to share her plan with me and Gen. We were leaving. Two days before she had met with Henrietta who had, yesterday, upon hearing the news of the abuse, arranged a home for us via her cousin who was a chef in a small town called Andrews, South Carolina.

Mama had also secured a car for us with her savings which she had been storing in Mary-Beth's driveway for the last day, who was going to be dropping it off at ten o'clock for us to make our getaway in. She wanted to be out of the house no later than eleven so we had two hours to gather our thoughts and sparse of belongings as possible into one suitcase each so that would fit into the car.

Upon the news, my head began spinning, as though I were in tune with the rotation of the world. This was the better she was talking to me about; I just didn't expect it to come so suddenly.

"Henrietta's cousin works at a restaurant where I'll be able to have a job, I already have a meeting set up with the head waitress. She arranged this all in one day for us. She also knew of the house we will be staying in on the outskirts of the negro neighborhood that just went up for rent last week and secured it for us to stay in. The key will be under the front mat upon our arrival.

"I have no idea what I'm getting us into, but I know what I'm getting us out of, and I won't stand by one more minute and allow him to ever touch you girls again. Whatever this place be, will be better than here and what you've been enduring. If it's horrible, we will go from there and move along. What's important is there is not here. I'm so sorry to spring this on you so abruptly, but in my mind there was no time to waste and Henrietta was in full agreeance.

19

"She was absolutely furious when I told her what had been happening to you two, I was afraid she was going to go and confront your father. Instead, she channeled her rage into productivity and helped to orchestrate us being able to flee as quickly as possible. My instincts are telling me we are doing the right thing. But here I am rambling on when we need to be preparing. Are you up for all this or is it too much?"

Both Gen and I stood there awe struck in the kitchen, shell shocked in a sense.

Gen cleared her throat, "I'm ready to get out of here. I'll go start packing right away," was all she said.

My mouth was dry as a southwestern desert, but I managed to spit out, "So, we'll never see Henrietta again?" my eyes robbed the moisture missing from my mouth.

Even though she wasn't our housekeeper any longer, I still visited her rather regularly, and was dismayed at this particular loss.

"I'm afraid not, sweetheart. She told me to tell you how proud she was of you for being strong, and to give you a big hug from her to you. Come here," she said and embraced me lovingly.

"Well, I want to keep making her proud. So, I better go get packing, too, I guess," I said into my mother's ear as she held me.

"That's my girl," she gave me an extra tight squeeze before letting me go.

Part 2

Chapter 6

October 8th 1965

She covered the sheets with the only blankets we'd brought for me and Gen: the quilts our Nana had sewn for us for our 8th birthdays. They were non-negotiable items to bring as we loved our grandmother from Maryland very much; indeed, as much as our father despised her. The feelings had been mutual.

We knew if we left them behind, he'd likely burn them or do something of the sort for revenge so both Gen and I—well mostly me, but Gen did chime in—begged to cram them in the trunk, which we thoughtfully ended up lining it with. I could see the sunlight starting to peak below the beige window coverings as my eyelids were growing uncontrollably heavy (and not from my thick lashes).

I had so many things I wanted to discuss with Gen, but they would have to wait, as I was asleep no longer than two minutes in Mama's freshly made new old bed.

I had a dream. I dreamed that a great storm hit Andrews and washed away our little dusty blue house. Somehow, this led to our father finding us and I remember thinking 'we are as good as dead', but thankfully, my mind spared me the consequences of what that death would look like, and I woke up. This time, the sunlight was billowing out from the side and bottoms of the curtains, and Gen was not beside me.

"Ugh!" I exclaimed aloud.

I had wanted to be the first one up, or at least to get up together. I didn't even bother changing out of my pajamas before taking the five whole steps it took to make it into the kitchen. The kitchen comprised of a narrow sink, a minuscule slab of counterspace, an ancient looking oven and an outdated fridge. Down way of this in a connected narrow enclave was a tiny round table set, looking as though it were made for a dollhouse with its size.

There Gen sat, dressed and ready for her day, and she looked up from her bowl to say, "What's the story, morning glory?" This was a favorite adage in my family as my middle name was Morgan which meant 'morning'.

"I overslept," I said, slipping into the chair across from hers.

"Nonsense!" said my mother, "You mightn't' have slept all day and you wouldn't have overslept! But now that you're up, how about some breakfast? I managed to bring a pot among our few treasures, and I made oatmeal with extra lumps just for you, my darling."

It was true, I liked my oatmeal with extra lumps, but this had just started a few years ago. I used to like cream of wheat. It was my favorite growing up. Suddenly, however, it started reminding me of what he used to force in my mouth and down my throat and I became unable to eat it.

Mama had wondered at this sudden change and put me through the wringer with questions which I aptly dodged until it was finally accepted that I now preferred lumpy oatmeal. Hopefully, you understand what I mean, and I need not explain more. I don't like thinking or talking about those times. Not even cream of wheat. It was history to me, now among the rest of it.

"Yes, please Mama, I'm actually starving."

"Of course you are!" Her voice was gleeful. "I'm happy to hear it. You and Gen had quite a night. All three of us did. And we have a day ahead of us getting settled in, so you need some fuel to start you off."

She smiled as she spooned two heaps of oatmeal into a bowl that thankfully must have been left in the cupboard here, along with the spoons. As I swallowed, I could feel the oatmeal sticking to my ribs. My mind was calm for a moment. I was soaking in my new reality with quiet jubilance.

"So girls, the plan for today is to acclimatize," (there Mama went with those big words) "Unpack, and we'll take a trip into town to grab some essentials and get a feel for this new place we'll be calling 'home'.

"Tomorrow, I'm to meet with Henrietta's connection, Joyce, about my new job. I still can't believe how lucky we are to have this all lined up. Whether I will be any good at waiting tables, only time will tell, but we are extremely blessed that I'll be able to provide for us. Henrietta is nothing short of being an angel on earth." She started tearing up.

"It'll be okay, Mama," I quickly consoled.

"I know it will be, and that's where my tears are coming from. Come here, both of you." Both Gen and I complied, and she embraced us passionately at once.

Unexpectedly, unto myself, I let out a deep sob. She pulled us closer without words. When her embrace dissipated and Gen and I headed off toward our room, she called after us.

"We're going to make it girls, I promise. Yes, I promise you that."

Before I could respond, Gen spoke with gripping conviction, "I know. I know we are," she said.

And with that we were off to unpack in our new room.

Chapter 7

October 8th 1965

Tucked into the corner of our tiny room stood a medium sized four drawer dresser that smelled like the rest of the house...like damp wood and cinnamon. Inside the wood was rough so I had to place my clothes just so, so they didn't catch and pick. Nonetheless, it was the most beautiful chest of drawers I had ever seen.

At least, that's how I felt as I placed my clothes into it. It was as though fate had planned Gen and I to have just enough space for our belongings, only able to pack one bag each. I had less clothes than Gen though because I had opted to pack my small record player and a few of my favorite records as well which took up a significant amount of space in my suitcase. I figured if I shared my music Gen would share her clothes and it would all be worth it. I never regretted this decision.

I unpacked the record player first and put on an old Everly Brothers record to please Gen as it was her favorite. As the song '*Dream*' began to croon out, I could hear Gen faintly humming along. I decided to muster up the courage to ask her what I'd been wondering for some time.

"Does this song make you think of someone in particular?" I drew in a breath and held it.

Had I crossed a line? Gen was a closed book in many respects, and rarely, if ever, did I pry about such personal matters. Much to my relief however she smoothly broke her hum, continued to unpack—unfold and fold her clothes on the bed—and answered rather tranquilly.

"No, no one in particular. Just what love will feel like when I find it."

Will find love! I was shocked at her positivity! Not that I didn't think she would find love. Gen was gorgeous. Her naturally blonde hair that she curled at chin length (a style which I admittedly imitated with my chestnut locks). Her sky-blue eyes (versus my brown ones). Straight teeth (we'd both lucked out in this genetic department), and perfectly symmetrical face (I suppose mine is too, though I feel like a braggart to say so).

I've digressed from my point. Gen was beautiful and I was confident she'd find love, but she was just so generally pessimistic—or she would call it 'logical'—about everything, I was surprised her outlook on love was so rose colored. I was happy for it. It made me hopeful for her.

Did I think *I* would ever find love? Ah, this question plagued me far beyond what most fourteen-year-olds should be preoccupied by. It wasn't recent, it had for years. I spent many countless hours meditating on what love would feel like and imagining who my prince charming would be. In reflection, this had intensified when the abuse started, as I would picture the love of my life rescuing me and us running away from it all, together into the sunset.

It turns out I didn't need a prince charming to get away, but I would be lying if I didn't say that it had crossed my mind perhaps, he'd be waiting for me in the throes of my new adventure, my new life. I didn't know what love felt like because I'd never been in it before.

I'd had my share of boys pursue me; I will admit. But even though I'd kissed one, it was nothing close to love. My heart didn't beat faster, I didn't want to hold him closer, in fact, on the occasion, I'd wanted it to be over.

It was in Nicky O'Brien's basement playing 'Seven Minutes in Heaven'. I'd gone in the closet with Mel Brooks, who I thought I had a crush on. When he kissed me, he immediately forced his tongue in my mouth—straight and hard and full of saliva. I was quite put off. As I was trying to process the erasure of my crush based on this action, he had already stuck his hand up my shirt.

This is part of why I was popular with the boys; I had developed early, with the breasts and shape of a young woman not a girl like every other female at the party. Further repulsed, I shoved his scrawny body off of me and snapped him out of whatever creepy daze he was in and gave him the ultimatum of staying in the closet, hands off for the rest of the time to save face (for him, not me, I didn't care), or if he couldn't handle that, I'd just leave.

He snorted and said, "What, so you're square?" to which I responded with silence, and an opening of the closet. To the crowd's reaction of our premature exit, I felt no need to protect him.

So I said, "I only kiss boys who know how," which I thought to be snide and classy.

It backfired, however, with every other guy presenting themselves to me and I wasn't interested. Ultimately, I ended up leaving the party early, feeling a vague version of the dirtiness I would feel after my father would assault me.

So, what was love? To me, it would feel like the song *Sleepwalk* by Santo and Johnny sounded; no words needed, just the melody strong enough to carry you into a state of bliss. It would reach down into your soul and caress it, hold it firmly yet gently at the same time.

Love would be the cliché butterflies in your stomach that rose up to tickle your throat. It would feel like stepping into a hot bath after being soaked outside in a winter's rain—that sweet unburdening thaw. One thing I knew was I would never settle like Mama did, not for any reason, including a child. I was prepared to wait, but desperate for love to be waiting just around the bend.

I couldn't go looking for it though or it would elude me, this I knew. So, I had to maintain my semi-obsession with necessary optimism but even more necessary distance. It was a complicated dance in my young teenage mind, a war of sorts, but I was used to sustaining a delicate balance which would hopefully bring my true love to me.

I'd successfully unpacked the six outfits I'd crammed into my suitcase around the record player into my two drawers and I fell asleep again on my bed. I don't know for how long I napped, but it was later in the afternoon when Mama stuck her head in the door frame.

"Are you girls up for a ride into town?"

"Yes!" I said springing off the bed, with Gen in agreeance, though outwardly less excited than I.

"Get ready and we'll convene in five. I need to get some general supplies at the grocer. It will be our first adventure here in Andrews. Are you excited?" she asked.

"I most certainly am!" I responded, making my way to the bathroom to check the mirror, and put a red ribbon in my hair.

"I'm stoked," Gen added.

I crinkled my nose at her new-fangled slang from one of her magazines. It definitely was not one of Mama's words.

After tying my ribbon, I made my way outside to claim the front seat. Gen had had it all night and I wanted the best seat in the house for this grand tour of our new hometown. The air was dense, and the clouds were the kind that you could stare at and swear they were shaped like a pony or a rocket ship, or this or that.

A slight breeze moved the thickness almost like a paste across my face making it hardly refreshing. I was hot but not at all bothered. It wasn't that different from Virginia really, and besides, I welcomed the stickiness as a sign that I was no longer there and no longer near him. Yes, I liked it just fine.

I stared down the road toward the other houses, which were spaced quite a descent amount apart, and noted they were much the same size as ours. It was obvious we were in the poorer area of town, though I hadn't seen the rest of it. Not to say the street was run down by any means; it was just humble.

It appeared, however, from my vantage point, that people took pride in the property they did have and cared well for their tiny houses giving Dogwood Street a quaint vibe which I reveled in. It was part of me now, and as I stood there, I was absorbing my surroundings into my being. I, me, mine, now.

When Mama stepped out into the daylight, I could see the dark circles beneath her emerald eyes. You'd never know it though by the bounce and quickness in her step as she made her way toward the car, her red and white rayon dress faintly floating out behind her in a regal fashion. Gen got in the back without complaint; perhaps appreciating my previous night's sacrifice or maybe simply too tuckered out to kick up a fuss.

Whatever the reason, I was satisfied and ready to go.

Chapter 8

4:30pm Friday October 8th

The leaves were only hinting at changing yet, barely fraying yellow and orange around the peripheral of the green. I marveled at the tree lined streets, though there was technically nothing particularly special about them as we made our way into town, which was less than a five-minute drive. I noticed, as we turned onto the main street, it was called 'Morgan Ave'.

How fateful! My middle name! I knew we were where we were supposed to be in that moment.

"Look! It says Morgan Ave." I exclaimed from the coincidence.

"Ahh, synchronicity," said Mama literally echoing my own thoughts. I flung myself back in the seat.

"I just can't believe it."

"But I do," my mother interjected. "The universe has a funny way of working things out, and this is just one of the ways it's letting you know that the path you're on is the correct one. As for me and Gen, we're connected to you, so we'll take it as a sign too."

"Well, it's not like we're going to run across a Genoa Street, so I guess I'll have to take the second-hand coincidence."

"Gen," my mother spoke lower, "No need to be salty. I mean it. This speaks to us as a family not just Kim. Chin up, my sweetheart. The universe loves you just as much."

Mama checked the rear-view mirror to see if Gen had cracked a smile which she inevitably did. My mother had a way with her like no other. She could break down her walls in one fell swoop. A remarkable feat really. From my standpoint at least.

With that, we'd arrived at the grocers and stepping in it didn't look much like ours back in Virginia. There was no produce section—no fruits or vegetables to be found.

My mother inquired and was told, "Around here miss, we done mostly grow our own fruits and veggies. If not, you can get them from the few stands at the side of the road," and directed us to some that he knew of.

With that, we gathered what we could, mostly canned goods and meat, and set out on our way. Back in the car, we decided to venture out to one of the stands the man had pointed us toward as to explore Andrews a bit more and came across one with a young man who looked about my age running it.

When I first saw him, my heart skipped a beat, and I had that feeling often described as deja' vu. All of these feelings came on so strongly, I hadn't even left the car yet, and I needed to make sure they didn't show. It was more than likely I was the only one who was going to have them. I couldn't count on him reciprocating the inexplicable rush of emotions I was experiencing.

Besides, I most definitely didn't want Gen or Mama catching on to be able to pester me about being lovestruck afterwards. Getting out of the car to approach him, my legs felt like jelly and I had that *Sleepwalk* feeling with butterflies tickling my throat.

When he spoke, his voice was like a reverberation from a thousand lives past. I'd heard it before, I swear. In my dreams? That must have been where. This is all very dramatic, I know; but this was truly my experience.

"Well, good afternoon ladies, what can I help you with?"

After Mama prattled off her list of what we needed and he was packing them up he paused for a moment, leaned over the stand closer to me, and in a hushed voice said, "I like your ribbon."

I felt my face turn crimson like two waterfalls down my cheeks. "Why thank you," I answered with an equally quiet tone and a smile.

Everything around him in my field of vision was vignetted as I soaked in his dark strawberry blonde hair, his tanned skin, and his perfect mouth with an accentuated cupid's bow. I hadn't yet the courage to look him in the eye so, I couldn't report to you their color.

Before I could gather myself from the ribbon comment, he spoke again, this time to the three of us, though I could feel the thrill of goosebumps each time his eyes passed over me.

"Before you go, I thought I might ask you if you would be interested in looking at a few kittens we have up at the house just yonder," gesturing to the farmhouse behind him and to the left.

"They're desperately looking for homes, but I won't give them to just anybody you see. I've got a good feeling from you folks, so I thought I'd offer if you'd be obliged."

Both Gen and I turned to Mama with pleading eyes.

"Please Mama?" I begged, desperate for this fateful meeting to continue to unfold. I don't know which one I was hoping for—more time with this familiar stranger, or the thought of getting a kitten. It didn't take but seconds for our mother to concede.

"Oh, alright we can go look, but I'm just saying look for now. No promises."

I was elated and much to my own dismay let out a squeal, at which the boy laughed.

"Pleased to please you," he said.

It was a long dirt driveway littered with pebbles here and there, lined with trees, evenly spaced along the way, whose leaves, much like the others I had seen, had not made up their minds to turn yet.

The house we were heading to was one story and by no means large, though it was certainly more sprawling than ours, with a weathervane attached atop it. In the distance, I could see a small red barn and the view reminded me of something I'd see in a painting of a pastoral scene.

"Might I ask the names of you lovely ladies? I haven't seen you around these parts before. Not that I've been here that long myself."

I froze. Names. We'd spoken about this in the car and decided it was best to change our names completely to avoid detection from our father, in case, he tried to trace us somehow and began asking around we wouldn't be identified. It was kind of fun getting to pick a new name! Not many people get to do that. Remembering was going to be something though. Such a strange thing to get used to. I spoke first.

"I'm Gina, pleasure to meet you. What's your name?"

"Well Gina, the pleasure's all mine. I'm Ronnie."

My mother then added, "I'm Matilda Owens," And then Gen, "I'm Venus, but people call me Vee."

It took all my self-control to not burst out laughing at Gen's choice of name. I mean, Genoa is unusual but it's not odd. Venus? Give me a break! But I was going to have to get used to it. That's the way the outside world would know her from this point forward, so I'd have to get past the humor. Still, I involuntarily giggled to myself. Shoot! Now was not the time for daydreaming. I wanted to impress and being in my own world was likely not the way.

Thankfully, my laugh wasn't questioned and instead he asked, "Where'd y'all come from?"

"Virginia," I blurted out and felt Gen's fingers jam into my ribcage.

Oh, no! I thought. *I've blown it.* The story was supposed to be that we came from North Carolina.

Fix it! Fix it Fix it! I thought rapidly. "I mean originally," I quickly corrected. "We just moved from North Carolina."

Thankfully, Ronnie didn't seem to catch the slip.

"Ahh, North Carolina. My sister just moved there. Big city, Wilmington."

"How nice! We're from a small town off the coast," my mother lied easily.

"What brings you to Andrews?"

"Oh just a few friends and change of scene," my mother, here, almost faltered having not thought of a proper explanation.

"Well, I hope y'all find what you're looking for. Welcome."

"Thank you young man," Mama said, glad to close the conversation.

"Don't worry about your shoes," he said as we entered the house, and he led us toward a bedroom. The walls were whitewashed wood paneling, giving the inside a bright charming feel. It was decorated with trinkets and had blue carpet that accentuated the walls.

"They're in here," Ronnie said, and he opened the door to reveal a mama cat and four baby kittens. I was instantly in love! And not just with Ronnie, with the kittens too. The mother was a sleek gray tabby with slanted yellow-green eyes. She emanated love toward her brood as she licked the behind of the one.

"I'm pretty sure their daddy was orange, that's where that one little girl gets her coloring from."

The other three were gray like their mama. I sat on the ground and a chubby little one came wobbling over to me. My heart melted as he climbed into my lap.

"That one's a boy," Ronnie pointed out.

I picked him up and cuddled him close. I didn't just feel like I wanted him, I felt like I needed him. He was filling a hole in my heart as I held him up in front of me and touched his nose to mine. I looked up at my mother, legs crossed, little man clenched close to my chest.

She smiled, tilted her head to the side for a second, then nodded yes. I was ecstatic! In that moment, I felt like life couldn't get any better. I was free, I'd met a cute boy, and I had the most adorable kitten in the world I'd ever seen.

Wrapped up in my ecstasy, I turned my attention to Gen to see if she was sharing in any part of it, (hopefully not the boy part…I didn't need the competition). I could see that her world too had been made a little brighter as she had bonded with the little orange one.

Clearly, Mama had already indicated her seal of approval to her as well because she came right out and announced, "I'll call her Sal. Yes, Sal. She just looks like a Sal to me," she said kissing her forehead.

Off to the side, I could see Ronnie beaming with pride. It made him all the more adorable to me.

"I hand raised them," he said, "and that one," gesturing toward 'Sal', "almost didn't make it. She was the runt, that's why she's the smallest of the bunch, and had trouble nursing. I had to use a syringe and coax her to take formula in. She's a real sweetheart. You're going to love her. As far as the little man you've got there Gina," (when he said my name it made my body tingle) "he was the first to nurse and the first to eat solid food. I'll send you with some food by the way to get you started."

"That's very generous of you, Ronnie. Thank you," my mother said. "Now, how much are you looking for the two cats?"

"Oh, I'm not looking for anything but a good home for my babies."

He looked embarrassed for a split second for having called them his 'babies', but I thought it was sweet. In fact, I was falling harder for him by the second.

"Well, that's awfully generous of you, but I just don't feel right about not compensating you somehow. How about four dollars for the two of them?"

I could see the temptation fleetingly flash across his face, however, he responded, "No ma'am, I wouldn't dream of it. They're all yours, and this too." He turned and headed toward the closet at the back of the room having retrieved a litter box and half a bag of litter.

"It's a spare, and you'll be needing it, so please, take it with you."

"Why don't you come by our place tomorrow to see how they're settling in?" I bravely offered without consulting Mama or Gen. I glanced nonchalantly at Mama who didn't seem to have an issue.

34

"Well, if you wouldn't mind, I'd love to see these little tykes in their new home," he answered promptly with a big smile that crocked slightly to the left.

"Being pretty new around here myself I don't get to do too much so visiting would be a real treat."

"Our address is number eight Dogwood Street, it's off County Road 22. Do you think you can find your way? How about around three?" I asked.

"Oh, I'm sure I will. I've ridden my bike all over these parts since I've been here, probably right past it and not even known. Three sounds perfect. It's a date," he said giving me a barely discernable but deliberate wink, sending those butterflies back up into my throat.

"Okay, that's all set then. Why don't we get these little ones on their way? Not to rush but we've got some meat in the car I don't want to go bad," Mama said.

And with that, we headed back to our new old car, kittens in tow, back to our new old house and our new life. I was happier than I could remember being since before Henrietta was let go.

Life was back on track. Quite different from our old one—and I liked it.

Chapter 9

Saturday October 9th 1965

I woke up early the next day, even before Mama who was going to speak with the lady about her new job. Thank God Mama had packed the hair dryer bonnet among the essentials. I was eager to shower and fix my hair just so before Ronnie came, though I had plenty of time to do it. First, I stepped outside, and the sky was pink like bubble-gum with wispy clouds standing guard across it.

As the sun was making its rise, the air was fresh and dewy, and I felt no chill standing there in my cotton pajama shorts and matching top. I felt so at peace in that moment, on our tiny front porch, that I wanted to wrap it up with a bow. I didn't feel afraid like I thought I would. I felt a million miles away from my father.

I wondered what he was doing…He would have arrived home yesterday morning from the police station to an empty house. Once he realized we were gone he would have noticed things like the pot, the pan, my record player and our suitcases—gone, gone, gone. I wished I could see the panic on his face when he realized his reign was over. It would have been priceless. Would he contact his fellow police friends to enlist them in the search?

I had originally assumed this. Or would he be too embarrassed to say that his wife and two daughters packed up and left him in the middle of the night? Quite the dilemma he was in. Ha! It brought me joy. Of course, I hoped for the latter outcome. The thought of state troopers out looking for us *was* terrifying.

That's why we left Virginia though, so we weren't in his jurisdiction anymore. I didn't know how far his power extended; because he always exaggerated his importance it was impossible to know. I could only hope news of us missing would not trickle down to this sleepy town just off the coast of South Carolina. It was so inconspicuous (Mama's word), I didn't see how it could.

Either way, we'd taken the precaution of our new names, and I just had to tell myself we were safe. I felt it in my bones that we were, so it didn't take much convincing.

After a few deep inhales of the moist air, I returned inside to find Mama putting breakfast on the griddle.

"You're up bright and early my girl, what stopped you from sleeping in?"

"I'm just so happy I couldn't keep sleeping."—which wasn't a complete lie, as I was so excited at the prospect of my day I'd woken up with the sun.

I wished, however, on second thought, I'd slept later so there weren't so many hours to pass before seeing Ronnie.

"Sometime this weekend, we'll go to get a TV so your hours won't pass so slowly, and as of Monday, you'll have school to keep you busy too! How exciting," She said as she flipped the angrily popping bacon over in the pan.

"Now, it's imperative Kimberlie, imperative, that you remember your alias. I know it will take some time to get used to but eventually, it will become second nature."

"I know Mama, I will remember." I tried to say it with the confidence that I felt. I was not going to mess up our freedom.

"Depending on when I start work next week, I'll be going to the DMV—I'll have to ask where the closest one is—to get a new license with my new name on it. I pray I can talk my way into it."

There was a nervous strain in her voice. I knew she just wanted everything to be set.

"I'm sure it'll work out. You're very persuasive," I encouraged.

"Thank you for your faith in me Kim. You're sweet." She brushed by me and kissed my forehead.

"Any advice for me meeting with Joyce today?" I had no idea what to say. I knew nothing about waitressing.

"Well, just be yourself and remember your experience with customers at the sew-shop. I know it's not the same thing, but it's something." It's the best I could come up with.

"You know what? You're right. I have people skills. I'm not a complete amateur! I can learn to carry plates and write down orders. I just hope this Joyce woman is kind. She must be if she respects negros enough to help me get this job. That shows character. It's one of the cooks that are in in the chain that link back to Henrietta through which I was connected to her. I'm so grateful for the web of people who have made our new life possible, I haven't stopped thanking God since we arrived."

"Me neither," I said moving to give her a hug.

By this time, breakfast was ready, and Gen came sleepily wandering in at its smell. Feeling particularly joyful, I burst over and hugged her too.

"Hey there, morning glory. You're up and at'em early today."

"Just eager to start the day," I repeated.

Mama left for her interview just before 10am and got back about an hour later, uniform in hand and she was beaming.

"This is it girls! Our new way of living—I start on Tuesday. I was going to start Monday but then I mentioned bringing you girls into school and Joyce was so considerate that she said to take the day to make sure you got registered and settled in. Plus, that will leave me time to drive out to Georgetown to get my new license. Joyce said that's where the closest one is. Do you want me to try on the uniform for you to see?"

"Yes! Yes!" Gen and I both called out.

When she exited the bedroom, she did a delicate spin. It was a simple light pink frock, collared, with white cuffs on short sleeves. There was a short apron with the shape of three petals on the front that stopped about mid-thigh, and the frock just at her knee flouncing out. On her head was a little white headband that mirrored the shape of the apron, like a small white tierra.

"Mama, you look gorgeous!" I gushed.

"Just perfect," added Gen.

"I want an outfit like that," I said only half lying.

"You think it really suits me?" she asked.

"Oh yes," we both echoed each other.

"Why don't you just leave it on, and you can serve us lunch!" I joked.

Gen gave me a playful shove and I giggled.

"You sound so demanding!" Gen said.

"I didn't mean it of course," I was still laughing at myself.

"I will get you lunch, but not in this! I'm not risking spoiling it before I even start. How about peanut butter and jelly?"

We were fourteen and sixteen years old, and more than capable of getting our own lunches, or any meal for that matter. But last time I had rejected my mother's offer and opted to do it myself, she seemed extremely hurt, so I of course obliged. Besides, everything always tasted better when Mama made it.

The next few hours crawled along like molasses on a winter's day. I got worried Ronnie wasn't going to come. When ten after three rolled around I thought for sure he wasn't coming, and my hopes were completely dashed.

What a fool I had been! But then around 3:15 a rap, rap, rap came at the door. I can't explain it, but I felt my life shifting with the noise. Like it meant something bigger, more profound. Something cosmic.

It was more than just a knock at the door, it was a knock at my heart. I rushed to the entry, smoothed out my clam digger pants, and pushed up the sleeves of my cardigan to just below the elbows. This was it. I felt like I had waited a lifetime to see his face again, though it had been less than twenty-four hours.

I opened the door and he was looking down with his hands in his pockets. He glanced upwards without moving his head until his eyes met mine, and when they did, a big grin spread across his angelic face.

"I found you!" he said enthusiastically.

"Sure did!" I responded, "Come on in."

As he passed, I smelled the subtle scent of the most delicious butterscotch.

"Do you want some lemonade?" I offered as pleasantly and causally as I could.

"That'd be awful nice, I'm parched."

"Well then this time, I'm pleased to please you," I said flirtatiously, hoping he'd remember what he'd said to me the previous day.

Suddenly, I was aware of how barren the house must look and felt the need to make excuses.

"I'd offer for us to watch television, but ours broke on the way here."

"Well, that's a shame. I'd hate for you to miss Ed Sullivan. Do you watch him too? He's my favorite."

"Well we're getting a TV this weekend, so I'll be able to see it," I unthinkingly spoke out, at first missing his hint at an invitation, thinking only of the show.

Then quickly my mind computed how what I was saying might be interpreted as rejection. I promptly corrected myself.

"But I'd love to watch it with you—me at your place or you here," unsure whether Mama would let me go.

"It's another date then!" He stuck his hand across the table to shake on it.

His grip was dry and strong. A voltage shot up my arm from his touch. We finished our drinks, and he inquired where the kittens were. They were in my room with Gen, who I wished would just go away so I could have alone time with him, but, there wasn't anywhere for her to go besides the living room, to where I was hoping she'd take the hint and skedaddle.

Of course, she didn't, she was laying lounged out on the bed on her back reading with Sal curled up on her stomach.

"Where's Bobbsey?" I panicked when I couldn't see him.

"He's been hiding under the bed all afternoon," she answered.

"Aww," Ronnie said, "what's the name you've given him? Bobbsey? Like the *Bobbsey Twins*?"

"Yes exactly!" I responded, surprised, and delighted he knew why I'd picked the name.

"I love reading them. Great taste. Great name. Now let's just see if we can coax this little man out."

Ronnie got on his hands and knees and peered under the bed.

"Bobbsey," he said in a higher pitched voice than his normal one, making a clicking noise with his tongue. No more than ten seconds had passed, and the kitten was out and in his arms.

"That's the first time all day we've seen him," Gen pointed out.

"Ah, he's just a bit shy, the tiny fella. Here Gina, come hold him," and he slowly passed him off to me. I could feel his resistance to leave Ronnie's safe handling, but he curled up in my lap and looked up at me with his big green eyes that told me he knew he belonged to me now, and further nestled in.

"See, he adores you. Who wouldn't?"

Those butterflies went up in my throat. I wasn't sure if it was just an off the cuff remark or if he meant it. When I looked up with burning red cheeks, I was met however, with his dark brown eyes—not unlike my own—piercing straight at me again, and an impish but heartwarming smile.

He meant it, I thought to myself, which deepened the hues of my cheeks.

Just then Mama came through the door from the errands she'd been running. She'd gone out to inquire about salons in town and stop by the general store and grocers again.

"I see an extra set of shoes!" She called out and then came around the corner into our room.

"Isn't this just the sweetest thing," she said observing Bobbsey on my lap and with Ronnie petting Sal all curled up on Gen.

"They seem to be adapting well, wouldn't you say, Ronnie?"

"Yes Ma'am. I picked the best family in town for them to go to, that's no doubt."

"How would you like to stay for dinner? We'll be having meatloaf, so if you object to that, my apologies. If not, you're welcome to stay. As long as it's okay with your parents." She paused for half a second before it dawned on her.

"Oh rats, we don't have a phone for you to call and check."

"Miss, don't worry about that. I live with my grandparents, and neither of them take much mind where I am, unless I'm supposed to be tending to the produce stand. Heck, one less mouth to feed I'm sure they'll be happy."

"Had you mentioned living with your grandparents before and I forgot? If so, I'm sorry. My brain is all over the place from the move. If you say they'll be okay with it, then we're glad to have you."

When dinner was served at our cramped little table, Gen decided to put Ronnie on the spot. Not with any malicious intentions of course, just out of curiosity.

"So, Ronnie, you say you've only been in Andrews a little while yourself, what brought you here?" He waited until he was done chewing and took a drink of milk.

"I followed my sister here," he said clearing his throat. "But she's gone now. She and her boyfriend moved to Wilmington."

"Oh, that's a shame," Mama chimed in.

"Nah, it's alright, she's happy and I'm happy with my grandparents. They're good people though they don't mind putting me to work! I like it better here in Andrews than in Indiana. I didn't get on with my mom's boyfriend. We didn't see eye to eye, so it was for the best that I left."

He let out a heavy sigh that implied there was more to the story than he was telling. However, he was holding back for a reason, and the three of us knew it was not the time or place to push him to expand.

Mama drove him home and I tagged along. Before he got out of the car, he asked if he could walk me to class on Monday. He said he'd wait outside the office while I got registered, so long as he didn't get kicked out of the hall. I felt like my dreams were coming true. He was returning my feelings.

I tried to contain myself, so Mama didn't know how excited I was, but I think she had an idea. First, Ed Sullivan, and now school. But wait? How would I see him for Ed Sullivan? We didn't have a phone and we hadn't solidified plans. I started to panic again. I wanted to get out of the car and chase him.

Well, I guess we'd shook on it, so it had to happen somehow. The universe had been working for me so far, I had to trust it wasn't going to start letting me down.

Chapter 10

October 10th 1965

I was distracted when we were picking out the television, much to the annoyance of Gen.

"Come on, be happy, we're getting a new TV," she prodded at me; but nothing could get me out of my funk of worry.

I was a wreck by the time 7:30 rolled around, but then a familiar rap, rap, rap came on the door and there he was. Oh, sweet relief!

"I was banking on you having gotten that new TV you were talking about," he said as he handed me a daisy.

"Thank you," I said accepting it as graciously as I could.

"Yes, we got it, antennae and all!"

"You don't mind a little company, do you?" he asked.

"Oh no of course not. I mean, I was hoping to see you."

I fumbled for words and prayed I was not coming across as sounding silly. He grinned that smile I was coming to adore. Eight O'clock rolled around and he, Gen and I crammed on the couch—me in the middle—and Mama was in a worn chair off to the side. All of us were in close quarters to the TV as the room was so small.

I hoped Ronnie didn't mind. He didn't seem to. What I mean is, he didn't seem to be judging. Our house may be small, but we did have a color TV thanks to the money Mama had stashed away from the sew-shop over time. I just wanted to be good enough for him. Then it happened. He reached for my hand. In front of Mama and Gen and everything. His grasp was firm but gentle.

I was worried he would feel mine trembling in his, and I think he did, because every so often he'd give it a reassuring squeeze. Petula Clark sang her heart out, Woody Allan told his jokes, but all I could think of was his hand in mine. I was only conscious of this; everything else was background noise. Was he feeling the same way too? I found myself wondering yet again.

Was he feeling the same current of electricity between our arms? He must! Electricity is tangible. It could not exist for one party and not the other if it existed at all. If it was there, it was there. And it was *there*.

When time came for us to part, it felt almost unnatural, like the separation of magnets. I wanted to kiss him, but wouldn't dare in front of Mama and Gen. Besides, I didn't want to rush what would be, what I so wanted to be, a forever thing. No need to rush what you could have for infinity.

October 11th 1965

The next morning came quickly and there was a slight feeling of fall in the air—a crispness that had not been there in the days before. We arrived at the school before the bell to register, and I was nervous about this next step in our new venture. Mama introduced us and the secretary did the necessary paperwork. The principal stepped out and introduced himself.

"Welcome to Andrew's High, ladies. I'm sure we are much obliged to have you here."

He was tall and round around the middle with thinning silver hair that reflected under the fluorescent lighting. We were lingering in the doorway to the office, and I could see Ronnie off to the side.

"Now, if you'll excuse me for a moment," the principal exited and approached him. At first, it looked as though he were reprimanding him, but then, after a moment, he put his hand on his shoulder and swiveled toward us beckoning us over.

"This young man is here to show you to your classes."

"Oh yes, Ronnie is a friend of ours," I was fast to alert him.

"Stand-up fellow, just the kind of student we pride ourselves in here at Andrew's High," and sent us on our way.

We said goodbye to Mama and set out to Gen's homeroom first. She didn't seem one bit uneasy, but she was skilled at masking her emotions, so it was hard to say how she was really feeling. Ronnie and I had the same homeroom, fatefully, History with Mrs. Ellis.

"Just listen, mind your homework, and she's a steady lady. You'll like her. Better yet, she'll like you. Like I said before, who wouldn't?" He said bumping his shoulder into mine as encouragement.

He knocked on the door, explained to Mrs. Ellis how he was helping me find our class and that's why he was late, and handed her a note from the office.

She was middle-aged with half-graying hair up in a meticulous bun. Her mouth looked stern, but her eyes were kind and crinkled at the edges when her mouth gave way to a smile.

"Welcome Gina, come in and I'll introduce you." I felt my insides sink. I hated public attention.

Ronnie seemed to intuit my anxiety and whispered, "It's okay, just keep your eyes on me." I looked at him as he made his way to his seat.

As I stood at the front, Mrs. Ellis announced, "Everybody, can I have your attention please. This is Gina Owens. She's new to Andrews and will be joining our class. I trust you will all make her feel at home."

With that, she handed me a textbook and I was able to sit down. I was pleased and relieved I didn't have to answer any questions about my background in front of the audience and prayed the same scenario would play out in my following classes.

Out of my five classes, Ronnie and I had three others together, plus study period, which for us, fell at the end of the day. I did feel lost without him in my other classes, but I supposed it was an opportunity for me to make some new friends. Or at least, that's what I tried to tell myself, though to be honest I wasn't that interested in the prospect. They were Home-Ec and Gym, so I was destined to be without him.

Our buses were different too, but he still walked me and Gen to ours at the end of the day to make sure we found it alright. It was the strangest matter. Here, senior students were the bus drivers! I thought it awfully bizarre and was slightly fearful for my safety. But I made it home just fine and found Mama sitting at the table upon our arrival, ready to burst.

"I got it girls; I got my new license! Well, a temporary one until I receive my actual one in the mail, but it worked. It worked! And at the bank, too, afterwards with my paperwork with me. I told them I'd lost my documents in a fire and they didn't even question me. Matilda Owens."

She presented the typed sheet of paper serving as her in-between license to us.

"I'm so proud of you, Mama, that's great," Gen said.

"Me too!" I added, wishing I'd been able to express my pride first.

"Oh, how selfish of me! Here I am going on about me as you two are coming home from your first day of school. How was it? Tell me all about it."

"You're not selfish," I swiftly interjected, "We're happy you got your license and a bank account too. Both are so important."

"Yes, me too—I'm elated, truly elated. But now school. Spill the beans!"

"Well, I met some new friends, and even got invited to a meeting," said Gen.

"A meeting!" My mother exclaimed suspiciously. "What kind of meeting?"

"A civil rights meeting. It's kind of on the lowdown with a few kids I met in Science. We got to talking on the way to Study Hall, and I told them I was interested. I think it's one of those hot and cold things, so they really took a risk asking me. I was impressed."

"Civil rights! Genoa, are you sure you want to get involved in that? I mean it's a worthy cause, but South Carolina isn't like Virginia. It's even more conservative, and Virginia was bad enough. It's a very divided place, with most leaning to the right. You could really ostracize yourself getting into that movement."

"From what I understand, the meetings are held in secret. It's a chance I'm willing to take. Think of Henrietta. We wouldn't be here if it weren't for her, right?"

Gen's personal note was an attempt to strike a chord in Mama which it did. Still, she didn't completely lose her hesitation.

"Of course Genoa,"—her continued use of her full name highlighted the seriousness of the conversation to her—"I'm just thinking about your safety. I hate that I must, but it's the reality of the situation."

"But," she paused for a moment in thought, "If you feel passionate about it, I cannot discourage you from following your heart. That's how I raised you girls, and it makes me proud to see you standing by your convictions."

"Thanks Mama," Gen went over and gave her a hug.

"My little Gen," she said hugging her back. "Always blazing trails."

Gen laughed, and then seemingly wanting the attention off herself, shifted it to me.

"How about you, Kim? How was your day as Gina?" she asked.

"Pretty good," I offered; but this was not enough.

"Pretty good? That's all you're going to give up? Details! Details!" Mama pressed.

"I had History, Math, English, Gym, Home-Ec then Study Hall. Ronnie and I have History, Math, and English together as well as Study Hall. We don't have the same bus, but he walked me and Gen to ours."

"Did he hold your hand again?" Gen asked.

This was the first acknowledgement that either she or Mama had seen him last night while watching Ed Sullivan. Mama turned away hiding her smile and my ears flushed burning hot. I was so happy about it. Must they tease me? I figured the best way to combat any mockery was stoic honesty.

"Yes," I said, keeping my voice level and casual as possible. Like the sky is blue, so what? That's the degree of nonchalance I was aiming for.

"Well, isn't that nice, sweetie?" Mama said. "I'm glad you found a friend so fast here; you deserve the companionship. You too Gen. I'm glad you're finding people on your level. It's quite miraculous, really and makes me so gratified."

She let out a contented sigh, one which juxtaposed Ronnie's heavy one at the table the night before.

"Tomorrow, I'm hoping to use the phone at the restaurant to get the telephone company lined up to come and install a phone line for us. We simply can't go on without one. I need to call your Nana, or she'll be worried sick. I wrote her, but who knows how long it will take to reach her. Plus, wouldn't it be nice to be able to call Ronnie?"

"Sure it would be," I pushed back continuing with my stance, certain they were on a mission to embarrass me.

To distract, I saw Bobbsey by the foot of the couch and picked him up, holding him to my cheek. He was so soft and innocent. I admired his purity. He'd never done anything malicious in his short little life, all he'd ever done was just be. I sat down and he nudged his head into my lap and purred.

All he knew how to do was love. He was mine. Bobbsey and Ronnie. What more did I need?

Chapter 11

October 12th 1965

The next day at school, Ronnie was waiting for me when I got off the school bus.

"Can I carry your books, pretty lady?"

"Why sure," I said, handing them over and feeling a little guilty piling them onto him.

"Also, I wanted to ask you before someone else did—would you go to the football game with me on Friday night?"

"I don't think anyone else was planning on asking me, but yes, of course I'll go with you!"

"It's a date then," he said his now infamous saying with his cute little wink.

My heart skipped a beat I felt so excited. I had never had someone focus their attention on me the way Ronnie did. Someone whose attention I wanted that is. It was like being queen of the world. I was invincible, untouchable.

I was on a different plane than everyone else, hovering above them like a frog on a lily pad. It made it easier to talk to people when Ronnie wasn't around, for I knew I had nothing to lose. I had him. If I was rejected, it didn't matter because his arms were waiting for me. I ended up talking with a girl named Brenda Bremer who was in my Home-Ec and Gym classes, and we got on with rather well.

She was a bit overweight but still pretty, with sympathetic eyes you could see through her glasses. She offered to be my partner in Home-Ec, so I was grateful for that.

When I told her about going to the football game with Ronnie, she said "Oh, that's serious around here," with a smile and a girlish laugh. I hadn't thought of it that way, but I hoped it was.

Just when I thought things couldn't get any better, Ronnie passed me a folded piece of paper during Study Hall. What would he be writing me that he couldn't say out loud? I could tell that he had tried to make his naturally childlike handwriting look even and neat. It was a simple six-word sentence that carried the weight of the world with it.

It read: "Gina, will you be my girl?"

My initial reaction was one of feeling like a fraud. *Gina* it began. He doesn't even know my name. If he knew Kim, the Kim who had been penetrated by her father, would he still want me to be his girl? A sense of disgrace washed over me like the waters of a Pentecostal baptism. Is it wrong to accept under these fraudulent terms? I had to regroup my thoughts.

I'm not a fraud…I had no choice. This is who I am now. I am Gina. Gina is Kim. They are two sides of the same coin, synonymous like two forks of the same river. Who was kidding anyways, though? Despite any feelings of inadequacy, was there a chance on earth that I'd ever say 'no'? Ha!

Even considering it was preposterous. From the second I'd laid eyes upon him, I'd wondered if a moment like this would between us might ever come; but of course I had reined myself back in. I ran my fingers across the words to feel the pen's indentations in the paper; then I realized that as I was sitting there grappling with my emotions, he was awaiting an answer.

He probably thought I was really having to think about it—like I might not want to—as it was taking me forever to respond and I didn't want to give him the wrong idea.

So, I promptly wrote, in my nicest cursive, "Yes, I'll be yours," folded it up the way it had come to me and passed it back.

He artfully took it without looking at me, backhanded, and I watched as he undid it to read. When he did, he turned around with the biggest smile I'd seen on his face yet, and he reached his hand back to hold mine for a second as if to consolidate the pact we'd just made.

So there our hands hung silently for a few seconds, in the middle of study hall, suspended in time and space, like our young budding love. I could hardly wait to tell Mama and Gen, even though I knew they'd hassle me about it, I didn't care.

I wanted to shout the news from the rooftops! I was no longer just Kim or Gina, I was Kim/Gina and Ronnie. I belonged to and with somebody now. I felt a sense of worth and purpose that I hadn't before.

The next day, Mama got home from her new job and was feeling rather similarly to how I was feeling.

"I just love it," she gushed. "I never knew there could be so much satisfaction in just bringing someone their food and coffee, but you know what? There is. And I didn't mess up on any orders. Not even the big ones. I got a dollar tip. Can you believe that? Joyce said that's unheard of. It all continues to confirm we're exactly where we're meant to be. Anything new with you girls?"

"Wow, that's great Mama, a one-dollar tip, that's out of this world!" I was sure to compliment her before dropping my news.

"Well, I've been holding it in since yesterday to make sure he wasn't going to change his mind, but Ronnie asked me to be his girlfriend."

My mother who had been bent over in her seat untying her shoe shot upwards.

"He straight out asked you?"

"He asked me in a note, and I said yes."

"Oh my goodness, my little girl is becoming a lady. You officially have a boyfriend and we've been here less than a week. I suppose some might consider that quite the accomplishment."

She laughed and took me in her arms.

"Genoa, are you hearing this?" she shouted to the bedroom.

"Yes, I'm hearing it, an accomplishment indeed. I'm not at all surprised though. You two were like lovebirds from the second you met. Might as well make it official." Her voice seemed genuine, and my new little world felt complete.

October 15 1965

That Friday night rolled around quickly and it was time for the football game. There was much pomp and circumstance, it was fun; it was bigger than what I was used to in Virginia. I almost forgot about having run away as we were in the stands cheering. I was fully Gina.

People were saying hi, and I was no longer Kim, and it was odd but wonderful. I loved being seen with Ronnie as one. I wanted to be associated with him. He introduced me as his 'girl Gina' which made me proud. When the game was over he hushed me, grabbed my hand, and told me to follow him. He took me through a secret passageway under the stands. The lights from the field flooded in like strobes through the cracks of the benches.

"I used to come here alone." he said, "But it's so much better to share it with you."

He then took both my hands and pulled me closer. My lips met his and that same now recognizable electricity that had shot through our arms on the couch shot through my entire being. I felt like moonbeams were coming out my fingertips. I felt the world stop spinning.

Again, I found myself wondering, "Does he feel it too?"

Then he asked, "Do you feel it?"

"What?" I inquired.

"That, that I dunno…magic?"

He managed to stammer out with his slight drawl. I giggled at his words because they summed it up perfectly.

"Yes Ronnie," I said looking deep into his brown eyes. "Yes, I feel the magic too."

He pulled me close, and we kissed again. Suddenly, the lights went out and we were stuck in the dark under the stands. We both burst out laughing as we groped our way through the murkiness. We had left Mama waiting and she wasn't very pleased. I could tell by her reaction when we got in the car.

"There you two are! I was starting to get concerned." I didn't have an immediate explanation.

"We just got caught up with some friends after the game," I managed off the top of my head.

"Well, I can't fault you for being kids," her tone softened a bit.

Ronnie spoke, "I'm sincerely sorry, miss, for keeping you waiting, I should have kept a better eye on the time. It's my fault not Gina's. Please forgive me."

He was so sincere in his apology, even the hardest heart would melt, and Mama's—being hardly hard at all—melted right away.

"I appreciate it Ronnie, your words mean a lot. No need for anyone to be blamed, everyone's got a blank slate here."

"Thank you, ma'am, you don't know how much that means. I want you to trust Gina in my hands, and I don't want to do anything to spoil that."

"Nothing's spoiled," she said as she pulled up in the drive-in front of Ronnie's home. "I trust you are a responsible young man and that Gina's safe with you."

"Thanks a million. And thanks for the ride, too. Come by tomorrow and I'll give you some fruit on the house. Bye Gina, it's been a real blast. Can't wait to see you again."

And with that, he was up and out and disappearing into the shadow of his doorway. I held my breath afraid of Mama's commentary now that we were alone, but all she said was "You've found yourself a fine boy Kim. They're few and far between."

"I know Mama, I will. I don't plan on letting him go anytime soon," and that was the truth.

That night, the sensation I'd had of moonbeams shooting out my fingertips kept me awake. I played the two kisses in my brain over and over. How he tasted like bubble-gum. How his lips were soft and full on mine and how they fit together like two puzzle pieces that had been waiting to find each other since the beginning of time. It completely redeemed my 'Seven Minutes in Heaven' experience. That kiss didn't count. This was my first kiss, my first kisses, and would be forever in my mind.

The next day we drove to the stand with the sun high in the sky so Mama could get her fruit—apples—and I could help Ronnie for a bit, as he'd invited me to during the game. When I arrived, Ronnie was talking to his grandpa whom I hadn't met yet.

"So, this is the young lady I've heard so much about," he said putting his hands on his hips.

He was short and stout with a ruddy face and no resemblance to Ronnie, except for his brown eyes. He had a thick accent which colored his speech and made Mama smile.

"Yes, this is her," she said and clasped my shoulders with both her hands.

I was embarrassed to be made such the center of attention and tried to divert it quickly.

"Thank you for the kittens, sir," I interjected.

"Oh, those little balls of trouble?" he laughed a hearty laugh. "I'm glad you're enjoying them. Ronnie took good care of 'em before they found you. Didn't think he'd ever give any of 'em up to be frank with ya! Just goes to show how much he took to you."

Ronnie was blushing off to the side.

"He's right. I was real attached to them, but like I said, I could just tell you were good people, and look how happy they are now. Sal and Bobbsey, living the dream!"

His grandfather let out a howl.

"Sal and Bobbsey? How funny is that. They've got names now. Funny little buggers." He slapped his leg in amusement.

"Well, I've got to get going, got some chores to do around the barn. Can I trust you to hold down the fort here, Ron?"

"You've got it Pa."

He turned to me and said, "Don't let him get away with any shenanigans, it's up to you to keep him in line."

"Oh, I don't think I'll need to but I'll keep an eye," I said.

"It's been nice to meet ya'll," he reached out his hand to Mama.

"Matilda Owens," she said as she shook it.

"Gina," as he shook mine, though he already knew it.

He turned to leave, looked over his shoulder and shouted, "Don't forget to have a little fun!"

"Impossible not to with Gina!" Ronnie yelled back.

He then turned to me and said, "You'll have to come inside and meet my grandma before you go."

"As for leaving," Mama half interrupted, "how about being home in time for dinner? Say I come back around 4:30?"

"Sounds great. Thanks, Mama. I appreciate the rides."

"No problem sweetheart, see you then. Enjoy yourself." And with that, Ronnie and I were left to man the stand ourselves.

There was a steady stream of customers throughout the afternoon and at one point, a negro boy a year or two older than the two of us stopped by which excited Ronnie greatly.

"This is my friend, Jeb. He helps us out around the farm. Jeb, this is my girl, Gina." He introduced us, and then they proceeded to talk about their football games.

The black school, 'Rosemary' I was informed, used the same stadium on Thursday nights and Ronnie said it was habit for Jeb to come by and have these chats post-game nights. As they were talking, it occurred to me how sad it was that we had to have separate football nights, separate schools at that.

Why couldn't we all play and learn together? It made no sense to me and made me angry. I was impressed that Ronnie seemed colorblind and was interacting with Jeb just the way he would with any of his white friends. I thought of Henrietta and my heart swelled.

I couldn't believe I'd never see her again, and moreover, that without her, I wouldn't be free, standing here selling fruits and vegetables at the side of the road with my new boyfriend. Maybe Gen was onto something with those civil rights meetings she was going to. I mean I'd leave it to her for now—not that she'd have it any other way…she wouldn't let me tag along with her new friends and all—but maybe once she's found her footing with her peers, she'd let me in on it.

I wanted to help somehow. Indeed, I felt helpless in a sea of unrighteousness. I wanted to change the world all at once but knew it to be impossible. This made me feel aggravated and restless inside.

I guess it must have shown because Ronnie asked me, "Are you alright? Pa should be back from the barn any minute," misreading my discontent.

"I'm fine, just off in a daydream," I replied taking his hand, which he responded by kissing mine.

He started counting out the money and said, "Looks like having a beautiful girl on the sidelines is profitable. We made nearly half more today than we did last Saturday. You're my good luck charm."

This time, he kissed my lips and sent my spine tingling. "Look, see, there's Pa now! We'll head inside once he gets here to meet Grandma."

Pa expressed his delight at our afternoon profit before we headed to the house.

"By golly, Gina, you some sorta witch?" He said laughing at his own joke.

"Amazing job, kids. You're officially off duty. Go on inside, your grandmother's got a treat for you."

So, we headed into the house to be met by a waft of apple pie scent in the air.

"There's my special boy," Ronnie's grandmother came out from around the corner.

She was frail with thinning gray curled hair; slightly hunched. Her glasses sat perched on her small nose just so, framing the look of adoration in her eyes.

"I made something for you, your favorite."

"You made apple pie, didn't you, Grandma?"

"Yes, I did! Just for you and your friend." She reached out her hand to me revealing spindly arthritic fingers.

"Pleased to meet you, young lady."

"I'm Gina," I said shyly; I was intimidated by her apparent love for Ronnie and worried I wouldn't measure up to her affection.

She laughed, "Oh, I know who you are—he's been talking our ears off about you! Welcome to our home. Pull up a chair and enjoy a piece of pie," she said cutting into it and slicing it out for us.

"It's delicious," I said as I took my first few bites.

"It's my mother's recipe, goes way back," she boasted proudly.

"Well, it's awfully tasty," I affirmed finishing it up, hoping I was winning points with the compliments.

"Gina came all the way from North Carolina."

I started to squirm as my history was brought up. I hated having to lie and was afraid I'd stumble over the details.

"Is that so? Our granddaughter's up there right now in Wilmington."

"Yes, I heard." I glanced at the clock.

"Oh shoot, look at the time. Mama's probably outside, it's 4:30. I hate to eat and run, but I better get going."

"That's perfectly fine. I'm glad you enjoyed your pie. It was nice to finally put a face to the name meeting you."

"It was my pleasure ma'am. Thanks again for the pie. It was the best I've ever had." She glowed at my comment and Ronnie walked me to the door.

"I'll meet you by the buses on Monday morning?" he said.

"Like always."

He took my hand again and kissed it, and I was on my way.

Christmastime 1965

A few weeks before Christmas Mama got a letter from Nana with a check in it. I don't know how much money it was for but it made her cry and call her right away so it must have been a good amount. She gave me a whole twenty dollars to buy something for Ronnie for Christmas, and I couldn't have been any more excited. I wanted to get him something special that he could keep; something that he could look at and think of me.

So naturally, I settled on a watch. I took Gen with me to the department store to help me pick it out. She had a discerning eye, and I knew she'd be of assistance. We decided on one with a real brown leather strap and refined looking black numbers with the outer face being gold plated. I didn't want one with roman numerals because I knew Ronnie didn't know how to read them.

All around, it seemed like a gentleman's watch, but casual enough to wear day to day which is what I was aiming for. Gen gave her seal of approval, and they tied up the box with a little red bow for Christmas. I wondered if it would remind him of the one I wore in my hair when I met him. By this time the leaves had turned brown and had fallen from the trees.

A few straggling ones tumbled around the tires of the car on the way home. It was chilly out, but not as cold as Virginia. It was a bit hard to get into the Christmas spirit when it felt like October outside, but I was determined. We managed to fit a little tree into our small living room.

Mama had to buy some new decorations at the Five and Dime and department store, but it was fun to have that fresh start to our old tradition. Sal and Bobbsey sure had fun with the tree! Sal even tried to climb it. She was so tiny she just scurried up it like a fire pole, silly little thing.

Bobbsey wouldn't stop growing, and my chubby boy couldn't fit in between the branches if he wanted to. Not agile enough. Oh, how I loved my big ball of fur.

I had chore money saved up to get Mama and Gen their presents. For Mama, I got what I felt to be a striking pink scarf with little white flowers on it, and some new perfume called *Shandoah* that had a spicy floral scent to it. It came in a little white bottle with one of those bubbles you had to squeeze to spritz yourself. I thought it was quite elegant.

For Gen I, got her a leather-bound journal with a special lock on it, since I knew how important privacy was to her. I felt all around satisfied with my presents and hoped they'd be received with the same love as I'd put into them.

When Christmas day came around, Mama told us one of our presents couldn't fit under the tree and that we'd have to go outside the front door. What we found was a red bicycle for me and a blue one for Gen. I could hardly believe my eyes! I jumped into Mama's arms like a child. A bike meant freedom. Freedom to come and go and get around without having to rely on anyone.

"When summer comes and you're home all day without me being able to drive you, they'll come in handy," she said.

Now Ronnie and I could go exploring together. He had a bike but never used it when we were together because I couldn't keep up. A whole new world!

"Thank you Mama! Thank you, thank you, thank you," I kissed her all over the face.

"Now my present to you doesn't seem enough," I said.

"Of course, it will be. Anything you put thought into is enough for me. Besides, I don't need any gifts at all. You girls and your safety are my presents. I couldn't ask for anything more."

Gen then proceeded to thank her, though she was more in silent awe of her surprise. We resumed in the living room to finish opening. Gen got me a form fitting white sweater which I could barely wait to try on, and Mama, a new pair of leather gloves.

It turned out Mama did like the scarf and perfume, even though it didn't hold a candle to the bike. She sprayed herself immediately and said the scent was 'heavenly'. Mama also got me a new pair of pants and a skirt, the latter of which I wanted to change into immediately, with Gen's sweater, before I saw Ronnie.

Now that we had a phone, it was easy to arrange things. He beat me to the call though at about 10:30am.

"Merry Christmas Gina!"

"Merry Christmas Ronnie," I said my voice full of the love I felt for him.

"Do you mind if I come to you? I have something for your Ma and sister too."

"How thoughtful of you. Certainly. Come by anytime."

"How about twelve then?"

"Fine by me!"

"Alright, see you soon." I'd wrapped up his watch box carefully as to not smoosh the red ribbon too much.

I pulled out one of Mama's Christmas greeting cards and pondered on what I should write inside of it. I felt it to be of the utmost importance.

Finally, I decided on the rather dramatic: "To Ronnie, Merry Christmas. When I look at you, time stops. Love Gina."

I almost accidently wrote Kim and corrected myself. Putting love was quite the choice, but it what was in my heart and there was no denying it.

To write 'From Gina' would have felt so cold and unnatural; so, love it was.

He arrived wearing a red seater with a white collared shirt underneath it, looking rather festive and dapper. He noticed my new outfit immediately.

"Gosh Gina, you look extra beautiful today if I may say so myself. Are those new clothes?"

"Yes, they are, thank you for noticing!" I said doing a twirl to model for him, and we went and sat down.

"You sure wear them well. You look so pretty." Ronnie pulled wrapped presents out of his satchel. They were wrapped poorly, though you could tell he'd tried his darndest.

"This here is for you, Miss Owens."

"Oh, please Ronnie, call me Matilda."

"Okay, Miss Matilda," he said.

As she unwrapped, an ornate little teapot was revealed.

"Ronnie, it's gorgeous. You noticed how I love my tea, I see?"

"I picked up on it some of the times I've been around here," he smiled.

"That was so thoughtful of you. Thank you."

"You're always having me for dinner and giving me rides, I wanted to give you something to show my gratitude."

"Well, gratitude received." Then came Gen's. She opened hers to find a fancy jar filled with catnip.

"For you and Sal. I figured once the catnip's done you can use the container to put some of your knick-knacks in."

She laughed, "That's great, thank you Ronnie, you really shouldn't have."

"You might want to be careful using that catnip around the tree though, they go a little crazy on it," he warned, and we all chuckled.

"Now, it's your turn, Ronnie," I said pushing the watch box across the table. He gingerly picked the tape as to not tear the paper. When he finally opened the box, his eyes widened like two bright brown saucers.

"Gina!" he exclaimed pulling it out and strapping it on his wrist. "It's the most handsome watch I've ever seen." He read the card and was tearing up, which in turn made me start to silently cry.

"I'm so glad you like it," I said wiping away my stray tears.

"I couldn't have found a better one if I'd designed it myself," he said, sticking out his arm to admire it. He leaned in and gave me a heart hug—the kind where both your hearts line up on the left side—and it truly felt as though they were beating as one.

"How about you open your present now," passing mine toward me with a little card attached.

The card read: "I hope this gift is as special to you as you are to me. You have my heart, so here's one for you. Love Ronnie." I was so exhilarated by the fact that he wrote 'love' too, I didn't even need a present.

The wrapping paper was silver foil and it crinkled as I hungrily tore it open. I didn't think until after the fact that I should have been dainty about it. Inside the box was a small gold locket with some decorative engraving on it, and it hung on a delicate chain.

"Oh Ronnie," I said, "I'm speechless. I love it, I love you."

I wasn't planning on first declaring my love in front of Mama and Gen, but in that moment, it was like we were the only two in the world and it just came out.

"I love you, too, Gina. Love you a million times over. Merry Christmas." And that was it.

We'd both said, "I love you." There was no turning back now! But had there ever been? Not from the second I saw him at the fruit stand.

"Who would like a very special treat?" Mama interrupted my sentimental thought flow. "Eggnog with a splash of rum?"

Oh, this was a treat! All three of our hands shot up like we were in school.

"Yes please," we all said in near unison, then laughed self-aware of our eagerness.

The rum felt warm as I swallowed, and bringing my inhibitions down, made me all the more aware of my blessings. Yes, I was in a tiny house, with a tree not much bigger than Charlie Brown's (we'd watched the special together), but I was free and in love. No more being forced down by him, being afraid of his footsteps.

Footsteps were normal to me now. They didn't symbolize terror. I felt safe, a feeling whose power I think that is underestimated by many. As much as I hated to admit it, it was kind of a comfort waking up and Gen being in the bed beside me. Sure, she was sometimes known to give me a few kicks in her sleep under the covers from time to time, but overall, it was a solace.

Sometimes, I'd still awake from nightmares of him suffocating me with the weight of his heavy body, me gasping for air—thirsty for it, gulping it down. But footsteps no longer pre-empted horror, and I felt blessed by that.

"I have something for your grandparents too," I told Ronnie.

"Well, I'm assuming you want to be home with your Mama and Gen for dinner, so why don't you stop by after it if that works for you?"

I looked to Mama for approval who nodded, "Yes of course."

"I hope they'll like my present. I've been working on it for over a month." It was a cross-stitch of their barn; I wanted it to be something personal that they could share.

"Do you want to see it?" I asked Ronnie.

"Certainly!" he said.

I ran to my room and pulled it out. Each little red stitch of the barn had been done with such careful precision out of love for Ronnie, and extension, his family.

I thrust it onto his lap, "What do you think?"

"Hey look it's our barn!" I was impressed with him for recognizing it and with myself for stitching its likeness.

"I'm so glad you can tell! Do you think they'll like it?"

"Think? Nuh-uh, I know they'll like it. You're so talented. You got anymore hidden talents you're hiding from me?"

He reached over and started to tickle me.

"You'll have to wait and see," I said through my laughter as I half shoved him off me and half held his hands.

"Do you want to go outside for a bit and check out your new bike I noticed on my way in?"

"Yes!"

"Hey Gen," Ronnie said, talking a little louder than normal because of the rum, "How about you? Wanna come outside with us and fool around with your bike?"

Gen had Sal on her lap like a perfectly content tiny little tiger.

She hesitated and Ronnie interjected, "Come on, I want to see you ride it."

"Oh, alright, let's go," she said carefully placing Sal on the back of the couch who let out a full-mouthed yawn revealing her sharp baby teeth.

I changed into some jogger pants which did not match my sweater—a point which the rum helped me get around (normally I wouldn't have been able to tolerate it). Ronnie suggested we race, which we did. Gen beat me by a fraction of a second. Gen then let Ronnie use hers and I beat him! Though in reflection, I'm not convinced he didn't let me win.

Just when Ronnie was about to race Gen, Mama stuck her head out and said, "Ronnie, you need to get home for your dinner, it's getting late. I'll make sure Gina gets over when you're finished but I think you better go now."

In slight defiance I peddled to the end of our road. The scent of burning wood from fireplaces in town lingered in the air. It was 70 degrees and hardly cold enough for a fire, but it made it feel more Christmas like, and I guess 70 was cold enough for Andrews folk. Then I played a little game with myself. I pretended my father was chasing me and I peddled back toward the house.

I peddled so hard my upper legs pulsed and burned. The wind pulled my hair tightly back from my face as I challenged the air with my speed. Ronnie was cheering for me, knowing, of course, nothing going on in my mind, and the strange little game I had been playing.

"Look at my girl go! The wind ain't got nothing on you Gina!"

My mother came all the way out this time.

"You should have seen her Miss, she's a real speed demon!"

"I don't want too much of that, Gina," my mother scorned, "I expect you to ride safely and responsibly. Soon, you'll be driving a car, and we can't have any of that."

Her hands were on her hips. I thought she was being a bit strict, but better not argue.

"Sure, Mama," I agreed laughing her off.

I arrived at Ronnie's after we'd both finished our Christmas dinners with my cross-stitch. His grandmother became emotional and even took down a picture in order to hang it up.

She said, "Welcome to the family little girl," which made all the hours I'd put into the needlework worth it.

All in all, it was the best Christmas of my life. I was in love. I was with the ones I loved, not tainted by the toxicity of my father spoiling the environment. And oh, how could I forget? I had an adorable kitten. Who could ask for anything more?

Chapter 12

February 14th 1966

Valentines Day was a Monday that year, and Ronnie's grandparents had given him the day off from any farm work, so we had the whole day to spend with each other, during and after school. With the help of Mama, I'd bought Ronnie a ring. Just a simple thin gold band because it's all I could afford—I was using all my chore money I'd saved up since Christmas plus Mama was helping me make up the difference.

I wanted it to be like a promise ring. I guess a promise ring in reverse. For as he wore it, it was a symbol of my devotion to him. Having packed my present in his purse for when school was over, I just went home with Ronnie on his bus to his grandparents. It was cold out that day, so Ronnie's grandma made us hot cocoa when we got in.

It was rich and creamy and filled me up where I was no longer hungry, so when she offered sandwiches, I had to turn mine down. Ronnie, despite his slight figure, was a bottomless pit! He accepted and I had to wait through his eating before exchanging our gifts.

After much ado and his final bite, he said, "Wanna take a walk with me to the barn Gina?"

"Surely," I replied, my heart starting to pitter-patter with anticipation of giving him his present. He held his hand out to help me down from the stool at the counter.

"Hold on though." He left and came back with his red and black checkered wool jacket.

"Put this on, it's too cool out for just your school clothes." I gratefully slipped into it, and off we went, hand in hand across the field to the picturesque red barn at the corner of his property.

We sat down on some wooden planks used to store hay and at the same time said, "I've got something for you."

"Jinx, owe me a coke," he laughed.

"Who wants to go first?" I asked.

"Let's do it at the same time. On the count of three."

"Okay," I said.

"One," he counted, "two, three."

I reached into my purse and he into his coat pocket. Much to my delightful surprise, he pulled out a ring box too.

"Happy Valentines Day," he said popping open the lid to reveal the ring.

It was also a thin gold band—thinner than his—that melded into the shape of a heart in the middle.

"Oh Ronnie, it's perfect!" I said slipping it onto the ring finger of my right hand. It fit like a glove.

"Here's yours," I opened the box as he had for me.

"I thought it would be like a promise ring...like I'm promising myself to you with that ring."

"Well then, I promise myself to you with that ring." He said pulling me close and kissing me.

"You are the best thing that's ever happened to me, Gina. I swear to God Himself." He uttered in between kisses.

I took his hand and put it on my breast without thinking, out of mere instinct. I could tell he'd never done anything like that before and I was glad to be the first one. Our kissing grew more passionate, and he became more comfortable. When we finally stopped, he put his arms around me, and he took off his jacket to put behind our heads on the wood.

"It was a year ago today I left Indiana you know," he said breaking the silence of our fervor.

"No, I didn't, but you like it here just fine now huh?"

"Sure do." He paused before beginning to speak again in a careful tone.

"I left to follow Glenda because my mom's boyfriend had broken my arm. I was trying to defend her because he was beating on her. I called the police, and she turned it all around on me and said I had started it all. They believed her, and him, and they reprimanded me.

"Acted like they were doing me a favor by not taking me in. When they left, she told me I was no longer welcome there, so I came out here to be with my grandparents. She picked him over me and it hurt, hurt more than my arm."

"Oh my gosh Ronnie, I'm so sorry. Why didn't you leave sooner? Before it got that bad?"

"Like I said, I was trying to protect her—my mom—but it never worked anyways. In fact, it usually made it worse. He's an evil man, but she picked him over me every time. Luckily, I'd been helping out in an auto-shop, so I had some cash, and last year, on this day, I packed my suitcase and caught a bus. It took more than one, but I made it alright.

"My grandparents were so good to take me in, especially with Glenda still here at the time. I had to sleep on the couch for a while, but they didn't seem to mind. That's why I like to help out on the farm as best I can as a way of showing my thanks."

"I'm sure they appreciate it Ronnie. You can tell how much they love you just by the way they look at you."

"Ya, they were sad to see Glenda go, but I told them they're as good as stuck with me, so they needn't worry about me going any place."

"Me neither," I snuggled him closer.

"Since we all have yesterdays, do you mind telling me about yours?" My body went rigid and my breath stilled.

"Hey there little missy," he said shaking my body a bit with his arms still around me.

"You don't have to tell me if it's going to upset you. Take a deep breath," which I did, then suddenly blurted out, "My name's not Gina."

"Pardon?" He said, immediately perplexed.

"My name's not Gina it's Kim."

"Okay, wow, I wasn't expecting to hear that. Kim's a pretty name—why'd you change it?" He wasn't understanding.

"Because we're on the run from my father who's a police officer in Montross, Virginia. We thought changing our names would make it harder for him to find us."

"I suppose it would. Smart decision. Might I ask why you're running away from him? Same reason as me?"

"No. He was raping me and Gen." I'd never said it out loud before. The words sounded hollow and far away as I communicated them.

"Jesus Christ!" exclaimed Ronnie.

"Do you need me to go take this guy out? I'll find a way. Pa has a shotgun and rifles. I'll hunt him down I swear to God above."

"No, I need you here with me," I said taking his hand and intermingling our fingers, and there was silence as he took it all in.

"Does that mean your full name is Kimberlie?"

"Yup, Kimberlie Morgan Mair."

"Kim," he repeated. "So, can I call you Kim then? In private I mean."

"Sure, I guess that makes sense."

"Are you going to tell your mom you told me?"

"Oh Lord, I don't know. She's not going to be happy."

"But it's me! You can trust me. I won't tell a soul. I think you should tell her."

"Okay, if you think it's best. You promise you won't tell anyone? Not your grandparents, not Jeb, not anybody?"

"Not *anybody*. It's between you, me God and hopefully your family." He stuck out his pinky to do a pinky swear.

"Let's make it part of the promise rings. They're a promise to each other, but a promise to the secret too."

"Alright." I was feeling more at ease. We sat up.

"Come here." He hugged me long and hard.

"You're so strong you know that?" he said to me. "I never really thought about it."

"Well, you are. Think about all you've gone through, where you are now. You're a warrior. My warrior. I'm so proud you're my girl."

"Thanks Ronnie." I said looking him in the eye, searching to make sure his words matched his sentiments which they did.

"How's about getting out of this drafty barn? Would you go for some more hot cocoa? I sure could."

"Sure, why not," I responded.

"Let's go Kim," he grabbed me under the arms and helped me off the shelf and we headed through the setting sun—red and orange and yellow strewn across the sky—and headed back to his house.

I couldn't hide it from Mama for long. She was lying in bed reading when I came to her door. I knocked lightly.

"Kim! What is it sweetheart? Come in and sit down."

"I'm afraid you might be disappointed in me," I started out.

"Whatever for?" She inquired putting the marker in her book and closing it. Her brow furrowed; she looked up at me. I bit the bullet and said it.

"I told him. I told Ronnie about Daddy and about my name. I'm sorry, I just couldn't keep lying to him, we've gotten so close. I just felt like he deserved to know my who I really was. I'm sorry if you're angry with me."

She sat in silence for what felt like eternity then finally spoke.

"I figured just as much—that you'd told him. When did you tell him? The other day? You were harboring a lot of nervous energy."

"Yes," I said, amazed at my mother's intuition.

"I'm not mad. I'm a little bit scared that anybody knows outside the family, not in particular Ronnie. In fact, I trust your judgement. If you believe him to be trustworthy, I stand by your decision. I understand spending so much time with a person why you would want them to know the truth."

"I felt like a fraud. Like I was tricking him. It just felt wrong. Especially after he gave me the ring."

"I understand. Just don't expect your sister to be so forgiving. You know how she is," she said opening her book back up. Oh God, Gen was going to be furious. "Do I need to tell her?" I asked Mama.

"Well, if he's going to be calling you Kim you're going to have to explain yourself." She was right. I had no choice. It was going to be like pulling off a Band-Aid.

"Thanks, Mama, for being so kind about it," I said bending over to give her a hug.

"Of course, baby. It's all so difficult to manage. You've done very well."

I headed to our room bracing myself for the divulgence.

"Hey Gen! I haven't got the chance to show you what Ronnie got me for Valentines. Look!" I stuck out my hand to reveal my ring.

"Wow, it's lovely," she said, taking my hand in hers to inspect it.

"So, you guys got each other matching rings and didn't even know it?"

"What a coincidence huh? They're promise rings, promising us to each other."

"Ah, I see. Very romantic." I couldn't tell whether she was being genuine or facetious, but either way I had to move forward with my confession.

"After promising ourselves to each other, I didn't feel right about continuing to lie to him, so I told him my name was Kim." I braced myself.

"You told him *what*?" her head shot u from nuzzling Sal.

"I told him my name was Kim and that we were on the run from Daddy."

"Holy shit Kim—you've compromised us. Do you realize you could have blown everything?"

"He won't tell it's Ronnie. You know as well as I do, he can be trusted," I defended. Gen's breathing slowed a little as she gave this some thought.

"He's a good kid, and I don't think he'd do anything on purpose, just if it gets out in any way we're screwed."

"You'll see, it won't," I reassured.

"We'll see, I guess. We don't really have a choice." I felt guilty, but not so guilty that I regretted my decision. The phone rang intercepting any further comments from Gen. It was Ronnie.

"I just wanted to say thank you again for sharing what you did tonight and assure you that your secret's safe with me. So just sleep well knowing that."

"Thanks baby," I said, "I trust and love you."

Then hung up and went to bed. As I was falling asleep, I felt as though a weight had been lifted off my chest; everything felt more aligned than ever. I knew in my heart of hearts I had made the right choice and I was at peace with it.

Indeed, I was at peace with life as I twirled my promise ring on my finger. He still wanted me, even after knowing I'd been tainted by my father. I felt clean and whole. I was the luckiest girl in the world by my estimation, and I couldn't wait to see what tomorrow would bring.

Chapter 13

May 5th 1966

Winter passed by like a swift current, and spring was fragrant in the Southern air. On this day, Mama was working a later shift than usual, and Gen was at one of her meetings, so Ronnie and I had the house to ourselves. What started off as soft gentle kissing, quickly progressed to heavy caressing, to us taking off our clothes. We'd never gone this far before, but it felt right.

Our bodies moved together as one, in and out, up and down. 'Electric' like on other occasions doesn't even begin to describe it. Two celestial beings melded together in ecstasy. It was the complete opposite of when my father would assault me. My body responded to his touch instead of recoiled. He was tender but strong.

Feeling him inside me was blissful. I never wanted it to end. We had passionately consummated our love. Afterwards, we rode our bikes into town and got some penny-candy and ate them down by the creek besides this little old bridge that looked like it was from a storybook. Down a little way the creek got wider and there was a rope tied to a tree for you to jump in it, I think tied there by some senior kids.

The water was still a bit too cold for that yet though, but we took our socks off and dipped our feet in the creek and felt the cool water rushing past our toes, resting them on the smooth rocks beneath.

"Today was the best day of my life," Ronnie said.

"Me too," I returned honestly, resting my head on his shoulder.

"Kim, you mean everything to me, I don't know what I'd do without you."

"You either Ronnie."

"I mean it, you complete me, complete my world. I don't even know who I was before I met you. I don't even want to remember."

"I know who I was, and I was half the person I am now. You complete me too. I love you Ronald Tisdale to the moon and back. There then back again."

He flung his arm around me in a playful manner and pulled me close laughing.

"I can't believe you called me Ronald. No one's called me that for years! Let's get outta here."

So, we got up from the river and headed back into town on our bikes, deeper in love than we'd ever been, and falling even harder by the second.

When we got back to the house Gen was home and I started to change the sheets which she thought was suspicious, but she was on a high from one of her meetings, so she didn't have it in her to pry.

"Ronnie, I met a friend of yours, Jeb?"

"Oh, you met Jeb, huh? He's a good friend of mine. He helps us out in the fields."

"He's just as passionate about civil rights as I am and willing to fight for it. We're planning a rally in one of the big cities. I think he's brave being African American and being willing to stand up. It's easy for me, being white, to say how I think it should be, but for him…I mean he even said he's participate in a sit-in if the opportunity ever came up. What a guy! We had a really good conversation. I like him a lot," said Gen.

"Ya, he's a stand-up fella. He's indispensable around the farm too. I didn't know he was into civil rights though. We never got to talking much about that kind of thing, but I'll be sure to bring it up now," Ronnie responded thoughtfully.

The next Monday at school Ronnie told me how he'd talked to Jeb that weekend about the civil rights meetings. He said he spoke about how demoralizing it is to have to be served out the back of the restaurant and the grocers, and to have to drink from different fountains and use different restrooms. He said it made him feel 'dirty'.

This made me think of the way my father made me feel and couldn't imagine being faced with it every day, at every turn. I wanted to do something to change it and made up my mind to talk to Gen about joining her meetings, though I was intimidated to intrude.

That same day after school, Mama came home in a particularly good mood. She was humming around the kitchen with her uniform still on, which was odd as taking it off was usually the first thing she did.

"What are you thinking about Mama?"

"Oh, just my day. It's been a good day, Kim. I met someone. Someone special, I think."

Then she returned to humming.

"Who?" I naturally inquired.

"His name is Marshall Green. Do you know that big white house with the Greek like columns down the road from Ronnie's?"

"What, the one that looks like a mansion?" "Yes, that one. That's his house. He owns that big farm. He's been coming in regularly since I started at the restaurant, and I'd had my eye on him because I thought he was handsome—I had no idea where he lived until one of the other girls told me.

"He's always been the most generous tipper. Remember that one-dollar tip? That came from him. Anyhow, today he asked me to dinner this coming weekend. I accepted. Can you believe it Kim? I'm going to be going on a date! He says there's a place in Georgetown he'd like to take me. I might need to buy a new dress. Do you want to be my shopping partner?"

Of course, I couldn't say no, though I was hesitant about the whole thing. I didn't know how I felt about Mama going out with some strange man. I liked to see her happy though, so I went along with her to Ruffins, the department store. She didn't want to be too dressy or too casual, so she settled on a pink swing dress with black polka-dots and a little collar on top. She was a vision no doubt, any man would be lucky to have her.

May 7th 1965

When the farmer came to the door, I sized him up. I was the only one there to do so as Gen was off with some of her friends. He had a bouquet of flowers which Mama put in a vase in the living room, even though I knew the kittens would get at them. He was scrawny—tight and tanned, a brass complexion with clear blue eyes. They were kind eyes; I'll give him that. His lips were thin and muscly, and his ears stuck out from under his cowboy hat.

"Nice to meet you, little lady. The name's Marshall," he said tipping his hat to me, revealing a head of dark hair when I came out from the kitchen.

"The pleasure's mine," I said, feeling rather mature in my response, having heard many adults use the same phrase.

He laughed at this and responded, "Ain't that sweet," nervously shuffling from foot to foot.

I was glad to see he wasn't busting with confidence, as my Mama was a prize and wanted him to see her that way. Just like with Daddy, she was more beautiful than he was handsome, no matter what she thought, so how he handled it was pivotal. He seemed humbled by it, but this was in my brief estimation. I hoped I was right.

"I see you're ready to go," he said to Mama as she approached the door with her purse.

"Yes, I'm set."

"I might say, you look supremely lovely this evening."

"Why thank you," she said.

"Kim, I'll be home in good time. I hope you don't mind getting your own dinner. Feel free to have Ronnie over if you like."

"Okay, thanks Mama. No, I don't mind. Have fun. I'll see you soon."

"Thanks sweetheart, see you shortly. Bye for now."

I did call Ronnie to come over because I was feeling anxious.

"What's the matter baby?" he said pulling me close once he'd kicked off his bike. "I see it all over your face. You're stressing."

"I just don't want him to be like Daddy," I said and surprised myself by starting to cry.

"Come on inside, let's sit down and talk this out." He kept his arm around me the whole time.

"Now Kim, I never met your father, but what I know of him he's a wicked man. Men that evil are few and far between, despite our experiences. It just feels common for you because it's all you have known. Think of church for example. Think of all the men there. How many are like him? None.

"None that we know of at least. But my point being, even if there is one among them, that's still just one out of dozens. The numbers are against it. The good outnumber the bad. You and I have just been unfortunate. We've encountered the bad ones. By random chance. The odds are in your favor that this Marshall guy is a good man.

"Anything I've ever heard of him has been positive—that he runs a fair farm. Besides all of this, things have been going pretty well for y'all since you've come to Andrews, I don't see why your streak of luck would stop now. Who knows, this fella' could be the best thing that ever happened to your Mama. Besides you and Gen of course. Did you think of it that way?"

"No," I said sniffling and giving it some thought.

Maybe he would treat her well and make her feel loved and worthy—everything my father didn't. Everything Ronnie made me feel. She deserved love.

"Are you afraid he's going to take her away from you?" I hadn't consciously thought about it, but I supposed on some level I was. Perhaps that's where my tears were coming from in part?

"Oh Ronnie, I don't know. Maybe a little."

"It's alright to be afraid baby. But your mom loves you so much, no one could take you away from her. Look what she did! She brought you and Gen down here not knowing a soul, started a strange job. Man, she was brave for you guys. If she loves you enough to do all that, there's no way she'd let a man ever come between you, I promise."

"Thanks Ronnie," I said, laying my head down in his lap as he stroked my hair in loving caresses, lulling me into a sleep from his soothing touch. The next thing I knew I was waking up to Mama's voice.

"Angel, I'm home," she stooped over and kissed my forehead as I was orienting myself.

"Thanks for keeping her company, Ronnie. Do you want to leave your bike here and get it tomorrow if I give you a drive home? I don't feel very good about you riding in the dark."

"No need to go to the trouble, Miss Matilda. I've been riding this route so many times now I could do it with my eyes closed."

"Honestly, Ronnie, I'd really prefer it. I'll come pick you up tomorrow too to come back here to get it if that's what you're concerned about. I just would never forgive myself if something happened to you riding home at this hour."

"That's not what I'm worried about at all, but, if you insist, I won't fight ya! Don't worry about tomorrow though. I'll find my own way, I'm sure."

"Well, be in touch about it. For now, let's get you home." I came along for the ride.

"Goodnight, Miss Matilda, goodnight Kim. I'll grab my bike tomorrow at your convenience," he said shutting the car door behind him.

"Such a polite boy. I've said it before, but a good kid you've got there Kim."

"I know. I love him," I said.

"Love is such a strong word that means so many things. Do you feel love for him, or are you in love with him?"

"The latter." I felt clever in my response.

"And I'm assuming he feels the same way?"

"Don't you remember Christmas? Yes, he feels the same way!"

"So this is as serious as I thought," she said, as we made it down the County Road back to Dogwood.

"Well, I hope to be in love one day too again Kimberlie, and who knows, it might be in my cards. Not to jump any guns."

"Oh yes your date Mama, how was it?"

"It was nothing short of wonderful. He was a true gentleman—opening the car door for me, pulling out my chair. I didn't understand the wine selection and he helped me order without making me feel or look inferior. The conversation flowed freely.

"He was open and honest. I didn't have to pry, yet he didn't overshare things to the point of being draining. I hate to say it, because I don't want to jinx things, but I feel like he might be the one."

I could tell by the excitement in her voice that she meant it. My insides did a little flip, as there was a part of me that was hoping it would fail and I'd be keeping Mama all to myself like I'd talked about with Ronnie, but that was not in God's plan.

Chapter 14

End of October 1966

Five months after Mama met Marshall Green, we were moving our belongings into his rich, Greek columned farm home. Gen and I had got to know him over family meals and a shopping trip into Georgetown—his treat—and I can't say I didn't like the man. He had a non-imposing demeanor and a dry sense of humor. It made Mama laugh a lot which brought joy to my heart.

As we left behind our dusty little blue house of cinnamon and damp wood, I felt rather nostalgic, even sad to let it go. It had been our haven, our first place of refuge and freedom. It's where Ronnie and I had first made love. Where we had brought the kittens home to. So many positive memories.

However, I'd have my own room now; it was huge with white walls and a tall window that faced the east so I could watch the sunrise. Mr. Green said I could paint it whatever color I fancied, and he'd get one of his men to do it for me. I eventually settled on soft pink. Plus, I was just down the road from Ronnie now!

Yes, I was moving on up. We'd have the same bus now too. The downside of it all was that the only time I was Kim was when Ronnie, or Gen and Mama and I, were alone, because Mama didn't want to tell Marshall about our secret. He had proposed to her one Sunday in late September. We'd just finished dinner together and he got down on one knee in front of her.

He was wearing tan slacks and a flannel shirt, and a fancy belt buckle. He took off his cowboy hat that he didn't even normally remove at the table. I could see his hands were shaking, which made me feel sympathy for him, and in the moment, I wanted her to say yes just to ease the poor man's nerves.

When he asked, he said, "With the permission of these two girls that is," and seemed to mean it.

Gen and I simply nodded and said, "Yes, of course."

"It's whatever you want Mama."

"Well, then it's a yes from me," and he slipped the biggest diamond ring on her finger I'd ever seen.

They then stood up and kissed and embraced. I could see Mama's face over his shoulder as they hugged, and it was full of happiness. I could tell she was saying yes because she was in love, not out of obligation.

As I sat there looking at the beef and gravy remnants of my plate, I let it sink in that this was yet another new chapter in the new book of my life. I didn't know how getting married was going to work, considering she was still married to my father, but I was sure she'd figure it out. And she did.

November 19th 1966

Because of the name change and her paperwork there was no trouble. Two months later in a small ceremony they were married at our church. There were just a few friends of hers from the restaurant there, and he had his brother come from out of town to be his best man. He looked stylish in his suit, and didn't, for once, bother to wear his cowboy hat. It rained hard that day, the kind of rain that pelts down and assassinates the earth.

Though inconvenient, Mama sloughed it off saying it was supposed to be good luck. They went on a honeymoon to Key West Florida for a whole week, leaving Gen and I alone in that big house—with Sal and Bobbsey of course. I can't say that Ronnie and I didn't take advantage of the freedom. What can I say? We were young and in love, so we made lots of love. Lots of it.

There are no words to describe the thrill of when we were together. In those moments of rapture, the whole world melted away, every pain from the past, every worry from the present. All was atoned. What was so special was that we learned from each other, not from previous partners. I was only acquainted with lying there, being forced upon, I had no experience in the dance of lovemaking, and neither did Ronnie.

So, we maneuvered the steps together, getting better and better every time. I loved it when he would breathlessly say my name—especially since it was used so sparsely anymore. He was conscientious, but not to the point of annoyance. Checking in if what he was doing felt good or if he was hurting me, (which he never was).

I remembered when I had wondered during the Ed Sullivan show, if he'd felt the electricity too; I now knew that he must have. The way we moved together so in synch. There must be a common currency running through you to create that sort of rhythm. I still felt it when we held hands too.

Nearing the end of the week I got a frantic call from Ronnie. It was his grandpa. He'd collapsed in the field. By the time the ambulance got there—it was run by volunteer drivers at the time—it was too late. His heart had stopped.

I hung up and rode right over. Ronnie was a mess. His grandmother too. They took him away and he was gone forever. What would happen to the farm? I knew they both were thinking it. It was going to fall on Ronnie. And it did.

November 26th 1966

The funeral was a somber affair. Seeing Ronnie cry broke my heart. It made his brown eyes glow like lanterns in the night sky. Gen made them a casserole dish to have for dinner, so they didn't have to cook, and I stayed behind to help clean up after the people left from the post-funeral gathering. I didn't know what to do to make it better.

I sat with Ronnie out in the barn and pet his head while he cried. He said his grandpa was the closest thing to having a father he'd ever known. He told me he was going to have to quit school to stay home and work on the farm which scared me to death. School without Ronnie? I only had one other friend. I begged him to reconsider but his mind was made up. I felt like my world was falling apart.

Why did this have to happen? Why did he have to die? I cried into Ronnie's shirt, and we held each other. He promised it wouldn't change anything between us. I believed him. Nothing could tear us apart, not even this. I told him this wouldn't break us; it would make us stronger. Another promise to add to our promise rings. When Mama came home that night I was waiting up and went bursting into her arms with a sob. I told her the story of the week, while Marshall kept his distance but was listening.

Out of nowhere he interjected into Mama's consolations, "He can have Henry help out. He's one of the best in the county, and I'm willing to part with him some for your little friend Gina."

"Who's Henry?" I whimpered. "One of the top farm hands this side of the Santee. He's the one I left in charge when we were on our honeymoon. He knows the ins and outs of everything, from harvesting to financing. Your buddy will be in capable hands. I'll talk to him about it tomorrow. And I'll keep him on my payroll, so your friend needn't worry about that."

"That's so generous of you Marshall," Mama enthused.

"Oh Marshall, thank you! That helps me feel better to know Ronnie won't be alone dealing with everything," I wiped my eyes and nuzzled into Mama's neck.

"Should I call him now and tell him or wait until you've talked to Henry?"

"You can go ahead and call him now Gina if that will ease your upset by any degree. It's as good as done so there's no harm in telling him that I see."

With that I raced to the phone. It was a little late to be calling for etiquette reasons, but I felt this overrode manners, so I did it anyways. Ronnie answered, his voice thick and swollen as though he's been crying.

"I've got good news for you. Marshall is giving you his right-hand man to work on his farm with you. He knows all about crops and money and it'll be the best help."

"Aw Gina, I hate to disappoint you, but we can't afford to take on an overseer like that."

"No, no—Mr. Green is keeping him on his payroll. Isn't it perfect?"

"Are you sure you've got this straight?"

"One hundred percent sure. I could get him on the line if you want."

"That's alright, I trust you. It's just a little too good to be true. I'll have to think of what to do in return to show my appreciation."

"I've got an idea!" I said, "Give him one of Ella-Mae's puppies!"

"Do you think he'd want one?"

"Yes! I think he could use a friend to follow him around the fields he works and checks in on. It's the perfect gift, trust me."

"Well, I'll have to talk to my grandma about it to make sure she hasn't promised them all to people yet. Since, she's making money off them, she's been reserving them since before they were even born. It's because they're game dogs—retrievers—and there's so many hunters around these parts. Hold on I'll go ask her."

I could hear muffled speaking in the background for what felt like forever, and then finally he got on the phone and said, "We've got two outta seven left. One boy one girl. Your pick."

"The girl," I said. "She's a little black baby, sweetest temperament as could be. He's going to love her. I guess I'll wait to hear from Marshall or Henry and once that's all settled, I can bring her over. Do you have a pretty pink ribbon we can tie around her neck?"

"You bet I do," I said, pleased that Ronnie had lost his nasally tone and seemed in brighter spirits than at the beginning of the conversation.

November 28th 1966

The next day was school for me, but Ronnie didn't come. I was worried about him all day and got off at his stop instead of mine on the way home to find I'd interrupted a meeting. It was with Marshall and Henry—a man of average build, bald as a billiard except for a thin rim of gray hair that encircled his head. He had small eyes and a wide smile.

You could tell he was one of those men that looked older than he was. He was sitting around the butcher block with Ronnie, Marshall and Ronnie's grandmother.

"Come on in Gina," she shouted when she saw me at the door.

"Pull up a stool and sit with officially my three favorite men on earth. Ronnie, of course, you're my number one," she reached over and pinched his cheek while the men laughed, and he did too.

Thank God! I thought, *This is going well.* Then the surprise came to mind! Oh no! what if it was ruined?

I mouthed, "Dogs?" across the table to Ronnie and he smiled and mouthed back, "barn." He was always on my wavelength.

"Well, then, we better be getting on our way Mrs. Knight now that we're all decided."

"I'll never be able to thank you enough Mr. Green she said taking his hand in both of hers.

"And you Henry, I'm so grateful for your willingness to take us on. I'm forever indebted."

"We're happy to make a difference under these trying circumstances. So, Henry will be by tomorrow morning to talk to Ronnie about the day."

That evening Ronnie brought the puppy, and I got my bow out. I came round the front of the house to knock at the door with Ronnie. Mama answered and we asked for Marshall. He came sauntering over, unsuspecting. The puppy was wiggling in Ronnie's arms.

"Mr. Green, I wanted to present you with this life friend as a token of my appreciation for your helping out with my farm."

Marshall's face lit up with amusement as he took the squirming puppy from Ronnie.

"For me?" he said.

"Yes, all yours," confirmed Ronnie.

"She's a purebred Labrador Retriever if you're wondering."

Marshall didn't seem put off by any impending responsibility that would come with the dog, and just seemed genuinely pleased with his gift.

"Thank you, young man, this is awfully thoughtful of you. I wasn't expecting anything in return so it's the most pleasant surprise. I'll take good care of her, just like Vee and Gina do with Bobbsey and Sal. I know they came from you too, and they've turned out to be fine animals in my estimation."

I felt proud of my boy when he said this. He was a 'fine animal'. So sweet and cuddly and kind as a cat could be. My little butterball. He let me cry into his fur, what more can I say? I hoped Marshall's new puppy would be just as loyal of a companion.

This same night was the night I overheard Mama's conversation with Marshall about continuing to work at the restaurant, even though they were married, and she didn't need to. Old habits die hard, and Mama still longed for that sense of independence and need to stay busy. She'd found a sense of belonging at the diner, too, which she didn't want to give up.

She started off defensively—I could tell she was ready for a battle due to the way my father had always acted about her working, but there was no resistance.

"Honey, whatever makes you happy, makes me happy. If it suits you to keep waiting at the restaurant, then that's what you shall do. Now, come here and give me a kiss."

I couldn't see them from my vantage point but I'm assuming she did.

"Thank you for understanding my love. To be honest I didn't know if you'd support me. It eases my heart so much to know that you do."

"Under one condition."

"Oh," I heard her voice sink in disappointment.

"You let me get you a new car."

"A new car?" she said excitedly.

"You and me, tomorrow after you're done work. Let's go check out the lot."

"Oh my love, yes, yes, yes!" was followed by silence which I think was another kiss. "Can I bring the girls along?"

"Of course you can. You never have to ask me that. They're welcome wherever you are. Well," he said after a moment in thought, "Except in bed," he snickered to himself.

"Let them tell them now!" I scrambled down the hallway into my room.

"I have some exciting news," she said sticking her head around the corner without knocking.

"Marshall is taking us to get a new car! Will you be around after school when my shift finishes to come along?"

"I sure will! Can I bring Ronnie? He loves cars more than anything."

"Of course, dear. We've got just enough room for him. He's like family anyways, right?"

My throat tightened in a good way at Mama's sentiment. I planned on one day marrying that boy, but unfortunately because we were too young that would have to wait, so her ultimate endorsement would have to make do in the meantime.

November 29th 1966

After many test drives and inspections of interiors and exteriors at the lot, Mama decided on a new blue four door Ford Galaxie 500 with a hard top. It was a darker blue inside and smelled a lot better than the car we'd been driving—although I hadn't minded that old cigarette scent that could be detected from time to time.

She said she felt like royalty driving it, and she looked the part. So sophisticated behind the wheel, she was majestic. Ronnie felt like he helped get her a deal, but I'm not sure he had made much of a difference. It was cute though hearing him attempt to barter. He did more talking than Marshall who, excuse the pun, really took a backseat during the whole business; just paid when it came time.

Back at the house, the puppy was already following him around at his heels. He'd named her 'Lucy' after the Peanuts character because of her dark fur. Ronnie was still grieving his grandfather, and I didn't know what to do to cheer him. At loss, I put on one of his favorite records, *Can't Take My Eyes Off You* by Frankie Valli and the Four Seasons and forced him up to dance.

Soon, his tears were drying, and he was laughing as I dragged him around my room to the beat, cheek to cheek. I'll always remember how his cold tears felt on my face and how badly I wanted to erase them; I felt so deeply for him it was as though his sadness were my own. Our love was that sacred.

Chapter 15

January 8th 1967

I first heard it from Ronnie, and then from Gen. Ronnie called me Saturday afternoon and told me that Jeb hadn't come by the stand (even though football season was over, he still always came by), and he was concerned. I told him not to worry about it; not to downplay the importance of their meetings, but perhaps Jeb just got busy, was sick, or had something more important to do.

Still, Ronnie insisted there was something wrong and ended the conversation. A few hours later, Gen came to my bedroom door knocking and talking at the same time.

"Jeb is missing Kim."

"I heard he didn't come by and see Ronnie this morning, but I'm sure everything is fine."

"No," said Gen, "like really missing. His family can't find him. They say he went out last night and they haven't seen him since which isn't his character. I'm worried it has to do with Debbie Howard.

"He's been getting too friendly with her around town, and I'd warned him against it with her family's connections to the Klan, but he wouldn't listen to me. He said the only way to fight hate was with love, that was his attitude with everything. I'm scared Kim. I just have a sick feeling about it."

I started to have a sick feeling too. The Klan scared me to death, and I couldn't believe that Jeb would risk messing around with anyone of their kind.

"Last time he said he was talking to her was about her shoes outside Ruffins. Kept saying she isn't that bad, that the apple *can* fall far from the tree. He said he hoped to talk to her again to make a point. I don't know Kim; I just don't know."

It took two days, but they found him. Lynched in the woods just outside Andrews. All signs pointed to the Klan, which meant nothing would be done. Poor Jeb! So young and vibrant and full of life! All because he talked to a white girl about her shoes. It was unfathomable to me. The loss hit Ronnie hard. First his grandfather, and now Jeb. Gen went to an 'emergency meeting' at her civil rights group before the funeral. It was decided that the whole club would attend—black and white—it's what Jeb would have wanted.

I went with Ronnie to support him, and to say it was upsetting would be an understatement. Jeb's mother could hardly stand she was crying so hard, having to be supported on both sides by his brothers. The police lingered around the outskirts as though they were expecting a conflict, but it just made it feel uncomfortably supervised, or like Jeb had done something wrong.

I felt scared and clung to Ronnie. I don't even know what I was afraid of…hate? I was afraid of hate I suppose. It hung heavy in the air, infiltrating the whole event. There was deep singing as Jeb's casket was lowered into the ground, which made the scene very macabre to me (a word I'd learned from Mama).

I wanted to run away from it all, but knew I had to stay strong for Ronnie. When it was over, I went home and snuggled with Bobbsey whose innocence helped revive my faith in the world, even just for a moment. Gen came in despondent, and wanting to help somehow, I asked if Ronnie and I could come to her next meeting with her. She agreed and then went straight to her room. Mama hugged me and told me to let her be her.

All I could think of was Henrietta and someone hating her because of the color of her skin. It just made no sense to me. I couldn't wrap my head around the concept of seeing people on such a superficial level. I cried into Mama's shirt until it was tear-stained.

She explained to me that my heart was good, but that most other people didn't have hearts like mine, or eyes like mine either. She said the world was on its way to changing but it was going to take a long time, and that the last place it was going to change was going to be the South. This land of such beauty—of Spanish moss and cherry blossoms, would be the last to see the light.

February 27th 1967

With the horrific events of the last month behind us, the 27th of February was Ronnie's sixteenth birthday, and redirecting my emotional energy, I couldn't have been more excited because now he could get his license. His grandfather had taught him how to drive already on the backroads so he was good and ready for his road test and neither of us could wait. I got him a Saint Christopher medallion necklace, the patron saint of traveling since he'd be driving around and needing a little extra protection.

The medallion was gold and engraved 'Protect me St. Christopher' on the backside. I called him and he said he'd already made his driver's test appointment for Wednesday. Two more days and yet another new chapter was about to be opened in the book of freedom that'd been being written since arriving in Andrews.

On Wednesday, Gen and I got off the bus to find Ronnie parked in the driveway, sitting on the back of his grandpa's old pickup. He looked at me, grinned, and opened his arms wide.

"I got it!" he exclaimed. I ran over and jumped off the ground into his arms.

"I'm so proud of you Ronnie!" I said, kissing him.

"Was it hard?"

"Nah, piece of cake. Except for parallel parking. That part's a bitch, but overall, not a problem."

"Do you think I'll be able to pass?" I asked anxiously.

"With me as your teacher? Hands down. Home run. You'll pass with flying colors like me."

"I'm so excited! When can you start teaching me?"

"Well, there's no better time than the present—how about right now?"

"Are you serious?" I burst out. "Heck ya I am, are you up for it?"

"You bet I am!" I ran into the house to Gen's room where she had already retreated, frantically knocking.

"Tell Mama, I'm out driving with Ronnie and will be home for dinner."

"K." She said not looking up from her book. I didn't even know if she'd registered what I'd said but didn't care. I gleefully jumped in the truck and Ronnie revved it up.

"It's not the smoothest ride, I warn you, but it gets you from point A to point B. I've been saving for a while now and should have enough to get my own by mid-spring I'd say."

"That's wonderful Ronnie!"

"Obviously, it won't be new like your mom's, but I know a thing or two about cars so if it needs some fixing up, I'll be up for the job. Like I said before, I used to help out at the garage back in Indiana. I loved it, it was the best part of living there. Since I was just a kid, I didn't get to do too much hands-on stuff, but I watched and learned and caught on pretty well. It comes naturally to me. This here truck conked out on Pa and I got 'er going again all by my lonesome."

"That's amazing—maybe you could try and work part-time at the auto-shop here in town if you get everything lined up on the farm?"

He paused for a moment in thought.

"You know what Kim, that's not half a bad idea. With Henry around, I just might be able to swing it if they'd accept me part-time that is. That way I'd be bringing in more money too."

He drove me to the back roads he used to practice on, and we switched places. He explained to me about the clutch and the gears, and it was difficult for me to get it going. I hadn't imagined it would be so hard, Ronnie made it look so leisurely. After quite a few jumps and false starts I got it cruising and wow, what a feeling. Freedom squared!

The steering wheel was thin and tall, just at my eye level, so it was a bit tricky steering and seeing past it. Ronnie calling out to me when I was to shift gears was also a little overwhelming, but I did it. After driving for about five minutes, I pulled off to give Ronnie his throne back—I'd had enough for one day. But boy, was it exhilarating.

Ronnie gave me a kiss in passing around the truck.

Once in and headed home he said, "Good job babe, you'll be a natural in no time. Besides, I think I'll get a manual when I get my car which will be way easier for you. Hey, maybe your Mama would let you practice on her new Galaxie?" He said jokingly.

I playfully punched his arm.

"That's her third child, I swear, no one's getting near it with a ten-foot pole."

"Just give me a couple months and you can practice on mine until your heart's content."

Though my heart felt as content as it ever could be already.

Chapter 16

March 1967

The house wasn't much bigger than our house on Dogwood and everyone was gathered into the living room. Gen was already there and greeted us.

"Hey, glad you could make it," and introduced us to a few of the people there. They were mostly just juniors and seniors from our school and from Rosemary, but there were a few older people there too. There were snacks, and some individuals playing board games like Yahtzee. Ronnie got to talking to one of Jeb's brothers which I think did his heart good. I slowly realized it was less of a meeting, at least on this occasion, than a get together where blacks and whites came together to interact without judgement from the outside world.

A girl named Sandy from Rosemary got to explaining the Civil Rights Act of '64 and the Voting Rights Act of '65 to me which I hadn't previously heard of. It made me feel enlightened and important that she would take the time to break them down for me. We exchanged phone numbers, and I told her she was always welcome at our house.

She told Gen that she had a 'gem of a little sister', and I was happy and relieved to have fit in with the crowd. Things started to break up and Ronnie offered to drive Gen home with me, which she accepted. Before we left Ronnie made the bold move of raising his cup of soda to Jeb.

"To Jeb, who lived and died with his heart on his sleeve in the name of justice."

Thankfully, it was well received by the crowd who raised their glasses in response and proceeded to talk about Jeb as we all dispersed. I looked forward to getting together again with the group and had a sense of hope that together, this band of kids from small town in South Carolina, could make some sort of mark on the world even if it was just through microcosmic solidarity.

April 5th 1967

After saving since he'd moved into his grandparents, Ronnie finally had enough money to buy himself a car. I went with him to the lot, and he was like a kid in a candy store. He only had enough for a used one of course, but as soon as he set his eyes on a golden '58 Chevy Impala it was love at first sight.

You should have heard him bargaining away with the salesman—it was something else. He got it down to one fifty which really was quite a steal. Like I said, it was gold on the outside, and the interior was tan leather with embroidered lines down the seats. The wheels were white and black with a little red symbol in the middle.

It wasn't a bench seat in the front, they were separate, and it had a large thin steering wheel with three prongs. The only other time I remember seeing Ronnie this proud was when I first met him, and he was showing us the kittens. This was a different pride though. The previous was a nurturing pride, this was a confidence pride which I loved to see in him.

He asked me if I felt comfortable enough to drive his truck home from the lot behind him—which I did not—but agreed to without letting on. He'd worked tirelessly with me this winter to learn how to drive, yet at best I still felt mediocre. Nonetheless, I made it back to Ronnie's without an accident or being pulled over without a license.

When I hopped out of the truck, Ronnie was inspecting his new ride as though he hadn't already gone over it one hundred times at the lot, and he said to me, "So, what do you think about me going down to the auto-shop and asking if they might need a little bit of help? You know, just a few hours here and there. I don't want to neglect the farm, but it'd sure be nice to get to doing something I'm passionate about."

"I think it's a swell idea Ronnie. You need to take care of you. I support you one hundred percent. Let me come with you when you go over there, for moral support."

"Okay, I'll pick you up after your classes tomorrow and we'll head over. I'm right nervous about it Kim. I'm not that good at presenting myself."

"You're plenty presentable, don't you worry about that. Just have a little faith in yourself, and it will work out. Take the faith I have in you and make it yours."

"Thanks babe, I'll try. It's all I can do, I guess. I want it, so I've got to go get it."

The next day, he came to pick me up at school, and a couple of his old friends had found him and were admiring his Impala.

"Clear the way boys, my lady's coming through," he said reaching out to me and grabbing my hand, his arm outstretched. They all started disbanding, slapping Ronnie on the back, shaking his hand, congratulating him on his new ride.

"She makes her all the more beautiful," he said, pulling me close and giving me a kiss. I felt my cheeks flush scarlet.

"Ya, you're definitely a winning man," one guy said as others echoed in agreement. I was feeling flattered to be included in their compliments, but also shy and decided to slip into the front seat.

As soon as he got in, he said, "How about some air conditioning?" satisfied that his vehicle touted this feature.

"I named her for you," he said, referring to the car.

"Thanks baby," I said with a giggle, but quickly realized it was no laughing matter.

"I'm truly honored and hope she loves you back as much as I do."

I said reaching over, holding the back of his head, and kissing him.

"Are you feeling nervous about talking to the men at the shop?" I asked, wanting to check in on his state of mind before we got to the garage.

"A little," he said, then hesitated, and said, "okay, a lot nervous. Kim, I'm not that good a talker."

"First of all, not true. Think about how you helped my mom get her car," (a bit of a white lie), "and you with yours. It was your way with words that got both deals. You charmed me and I'm not that easy to please! Have the attitude inside that they'd be lucky to take you on. And they would be!"

"Thanks babe, you're the sweetest. I've just got to bite the bullet," he said as we pulled up in front.

"Just remember, no matter what, I'm here in the car waiting for you, okay? I'll smuggle a couple beers from Marshall and we can celebrate your bravery for going to do this no matter how it turns out." This seemed to truly motivate him as he reached for the car door, then turned his head back.

"One more kiss for good luck?"

"Always," and planted as romantic of a kiss as I could muster.

He seemed calm as he said, "Alright, I'm ready now," and headed up to the garage.

Twenty minutes (long minutes when you're waiting keenly for a person), passed and finally Ronnie emerged and came back to the car.

"Well," he said, with a hang-dog look on his face.

Oh no they've rejected him, I thought and began preparing myself for damage control, "They're willing to take me on for twelve hours a week to start—his face totally shifting and lighting up like a Christmas tree."

"You bum!" I hit him light-heartedly.

"You had me thinking something bad had come of it. Twelve hours a week is perfect. It will still give you lots of time at the farm, but you'll get to do what you love to."

"I'm pretty excited about it. Thanks for your pep talk, I definitely think it helped."

"Anything for you," I said and meant it.

There was nothing in the world I wouldn't do for that boy, and it was a satisfying feeling to have to know that I'd been of support.

Chapter 17

Saturday May 27th 1967

The school year was winding down and it was my sixteenth birthday. Mama got sixteen plastic flamingos and put them on our front lawn with a sign that said 'Happy Sweet 16 Gina'. I didn't want a party though, I just wanted family and Ronnie.

Marshall barbequed us hamburgers, and hotdogs, my favorites, on his big grill in the backyard and Mama made me chocolate cream pie instead of cake because I requested it. Ronnie got me a beautiful new jewelry box that played music when you opened it.

I didn't know the song but it was soft and dreamy and made me want to waltz around the room when I heard it. He said it was called *Clair du Lune* and that the melody reminded him of me.

I booked my driver's test for the upcoming week, though I was quite nervous about it. Driving didn't come naturally to me like it did to some. Gen and Ronnie both got it on their first tries, so I felt the pressure to get it on mine.

When the day came, I had a female tester—though she had a detectable mustache above her upper lip. She refused to engage in any conversation besides her driving instructions, which I felt to be demeaning.

"Hi how are you?" Radio silence.

"Pull off and make a left-hand turn."

Straight down to business. She was overweight, it was hot, she was sweating and had that type of body odor where you couldn't discern where it was coming from and didn't want to. After taking me for a drive through town, she directed me to a side street to parallel park. It was at this point I froze up—my mind went completely blank, and I couldn't remember which way to turn the wheel, let alone how far and when to start backing up.

It was a disaster.

After about five minutes of struggling—which felt like a lifetime—she said, "I've seen enough, you can head back into town."

I parked, sat there anxiously as she wrote things down on a form, balancing the clipboard on her stomach. She was making these God-awful wheezing noises as she breathed where part of me wanted to ask if she was okay, and another part of me hoped she wasn't.

Finally, she signed the bottom of the paper, unclipped it, undid her seatbelt, shoved the paper toward me and said, "Better luck next time sunshine, today was not your day. You've got to wait a full week to re-book."

And with that opened the door and maneuvered her hefty body in one deft movement out of the front seat. I immediately burst into tears. I failed? Failed? Ronnie came over from across the street where he'd been waiting. I got out and hugged him, burying my face in his chest.

"Oh no," he said. "They failed you?"

I simply nodded and continued to cry.

"Hey, why don't we grab a couple of Marshall's beers, and we'll go down by the creek and spend some time in nature. We'll ride our bikes like old times, what'd ya say?"

"Okay," I got out in between sobs.

"Bring the paper with you down to the creek so I can take a look at it. We'll fix what you need to fix. You'll be behind the wheel in no time, I promise you that. Do I ever break my promises?"

"No," I said, as my crying ceased, but having gotten in the car, sulking out the window.

"So, there you have it. You'll be driving before you know it. Not to change the subject, but I do feel a little guilty taking from Marshall. He's so good to us, you don't think that taking a couple beers puts him out too much do you?"

I laughed half-heartedly.

"Marshall's got money growing out of his ears, and an endless supply of alcohol—which is odd now that I think about it because he doesn't drink that much. Maybe a beer or two coming in from the fields or a glass of whiskey, but nothing excessive.

"Either way, the short answer to your question is no, it doesn't put him out. Besides, I think he knows we borrow from him from time to time and he doesn't mind. If he did, he would have said something before now."

"Borrow," Ronnie laughed, "I think the word you're looking for is 'steal'. But if you say it's alright, then I say let's go for it, especially today. You deserve a break."

So, we went down to the creek and it turns out all I needed to improve was my parallel parking.

"They shouldn't have failed you just for that. That woman you had was just a bitch," Ronnie said taking the swig of his can and then crushing it.

"I know right? Totally unfair. Hopefully I won't get her next time."

"Well, there's only a few who do the tests, so fingers crossed. In the meantime, let's practice that parallel parking missy. The Impala's rather long so it makes it a bit hard, but you can do it, I have faith in you."

June 5th 1967

Since school was over that week my schedule was wide open, but Ronnie started at the auto-shop that Monday morning from nine until one and then had some farm chores to do, so we didn't get practicing until Monday evening. We tried using trees as markers because we didn't want to risk me hitting anything with Ronnie's car, and I struggled.

On a positive note, his first day on the job had gone swimmingly! He said the guys treated him like a little brother, which he didn't mind, and that they already let him change the oil on a car.

"You know that feeling when you put your feet into an old pair of shoes, and they fit just right? That's how I feel when I'm working around cars. I feel like it's my calling if there is such a thing."

"I believe there is such a thing," I encouraged. "I'm so glad you're finding something that fulfills you," (I felt like I was using a Mama word).

"The only time I ever feel fulfilled like that is when I'm doing art—drawing, painting, cross-stitch—and who can make a living out of that?"

"Kim, your drawings are amazing. Someone out there needs something drawn for them, it's just a matter of finding those people. Commissioned! That's the word I'm looking for. Someone out there will commission your art."

Talk about a Mama word! I was impressed. Impressed and hopeful. I'd never thought of it that way. He took both his hands and cupped them around his mouth and shouted as loud as he could 'my girl's an artist!' It echoed off the forest walls.

"So, what do you say we go for a dip?" The beers had got the best of him.

"Oh Ronnie, I don't know, it's kind of cold and getting late and—" the next thing I knew he had me in a bear hug and we were jumping in. I felt the slippery mossy stones beneath my feet.

"You brat!" I exclaimed as my head bobbed up.

"I didn't want to get my hair wet!"

"Well, you're done like dinner now. Good thing you look super-hot when you're wet."

I jumped on his back as an attempt to dunk him, in exchange he just took my legs and started swimming around with me. Another moment when 'freedom' hit me on a conscious level. Two years ago, I was enduring the weight of a two-hundred-pound man forcing himself inside me, feeling so alone in the universe and so trapped.

I had been thinking about the various ways I could end my life. Today I had a boyfriend who I was madly in love with, romping around in the woods, hundreds of miles away from that man who had no idea if I even existed anymore.

The creek was freezing so I told Ronnie we had to get out and he of course obliged, wrapping me in one of his grandmother's towels we'd brought along and had been sitting on, rubbing it up and down my arms to warm me.

"Here," he said, tossing his black hooded sweatshirt at me, "Put this on until we get back to my place and then I'll get you outta all those wet clothes and into some of my pants too."

He was trying to hide it, but Ronnie was a shivering mess by the time we'd made it back to the farmhouse and we both immediately changed. He gave me a pair of his boxer shorts and track pants that matched his sweatshirt. They were a little big on me which for some reason endeared me to him.

"Aw, you look so cute in my clothes, come here."

We cuddled on his bed for a bit, warming each other up before I headed home. Mama picked me up and Ronnie said he'd bring my bike by in the truck tomorrow.

The next day, Ronnie called me and said the truck wouldn't start. He said it was so old it was just good for parts anyhow, now that he had his Impala. He told me he'd ride my bike over to my place for me, so I didn't have to worry about it, which he did. Mama was feeling pretty badly about me failing the test, so she offered to take me out in the Galaxie to practice my parallel parking.

We could tell how much this secretly pained her though, so Ronnie just asked for a ride back to his place to get his Impala since that's the car I'd be using as our excuse. She promptly agreed to this compromise. So, I practiced, practiced, practiced until I could do it with my eyes closed.

June 19ᵗʰ 1967

I made my appointment for my next test for the following week and prayed I didn't get the same lady. I didn't. I got a man who was miniature—everything was small on him. Small ears, small nose, small fingers. He was nice enough though, much friendlier than the last tester! He actually responded when I spoke to him. We went through the same routine as the previous time, and when it came to the parallel park, and I nailed it! I just knew I had passed.

"Excellent job young lady, you're officially a licensed driver, hereby the state of South Carolina," and handed me the paper.

"Thank you!" I said exuberantly.

I wanted to kiss his cheek but felt it to be inappropriate, so I restrained myself. I got out of the car and Ronnie was walking toward me. I ran and jumped on him.

"I did it!" I proclaimed, "I can finally drive too!"

"I'm so proud of you, I knew you could do it," he said kissing me on the forehead and then the lips.

"Now, do you want to drive us to get some ice cream?"

"Absolutely!" And that's how we celebrated, with a banana split.

That was the beginning of the summer of 1967, which is when I started working part-time at the restaurant with Mama. One of my favorite moments in life was getting to serve Ronnie.

"I'll take a number two, bacon, white toast please pretty lady."

I wondered if other customers heard him call me 'pretty lady' and what they thought. I caught on rather quickly and made good tips like Mama did. Not to be arrogant, but I think it was at least in part because of my looks, and I suppose, my polite demeanor.

It made me mad we weren't allowed to serve black folk except out the back. I mean we had a black cook, why weren't they allowed in the diner? I always made the point to deliver to them when I could, even though I knew I wouldn't get a tip.

Gen had taken a job at the 'Five and Dime' store part way through the school year, working evenings and weekends, and now fulltime. She said she hated it and was just doing it to save money to take with her to college. I was dreading September when she was going to be leaving. She'd been accepted into the College of Charleston about an hour away and was majoring in Elementary Education.

I'd felt betrayed when I first heard the news. How could she leave me? We'd beaten our father together. Started a new life, new identities. We'd shared a bed! I was scared to think of my world without her around. Since birth she'd always been there for me to look up to, how strange it was going to be to not have her as my lighthouse in this vast sea of existence.

That summer was extra hot, the kind of humid where it feels like you're chewing on the air. Ronnie and I spent our free time making love, swimming in the creek, and drinking Marshall's beer. I wanted time to stop, I was having so much fun, it felt like life was just as it should be.

I, myself, had started saving for a car of my own, but knew I wouldn't have enough at least until winter. Marshall offered to help me out, but Mama wouldn't let him, much to my dismay. She said I needed to understand the value of working hard for my money and the rewards of such. That was so frustrating and made me a little mad at her to be honest. I comforted myself by the fact that that's what Ronnie had to do, so I could do it too.

Along with working at the diner, I got in as much time with Ronnie as I could by helping him out at the stand and around the farm. I loved being able to do this. Just when I thought our relationship couldn't get any stronger, it did. We were growing up, maturing, and so was our love. Almost two years together and we'd never fought, not once. We talked about marriage all the time, and agreed that when we turned eighteen, we'd tie the knot.

I dreamed about it, but also had bad dreams too. All the time. Dreams about my father finding us, hurting me like he used to. I would try to scream but had no voice or try to run but my legs wouldn't work. When they were really terrible, I'd creep down the hall and crawl into Gen's bed. She'd move over and give me some of the covers. Sometimes I'd just stay until I could shake it off, others I'd remain until the morning.

The next day, she'd ask me what the dream was about, and I'd recount it to her. Sometimes in tears. She'd reassure and remind me that we are safe now;

that if he were going to find us, he would have already. She only hugged me when it counted, and she would hug me then. Anyhow, I digress.

Ronnie and I would talk about how Gen would be my maid of honor, and how Marshall would walk me down the aisle. We decided our wedding song would be 'Sleepwalk' because we loved to slow dance to it ever since I'd explained to him about how it sounds like how love feels, and he agreed. We even started a stash of money for our honeymoon.

Every pay check—him from the garage, me from the restaurant—we'd put a little bit away so by the time our wedding came, we'd be able to take the trip of a lifetime. Both of us were set on Hawaii, and it wasn't cheap, so we had to get to saving. It was rewarding watching our jar grow fuller and fuller every other week, closer and closer to our future together as one. I guess that's what Mama had meant when she talked about reaping the rewards of hard work.

As the summer wound down, and it came time for Gen to go, I was a wreck. She had all of her bags packed and was standing in the foyer when it truly hit me, she was going.

"Oh Vee," I said, as Marshall was in earshot, "Please, don't leave me!"

I burst into a sob, covering my face with my hands.

"I don't know what I'll do without you here."

"Aw Gina, come here." I approached her with slow begrudging steps.

"I'm not leaving *you*. I'm leaving Andrews. And I'm not even far, just an hour. Once you get your car, you'll be able to drive down and see me all the time. Plus, I'll come here and visit as often as I can. It's only 'til April, not the whole year, then I'll be home for the whole summer again. Do you think I'm going to completely abandon Sal?"

This was true, there was no way she'd let Sal forget her, so maybe she wouldn't be as 'gone' as I was envisioning. She embraced me and I saw our childhood flash before my eyes in an instant. I helped her bring and fit a couple boxes into her red 1960 Chevrolet Covair Monza, which really wasn't that big.

She had just bought it two weeks before with some of the money she's saved from the 'Five and Dime' gig. I knew I'd never be able to fill her shoes— work and pull off good grades (Gen was honor roll) and thinking about it made my nerves twitch. I didn't want the spotlight to be completely on me. Way too much pressure.

I was quite content standing in the shadows of Gen's achievements, so long as I didn't get hassled for needing to do better. That never happened though, usually Mama ended up feeling guilty for making such a fuss over Gen's, she'd glance at mine, note it's mediocrity, and fold it back up and act as though I'd aced everything.

"The Lord blessed me with two intelligent and beautiful girls. Who says they can't have it all?" was her reaction to our June reports.

If grading, I'd give her an A plus on hiding what I can only assume to be dissatisfaction in me. Not that I did extremely poorly, I just didn't excel.

Once Gen's suitcases were tightly squeezed in, we said one final goodbye and she was off. I felt dreadfully lonesome standing there in the driveway watching her car fade into the distance. At least I still had Ronnie, I told myself, and went inside to call him. His grandmother said he was working the stand, so to distract myself from my emotions I decided to just bike over.

Surprised but happy to see me he said, "Hey baby, what's going on?"

"Gen's gone," I responded, again, bursting into tears.

"Come here," he drew me close, and I cried into the collar of his shirt.

"We'll plan a road trip to go see her soon, okay?"

"Alright, but it's just not the same, it'll be me alone in that big house, I won't know what to do with myself."

"Get to drawing more. Or painting. Turn to art. You're so good at it. Use this as an opportunity to express your artistic side."

"I guess," I said moping. "And hey, look who you've still got. I don't live there but I sure don't mind hanging around more. Little ol' me," he said, smacking my back in good humor.

"Cheer up buttercup, it's going to be just fine."

"I suppose," I said with hesitancy but inherent trust in my love.

Chapter 18

September 1967

I just couldn't shake the feeling that something sinister shrouded that September. Every unkindness and bad word hung in the air like ripe fruit. The customers at the restaurant seemed extra sour, and I didn't have Brenda in any of my classes at school. Even Marshall and Ronnie's crops weren't harvesting right.

Near the end of the month, I received a call from Gen that there was going to be a rally next Wednesday, the 27th about desegregating her college, and that we just had to come. I thought this might turn the vibe of things around and said I'd bring it to the next civil rights meeting on Monday and see how many others could go. Wouldn't you know it, Ronnie's Impala broke down that weekend and he had to get it towed into the shop, which he couldn't until Tuesday.

So, we rode our bikes to the meeting on Monday with the hopes someone else would be willing to go to the rally and we could hitch a ride. We met a nice seeming man named Greg we'd seen around the meetings before, but not spoken to. He was a factory worker, passionate about getting equal pay and promotion opportunities for his fellow negro workers which I thought was quite admirable.

He said he'd be happy to drive us to the rally, so we were relieved. I was going to get to see Gen and participate in something that could actually make a difference! I was so excited. Plus, I'd get to skip school for it, Mama had already approved. So, Greg gave us his address and we said we'd be there 10am sharp on Wednesday. A few of the other kids who had their own ways cramming into each other's cars together were going too; it was going to be a blast.

I started making signs to bring for me and Ronnie and had a lot of fun with my paints. It was hard to fit the word 'desegregate' but I managed to. I showed Ronnie and he gave me a big kiss, repeating his mantra, 'my girl is an artist'.

He had a way of making me feel proud of myself like no one else did. His love for me became my love for myself. It's part of how we completed each other. I liked to think I did the same for him.

September 27th 1967

On the day of the rally, I stepped outside to ride my bike to Ronnie's and noticed how there was absolutely no breeze. Everything was still. The cicada bugs hummed their exotic tunes from the trees as I hopped awkwardly on my bike with my signs under my one arm and headed his way.

By the time I was there, I was so hot I wanted to unbutton my shirt, but of course I knew that would hardly be proper. Ronnie brought a canteen, some of which I poured on my face to wash away the beads of sweat that were out numbering the freckles on my nose.

"Hey," Ronnie said as we peddled "Something big is about to happen. I feel it. And we're going to be a part of it. Don't you just feel it coursing through your veins?"

"I do, I feel it too. Plus, I'm so eager to see Gen—this is the longest I've gone without being around her in my whole life. Even though it's only been a few weeks."

We arrived at Greg's after about a fifteen-minute grueling ride, though Ronnie had taken my signs for me, and when he answered the door, tall and gangly, partially bald, and he reeked of alcohol. I tried to give Ronnie a look, but I couldn't catch his eye. As we entered, I saw the bottle of gin sitting on his butcher block.

Suddenly, I didn't want to go. Well, I still wanted to go, but not with him. Something inside of me was telling me it wasn't safe. Maybe there was a way to find a ride with one of the other kids. There had to be some other means to get there. I just didn't know how to get out of it. Hopefully Ronnie would take my lead. I know, I would fake sick. That's what came to me.

"I'm not feeling very well Greg, I don't know if I'm going to be able to make the drive."

"What?" Ronnie said, "Are you really feeling that bad?"

"I'm really feeling unwell," I responded. "Well shoot, we better get you home then. Maybe Greg can drive us." He hadn't caught on.

"No! I mean, no, I'm fine to ride, but I do think we better get home."

Ronnie was confused no doubt, and disappointed, I could tell by the look on his face, but my alarm bells were going off.

"Why don't you come over here and have some pink lemonade to hydrate yourself before you go if that's your decision. You, young man, can just make yourself comfortable on the couch over there." Greg slurred.

"Sure thanks," said Ronnie.

"Okay," I accepted his offer, despite wanting to get out as soon as possible, and stepped behind the butcher block to get the glass he was offering me. I took a few sips and felt his eyes penetrating me as he stood much too close for comfort. I tried to shift away, farther down the counter, but he followed.

Out of nowhere he said, "Pull down your pants." I spit my drink back into the glass.

"What?" I said. "Pull down your pants," he commanded "Or I'll pull them down for you." His voice was vicious and he spat while he spoke.

"Hey man what the fuck are you talking about?" Ronnie got up from the couch and started to approach the kitchen. That's when Greg opened the drawer beside the fridge and pulled out the gun. First, he pointed it at Ronnie.

"Stay back kid and stay out of this, or I'll blow her brains out right in front of you," he said turning it on me. I was frozen in fear. Ronnie threw his hands up.

"Listen man, we don't want any trouble here. Just let her go and we'll be out of your hair," he tried to reason.

"Sit down and shut up. And you. I said pull down your pants or I'll pull them down for you."

My hands were shaking and all I could manage to do was place the lemonade down on the butcher block in front of me.

"I guess you're going for option number two," he said lunging my way and tearing my shorts down in a dexterous movement.

He got up behind me and wrapped his arm around me so that his hand was covering my mouth while grabbing my breasts with the other. He proceeded to rape me from behind. It felt like a thousand knives jabbing into me. It, of course, was not an unfamiliar feeling, but what was unfamiliar was the humiliation.

"Stop it, please!" Ronnie shouted, begging.

Greg used the hand not covering my mouth and grabbed the gun shoving it into my temple.

"Don't tempt me, son. Keep your Goddamn mouth shut," he said as he rammed himself inside of me.

The cold feeling of the gun on my face only added to the terror. I tried to detach like I did with my father, but I felt anchored to the time and space and to my body. I could not escape. And I couldn't breathe. That familiar struggle for breath, my nostrils automatically taking in oxygen subconsciously to survive was back to haunt me.

I don't know how long it lasted, but it felt like a lifetime. Ronnie was sobbing and standing there helpless and mute. Although I was glad I was not alone, it hurt me to see him almost as much as it hurt to have this strange man forcing himself fiercely inside me. When it was over, and he stepped away and wiped his mouth from panting with the back of his hand, keeping the gun in the other.

"Now, if I hear either of you two have said one single peep about this, I'll make you sorrier than you can imagine. I'll turn the tables so quick your heads will spin right off them their bodies. Do ya copy?"

I was pulling up my shorts and mumbled, "Yes," which apparently wasn't good enough because he took the gun and repointed it back at my temple.

"I said *do you copy?*"

"Yes sir," I said as loudly and confidently as I could muster.

"Yes, Greg we hear you loud and clear," Ronnie added, having composed himself enough to make the statement.

"Now get your asses outta here. I don't want to be seeing any more of them today," like there was a chance we'd stay or be by again. I was shaking from head to foot and bleeding from the assault.

Ronnie tried to stop and hug me outside the door, and I said, "No ride away from here first. I want to get away down to the creek."

It hurt to sit on my bike seat, and I felt nauseous and dizzy. We made it about five minutes, and I told Ronnie, who was riding by my side, that I needed to stop. I threw up all my lucky-charms from breakfast and that pink lemonade I had before the attack. Ronnie held my forehead as I heaved over in the ditch praying no one could see me.

Ronnie, again, wanted to hug me, but we weren't far away enough for that indulgence yet. Once we got to the creek, I collapsed into him and started balling. Right then and there he stripped down and gave me his boxer shorts to put on instead of the bloody mess I was currently wearing. After he buttoned his jeans back up, he just held me as we laid in the bygone leaves.

"I'm so sorry Kimberlie," (he never used my full name, which spoke to the gravity of the situation).

"I didn't know what to do, he seemed so unhinged that he might actually shoot you and I couldn't lose you so I didn't know."

"You did the only thing you could have done. Well, I guess you could have ran, and I'm glad you didn't do that. It was a comfort—a cold comfort no doubt—but a comfort nonetheless knowing you were right there with me although I was so embarrassed at what you were seeing. If I'd been alone, I'd mightn't have died from fright."

"Well don't you worry—this is far from over. That Greg's got another thing coming if he thinks he can just do that and get away with it. I'll be paying him another visit."

"Ronald Eugene Tisdale," now it was my turn to use full names, "you will not be doing *anything* of the sort. I don't want you around that man ever again. Not for any reason. You heard what he said."

He hesitated and let out a sigh, "Okay, I'll let it be. Just know it goes against every grain of my being to do so."

"I know it does Ronnie, but for me, please just stay away."

"Alright," he said, skipping a stone across the water. I began crying again.

"Ronnie, I don't want to be here anymore. This whole town is tainted for me now. Everywhere I go I'll have to be looking over my shoulder for him. He's gone and ruined everything. What am I going to do?"

"What are *we* going to do is the question. We're in this together Kim, you're not alone," he said taking my legs and putting them across him.

"Let's run away. We can go up to my sister's place in Wilmington for now, but then we can go anywhere your heart desires. We'll use our honeymoon fund, plus my regular savings to support us 'til we can get jobs which won't take long. We'll get married along the way. What do you say?"

I think he was expecting me to reject his plan, but I saw no other way out, so I agreed whole heartedly.

"Yes Ronnie, I think that's a fantastic idea. But what about the farm?" He thought for a moment about it.

"Some things are just more priorities in life and you're my number one, so they'll just have to figure it out without me. They'll just need an extra farm hand or two. They have Henry. Grandma will survive. If I'm being selfish, so be it. I don't care."

"Oh Ronnie, thank you," I said untangling my legs from his and reaching up to hug him. My heart was beating so fast as he held me, but it gradually slowed to a more average tempo.

"Shit! My car! We need my car! I'll get you home and then I'm going to slip into the shop even though I'm not scheduled and work on it and it should be ready by the morning. Will you be ready to go at say, 9am tomorrow? Does that sound reasonable?"

"Sounds like a plan," I said in a choked and raspy voice that was all which could come out.

"Is it easier for you to walk than to bike?"

"Yes."

"Okay, let me walk you home with your bike and draw you a bath before I head over to the shop. Oh, and do you want me to try and call Gen and tell her you're too sick to make it to the rally?"

My heart sank further into my stomach as I remembered what I was supposed to be doing that day. I would have been in Charleston by now if everything had gone according to plan. I'd just left my signs at Greg's house as there was no need to struggle with them on the bike for no reason. All that hard work for nothing.

The pain was bad. He had torn me open. Even walking was difficult. Ronnie was patient with me as I shuffled along taking baby steps down the road to my house. I must have been a sore sight in his boxers. No one was home, so we had the place to ourselves once we made it there.

Bobbsey greeted me at the door as though he knew the trauma I'd just been through. I picked up the now twenty-pound cat and snuggled my nose into his soft fur as he purred. I brought him in the bathroom with us.

"Now, I want this to be warm to soothe you, but not so warm that it hurts whatever he did to you down there, so I'm going to get it the perfect temperature. Are you shaking because of what he did to you or because you're cold?"

"Both," I answered.

The shock had made me cold in spite of the sweltering heat.

"Oh, baby come here," and he took me on his lap as he sat on the edge of the bathtub and held me through my tremors. He slowly undressed me and took my hand as I slipped into the cozy tub.

"It stings Ronnie."

"I'm sorry sweetheart. Give it a minute and maybe it will fade." And it did. I lay back and let the warmth engulf my body. My mind was reeling from what had just happened, and I was so glad to have Ronnie by my side.

"Does it still hurt?" he inquired thoughtfully.

"Yes, but not as bad."

"I'm glad to hear it." He paused.

"Kim. Are you sure I can't go back?"

"I'm positive. Ronnie, do not go back there under any circumstances do you hear me?"

"Yes, I hear you," he said in a low voice.

"Do you want me to call the police?"

"No, they're just like my father. I can't trust them."

"Okay, if that's how you feel about it, it's totally up to you." I got out and dabbed myself gently with a towel.

"Do you mind if I step out and try Gen?"

"No, go ahead. You know where the phone is; her new number is posted on the wall beside it."

"I'm just going to tell her that you're sick, right?"

"Right," I responded. I wanted to tell her, I would tell her, but not now. Not until I was far away from this now contaminated town. From him.

Gen was living off campus with a couple of other girls, and one of them answered the phone when Ronnie called.

Gen wasn't in, she was at the rally, but they said they'd be sure to get the message to her ASAP as they were heading over there soon themselves. I hoped she wasn't mad at me, or worried, but it could not be helped. It was well past noon now and Ronnie was eager to get to the shop to get working on his car so it would be ready for the morning.

"I hate to leave you Kim. It breaks my heart. But for us to get away, I've got to fix the Impala."

"I know baby, I understand."

"Maybe I'll walk you down to the shop then come home again. Just to kill some time."

"If that would make you happy, you're more than welcome to accompany me."

It was about a twenty-five-minute walk into town to the shop, especially since I was so slow moving from the pain, but I pushed through it to get to spend that extra bit of time with Ronnie. When we got to the garage, I stayed around for about a half hour, I wanted to longer but didn't want to intrude or get him into any trouble.

I loved watching Ronnie work. He was in his element, and I could tell he felt confident in what he was doing. He consulted with Mark, who ran the garage, over a few things, but got started right away on the Impala himself. He told me it was going to take a while, so we solidified our plan for tomorrow at 9am, and how he would pick me up. He asked me to get a map at the gas station on my way home for our trip up north, which I did.

When I got home, I packed my suitcase with as much of my clothes as possible around my record player in somber silence. Just like old times. I couldn't believe I was having to run again. That my safe haven had been compromised. I started to feel angry—it was so unfair.

Why should *I* have to leave. It should be Greg. Greg should be exiled! But no, the victim was being displaced. However, there was nothing I could do about it but accept my fate. I had Ronnie and we would marry. We might not get the honeymoon we'd planned for, but we had each other. That was most important.

Chapter 19

Gen called around eight o'clock that night. She told me all about the rally, and how, "I should have been there."

It took everything in me not to break into tears and tell her the truth. I had no appetite and could barely swallow any of my dinner.

"What's the matter Gina?" Mama asked as I pushed around the food on my plate.

"I just have a stomach-ache. I can't eat I'm sorry."

"Don't be sorry honey, I'm sorry you're not feeling well. Would you like to be excused to go lie down?"

"Yes please," I responded in relief.

I went and laid down on the couch and put *The Jetsons* on. Anything mundane to distract myself. When Mama finished dinner, she came over to me and put her fresh hand on my cheek.

"Well, it doesn't feel like you have a fever at least, that's a good thing. But you look awfully pale. Like someone's taken the life right out of you."

"I might need to stay home from school again tomorrow if I don't start feeling better."

"Of course. We'll see how you feel come morning and if you're not better I'll call in for you," she said stroking my hair.

Oh Mama! How I was going to miss her! Why did she have to be a part of this Godforsaken place. And Bobbsey! My sweet boy! How I wished I could take him along. All I could console myself, over and over, was with was Ronnie. At least, I had him. Time crawled along until bedtime, and I throbbed in pain as a reminder of the day's earlier events.

It kept flashing in my mind like constant lightning bolts without thunder. I wondered if Ronnie had fixed up his car but couldn't risk calling to ask with the party line and all—someone might overhear our plans. So, I waited in silence and went to bed assuming it would be my last night in this house. I cuddled Bobbsey close and cried bitter tears—bitter that things had to be the way they were. This is what bitterness truly felt like.

I fell into a sound dreamless sleep that night, my soul exhausted from my day. I was woken up by Mama at six-thirty, asking how I was feeling. I lied that my stomach still hurt, so she said she'd call into school for me. I stayed in bed for a while, feeling like dead weight, but got up to say goodbye to Mama. I held her extra tight and tried not to cry.

"What's the matter baby? Are you feeling that unwell?" she said to me. Obviously, I was unable to hide myself from her.

"I just feel really sick." I didn't know what else to say.

"Don't worry, I'll hurry home at the end of my shift. I'll bring you some soup too!"

"Thanks Mama," I said with extreme guilt for lying to her in that moment, knowing I'd be long gone by then.

"Now go back and lie down. Rest up, that's all you can do."

"Okay I will," I said starting to head back down the hallway to my bedroom. I stopped and turned around.

"I love you Mama,"

"Oh sweetie, I love you too. I hope that you're feeling better by the time I see you next."

Little did she know I had no idea when that would be.

When she left, I made sure I had everything packed that I needed. I checked then double checked then nine o'clock rolled around and I took my suitcase out to the driveway, praying Marshall would stay in the fields. Ronnie was late but I tried not to stress. Then he was really late, and I became concerned.

When nine-thirty came, I put my suitcase back in my room and decided, despite the pain, to get on my bike and head over to his place. Maybe he didn't get his car fixed? But why hadn't he called? I pushed through the pain and the fright—where was he?

It was so unlike him to break plans. I made my way down his dusty driveway and felt my heart pounding deep and hard in my chest. Something was wrong. I could feel it. There his car was. I frantically knocked at the door and his grandmother answered.

"Gina! What are you doing here?"

"I'm looking for Ronnie."

"Dang nab it, I'd hoped he was with you," using the phrase he so often used himself.

"What do you mean?" I said. "Come in, come in," she beckoned.

"I mean I haven't seen him since last night after the police left, and I thought he'd gone to find you. I thought he was with you this whole time."

"What do you mean the police?" I said panicking. We had agreed to not get them involved.

"He went over to that Gregory Steven's house with his grandfather's shotgun to 'teach him a lesson'. He wouldn't tell me about what, just that he had to do it. I tried to stop him, but there was no interfering with his mission. I don't know what went on over there, but he came back, and within the hour we had the police knocking at our door.

"They talked about how you two had been there earlier in the day, and that Stevens had seen him roughhousing you. I tried to interject and say there was no way, but they wouldn't let me speak. Ronnie said he never touched you and that it was Stevens who had hurt you.

"The police didn't seem to take much mind of that and diverted the conversation back to how Ronnie was threatening Stevens with a gun that night. Ronnie admitted to doing it, and said it was because Greg had hurt you previously. They said they weren't buying what he was selling, and said he'd gone back to rob him."

"Rob him," Ronnie said, "Rob him of what? The guy's got nothing."

"He's got a ring that he said you had your eye on."

"He's lying," Ronnie said. That's when they said they'd stopped to talk to you and you didn't want to be seeing anymore of him after that stunt.

He said, "Are you sure she said that?" and they retorted, "We're positive, she was pretty angry with you for going back."

He repeated, "She said she didn't want to be seeing anymore of me?" and they said, "That's right. You should have never gone back to Stevens'."

Then they asked if he was going to stay away from you and Stevens or if they needed to take him in. He was only half present then, after the news about you, and listened, but I don't think heard the rest of their lecture.

"So, she's gone?" he asked at the end, and they just said, "I guess that's the consequence of your actions son. Consider this a warning and yourself lucky that we're not booking you."

"He raped her," he finally said, and the police responded saying, "Well, if that's the case, she needs to come down to the station and report it then. As for you, I strongly advise you stay away from both Mr. Stevens and Miss Owens. Have a good rest of your night."

And with that they left.

"But they never spoke to me!" I exclaimed. "They're liars, they never spoke to me, I never said I didn't want anything to do with him, I'd never say that! Mrs. Knight—where is Ronnie?"

"I don't know, sweetheart. I knew you'd never say those things. After the police left he was crying up a storm. He said he was heading out for a bit, and I just assumed it was to go find you and straighten things out."

I burst out of the house.

The sinister feeling that had permeated that September became all concentrated into that one moment. He'd been gone all night, this wasn't good. Where would he go? His bike was missing. The creek. Perhaps he had just camped out there for the night. I got on my bike and started peddling madly, up and down the hills into the forest. I saw his bike first which was initially a relief.

"Ronnie?" I called out. And then I caught a glimpse of it, the limp figure dangling from the bridge. No. It couldn't be. I peddled closer and jumped off tossing my bike aside.

"Ronnie?" I said again, this time more strained and frantic.

As I got closer, every worst fear in my body came into fruition. The limp figure suspended from the bridge was him. My love. My one and only. My other half. Lifeless, hanging, dangling like a puppet on a thread. I literally felt my heart stop a beat. I froze. I couldn't move my body.

I wanted to run to him, but it was like in my nightmares when I lost all my mobility. What if he's still alive, I have to go to him! I picked up one foot, it was like cement, and then the other.

"Help!" I screamed hoping someone, anyone could hear me.

"Help!" I yelled again at the top of my lungs.

I simply couldn't get my feet to keep moving. When I was finally able to, I stumbled down the embankment and into the creek. I reached for his wrist praying there would be a heartbeat, but it was cold and clammy and dead. I shuddered and tore my hand away.

I trudged out of the creek and ran up the hill. I stood there for a minute in a daze knowing what I needed to do next but not wanting to. Slowly, I made my way back to Ronnie's grandmother's house and knocked on the door.

"Mrs. Knight, I found him," I stuttered.

"You've found him!" she exclaimed, but I cut her off.

"No. It's not good. He's hanged himself down by the creek. He's dead, Mrs. Knight, he's dead!" I broke down sobbing.

"What?" she said not comprehending what I was saying.

"He's *dead*?"

"Yes, Mrs. Knight, I'm sorry." I collapsed to my knees with my face in my lap. I couldn't believe my baby was gone. Why did he have to listen to them? Why hadn't he consulted with me? Were his abandonment issues that bad?

"We've got to get Henry to cut him down," I said. His grandmother agreed through dismayed tears herself.

"I'll go fetch him from the fields," which she did.

Henry carried him back to the farm with us and placed him on his bed. I wouldn't look at him. I didn't want to see the marks around his neck or what it did to his face. I didn't want to remember my love that way. All I knew was that I needed Mama, and I needed her now.

I decided I would bike to the restaurant. I hugged Ronnie's grandma and left. It felt like I had a hard brick inside me sitting on the hard seat. I peddled madly. Faster than I'd peddled in my life. My legs burned like the time I had pretended to be riding away from my father, and I wanted them to, to divert my attention from all the other pain, inside and outside. I showed up, half delusional, into the diner, tear-stained cheeks, out of breath, dripping sweat. Mama was behind the counter.

"Gina! What are you doing here?" she said coming out from behind it.

"I need you, Mama," was all I could articulate. She took my hand and led me to the back.

"What is it baby, what's the matter?" she whispered so the cook couldn't hear.

"Ronnie's dead!" I burst out and flung myself onto her, disregarding completely that she was at work. She embraced me back.

"What? *Dead*? How?" she continued to use a hushed tone despite my less than quiet outpouring.

"I can't tell you here. It's too long of a story. I've been hiding something from you. Can you please come home?"

I knew how seriously Mama took her job and how heavy a request this was.

"Let me talk to Joyce, I'm sure she'll be okay with it if I tell her it's an emergency. I'll call Brooke right now and see if she can come in early. Come sit out here and I'll get you something to drink. Do you want a milkshake? How about your favorite, chocolate? Just for you," she attempted to comfort.

"Okay I'll try it," I said to appease her, gathering myself and going out to perch myself at the bar.

Mama made the milkshake, which I could barely get down my throat, then called Brooke who luckily agreed to come in. Joyce said it was fine for her to leave right away though.

I just didn't know what to do with my bike. Mama said she'd get Marshall to come back later for it and put it in the trunk of one of his cars with bungee cords, so we were on our way. When we got in the car, I came out with it immediately.

"Greg Stevens raped me, Mama, and Ronnie went back to teach him a lesson. Then the police accused Ronnie of trying to rob him and said that I didn't want anything to do with him anymore, and he believed them because I told him that I didn't want him going back. They said that they'd spoken to me when they hadn't, they lied Mama, they lied and he believed them and killed himself," I said through heaving sobs.

"We're going to the police, Kimberlie."

"No, Mama! Aren't you hearing me? If it weren't for them Ronnie would still be alive. Look at the mess they've made already!"

"Well, they need to clean it up best they can and deal properly with this Stevens man after what he's done to you. We're going to talk to them."

"Can we go back to the house first?"

"Okay, but then we're going."

We went back to the house, and I cuddled Bobbsey on the couch hoping I could convince Mama against going to the police, though part of me wanted to confront them on the mistruths they had told Ronnie. I was torn. Literally and figuratively.

Either way, Mama was hearing none of it, we were going to the police and that was the end of it. I felt acutely that she was overestimating them, what evidence did we have to trust them? My father? The men who had lied to Ronnie? Why were we bothering with them? I wanted justice just as much as she did but had already resigned myself to the fact that it was not to be.

Look what happened when Jeb died? Nothing. White men were privileged here and that was the end of the story. I could feel my anger boiling as we drove like a kettle about to whistle. When we arrived, I saw men who reminded me of my father, some big lugs in uniform, and a 'detective' in a suit whose arrogance was enough to make one vomit on the spot.

"Hello there, can we help you?"

"Yes—why did you lie to my boyfriend? Why did you tell him you'd spoken to me and that I didn't want to see him anymore?" "Whoa, whoa, slow down there miss. Who are you talking about?"

"Ronnie Tisdale," I was breathing as rapidly as my heart was beating.

"Oh yes, that boy from last night. Let me get the sergeant, he's the one who dealt with him." He went into a back office and emerged with a shorter man who had slicked back blonde hair and was chewing gum.

"You're here inquiring about the Tisdale boy?"

"Yes, I am. You told him I didn't want to see him again and now he's dead. Why did you say that? Why?" I started hyperventilating.

"Settle down there young lady. I said it for your own protection. First off, I'd heard he'd been roughhousing you earlier in the day—" I interrupted.

"Not true!" I yelled, "Greg was just saying that to take the guilt off himself!"

"Alright, alright, no need to raise your voice, I can hear ya. Secondly, he'd been acting very irrationally with a firearm later in the day and with the information I had, I thought it best he stay away from you. My intentions were good. I'm sorry it panned out the way it did."

"Sorry? You're sorry? He's dead! Sorry isn't good enough."

I broke down into tears and tucked myself into Mama.

She turned to the officer and said, "She's been through a lot. In fact, we're actually here to report a rape by Greg Stevens against my baby girl here Gina Owens."

"Okay then, if you'd just step back here and sit at the desk, we'll get a statement started."

So, I did. I recounted the details to these strange men, which felt violating all over again.

At the end of it, all they could say was, "We'll see what we can do."

I was right. I knew nothing would be done. Like I said, he was a white man, he had all the power. I was stuck. Stuck in this town with him now indefinitely without Ronnie or Gen.

I felt like there was a deep gaping hole inside me. What was I going to do without him? Ronnie had been my world since moving to Andrews. My soul ached. I was completely lost, like a broken compass.

The funeral was small and private. Gen came home for it; she even cried. Mama held my hand until I spoke. I felt I needed to say a few words about Ronnie because I knew him best, though I couldn't collect myself to deliver much.

"Ronnie was a compassionate boy who loved deeply. He was fun and silly and hardworking. He was there for me in my darkest moments, and I'll always regret not being able to be there for him in his. He was my other half, and I will miss him forever."

It was heart-wrenching seeing Ronnie's grandma so upset. I was glad she didn't blame me, she blamed the police, and Greg, but the comfort was small. I offered to help her out with the stand when I wasn't working at the restaurant or at school and she was grateful for that.

"My boy will live on through you," she said to me.

I hoped it was true. The sandwiches inside were stale tasting and made me feel sick. Ronnie would have wanted peanut butter and jelly was all I could think. I wondered in that moment if it was true that you could actually die of a broken heart, because if you could, death was upon me.

December 1967

But, I wasn't so fortunate, and I was forced to live in this alternate reality, without my love. Time marched onward. Christmas was dim and sad. Shortly thereafter I had enough money to buy myself a car. All I could think of was how I wished Ronnie were there to help me like he had been with Mama's and his own.

I settled on a 1958 Plymouth Fury in cherry red with a white top and white rimmed wheels. It was red inside too, with a white wheel. I felt Ronnie's spirit guiding me as I combed the lot and thought that he would have endorsed of my final decision. Red was his favorite color after all. I felt safer once I had my car.

No more biking to work or to Ronnie's to work at the stand. I drove everywhere. This is also when I bought my first pack of cigarettes. One day I was feeling anxious, and I thought I'd give them a try. It was love at first puff. I felt the release flow through my body. I wondered if Ronnie would have accepted. I'm sure he'd understand, I reasoned.

I had to keep it a secret though, I knew if Mama found out I was smoking she's freak out, even though she did herself. So, I smoked at school, and at Ronnie's and sporadically at home when Mama and Marshall weren't around. It was the worst at work when I felt like I needed them the most, but of course couldn't risk the other waitresses telling Mama.

Sometimes, when I couldn't get back to sleep after a nightmare, I'd sneak out onto the porch and have one. My favorite was when it was raining. Rainy night smokes relaxed me the most. I would talk to Ronnie like he was there, and maybe I'm crazy, but I could swear his spirit was. Sometimes I'd hear his voice answer me back in my mind. The pitter-patter of the raindrops in the background of my conversation.

I asked him if he regretted not coming to me and he said, "Yes, with all his heart."

I don't know if it's just wishful thinking, or if it was actually him, but the thoughts didn't feel like my own.

He said it was an 'impulsive act of heartbreak', and a 'reaction to perceived abandonment'. I'd look and swear I could see him out of the corner of my eye, but then I'd glance over, and he'd be gone. I wanted to reach out and grab him, to touch him one last time. Oh, what I'd do for one last kiss!

It crossed my mind to take one of Marshall's guns and go and shoot Greg, that officer that lied to him, and then shoot myself, and then Ronnie's voice, clear as a bell in my brain, said "No, just like you said to me but I didn't listen. No, I need you to stay. To stay alive. God has plans for you still."

So unlike Ronnie, I hung on and resisted my urges to seek revenge and escape the heartache.

As expected, nothing ever came of my report. No repercussions for Greg, who essentially killed Ronnie. If he hadn't done what he did to me, Ronnie would still be alive. So yes, the police lied, but that was later in the chain of events. The original link began with Greg, I couldn't forget that. I decided that even though I wasn't going to shoot Greg, the officer or myself, I still wanted a gun.

I was still looking over my shoulder at every turn as I had expected and was afraid falling asleep. I wanted the security to protect myself. I picked one that was easy to use, and small enough to fit in my purse. It was shiny and I liked it—I felt more in control immediately. When I went to bed, I put it in my nightstand drawer, locked and loaded.

Mama didn't know about it, and probably would have shunned the whole idea, but I needed it, or at least I felt I did. Of course, I didn't bring it to school; though I would have if I could. School had become frivolous business and frankly, I'd had enough of it. I was no Gen.

I did not excel in any area, and I didn't plan on going to college. So, the time came when I asked Mama if I could drop out and work full time at the restaurant. At first, she was fully against it. However, I pleaded my case; I explained how my heart wasn't in it and how depressed it made me feel, and she finally gave in.

Luckily, the diner was able to take me on full time as Betsy had just retired. Perfect timing. And so, I fell into a mundane routine, but at least I was getting paid for it.

Part 3

Chapter 20

December 31st 1969

It was Gen's final year in college and she was having a New Year's party. I drove down to Charleston for it, with nothing else to do. I met a guy named Mike who was studying chemistry. He was attractive with sandy blonde hair and the kind of green eyes that change color in the light. After too many drinks I ended up in bed with him and one thing led to another. He left right after we were finished, it was very unromantic—nothing like with Ronnie.

It was my first time being with someone since him and it made me nostalgic for our bond, nothing like the crude lovemaking I had just experienced. It left me cold and wanting nothing more. I didn't even get his last name, and Gen only vaguely knew who he was. Oh well, what did it matter!

In that moment, not at all. But a month later, when I missed my period, it mattered a bit more. Then another week passed, and it still didn't come. Plus I was sick every morning. I went and called Gen.

"Holy shit, you're pregnant," she said seemingly more shocked than I was.

"Yes, it's been two months," I said. "I don't think I want to tell the father."

"Good luck finding him if you do. I mean, I'm sure I can track him down if you want me to. It's a pretty big deal, are you sure you want to do it all by yourself?"

"I'm sure," I said with conviction. In that moment, I'd never been surer of anything in my life. It was my baby, and I didn't want to share it with some stranger. I didn't want the interference and that was my final decision. Now, to tell Mama. I did not expect her to be happy, but she responded with more joy than expected.

"You mean there'll be a baby Kim coming into the world?" was her retort. "Well—yes…"

"Oh Kim, I'm delighted! Who's the father?"

"This guy named Mike from Gen's school. I don't know his last name and I don't really want to tell him anyhow."

I winced waiting for her reaction.

"Okay, so this was a casual encounter. Is there any reason you don't want to tell him?"

"The baby is mine and I don't know him, and I don't want to have to trust him with my child."

"Well, that's perfectly understandable. Although, I personally can't help but feel he has the right to know, I support your decision to keep him uninvolved. It's your body, your little one, and your choice."

"Thank you, Mama," I said and gave her a hug.

It was a new and strange sensation to think something was growing inside of me. I tried to pretend to myself that the baby was Ronnie's which made it a bit easier. I had to go into Georgetown to the hospital there, to see the doctor for my prenatal appointments. The doctor was tall with a full head of white hair.

He had a caring, unassuming face, with a bulb shaped nose, blue eyes and a gentle smile. He was a gentleman and never questioned me about where the father was, though I was sure he was wondering it. He reassured me that my morning sickness was normal, and I needed reassuring because it was bad. He said my iron was low and I was told to eat foods like spinach and liver.

Yuk! But, I had to do what I had to do. I wanted a healthy baby. I even gave up smoking; that was the hardest thing. Plus, I was tired all the time, making work quite difficult.

I wanted to scream at customers, "Can you hold on a minute, I'm pregnant!" but we all know that was an impossibility.

Ironically, when I started to show is when I got my energy back, around sixteen weeks (late April), and the diner didn't want me working anymore—though they assured me that my position would be waiting for me once I'd given birth. I was clearly insulted by this, but there was nothing I could do about it.

Thankfully, Ronnie's grandmother continued to let me help out at the stand, so I still had some money coming in, but not too much. Luckily, since I'd bought my car, I'd not had much to spend on besides clothes, cosmetics and gas so I had plenty saved, and at the end of the day, I knew Marshall would step up and help with any additional baby costs.

He'd been involved and concerned from the get-go, buying me ginger ale when I was sick; he even insisted on coming to the doctor's when Mama couldn't make it. He was a good man I'd come to see over the years, and I trusted him and appreciated his presence in our lives. He'd only bettered them.

Really, he showed me what a father should be like, even though I don't think he was particularly trying to, which made it all the more genuine.

Shortly after I stopped working at the restaurant, I started feeling kicks inside me! Kicks and movement, little jabs here and there. The tiny person within me was alive and they were letting it be known! When I played music, the baby seemed to dance in my stomach. I would play it songs Ronnie and I used to listen to together.

I had this feeling that I couldn't shake, and didn't want to, that the baby coming to me was Ronnie's soul reincarnated. I felt like he was coming home to me in the only way that he could. One day, I was lying in my bed and my clock radio turned itself onto *Can't Take My Eyes Off You*, the song I'd used to cheer him up when his grandpa died.

There was no one else in the room to turn it on. No explanation. I just know it was the universe's way of telling me he was coming back to me. And as the song played, the baby kicked up a storm, hopping away in my belly to the beat, just as we had together.

September 1970

About a month before the baby was due, I packed up my Plymouth and decided to head north to my Nana's to have the baby, as she was a midwife. I hadn't seen her since I was thirteen, but had missed her dearly, and knew it was where I wanted to bring my child into the world. It was a seven-and-a-half-hour drive, so I started out early.

I got nervous driving through Virginia but reminded myself that my car was different so my father wouldn't be able to spot me, and I wasn't driving directly through Montross. Still, I refused to stop and pee which was a feat in and of itself. I arrived at Nana's to her warm embrace like I had never left it. Her soft white hair was blowing in the late summer wind as she came out to greet me.

She had a room set up waiting for me; a comfortable bed where I'd be giving birth next to a chestnut nightstand with a seashell lamp and a clock radio, not unlike my own. I turned it on and *Sleepwalk* was playing. I knew I was in the right place. What Mama so notoriously called a good old 'synchronicity'. *Another sign from Ronnie*, I thought. He's coming to be mine again. I rubbed my belly affectionately. My baby. My baby and no one else's.

October 4th 1970

The pains came on strong and steady, like a racehorse pulling ahead. As they became closer together, I started to panic, but Nana was there to calm me, and told me it was a natural part of the baby coming. When I felt it starting to arrive, and I needed to push, it was one of the scariest moments of my life.

I had no choice, even though in that moment I didn't want to. It was a strange mix of horrible discomfort and relief as I forced through it. I was hot and cold at once and screamed loudly as I released the baby from my body.

Once the baby was finally out, Nana cut the cord and announced, "You have a beautiful baby boy."

I knew it!

"Ronnie," I said, taking the newly swaddled infant in my arms.

"Ronald Eugene Owens."

My baby. I couldn't believe the miracle I was holding, how just moments ago he had been inside of me. No, I wouldn't be tracking down his father. He was all mine. I couldn't hold him close enough. I took off the blanket wrapped around him, so our skin was on each other's skin.

He took to nursing immediately, a time which I will always cherish. I hadn't been so happy since Ronnie was with me. He was alive again; I just knew it. I felt our souls connected as one as they had been in old times. I was complete again.

Nana crocheted him a pumpkin hat and sweater for Halloween. I delighted in the children coming to the door dressed as witches and vampires, thinking how in not so many years that it would be Ronnie out collecting candy. We went and bought a car seat and a stroller.

I relaxed in the autumn sunshine, and we took a trip to the ocean. I dipped Ronnie's baby toes in the water. I ate French fries with sea salt and ketchup and walked around with Nana while pushing Ronnie in his new stroller down the boardwalk.

"You're going to be the best mother of all time," Nana told me, and I believed her, because I felt like I loved Ronnie more than any mother had ever loved any child on earth.

He had a tuft of hair that was dark like mine with a hue of strawberry in it, and that same cupid's bow mouth as Ronnie had. A perfect blend of he and I. He was perfection to me. I stayed with Nana until November when I was fully healed from the birth, and then I felt it was time to venture home.

So, I said goodbye to the seashell lamp and packed up my Plymouth again—the stroller barely fit—and set off on our journey back to Andrews. I was excited to show him off. Gen came home for my arrival. They put up blue and purple streamers and had balloons to welcome us. Mama, and Marshall and Gen cooed over Ronnie and all three agreed he was the most adorable baby they'd ever seen.

Next on the docket was to introduce him to Mrs. Knight. I took him over that evening after supper. She doted on him and noted the similarities in the face with our other Ronnie. She said she'd gladly watch him whenever I needed her to with work and all, which was very generous of her. It turned out I didn't need her that much as Mama and I often worked alternating shifts; Mama in the day and I in the evenings.

So, when I was working it was either Mama, or Marshall or Mrs. Knight taking care of him, all of whom I felt dependable. I was still nursing, which made it difficult. I had to pump which I hated doing. It was funny to watch the animals with the baby.

Lucy wagged her tail and tried to kiss him, letting out a playful bark. Sal wanted nothing to do with him, and Bobbsey was curious but confused about how a human could be so small, ultimately sniffing and nudging him like the sweet boy that he was.

Christmas 1970

At Christmas Gen announced she was quitting her job at the department store in Charleston and moving to a commune where she'd find new work. Mama was not impressed by this news and asked her if she was planning on doing something with her degree, to which she responded coolly, "When I can." Gen had met this man named Tim who'd introduced her to the Bahá'í faith which she'd jumped into both feet first.

From what I understood, it taught the essential worth of all religions and the unity of all people. It was very tied into the civil rights movement, which is where she'd met him, at a rally. It promoted equality between men and women, universal education and the elimination of all forms of prejudice, among many other things that appealed to Gen's inner drive.

The commune was a set of small cottages off Old Highway #6. She brought Tim to the house to meet the family and attempt to set our minds at ease. He was tall and lanky with a braid at the side of his long brown hair.

Marshall called him a 'hippie' and he responded by saying, "Ya man, I guess that's one way you could categorize me. But I'm not a dumb hippie. I make decisions from an educated point of view."

"Glad to hear it," said, Marshall still skeptical of Tim's character.

"I'm all for living off the land. Like what you do here is amazing. Sustainable farming? That's what it's all about. I've got a liberal arts degree, but what does that get me in terms of serving humanity? Not much. Wish I could be more like you."

"I'm humbled by your words young man," Marshall responded, having softened, "You're always welcome to spend time with me here learning the ropes if you're ever interested."

"Oh wow, thanks, that's quite an offer, I really appreciate that. Thank you," Tim said putting out his hand to shake Marshall's. And he did come back.

One day, he and Gen showed up with the sun and he spent the day following Marshall and Lucy around, hearing the ins and outs of farming—not that he had anywhere substantial to use it.

From what I heard, the commune had a vegetable garden and a few fruit trees, but I think it helped that Tim showed an interest in the family business.

August 1971

When Ronnie was about ten months old, I took him for a trip to the commune and fell in love with it. I adored the little community of people, the five cottages with people of like minds who thought like me. I knew then and there I wanted to be a part of it, but didn't know how, as all the cottages were taken.

I was becoming more and more enamored with the Bahá'í faith as well, the more I learned about it, and wanted to immerse myself in it. Such ideas as the centrality of justice to all human endeavors and harmony between religion and science appealed to my heart on a fundamental level. I felt intrinsically drawn to it more than I had to church in years. Not that I had anything against church.

I loved Jesus and God and all that, I just felt that the Bahá'í religion elevated these relationships.

In the words of Bahá'u'lláh, one of the first two divine messengers of the Bahá'í faith, "He Who is your Lord, cherishith in His heart the desire of beholding the entire human race as one soul and one body."

So, Christ was still a part of the Bahá'í faith, which was important to me. Prayer was encouraged, just like with Christianity.

Again, in the words of Bahá'u'lláh, "Gather ye together with the utmost joy and fellowship and recite the versus revealed by the most merciful Lord. By doing so the doors to true knowledge will be opened to your inner beings and you will feel your souls endowed with steadfastness…"

The commune worked by pooling their money together and drawing from it as needed.

This was in line with the Bahá'í teaching of divine messenger Shogi Effendi, who said, "We must be like the fountain that is continually emptying itself of all it has and is continually being refilled from an invisible source. To be continually giving out for the good of our fellows undeterred by fear of poverty and reliant on the unfailing bounty of the Source of all wealth and all good—this is the secret of right living."

Something inside of me was pulling me to become a part of this community; it was where Ronnie and I belonged. The only thing I could think of was to get a camper. So, I went to our trusted car lot and lo and behold I found a 1965 Clark Cortez. It had a little kitchen, bed and shower. It was exactly what I needed. The only problem was it was far out of my price range.

I knew the only way I could afford it would be if Marshall would help me out and I'd never asked him for money in my life. I was worried because I figured he and Mama would probably disapprove of me moving to the commune in the first place.

There were two restaurants there, one literally right off the property to the right of the commune and then one across the street attached to the place where Gen had found employment called 'Bell's Marina'. She worked the front desk at the motel.

It was no teaching job, but she said she was able to teach the children at the commune, who were 5, 7, and 16, about the Bahá'í faith and general education which satisfied her, and made her feel as though her degree wasn't going completely to waste.

Anyhow, when it came to launching my idea, I was nervous. I waited until dinner on my day off; Ronnie joining us at table in his highchair was precious.

"Marshall," I began, trying my best to sound pleasant, confident, and casual all at once.

"I know you don't normally do this, and God knows I normally wouldn't ask, but I was wondering if you might help me pay for something upfront, and then I pay you back in intervals?"

"Well, you've got me intrigued Gina, and trusting you, my tentative answer is yes. But what is it you're looking to purchase?" Mama tried to interject in disapproval, but Marshall just put his hand up to show that it was between he and I.

"It's a Clark Cortez, it's down at the lot right now. I promise I'll pay you back, no matter how long it takes," I said removing Ronnie from his highchair and setting him onto my lap. Mama could stay silent no longer.

"And what exactly do you plan on doing with this motor home?"

Here it goes, I thought. "I want to go live with Vee on the commune." There, I'd said it.

"I'll get a job right away, and there will always be someone there to take care of Ronnie. I need a change, Mama. I want out of Andrews. I have for years now. Maybe just for a little while, I don't know, but I'm tired of it here. I'm, still always waiting for that monster to come crawling out of the bushes at any moment and I'm sick of it."

"I understand, honey. I just don't know if you've thought this through thoroughly. Are you really okay with the idea of you and Ronnie living in a van?"

"Yes." I replied steadfastly.

"Yes, I am. Besides, it's more than a van, it's a little home. Come down to the lot and I'll show it to you. You'll feel better about it once you see it I bet."

"I don't need to see it, my darling. And I can't stop you. If this is what your heart so desires, as I've always encouraged, then follow it."

"Oh, thank you Mama, you won't regret your approval."

"If your mother approves, then I certainly don't mind fronting you the cash."

"You two are the best parents anyone could ever ask for!" I said, truly meaning it.

I then saw Marshall wipe a tear from his left eye, something I'd never seen come from him in the past four years since we'd met him. I was momentarily confused and concerned I'd said something wrong. Gearing up to backtrack, I realized it was because I had referred to them as 'parents' and now didn't know what to do to break the awkwardness.

Grasping, I asked, "So, would you come with me to the lot tomorrow, Marshall?"

"I most certainly will. How does three o'clock sound?"

"Perfect. So long as Mama trusts us two alone to make the decision."

"Of course, I do!" she answered with a flip of the hand.

"You two will make out just fine without me. I'm excited to see what comes of it though."

August 31st 1971

So, at three o'clock the next day Marshall and I set out to the car lot with our goal in mind. As I already knew, he wasn't much of a bargainer, but he attempted to step up and we got it for $1500. Part of me felt super uncomfortable taking the money from Marshall, it was a lot, but I wanted it so badly, I pushed my feelings aside.

What complicated my feelings even more was when they handed me the keys, he said, "Consider this a gift kiddo. Don't you be worrying about paying me back. I want the money you earn to go toward you and Ronnie. And no need to be telling your mother neither. You hear?"

"Oh Marshall, it's such a substantial gift, are you sure I can't repay you somehow?"

"Repay me with your happiness. I've been seeing you down ever since your Ronnie died, though the little one's brought some light back into your eyes, I haven't heard you laugh like you used to with that boy. I want that contentment back for you. Maybe, you'll find it with your sister on that commune of hers."

I was overwhelmed with gratitude.

"Thank you, Marshall, I don't know what to say. It's mighty generous of you and I appreciate it with all my heart."

"You're welcome Gina. Just put it to good use, that's all I ask." "I will, I promise."

I had Marshall drive it home from the lot as I hadn't driven a stick shift since Ronnie's old truck, and he had to re-teach me how to drive it. But where there's a will, there's a way! It was a real change from driving my relatively tiny Plymouth Fury to this big lug of a vehicle, so I practiced around town for a bit before taking it out on the highway.

I took it over to show Mrs. Knight, who was fascinated by it, but upset by the news that little Ronnie and I were going to be leaving town. She started to cry and said she felt like she was 'losing Ronnie all over again'. It broke my heart to hear I was inflicting this upon her, and hardly knew how to respond.

I promised she wasn't losing us—that we'd be back to visit all the time and we'd always come to see her. She seemed generally assuaged by this and her tears ceased, thank God.

"You're like family to us. You're Nanny Knight to Ronnie, we could never forget about you!" I soothed.

What was worse was saying goodbye to Bobbsey. I wanted to take him with me but knew that living inside a van would be no life for him. He, besides Mama, would be my main motivators, to make the hour's drive to come and visit.

"You're going to be a good boy for Mama and Marshall, aren't you?" I said in my 'cat' voice. He looked at me and winked.

"I'll take that as a yes, monsieur," I said hugging his big fluffy body again.

"And take care of Sal—she needs her brother," he nudged my breast which was sore because I needed to nurse.

"Oh, big boy, I love you so," I said and laid out my uniform for my last shift at the diner, which was uncharacteristically in the afternoon.

How bizarre to think I wouldn't be working there anymore. I had my resume typed out and ready for the restaurants by the commune. Gen said I basically had a job waiting for me at 'Bell's' restaurant (the motel/campground she worked for across the road) due to some strings she's pulled, so I couldn't have felt more ready to make the leap.

Something new but familiar. I nursed Ronnie, went to my shift, and said my farewells. I told them it was just temporary, though I wasn't quite sure it was. They gave me a piece of cherry pie, my favorite, on the house as my parting gift. Hardly a keepsake of any sort!

The smell of warm rain proliferated the air as I stepped out, getting into my Plymouth the last time before I left it behind for Marshall to sell or trade into the dealer; whatever suited him. I'd managed to get him to accept this as some sort of payment, so I didn't feel so indebted about the Cortez. It was just a spit in the bucket, but it was better than nothing.

I plopped Ronnie in the middle of my bed as I continued to pack. He was such a good boy and just stared at me in wonder at what I was doing. The only time he got fussy was when he needed to nurse, but I could usually intuit that before he got to a place of crankiness. I heard the phone ring out in the kitchen, and Mama coming down the hallway.

"Sorry to disturb you but Vee's on the phone for you."

"Thanks Mama," I grabbed Ronnie, put him on my hip, made my way to the phone and picked it up.

"You're coming for real tomorrow?" her voice was enthusiastic.

"Yes, for real," I said in return, "I'm just trying to get everything together tonight so tomorrow when it's time to go, all I have to worry about is packing it into the van with Ronnie."

"This van—wow! It must be something crazy if you're going to live in it. I can't wait to see it. And little Ronnie; I bet he's grown since I last saw him!"

"Oh, probably. He seems to grow like a weed every day. We're looking forward to seeing you too, but to make that happen, we've got to get back to packing." I said, trying not to be rude in cutting her off.

"I don't want to keep you, I just wanted to check in if tomorrow was still going down, or not. Can't wait to have my baby sister by my side again."

I wasn't a fan of when she called me her 'baby sister'. I was not her 'baby' sister, I was only two years younger than her. I did look up to her, but I wasn't that immature in comparison. However, I truly don't think she meant it in a condescending manner, but rather just to be cute so I brushed it off.

"What time do you work until?" I asked.

"Three," she said.

"Okay, so I'll aim to get there around three-thirty if that works for you?"

"Heck ya it works for me. I'll see you then!"

"Sounds like a plan, bye until tomorrow."

"Bye!"

The tiptoeing of summer rain had now transformed itself into an indignant storm, tossing things at the house, causing trees to bend over as though they were meeting royalty.

After a few particularly loud and ominous claps of thunder, Mama came to my room and said, "I think we need to head down to the cellar,"—a fact I was hardly impressed with.

"Here, take Ronnie then, I have to find Bobbsey and Sal."

I proceeded to find Bobbsey huddled under the back corner of my bed, but Sal was nowhere to be found, having tucked herself somewhere untouchable, frightened from the noise. Stepping outside, the wind howled like a wolf at the moon, as I held Bobbsey tight, and we slipped into the cellar.

It was musty and damp and Ronnie started to cry. The only way to mollify him was to nurse him, so I sat on a small hard stool in the corner and let him, hoping Mama and Marshall wouldn't take mind.

"Please Lord, don't let it ruin the crops," I heard Marshall say under his breath.

I hadn't realized this minor inconvenience I was experiencing could have much greater ramifications for the livelihoods of others, and I stopped feeling as sorry for myself as I was. The cellar doors rattled as you could hear them being pelted with rain as we waited in silence for it to end.

Eventually, Mama spoke, "How are you feeling about tomorrow, Gina?"

"Excited and nervous," I answered honestly.

"Well, you have nothing to be nervous about, because you always have a home here if it doesn't work out. And you know the diner would take you back in a heartbeat."

This reminder was actually a great comfort to me; I wasn't really risking anything. Everything I was leaving behind I could get back if I didn't like the commune. I took a deep breath.

"You're right as usual Mama, that helps me feel more positive about things."

"Baby girl, I think you're brave venturing out by yourself with a little one. But I have complete faith in you. You will make it work, and if for some reason it doesn't, it's just not meant to be."

"I'll try and think of it that way," I said.

By this time, the wrathful Gods had tamed themselves and the shelling had made way to a light tapping, and the winds weren't to be heard. Marshall went out first to check and came back in to say 'coast is clear' and help us out. There were tree limbs everywhere, but in the horizon, the sun was peeking through, causing an extraordinary rainbow that seemed to arch itself directly over our house.

After bringing Bobbsey in I took Ronnie in my arms, "Want to go find a pot of gold my special man?" I said playfully to him setting him down, "You can lead us to it,"—he had been scooting around for about three months now.

I took the rainbow as a sign of what was to come. I was feeling very hopeful and at peace with its colorful, seemingly magical, illumination of the sky.

Chapter 21

September 1ˢᵗ 1971

I started packing the van up right away after breakfast, though we weren't leaving until two thirty. I hugged Mama extra before she set off to work, and promised I'd be back with Ronnie on the weekend.

"When you were little, I'd kiss you before bed and when I was leaving, you'd say 'goodbye'. I'd have to correct you and say 'no, it's not goodbye, it's goodnight.' Right now, this isn't goodbye either, it's goodnight."

Mama's eyes started to well up and I so badly didn't want her to cry I embraced her immediately and said, "Definitely just goodnight. I'll drag Gen along with me some of the times too. See, there's a blessing in disguise. You'll get to see even more of her."

Mama quickly rallied.

"That's wonderful. Go get 'em, tiger. And please, find a way to call me tonight and let me know you're settled in?"

"Of course I will Mama, you don't even have to ask."

I kissed her cheek and sent her on her way, and was back to packing up the RV. Soap for the kitchen sink (Marshall had helped me get my first round of water set up). Shampoo and conditioner for the little shower. Blankets for the tiny bed when the time comes. Lots of food—snacks and non-perishables, plus coffee, a coffee press and coffee creamer: all a must!

Ronnie's stroller took up a fair amount of space. It would have to be kept outside when weather permitted. Marshall came in for lunch around one o'clock and I said goodbye to him then, again, thanking him profusely for the van.

"You'll be missed around here, and this little guy too," he said, gently grabbing Ronnie's nose who didn't even notice as he was so enthralled by Lucy.

"You have enough gas to get you there?" he asked.

"I think so, I filled her up yesterday, and I'm hoping one way won't take more than a tank!"

"Nah, you'll be fine." He gave me a sturdy hug.

"I'm expecting we'll be hearing from you tonight?" as he was walking away.

"I already promised Mama."

"Okay good, I'm looking forward to hearing how you've made out."

I put Ronnie's car seat in the passenger's side of the van because there was nowhere else to put it. Besides, I liked having him where all it took was a glance and I could see him. So, all packed up and ready to go, I reversed out of the driveway just past two thirty and on the road to the commune.

We got there about quarter to four and I wasn't sure where to park, so settled off side of an apple tree and got Ronnie out to go get Gen to ask her. She was in cabin #2. They were small, cubical and white. Each had two small beds and a bathroom; some with couples chose to push the beds together.

Gen shared her cabin with one of her three college friends who had joined her, named Charla. The other two, Doug and Laura, were in cabin #3. Gen rushed out of the small door frame.

"You're here!" she said. "I can't believe it! Where'd you park?" "I wasn't sure, so I just parked there," motioning behind me.

"Bring it closer to the cabins. You're part of the neighborhood!"

"Okay sure, here, hold Ronnie," I passed him over and moved the van nearer. She came in to look around.

"This place is *happening*," she said, "I love it, and you're going to love it here, and so is he," she said tickling his belly, causing him to giggle.

"Tim will be home with dinner soon. He knows you're here, so there'll be enough for you. Come on, I'll show you off you to all who is here. I know you met a few of them a while back when you visited but I want to formally introduce you. The others will filter in. Let's meet the kids first. They're over here playing."

We went over behind the cluster of cottages to find a little girl and boy kicking around a ball.

"This is Kory and Adelaide."

"Hello there," I said.

"Hi," they responded, briefly stopping their game to size me up.

The boy had straight blonde hair in a pageboy hairstyle and the girl had long brown hair with bangs. The boy, apparently seven, had an unwieldy way about him that made me want to laugh and the girl seemed more mature than her age of five. Gen said both their parents were at work but would be home by five.

Richard, Kory's—the boy's—father, worked at the boat sales/rental shop for 'Bell's Marina', the same establishment attached to the restaurant I'd hopefully be working at, and Sue-Ellen, the girl's mom, worked at their general store. Charla, who worked at the ice cream shop in town, came out from the cottage she shared with Gen.

"Welcome! You made it in time for dinner."

"Yes, thank you."

"And who's this?" she said fussing at Ronnie.

"This is Ronnie, it's his first birthday in a few days."

"What a cutie pie! We're so happy to have you here."

She reminded me of a pixie.

The next people we met were Nancy and Paul. I remembered them from the first time I had been by the commune. They worked with the horses over at 'Bell's' and down the road at a place, similar to 'Bell's,' called 'Rock's Pond'. They were only sixteen and eighteen years old. Tim had met them at a rally and introduced them to the Bahá'í faith.

Nancy was lanky with dirty blonde hair, and Paul was average looking in most ways with short dark hair and pock-marked cheeks. Johanna came home next from working at the diner next door. She was ethereal. She had long dark auburn hair and smelled like sweet flowers, despite having been around grease all day. She had high cheekbones and a slim nose that turned up slightly at the end. She was stunning.

"Hello there, you must be Gina," she extended her hand with long painted nails.

"Yes, that's me," I replied.

"I'm sure you've already heard this, but welcome. We are family here and now you are part of it. I'm so pleased that you chose to join us. What a blessing to have this small fellow in our presence too. His youth will serve us all well," she said pinching his toes.

"I don't know if Venus already talked to you about it, but we have prayer and song every night around the campfire. Will you be up for joining us this evening?"

"Yes! That sounds like fun!" I responded to the invitation.

"Perfect. An extra voice will be lovely."

I was enchanted by her for some reason but tried to not let it show.

Doug came next, he'd been working in the kitchen alongside Johanna. He had a mop of brown hair and was medium built. His bangs covered his green eyes, which I'm not sure was intentional or not as and he seemed shy. I vaguely remembered meeting him that same New Years I conceived Ronnie, and he seemed to remember me.

His girlfriend Laura worked for 'guide services' over at 'Bell's' and it was more unpredictable when she would return, but they all assumed she'd be back by dinner. Sue-Ellen, the little girl's mom whom I remembered from meeting when I had previously visited the commune, was twenty years old and seemed like a free spirit, but was wise beyond her years. Perhaps from having a child at fifteen.

She had black hair about halfway down her back and big brown eyes. Tim had met her at a Bahá'í convention. He was like the pied piper! And then there was Richard, Kory's father who was Tim's cousin. He had glasses and a close-cut red beard.

He worked at the gas station right in front of the commune. To be truthful, I got a bit of an uncomfortable sense from him compared to the others. He wouldn't give me eye contact and his handshake was flaccid and clammy.

Oh well, I thought, *one out of a bunch isn't so bad.*

Around five o'clock Tim came rolling in.

He gave me the biggest hug and said, "I'm thrilled that you're here. Just thrilled. I want you to feel right at home. The way it goes around here is what mine is yours, so if you need anything, all you need to do is ask. Promise me you'll ask?"

"Yes, I promise," I said feeling a little self-conscious about the idea.

"The way we run business is we pool our money together every other Friday, make a list of supplies we need, then someone goes into town and gets them.

"Groceries, toiletries, anything you need, you can think of, you've got it. Of course, you can keep some money for yourself; just consider it like a generous donation to the community. Are you comfortable with that?"

"Yes, I'm fine with it, once I have money to pool that is."

"Vee tells me she's got you good as all set up at 'Bell's' restaurant, don't stress. And we'll always have someone here to take care of this little buddy," he gestured with a twirling finger toward Ronnie in my arms who laughed in response and brought me relief that my little boy's radar was in favor of this place's 'leader'.

"How about burgers everybody!" he shouted out which solicited a mélange of positive responses from around the area.

Off to the side of the firepit which sat in the center of the front row of cottages was a barbecue which Tim fired up and started cooking dinner for all of us.

A few of them were having beers and asked if I wanted one. I had to politely decline and slip away to nurse Ronnie back at the van. The way the ray of sunlight came in the window hit his face made him look angelic. His hair was finally starting to thicken up and he looked more and more like my old Ronnie every day.

I then took the opportunity to call Mama and Marshall from the payphone by 'The Del Mar' (the diner next door) and tell them about my day, and how the van was working out gloriously so far. As it got dark out, Tim lit up a campfire at the center of the cabins. I loved the way it smelled and how it shed light on everybody in an almost gothic way.

Tim brought his guitar and we all sat around it singing. He seemed to know how to play everything, it was really mind blowing how talented he was. I requested *Everyday* by Buddy Holly, which he played no problem; most knew the words and sang along with me, Ronnie entranced by it all, sat on my cross-legged lap.

Johanna had the most soulful singing voice; I really admired her for it. Her range was unbelievable. After about half an hour of song, Gen passed me a joint. I'd never smoked marijuana before, and I was a bit scared.

"You'll be fine," she whispered, "you'll like it, just give it a try."

So, I took a few puffs and passed it on. I felt the sensation of relaxation pass through my body. The music seemed all the more enchanting, and I became hyper-aware of the sound of crickets surrounding us. I hugged Ronnie tight. It's like the weed reminded me of how much I loved him. I let the adoration pour through my veins.

Song made way to Bahá'í prayer, and then Tim said a specific one for us: "God and Bahá'u'lláh, please help Gina and Ronnie feel comfortable and safe, and let them soak in the love this commune has to offer. Let us each individually forge a relationship with them and help them become an integrated part of our community.

"I know she's worried about her job, so please Lord, help her slip into employment without stress. Please watch over her as she finds her place here as you watch over us. In your name."

"Thank you," I said for loss of words; my head buzzing from the joint and the kindness.

"I'll take you over to the restaurants tomorrow, okay?" Gen said to me as I was standing up.

"It's my day off so I'm all yours."

"Perfect. I brought my resumes, even though you said I wouldn't need it for 'Bell's'?" I asked hopefully.

"You won't, but you can bring it anyways if it suits you. Just focus on getting a getting a good night's sleep."

"I'm pretty tired so I should sleep well."

The aftereffects of the weed were kicking in and I was burning out and ready for bed. There were two twin sized beds in the van, but one was suspended so I did not feel comfortable with either of us sleeping on it separately, so we cuddled up together on the one little low one, under the moonlight. I was feeling completely content.

That recognizable sense of being where I was supposed to be. Ronnie nuzzled between my breasts, and I drifted off to sleep, only to be awakened by the rising sun, as I'd forgotten to close the curtains. Ronnie wasn't yet stirring, so I stayed as still as possible, for as long as I could, but then I got up and made myself my first breakfast in the van: peanut butter and jelly on toast.

A little homage to my original Ronnie. I marveled at the efficiency of our van…to be able to get up and get breakfast in it? So innovative! I really did owe Marshall; it was a priceless gift. Gen would flip her lid if she knew he just gave it to me, so I had to remember that when it came to money pooling time.

Not that I wanted to cheap out and be unfair, but I'd have to be aware of how close of attention she was paying. She hadn't brought it up to me, which was a good sign, a sign at least she wasn't picking up on any injustice done to her. I truly do believe he would have done the same thing for her if our positions had been reversed. Besides, he helped pay for her college, so technically we were even. I had that in my back pocket if it ever came out.

I reverted our bed into seats to eat and played with Ronnie for a bit before heading over to Gen's cottage. Luckily, she was awake when I knocked on the door.

She met me with her cherished phrase, "What's the story morning glory? Did you sleep well?"

"Like a baby. With the baby!" I reported proudly.

"Hey, are you okay if I use your shower, maybe tomorrow? I have one, but it's pretty small, and it will deplete my water supply quickly."

"Of course! Mi casa su casa," Gen said.

"So, are you ready to go to the restaurants?"

"Sure, but what about Ronnie?"

"Johanna is off. I'm sure she'll be fine to watch him, let me go see."

Gen sauntered off to Johanna's cottage and knocked on the door.

She asked her and Johanna beamed a big smile, "Yes, bring him here," she said calling to me.

"I'd love to watch your beloved boy while you're out. Come here little man," she took him from my arms.

He grinned and hugged her back. I was reassured to see him take to her, so I didn't feel so uncomfortable or unsure about leaving him, though I realized it was something I'd have to be getting used to.

"Let me grab my resumes from the van and I'm set," I said.

I hoped I was dressed appropriately. I was wearing a pair of bell-bottoms and a mauve knit top.

The first stop was the restaurant next door. A woman named Gladys was working, she was short and squat with close-cut brown hair.

"You're looking for work? Well, we can always use a helping hand around here. Can't promise you full time or anything like that, but if you're willing to work part-time we've got a spot for you."

"Yes ma'am I'm willing."

"That's great. What did you say your name was? Gina?"

"Yes, Gina Owens." "Come by tomorrow I'll have you on the schedule."

"Thank you so much Gladys! I look forward to working with you."

"Haven't heard that in a while," she let out a raucous laugh.

"See you then," she said. Then it was off to 'Bell's.'

"We're only able to fit you in part-time right now but that should change by winter, if you want it to, of course. We already have you on the schedule for next week, as Venus told us you were coming. Does that work for you?"

"Yes of course, thank you!" I answered, thinking how I would have to coordinate my two timetables but it would be fine.

The uniform for 'Bell's' was a burgundy color with a white apron, white collar and buttons, and was given to me on the spot. I went back to the van and copied out the scheduled and ran it over to Gladys so she didn't double book me. I didn't want to work too much, I wanted to be with Ronnie, so depending on how much 'the Del Mar' penciled me in, I'd have to talk to the restaurants and let them know I needed a little less if needed.

Johanna was thrilled I was going to be working with her.

"Hopefully they'll schedule us together sometimes, that'll be great. We'll have so much fun."

I wasn't used to having friends like this and it was a nice change.

"Ya that would be great!" I responded, thinking it would be, but also worried about who would tend to my boy.

I reminded myself Johnna was not the only one at the commune and eased my own concerns.

"Ronnie has been a complete sweetheart. I want to keep him," she said kissing his head and wrapping her arms around him in jest.

"Ah, he's mine! But I don't mind sharing," I laughed as I reached out my arms for him. He reached back to me coming willingly into my grasp.

"I guess he's ours now," I said rocking him.

"I'm so glad he's part of our little family," Johanna replied flicking his little nose.

"We're going to have a celebratory picnic I think," I said and took a deep breath of the fresh air.

With Ronnie on my hip, I headed back toward the van I made a sandwich for myself and got some yogurt and cereal for Ronnie. I brought a blanket and laid it out under the apple tree. Suddenly, Ronnie struggled to his feet. The next thing I knew, he was taking his first steps.

"Vee! Vee!" I yelled, hoping she could hear me.

"He just walked!" He stumbled, then did it again.

Oh my gosh, I was so excited, just a month shy of his first birthday and he was walking.

"Good boy! That's my good boy!" I cried.

I was watching him grow up right in front of my eyes. He smiled and giggled and fell on his bum.

"That's okay, try again," and he did. "Come to Mama," he toddled along a few steps and then tumbled again. At this point, he had an audience. Gen, Johanna, Charla, Nancy, and Sue-Ellen. They applauded and he lapped up the attention.

"Yay!" they called out, "Atta boy! keep going!"

He motored along and then would plummet. It was a proud moment for me, and I was fortunate to share it with my new friends.

We had dinner together again that night and gathered around the campfire. This time Tim read some Bahá'í scripture, the words of Bahá'u'lláh, which were very enlightening.

We sang *Sad Eyed Lady of the Lowlands*, *Times They are A-Changin*, and *There's a Kind of Hush*. I had some of a joint again and it was mystic. The whole experience was other-worldly. I loved how the marijuana gave me a full-bodied buzz. I blew the smoke out slowly making a design in the sky.

Laura brought her tambourines, so I really felt part of the music. I was one with everyone in the circle, it was a sense of belonging I'd never felt with a group of people before. Certainly not at school. I wished Ronnie, big Ronnie, were with me to share it. I knew he would love it too.

That weekend I went home to visit Mama, Marshall, Bobbsey, and who could forget little Sal of course as promised, and told them all about our adventure so far.

"I'm glad you're fitting in," Mama said, though I was unsure if she was secretly hoping I wouldn't and would want to come home.

"Me too. It's lovely."

"Glad the van is going to good use," added Marshall.

"Sure is—it's perfect. Couldn't ask for anything more," giving him an unsolicited hug which he received appreciatively, patting me on the back. I then went to visit Mrs. Knight.

"My little Ronnie's back," she said rejoicingly.

"He is! And guess what? He's taken his first steps."

"Wow, our munchkin's growing up. Doesn't he look more and more like our Ron every day? Don't you think so Gina?"

"Yes, I do," I agreed, and not just to please her, I truly did.

"Living up to his namesake," I added.

"Do you want me to leave him with you for a little bit this afternoon? I have some errands to run. I mean I can take him home to Mama, or I can leave him here, it's totally up to you," I offered.

"Oh, please Gina, leave him here with me. I'd love to spend some time with the tot."

"Okay, I'll come back in a couple hours."

I didn't really have errands to run, I just knew how desperate she was to be with him.

So, I left and went home to spend some quality time with Mama without Ronnie in tow, which was kind of alleviating to be honest. Not to say that Ronnie was a burden by any means, but it was different to interact without constantly having to pay attention to what he was doing. Especially now that he was able to get up on his feet!

Mama and I ended up heading into town for an impromptus shopping trip, Marshall giving us some money as a treat. I got a new paisley shirt and Mama got a new green dress that accentuated her eyes. She bought him a new blue sweater coat that vied at the front and had buttons below it. I helped her pick it out and anticipated he would like it. He smirked big when he took it out of the bag and tried it on, going straight to the mirror, so I think it was a success.

It fit him perfectly. He wanted to see what Mama and I got, so we tried our clothes on for him, the generous soul that he was. I loved my new shirt; it was blue and gold paisley, light and flowy, and had two tassels that hung by the neckline.

It, in and of itself, was worth the trip to Andrews! I went back to pick up Ronnie from Mrs. Knight's and she didn't want to part with him.

"We'll be back soon," I said in a sing-song voice to ease the departure.

"I hope so. I love this child."

"I know you do, and he loves you too. Never forget that."

I took him from her and arranged him in the car seat.

Chapter 22

I spent the night at Mama's but was ready to head back to the commune on Sunday, new shirt and all.

"Next time I'll bring Gen. I know she misses Sal, and you two too of course." I said, hoping I could keep my word.

It had become progressively more difficult to get her away from that place. I kissed Mama and Marshall on the cheeks and was off. Everyone was so welcoming upon my return.

"You're back! We're so happy!" was the general sentiment.

Tim had gotten word that there was going to be a sit-in later that week. How exciting! Sue-Ellen volunteered to stay behind to watch the kids which freed me up to be able to go, so long as I wasn't scheduled to work. I checked eagerly, and I wasn't—I was available to participate. I felt like I had been waiting for this moment since the day of the rape, the chance to make a difference.

I offered my van as a means of transportation, but Tim said we probably had enough with the cars. Thursday came around and it was time to go. We piled into three vehicles and headed off to Greenville. We met up with another group that had whites and negros outside of a restaurant. I still couldn't believe this place was getting away with still not serving blacks.

The plan was to go in with the negros and sit at the counter and defend against any antagonizing behavior toward them. The mass of us went in and I was seated next to a brave young negro boy, no older than eighteen.

"You aren't welcome here, get out," the server shouted as they took their seats.

"We just want service like everybody else," the boy beside me said.

"Well you aren't going to get it here. Leave."

"No," he said gallantly.

"Fine then, I'm calling the police."

He promptly picked up the phone.

The police? I thought, *Will they really do anything to support this establishment's out of date's rules?*

"Hi there, I've got two negros here at my counter who are disturbing the peace of my restaurant." He paused.

"Yes it's a scene alright." He paused again.

"Thank you."

"Get out now or the police will drag you out," he warned.

Still everyone stayed seated in suspense. When the police arrived Tim tried to step in front of them.

"You're interfering in state business, excuse yourself immediately," they said to him. I followed suit and tried to block the officer from arresting the other young negro, the one beside me.

"This is no place for a young lady like you. I'm going to need you to step aside."

"No," I said indignantly, then he forced me aside with his baton.

"I said step aside young lady," and he cuffed the negro boy.

"You have no right to arrest him, he's done nothing wrong!" I cried out.

"He's gone against the rules of this establishment by disturbing the peace and this is none of your business miss."

"It is too my business. The well-being of my fellow citizen is my business. You can't treat him like that."

"I can and I will," was his cold response.

"Let's go," he said, taking the negro boy roughly out of the restaurant.

"Tim, do something!" I hollered in anguish, but he was just as helpless as I was. He tried.

He stood in front of the door and said, "Sir, you have no grounds to remove these men from this restaurant. There was no scene caused despite the report. They just quietly came in looking for menus to order lunch!"

"I sure do. He's disturbing the peace with his presence and he's refusing to leave. Now get out of my way!" He shoved past Tim roughly with his elbows.

"I'm coming back for the other ones, so unless you want to be in my patrol car too, I suggest you get out of here stat."

He was speaking about the other two negros at the counter who refused to go and succumbed to the same fate. Our sit-in was fruitless. I felt so bad.

Tim comforted me afterwards, "We tried," but it didn't seem good enough. He said it was just part and parcel of the civil rights movement.

"Sometimes you win, sometimes you lose; today we lost. Try not to take it to heart."

I couldn't help it though. It brought back memories of Jeb. So many injustices. I didn't understand. Why did the color of our skin make such a difference? I couldn't comprehend it. I was so tired of situations in my life I had no control over. I guess that's what now days you would call a 'trigger'.

Things I couldn't control, lack of fairness and integrity. It made me want to quit. To not fight anymore. I know it was a bad attitude, but it was my natural reaction. Others were somehow looking at the bright side of it.

Johanna was like, "Did you see the press show up? That's amazing! It may not have turned out exactly as planned but we attracted attention to the injustice of it. That's half the battle."

Nancy agreed.

I sat in silence in the back seat taking it all in. Perhaps there were positives that I just wasn't feeling.

"Did you hear Charleston College desegregated?" Tim said.

I perked up at this news.

"No, I hadn't."

"Ya, our old school finally saw the light, isn't that amazing? You see, the things are changing, it's just a slow grind."

I was delighted at this update, though it reminded me of the protest I wasn't able to attend and that horrible life changing day.

"We'll regroup back at the commune. You did good today, Gina. You stood up to those officers all by yourself. I'm proud of you."

"What else could I have done?" I responded.

"You could have cowered away, but you didn't. You used your voice, and you deserve a big pat on the back for that."

Johanna and Nancy concurred.

"Ya Gina, good job," they complimented.

"Thank you, I tried," I repeated modestly.

"You went above and beyond, and for that, I salute you," said Tim, making a saluting gesture from the driver's seat.

I felt pride swell up inside me. Maybe it hadn't been such an awful day after all. I was glad to be back at the commune and hug my baby. I needed his innocence to refresh me from my day.

He reminded me, like Bobbsey did, of all that was good in the world; and after witnessing such nastiness, I needed his soft skin on my cheek. Tim brought fish and chips from 'The Del Mar' for dinner and boy, were they ever good!

Crispy batter and hot fries with ketchup, my favorite. It filled me right up. Ronnie ate some of the fish and seemed to like it, but it was hard to tell because he still preferred nursing over solid foods. I just couldn't bear to break the habit it contented him so much.

The next day I started my job at 'Bell's', and the day after I started at 'The Del Mar'. Both were much like much like the diner in Andrews, so it didn't take much for me to 'acclimatize' as Mama would say. There were different moods to the two places, it's hard to explain.

I preferred 'Bell's'. 'The Del Mar's' was a bit more stifling; perhaps because it was smaller and darker. I liked it when I worked with Johanna, but other than that my co-workers were rather crusty. 'Bell's' was brighter and friendlier and bigger. Also, the tips were a bit better there. The clientele at 'The Del Mar' were more of the truck-stop caliber, whereas 'Bell's' was a lot of families.

Besides that, Gen would come in on her breaks and visit which was a plus. All around, however, I was pleased to be working and able to contribute to the commune like everybody else. Of course, I kept some of the money for myself and Ronnie, as established, everybody did, but a majority went into our weekly pool. Tim insisted on less from me though because we didn't rent a cabin which was a nice break. He was good with our money, and never did I ask for something I didn't receive.

It gave a real sense of community, so I fully approved of the practice. There was always dinner prepared, though I kept my own stash of food for myself and Ronnie; ones that he would actually eat. Mainly cheerios, yogurt, bananas, and porridge. An easy to please boy he was! He liked grapes too, but I had to cut them up in tiny pieces so they were a treat.

October 1971

In just the few weeks that had passed since he took his first steps, he was already bombing around on two legs like he'd done it since birth. He'd tumble on his behind, then get right back up again like it was nobody's business and keep going. Thankfully, we had such an expansive yard around us, he could run and fall for days!

Nothing gave me more pleasure than sitting on the grass, legs in a vee, and having my baby totter his way toward me on bowlegs and fall into my lap giggling. Much was the scene that autumn. As the leaves began to turn crimson and orange and yellow, my little man's legs grew stronger and steadier like a strengthening baby deer.

For his first birthday on the fourth of October, Gen had surprised us with a cake that read, "Happy 1st Birthday Ronnie Love Your New Family." It was chocolate and rich and delicious. She said she got it personally made by the local baker, which is why it tasted homemade. As a unit, the commune bought him a new teddy bear, a blue blanket—not unlike Linus' from Charlie Brown—a little red pant suit and shirt set, and a toy key ring.

"So he can start driving for you," Laura joked. It was more than I could have asked for, and I told them that.

"You're part of the family and so is he. It's the least we could do," Johanna said. I hugged everybody and thanked them.

That night we sang him 'Happy Birthday' around the campfire, and I swear, despite his youth, he knew it was for him as he clapped along. It was a great celebration of Ronnie's life. I felt he was loved, and there was nothing I could want more.

Christmastime 1971

Christmas on the commune was a joyous occasion. The cabins were strung with lights and Gen got a little tree to put in inside hers. We all drew names from a hat, and I got Richard. I purchased him a Ralph Lauren cologne, which I felt to be a tasteful gift. I didn't know him as well as some of the others, so I felt it to be a safe choice.

Tim drew my name and we exchanged presents on Christmas eve day since Gen and I were going home for Christmas night. He got me a Levi's jean jacket—it was a faded blue color and felt worn in, so comfortable, it fit me like a glove. I loved it! I wore it home with pride, like a badge of love I received at the commune.

Everyone chipped in and bought Ronnie a red sweater. He looked so adorable in it! It was soft and not itchy at all, but I still put an undershirt on him first, just to be safe. He looked like a little Christmas ball! By this time he was running around, so I had to be on my toes to be aware of what was in his grasp. For instance, the fireplace at Mama's. There was a close call. When we arrived I set him down and he went catapulting toward it.

I had to lunge and grab him so he didn't go hands first into it. Christmastime always made me think of my other Ronnie. I fingered the locket around my neck which now held a tiny picture of him in it. I remembered that first Christmas together, how I'd gotten my bike, how I'd given him his watch. Such bitter-sweet memories. Those were the days in our little match-book house on Dogwood with our little Charlie Brown tree.

I looked up at the one before me. It was at least seven feet tall—such a grand sight reaching toward the cathedral ceiling with a glimmering star atop it. Mama had picked out a rainbow of decorations, and it looked marvelous with multi-colored lights twinkling. The air outside was sharp, for South Carolina that is, and it was overcast. I tried to imagine snow like I always did at Christmas.

As it darkened you could see the lights Marshall had artfully strung up and around the house, Ronnie loved looking at the colors. He had said his first word back in November.

Proudly, it was 'Mama.'

"Rainbow," I said pointing at the roof.

"Bainbow," he repeated back at me, and I hugged him close.

"Good boy!" I said, "Good talking!"

He wrapped his petite arms around my neck, and I felt as whole as I had since Ronnie's death. I felt him with me. I felt him through my son.

Christmas morning, we opened our presents and I was so delighted because the presents I got for everyone fit, just like my jean jacket. I got for a Gen a bomber jacket, which was a bit out of my budget but when I saw it, I just couldn't resist it suited her to a tee, similarly a beige wool car jacket for Mama and a thick black and red plaid jacket for Marshall.

It was a jacket Christmas! For Ronnie I bought him some new jammies, a few new outfits, and a Fisher Price telephone pull toy. Mama and Marshall got him even more clothes! She made him some shirts and a little track suit, as well as got him a pair of overalls, and a winter jacket. Gen bought him a hat with little teddy-ears on it and matching mittens which made him look so cuddly.

Marshall got Gen and I matching rings with our birthstones in them, mine being pink and Gen's being ruby for July. Mama got me a cashmere sweater coat, a jogger suit that matched Ronnie's (which I thought was priceless) and a pair of gloves. It was a very prosperous Christmas. We had our eggnog with rum and sang carols by the tree and fire (with Ronnie held tightly on my knee).

The cats and Lucy joined us. It was a true family affair. It was the best Christmas I'd had since Ronnie had died I'd say. I felt like I'd found my niche in the world for the time being, and it was great to be able to stay so connected to Mama et al. as I solidified myself in the new world of the commune.

On the TV, the movie *White Christmas* was playing, and Rosemary Clooney sang out, "When I'm worried and I can't sleep, I count my blessings instead of sheep," and I thought to myself, *What a novel idea!* And from that point forward, that's what I did. I'd count them out loud with Ronnie so he's learn the practice.

We stayed until the 28th and we were scheduled to work again. It felt like we'd been back home again for a lifetime to be truthful. It was hard leaving Bobbsey after half a week of cuddles. I missed him more than anything else, and hoped he knew how much I loved him. We were greeted enthusiastically back at the commune.

Tim said, "Hey, I like your jacket, where's you get it?" then laughed and gave Ronnie and I a hug.

Doug, Laura, and Charla had gone home too, but all three had beat us back so the whole gang was together again. Tim was so thoughtful and bought little earmuffs for Ronnie because we were going to be doing fireworks for New Years. I was so excited!

I hadn't been to a fireworks display since Ronnie was alive and I'd certainly never seen anybody set them off before. So, the night came, and everyone was passing around mushrooms to try. I was hesitant but didn't want to be left out.

They assured me that they wouldn't incapacitate me, "It'll just make the colors prettier," Richard said to me, handing the bag to me.

"We've all had some, the rest is all yours."

I didn't think I wanted the rest, so I decided on half, and if I wasn't feeling anything from them, I'd come back for more. As it started to get dark out, I could feel some effect coming on, but not too much, so I decided I'd try a bit more. Now, where had I left them? I thought on the table, but they were not there. So, it must have been the bench. I peered under it and Ronnie was sitting there eating them like they were potato chips.

"No Ronnie!" I screamed and grabbed them away from him.

I pulled him out from under the bench with the baggie and shoved the remainder in my mouth to assure he couldn't get them.

"Open up," I said, pulling chunks off his tongue. I gave him water and tried to get him to spit. I took him over to Gen's cabin frantically knocking at the door. She was obviously high already, but still reachable.

"He ate some. Some of the mushrooms! What do I do? Take him to the hospital?"

"No way man," Gen said, "They'll like see you as an unfit mother and try and take him away from you or something. No hospital. He'll be okay. They're only plants."

"Maybe, I am an unfit mother! I let my one-year-old eat magic mushrooms!"

Gen laughed and then straightened out her face when she saw my tears.

"Sorry, it just sounded funny. Don't cry, let's go talk to Tim, he'll know what to do."

So, we knocked on Tim's cabin and Johanna answered.

"Oh Gina, what's the matter? Come on in guys." The five of us crammed in.

"Ronnie ate some of the mushrooms!" I cried out.

"Little dude," Tim let out a half laugh, and then, like Gen, realized how distressed I was over the situation.

"How much did he have?"

"I don't know how to measure! I got the end of the baggy, then ate half of it, and left the other half. He ate about half of that. I got some of it out of his mouth, but I can't say how much he ingested. Oh, Tim what do we do?"

"Okay, let me think here."

Richard offered me the end of the bag and I said, "No, Gina hasn't had any yet, give it to her."

"And from what I could see there was only like 3 grams left in there. Then you ate half of that. So little man here, considering you got some out of his mouth, probably only ate about a gram. Is that what you're telling me?"

"I guess so."

"He's going to be just fine. That's literally nothing. Since he's so small, he might trip a bit, but that's all. He's safe, Gina, don't worry. You can't die from shrooms."

Almost simultaneous with my relief came Ronnie's discontent. He started to whimper at first, and I looked at him and his pupils had taken over the entire brown of his eye. He wasn't looking at me at first, but rather through me. When our eyes did meet he let out a proper howl and flung himself onto me.

He started feverishly grabbing at my breasts and saying 'nursy' in between giant sobs, so I figured the only thing to do was to get him back to the van and nurse him and see if that would settle him down. Selfishly, I so badly wanted to see the fireworks.

"Don't worry," Tim called after me, "I'll wait a little while before I start the light show to see if you can get him calmed down a bit."

"Thanks so much Tim. I really want to see it, so I'll do my best to get him simmered asap."

He was flushed and burning up, so I stripped him down to his diaper and got a cool cloth to put on his forehead as he was nursing. The hysterics stopped as soon as I let him, and what had been his tightly wound body softened. I rocked him slowly and held him tight. I just lay there with his nearly naked body against me as the sun went down on the final day of 1971.

I reflected how two years ago was the night I conceived this child in my arms. How he didn't even exist and through my careless act I now had a sacred human being I was responsible for, and I didn't regret it in any way. It was the best stupid mistake I had ever made.

Now that I had Ronnie, I couldn't imagine life without him and didn't want to. A feeling I'd had with my old Ronnie. It also reminded me there was some poor sod wandering around out there with no idea he was a father. Was it unfair of me to be keeping all this joy to myself? Well, either way it was too late now.

I wasn't going to find him and tell him, "You're a father and I've been keeping it from you for a year."

He likely wouldn't want to know anyhow. Ignorance is bliss. He was my child through and through. And besides, like I've already said, I liked to think of him as belonging to Ronnie too—like he was his—not some random guy named Mike whose face I could hardly recall.

"Knock, knock, knock," came on the van door. It was Johanna.

"We're going to start the fireworks soon. Do you think you guys will be up for joining us?" I took Ronnie off my breast and looked at him in the eye. His pupils had returned to their normal size, and he was breathing at a regular pace.

"I think we'll give it a go. I just have to get him dressed properly and put his earmuffs on."

"That's amazing, I'm so glad you two are going to come. Here, I'll wait for you, and we can go together."

So, I assembled Ronnie, who wasn't too pleased about the ear muffs, "Stop fussing honey, you need those," I redirected his hands and picked him up.

We all sat around the fire while Tim went off to the side and lit things up. I was feeling some effects from the mushrooms, so the colors looked spectacular, like exploding fairy dust. Ronnie's head tilted back into me as he watched them detonate.

He said, "Mama, Mama," and reached his hand to the sky opening and closing it.

"I know, they're called fireworks baby," not sure if he could even hear me through the protective earwear. At the end, Tim brought out Styrofoam cups and a bottle of champagne.

"I'd like to raise a toast to unity. To the Bahá'í faith and everyone on this commune. No matter what this world throws at us we know we always have each other and that's something to write home about. May this upcoming year present us with ways to make positive change in the world and continued opportunities to provide for ourselves. Happy 1972!"

"Happy 1972!" Everyone toasted and drank until the giant bottle was finished.

"I'll walk you back to your van if you want," Richard offered to me.

"Sure, why not?" It was only a few steps from the cottages, I didn't need an escort, but I figured he was just being kind.

"Okay, I've made it thank you," no sooner were the words out of my mouth than his hand was on my waist and his face was coming toward mine.

I pushed him away and said, "Richard I'm sorry. I hope I didn't give you that idea. I'm not looking for love or romance here on the commune. I apologize if you got that impression."

There had been no impression though, and we both knew it. We had barely spoken before I gave him his Secret Santa gift, and I only gave him that because I drew his name!

"I just thought…the cologne…never mind, I'm sorry to have bothered you," and with that, he slithered away into the night back toward his cabin.

What part of Secret Santa didn't he understand? I was obligated to buy him a gift, I had picked his name at random. I was going to have to tell Tim tomorrow I thought, but tonight, I was going to just have to make sure the Cortez was locked.

After such behavior I felt he couldn't be trusted. There was something off about the guy and I just couldn't put my finger on it. Oh well, I dodged a bullet that night at least.

The next morning after breakfast I knocked on Tim and Johanna's door. They invited me in and offered me some green tea which I accepted. I explained to them what had happened the night before and how uncomfortable it had made me feel—though I was unsure of how Tim would react as it was his cousin and all, and perhaps would take his side. Thankfully he didn't.

"Well, we can't be having any of that around the commune. This is supposed to be a safe space. I'm sorry that happened and can personally guarantee you it won't happen again. I'll have a talk with him. I'll get to it right after I'm done my tea here."

He took a sip.

"I'm so disappointed in him," Johanna said.

"I don't know why he'd needed to ruin things by acting so inappropriately." She shook her head.

"You did and said all the right things, though you needn't apologize to him. You're one smart cookie, Gina. Coming to tell us immediately is what needed to happen."

"Okay," Tim said. "I'm going to go find this bugger in a jiffy." He was gone about twenty minutes and came back.

"Poor bastard doesn't know what's up." He began.

"I had to set him straight, that's for sure. He started mumbling something about the cologne you bought him for Christmas, and I said that was Goddamn Secret Santa! She had to buy you that gift!

"I think he's just love struck by you Gina, and he's just going to have to get over it. I told him that hands down you're not interested and there was to be no more funny business to make you feel uneasy. So that's settled."

"Thank you, Tim, I appreciate your intervention."

"Of course, anytime."

And it would be needed again, in a far more dramatic situation.

Chapter 23

June 1972

It was a humid day, the kind where your clothes stick to your skin when you've been outside for more than five minutes. I was on kid duty and was preparing to bring them over to the beach at Rock's Pond's.

"Get your swimsuit on Kory," I called into his cabin.

"I'm not looking!" Then he said something suspicious.

He said, "Daddy always looks when I get changed."

I was caught off guard by the comment and responded by saying, "Well that's no good. You should ask him to please look away."

"I have and he said he'll look if he wants to."

"Hmmmm…" I pondered anxiously realizing the situation was escalating quickly to a dangerous place.

"That's not right Kory, I'm sorry that's been happening to you."

"Hey Gina," he said, coming out from around the corner with his swimsuit on.

"Can I tell you something if you promise not to tell anybody else?"

"Kory, I can't promise you I won't tell someone, but whatever it is sounds pretty important and I think you should tell me anyhow."

"Okay, well, I've never told anyone because it's embarrassing. But sometimes my dad touches me in places I don't want to be touched."

I felt like my ears were on fire. I didn't want to be the one hearing this. I felt horrible for the boy, but wished he's chosen someone else to disclose it to. However, he hadn't and it was my responsibility now. How to respond? I needed clarity.

"Touches you where?" I asked.

"Like where I pee from."

That's not what I wanted to hear.

"That was very brave of you to tell me that just now, Kory. Thank you for opening up."

"You're welcome," he said, looking a little proud.

"Does he ever make you touch him?" I inquired to cover all bases.

"Ya, that's part of it. I hate it."

"I'm sure you know this but it's very wrong of your father to do this and you don't deserve to be put in the position to have to do these things or have them done to you. Do you know that?"

"I kind of figured since it felt so bad."

"It felt bad because it is bad, but you're not bad. Your father's bad. Just remember that. You're not bad, your father is."

"He's nice other times," he said.

"Yes, but that doesn't give him the right to abuse you, Kory, and that's what it is, abuse. And I promise you, I will put a stop to it. It's never going to happen again to you. Do you trust me?"

I felt my words echo Mama's from the evening in my room sitting on the comforter.

"I trust you Gina, but how are you going to stop him?"

"I'm going to talk to your Uncle Tim and we will come up with a plan."

"I'm scared I'm going to get in trouble," he started cracking his knuckles and licking his lips anxiously.

"You won't get in trouble; I will protect you."

He paused for a moment, as though contemplating whether to believe me or not, and with a flip of his hair decided he did.

"Thanks Gina. I'm ready to go swimming now."

So, I packed the cooler with juice boxes and peanut butter sandwiches and headed with Ronnie, Adelaide and Kory to the beach for the day with this massive weight of information on my heart and shoulders. Adelaide was like a little mother to Ronnie, which was endearing to watch. She helped him make sandcastles which he enjoyed promptly crushing.

Kory was able to swim all the way out to the end of the dock by himself. This whole time I just wanted the hours to pass so Tim would come home, I prayed, to deal with Richard.

I felt violated that the man who abused his child was also attracted to me. Like all pedophiles liked me, not just my father. I was disgusted. Gen got home before Tim, and so did Richard. I pulled Gen aside immediately.

"Holy shit! What a fucking dirt bag! Right under our noses too. Tim will kick him out and keep Kory here with us. I can only assume. He is going to be *livid*. I honestly don't know how he's going to handle it."

Sue-Ellen came home so Adelaide didn't need to be watched over anymore and Gen said she'd watch Ronnie and Kory while I talked to Tim. I had to remember he knew nothing about my past, and that this was a, to use the word again, 'triggering' event for me.

I beelined to him as soon as he stepped on the property.

"Hey Tim, can we chat?"

"Of course we can, you know my open-door policy. Something urgent?"

"Yes," I said.

"Okay, well, let's get to it. Do you want to talk in your van or in my cabin?"

"Let's do my van, you're always hosting me. I got him a glass of sweet tea and we sat down at my little table nook."

"Tim," I said looking him straight in the eye, "your cousin Richard has been sexually abusing his son." He looked as if a sheet of wind had just hit him, and he went completely pale with all the blood draining from his face.

"How, I mean," he stuttered, "how do you know?"

"He told me this morning. It started out with him telling me how his dad would watch him change his clothes. Then he tried to get me to promise I wouldn't tell anybody if he told me something, which I wouldn't commit to, but I managed to get what he was going to say out of him. That's when he disclosed to me he touches him where he goes pee from and makes him touch Richard back.

"I didn't know what to do so I told him he was brave and that I was going to have to talk to you about it. He was worried he was going to get in trouble, and I reassured him he wouldn't, so whatever we do, we can't have it come back where Richard takes it out on the boy."

Without hesitation Tim said, "Oh, he won't be seeing Kory anymore to be able to get him in trouble. I'm removing him from the commune tonight."

He was angry. Deep angry. His hands were shaking slightly, the sweet tea quivering in his grip, and he was looking past me in a dense stare.

"I'm going to tell him leave Kory with us, and don't come back or I'm calling the authorities. I'll take custody of him. I'll take on the role as father. I'm ready for it. I won't allow this child to be hurt ever again. Please do me a favor when you leave the van, get Vee to take Adelaide, Kory, and Ronnie over to see Johanna at 'The Del Mar' next door to say hello?"

"Certainly. Look," I said, peering out the window, "there goes Richard right now."

"Okay, perfect," he said, cracking his knuckles loudly, mirroring Kory's action from earlier in the day.

"You go out first and have Vee remove the children, then come back and let me know when they're gone from the lot."

I swiftly moved and told Gen what he'd asked her to do, so I handed her Ronnie, and she corralled the other two and they went off to the restaurant. I ran back to the van.

"Coast is clear of kids, and I think Richard made his way to his cabin."

"Thank you, Gina. Thank you for all of this. He obviously trusted you specifically to tell you what he did, and you should feel good about that. Now, I'm going to go fix it once and for all."

Tim stood up and took a heavy breath. In through his nose and out his mouth and shook his body as though he were shaking off a layer of dust.

He clapped his hands together once, said, "Let's do this!" then exited the van. I followed as he approached the cabins.

To my surprise, he didn't go to Richard's, he went to everyone else's first, inviting them outside. About half of them were missing—Doug, Johanna and Gen—but those who were there came out on their front stoops.

"Hold on everybody, I'll be right back," He said sounding completely normal. He then went to Richard's door, knocked, and upon his answering, punched him across the face in a complete blindside. He grabbed him by the scruff of the neck and dragged him to beside the firepit.

"Ladies and gentlemen, can I have your attention please. Richard is going to be leaving us today because it was brought to my awareness that he's that rare type of specimen they like to call a pedophile. He won't have time to say goodbye because as soon as I let him go, he'll be packing up his shit and leaving without the little boy—his very own son—he's been touching."

At this point, Richard, who'd been standing limp since Tim's capture of him began to struggle and cry.

"You're going to take my boy from me?"

"Either I am or the police are, that's up to you. I'm ashamed to call you family. You make me sick."

He spit on him, and kneed him right in the balls, letting go of his neck. Richard doubled over in pain and shock.

"Now go get your shit and get outta here. And I mean now."

Richard started walking, but then turned back blubbering in an attempt to argue and Tim decked him across the face again.

"I said get out of here. What part of that are you not understanding man?"

Finally, Richard skulked away. His whole world had just been completely destroyed in less than five minutes. I went up to Tim and asked him if we should inquire if Kory wanted to say goodbye to his dad.

Tim decided it was the fair thing to do, and I volunteered to do the asking. I headed next door to find the kids eating some ice cream (even though they hadn't had their dinner yet, Gen knew today was an exception).

"Hey Kory, your dad is going to be going away from the commune and I don't know when he'll be coming back, if at all. Do you want to come with me and say goodbye to him? Or would you rather just stay here with Vee and finish your ice cream?"

"No thanks," he said between licks. "I'll just stay here."

"Are you sure? It could be a long time before you see him again."

"Ya, I'm sure," he retorted.

"Okay buddy just thought I'd check. See you at supper."

I reported back to Tim, making a cross with my arms from a distance and he nodded with satisfaction. That night at the campfire, (which always happened after the children were in bed except for Ronnie), he addressed the incident.

"I wanted everyone out of their cabins because I wanted to expose him for the piece of shit that he is. I'm sorry if I traumatized anybody, that wasn't my intention. I wanted to give him a taste of his own medicine and humiliate him. Maybe, I handled it wrong, I don't know."

People chimed in.

"No, you handled it fine—you did a good job, couldn't have done it better myself," And those who weren't there "Damn, I'm sorry I missed it."

"The important part is," Tim added, "is that Korey is safe now. He'll be needing a little extra support from all of us, and I hope ya'll can bring that to the table."

Again, unanimous support came from around the circle "yes," "for sure" "we're here for him." "I'll be staying in Kory's cabin to sleep, but in my regular cabin by day if you're looking for me."

I went over and hugged him. Together we had beaten him. To shift gears away from the day's horrid events we sang *Sweet City Woman*, *Sugar, Sugar, Sweet Caroline* and my favorite *Something* by the Beatles.

It made me think of my original Ronnie. I hoped he would be proud of me for the way I handled the Kory situation. I'm sure he would have approved of the way that Tim dealt with it, as I know the violence he wanted to inflict upon Greg.

There was a lighter mood around the camp without Richard there. I hadn't even realized it, but his sullen tone had been bringing the commune down, but it had. Kory seemed renewed, having a grand old time with Tim sleeping in his cabin.

It made him feel awfully important, and it was clear he didn't miss his father at all. He laughed and joked more than ever. One day, about two weeks after Richard had left the commune, he came running up to me and hugged my legs.

"Thank you, Gina."

"Whatever for?" I said.

"For getting my dad gone."

"Aw, Kory you're welcome. I'm so happy you feel safe now."

"Me too."

And he let go and continued playing. Shortly after this, Tim came home with a swing set in his trunk for the kids! He set it up and they absolutely loved it. It was so much fun pushing Ronnie on the swing.

Adelaide and Kory took turns too. There was a little seesaw swing on it and a basket bench swing too. It helped keep the kids occupied which was much appreciated. Tim really looked out for everyone.

Chapter 24

January 1973

In the newspaper there was an ad which read, "Looking for artist to compile pamphlet for local attractions. Please bring portfolio into 103 Journal Alley Summerville SC office #37."

When I read it, I just knew I wanted to apply. I could hear teenage Ronnie in my head, telling me how someone would want to commission my art, and hoped this would be an opportunity. Summerville was about forty minutes away, so I packed up Ronnie and set out on the road. I put on my paisley shirt and bell-bottoms and went into the office with my portfolio of drawings and paintings, Ronnie in tow.

I was hoping that he was with me wouldn't have a negative effect on them choosing me or not.

"Hello, may I help you?" the receptionist asked.

"Yes, I'm here to present my portfolio regarding the ad in the paper about the pamphlet."

"Oh great! You're the first one," she said. I felt immediately hopeful.

"Let me buzz Mr. Beckerman and see if he's available to review your work. Just take a seat."

I sat down with Ronnie on my lap and portfolio off to the side for barely a moment and the receptionist called over.

"He can see you now! He's down the hall, second door on the left."

I knocked quietly, "Come in!" said a booming voice. A bald man with long arms and squinty eyes sat across the desk.

"And who's acquaintance do I have the pleasure of making today?" he asked.

"Gina. Gina Owens. Nice to meet you sir."

"Call me Rudy. Now let's see your work."

I handed over my portfolio. It was a collection of sketches of people and paintings of places I'd done over the last several years.

"I dare say you're one talented young lady," Rudy said.

"No need to beat around the bush here, you're hired. If you're alright with the payment of thirty dollars that is."

"I am?" I said in gleeful disbelief. "Yes, of course I am okay with it."

"Absolutely. Let's get straight to your assignment then. On the front we'll be needing something about the Holiday Inn, but no picture. Just a few words in your nicest printing. Here's a paper and pen for you to write this down. Then we need a picture of 'Flowertown on the Pines,' about half the page both those things should take up.

"Next is our biggest paying advertiser, 'Camelia's Restaurant and Lounge.' Create a picture for that and say a few words about it. On the inside you might want to visit our park for some inspiration here. Just a scenic scape would be nice.

"And finally, our back page, I need this map, he whipped out a paper with a circular road map he'd drawn out on it, and a little street scape, maybe where we have our cobbled road would be a charming idea. Do you think you can handle that?"

I was a little overwhelmed by the wealth of information he'd just thrown at me but confident I could manage it.

"Yes sir. I mean yes Rudy, I do."

"I need it in two weeks. Is that enough time for you?"

"Of course."

"Okay, great, we're off to the races then. Don't worry about the dimensions, I can resize them. I'll see you in a couple weeks then, Gina."

He reached out his hand to shake mine. It was sturdy and tight. My first real job! Not that the restaurant wasn't, but this felt more like a career move, where I actually got to showcase my talents. I was so excited, I called Mama as soon as I got back to the commune.

"Good for you, baby, I'm so proud of you! I always knew your art would make you money someday. You're so talented, I don't see how it couldn't. So, it's going to be distributed throughout Summerville?"

"Yes!"

"Oh, that's just so amazing, I can't wait to see the final product."

"I'm going to have to drive there to sketch the scenery. And I'm not sure what to do for the restaurant. It's a girl's name, and I'm good at drawing people, so I was thinking of doing a fancy kind of psychedelic sketch of maybe one of the girls here? What do you think?"

"I think that sounds wonderful. You're a creative force. Trust your instincts and go with them."

I decided to ask Johanna, because of her haunting beauty to be my model. She was complimented and immediately agreed. She put on her flower headband and tucked a few additional flowers into her hair to add to the ambiance.

I was very pleased with the portrait of her and did a frame around it that was a half-circle at the bottom and straight across the top. Not knowing anything about the restaurant itself, I wrote "Camelia's Restaurant and Lounge…is essentially for people who have great respect for good living, fine dining, and for one another. Above the Flowertown scene, at the top." I wrote, "If all you want is everything…we invite you to experience the Holiday Inn."

The following day Ronnie and I headed back down to Summerville to do my sketches for there. I had to use my imagination a bit as nothing was in bloom yet, but for the front I did a close up of some cherry blossoms, which were a favorite of mine, and for the inside I found a spot in their infamous park that had a view of a pavilion and a little bridge.

It seemed like the perfect place to draw so I sketched it. Then it was off to the cobblestone street. I stopped at the press center to get directions and headed there. I parked at the top of the hill and drew the hardware store and livery, along with some surrounding buildings. All in all I was satisfied with my work.

I delivered it back to the press office and Mr. Beckerman, or "Rudy," who was equally as pleased.

"Excellent job, Gina. I like what you did with Camelia's! I'll Get Margret to print out your check for you."

"Can I get a copy of the final product?"

"Yes, of course, come back in two weeks, and they should be ready to go."

Margaret printed out the check and I looked proudly at the thirty-dollar amount. I took it straight to the bank and cashed it in, but decided I wanted to keep it for myself instead of pooling it like I did with my restaurant money. It was special money and I wanted to spend it on something personal.

When I went to visit Mama that weekend we went to Ruffin's and I saw this suede jacket with fringes on it I just had to have, also, Ronnie needed a new car seat so that's where some of the money went. I loved how the fringes swayed when I walked, it was my prize for my work.

Marshall loved it and said, "You need some boots to go with that jacket," and took me out the next day to get some cowboy boots, on his tab, to celebrate 'my first paying job as an artist'. I loved the way I looked in my new fringe jacket and boots. I hoped there would be more chances for me to be able to sell my art in the future as it felt so rewarding.

It turned out, Summerville had their Flowertown Festival that spring and I was able to set up a booth and was able to sell my art there. I wore my fringe jacket and boots, even though I was a little warm, and was amazed that people actually wanted my paintings (I didn't bother trying to sell my drawings) and felt very humbled by their purchases.

I made fifty dollars, more than I could have imagined! Ronnie was such a good boy too, spending the day at the booth. I brought along a little farm set that Marshall had given him for Christmas, and it kept him occupied for hours. It was a huge personal success for me, again realizing that my art was worth something. This time, I pooled half the money because there was nothing that I personally wanted or needed.

Tim was super grateful, but I told him it was the least I could do for everything he does for us. And it was true. He got us dinner every night, he'd got that playset for the kids—in general, we were never without at the commune. I loved Tim but was not in love with him. I loved him like a brother, and felt he loved me the same way back which was a solace.

Chapter 25

June 1973

The time came when I needed him again. There was this one customer at 'The Del Mar' who had taken a shine to me. He was about thirty, with a mullet and decaying teeth who always wore a baseball hat. He was always making passes at me that I had to ignore that made me feel uncomfortable, but Gladys told me to just let it slide.

"There's always one like that," she'd say.

He tried to pinch my behind, and even with that she still would say, "Just let it go. Usually, he came in the daytime, but on this one occasion, I was working the late shift, and he wouldn't leave. I'm closing up," I said.

"Alright, alright," he replied defensively and stepped out the door.

I could see that he wasn't going far, but I was trapped. There was nothing I could do. I had to go home. It was just next door, but he was between here and there. I held my breath and exited.

"You headed home miss?"

"Yes, I am," I said.

"Can I walk ya?"

"No, I don't need company, it's right there."

"Let me put it this way, I'm headed wherever you are, mind if I walk with ya?"

"I doubt you're headed my way, as you don't live in my neighborhood, and thank you, but I'd rather go alone."

"Well, I just don't feel right about you going anywhere unaccompanied at this time of night. I better walk ya," he persisted.

"It's literally right there," I gestured toward the commune, "I'm quite fine. You can go now."

"Let me walk you to your door."

He was relentless. I had already decided I was going to go to Tim's cottage rather than straight to my van where Gen was with Ronnie. I headed in his direction. The lights were out. Clearly, he and Kory were already in bed. I felt bad disturbing them but saw it as my only option.

I banged rather loudly and said, "I'm home!" and that's when I felt the knife at my back.

"Move to the side now."

I moved to the side of the cottage as he instructed. Just as Tim opened the door.

"Hello?"

"Tim!" I shouted before the man put his hand over my mouth. At this point, he had the knife at my throat. I heard Tim go around the other side of the cottage. He then came to our side.

"Gina! What the fuck man! Who the fuck are you?" The man got spooked and dropped the knife.

"Get the fuck away from her!" and he just bolted. I collapsed into Tim's arms.

"He had me at knifepoint," I cried.

"Here, come inside," he said sitting me on the edge of his bed.

"Sorry little man," he whispered to Kory, "there's been an incident."

"There's a mark," he said, "on your neck, from the knife. I'm so sorry Gina, that must have been terrifying.

"I seem to attract this type of situation."

"Hold on there. It's not your fault. Let me walk you back to your van, okay?"

"Alright." Gen was there with Ronnie. I told her what happened, and she said the same thing I did.

"I don't want any more of this blame talking," Tim interjected, "you do nothing to attract this sort of thing to yourself, it's nothing but bad luck. You're just a regular, pretty girl minding your own business, and if that attracts creepers, well, that's not fair."

"Thanks Tim, I'll try not to blame myself, although it feels like I'm doing something wrong."

"Well, you aren't, I promise you that. Keep your doors locked and have a good night's sleep."

With that, he and Gen were off and I was left to cuddle with Ronnie. I held him closer than ever, hyper-aware of any noise outside the van. I knew it was locked, that the man didn't know we lived there, and that we were technically safe, but I was still shaken up.

I let him nurse and it calmed me. Yes, he was 27 months old and I should have weaned him off the habit, but it brought us both so much comfort I just couldn't bear to do it. Soon I told myself, I just didn't know when.

The next morning, I was scheduled to work again, and Sue-Ellen was looking after the kids. I got Ronnie his peanut butter and jelly on toast and brought him over to her cabin. I was a little bit anxious returning to "The Del Mar," but figured I'd just explain the situation to Gladys and hopefully he wouldn't be allowed back in the restaurant. I put on my pale blue outfit and walked over.

Maybe, she would get one of the cooks to tell him? Raymond was large and intimidating. When I arrived, however, he was already sitting in the booth waiting. I pulled Gladys in the back and told her the story.

"Oh honey, that's horrible. I'll deliver his check and get Raymond to tell him he's no longer welcome here."

I had to walk by him to serve another table.

"Hey darlin'" he said. I looked down. He flipped a switch blade open under the table. I felt sick to my stomach. I was worried that making him leave wasn't going to be good enough.

"Gladys, I know I just got here, but can I take my break now?"

"Sure honey, go ahead." I grabbed my purse and beelined it back to the cottages. Tim hadn't left for work yet, thank God.

I told him what happened and he immediately said, "I'm coming over with you right now to have a talk with him." He was mad, but not at me.

"I can't believe this dude, having the nerve to show back up. I'll set him straight once and for all. Don't you worry Gina."

"I trust you. Thank you, Tim. But remember, he has a knife. You have to be careful."

"Oh, I will be. No need to thank me either. I see it as my duty to protect all of us on the commune and I plan to see it through."

We arrived at the restaurant and Dennis (the guy's name) was hamming it up with his buddy across the booth from him. Apparently, he hadn't been told to leave yet, or he hadn't abided.

166

"There she is," he said, "I thought you'd left me." I turned away and went behind the counter. Then he saw Tim.

"Ah, you brought your friend." Tim approached him.

"You, outside, now. We need to have a chat."

"Who? Little old me?" Dennis said with a grin revealing his rotten teeth.

"What would we have to chat about?"

"Just get up and cut the bullshit."

"Alright, alright," his token saying, "I'll come chat with ya if it'll make ya that happy."

He took the switchblade he's been handling under the table and put it in his back pocket. I watched out the window. Tim was using his hands a lot as he spoke and Dennis started getting up in his space.

Tim shoved him off and Dennis grabbed his switchblade from his back pocket and quickly stabbed him in the stomach, then jumped in his truck and sped off.

"Tim! Tim!" I cried. "Hurry! We need an ambulance right away!"

It took fifteen minutes for the ambulance to get there, and the closest hospital was Moncks Corner, about thirty-five minutes away. The ambulance sped and got us there in about twenty. He was bleeding profusely and finding it hard to breathe.

"You're going to make it Tim, it's going to be okay."

When we got there, they rushed him into the back right away for surgery. I waited anxiously for hours, unable to call anyone at the commune. I did call the police, however, and make a report on Dennis and his truck for the stabbing so they could be on the lookout for him—though my faith in them was minute. Finally, Johanna showed up, having gotten word from Gladys where they'd taken us. She embraced me crying.

"Is he going to be okay?"

"I think so," I said, holding back tears of my own.

"This is all my fault; he was protecting me."

"That's his job though Gina, to protect the commune. It's not your fault, no one sees it that way."

"My stepdad will pay for the hospital bill, all I'll have to do is explain the situation and he'll offer, I know him."

"That would be really helpful, but if not we'll find a way. Don't stress about that for now. Put our energy into sending healing forces toward Tim."

She took both my hands and looked at me earnestly. We waited two more hours then they came out.

"You can come in and see him now." Johanna went in and kissed him and I squeezed his hand.

"Hey trooper, so what's the news?" I asked.

"They said he just nicked my stomach lining. It could have been a whole lot worse. I was really lucky. They stitched it up and then me back up, and we're back on track. I'll be outta here in a couple days."

"I hope they catch him," I said kneeling down beside the bed as I was starting to feel dizzy.

"Me too," added Johanna.

"We'll call the police and check before we leave the hospital," she said sounding level considering the circumstances.

"I don't feel safe with him being on the loose—what if he comes by the commune?" I felt ill, then remembered my handgun which eased my concern slightly.

As if reading my mind, Tim responded, "You're going to have to rely on Doug and Paul. I know Paul's young but he can hold his own. Keep your doors locked and maybe a weapon on you if you're going to be wandering around. Just until I get back."

"Let me contact the police and see if they've got him," I interrupted, praying they had.

I called, and much to my surprise and delight they had apprehended him driving recklessly down Old Highway #6 and he was now in custody. They said he was being held for the crime. As they had already interviewed witnesses at the restaurant, and previous outstanding warrants so he wouldn't be being released anytime soon. What a relief! I reported the news back to Tim and Johanna.

"One for the good guys, bad guys, zero," Tim laughed then held his stomach.

"Be careful," Johanna warned, concerned, then kissed his forehead.

"Why don't you guys head back, it's getting late. I'm fine here. Come by tomorrow if you want but you need to get some dinner into you."

"Okay, if you insist. You're the boss!"

"I'm not the boss, I'm just looking out for you. Besides, I need to rest anyhow."

"Hey," I said, "Do you think they have a McDonald's around here? Would it be horrible if you and I just stopped and treated ourselves without the others?"

"You bet they do, and no, I don't think anyone would mind considering what happened if we got ourselves our own supper tonight."

With that, we were off until we found the double arches. We both got quarter-pounders with cheese, fries (with ketchup of course) and I got a chocolate milkshake. It was delectable. It felt like a guilty reward for what had unfolded that day, but I couldn't help but enjoy myself.

The next two days passed, and Tim came home from the hospital. Johanna and I went to pick him up. When we did, we had to go to the police station as they said they needed a formal statement from us. They called me over first, and I had flashbacks to the last time I made my statement when I was sixteen about Greg and what a fruitless horrible experience it was.

I tried to remind myself that these were different officers, and that the situation was distinct in that Dennis was already behind bars. I began with his inappropriate comments to me at the diner before anything had happened, progressing to when he followed me home at knife point, ending with when he stabbed Tim.

"So, we can add another charge to his repertoire, assault with a deadly weapon," was the officer's response to my story.

I felt so validated that I was actually being taken seriously and that my experience was being heard on a legal level.

"I think you were told, but this guy has priors," the officer said. "He's on probation, and wanted on a robbery, and other assault charge. It's back to the slammer for him. And likely for quite a while."

Oh, what liberation it was to hear those words. Definitely one for the good guys, as Tim has put it, for once.

Chapter 26

June 26ᵗʰ 1973

I needed to go home. I needed some home cooking and Mama time. Even Mrs. Knight. I needed Bobbsey! So, I took a few days off of work and headed to Andrews with Ronnie. Everything was in full bloom so the farm was bountiful and beautiful. Ronnie was putting words together now, like "Mama up please," or "Mama nursy" which was splendid to all of us.

Marshall had fired up the grill and put some ribs on it and was about to put on some corn. He came in to ask us how many pieces we wanted, and he started slurring his speech.

"What's wrong honey?" Mama asked him.

"I don't know, I just I can't, I can't feel my arm."

"What do you mean you can't feel your arm?" she said sounding panicked. The right side of his face started drooping as he attempted to speak.

"I mean, I mean, no feeling," he started to stumble.

"Sit down," she said pushing a kitchen chair toward him and he collapsed into it.

"Gina, call an ambulance!"

"Mama what's happening?"

"I think he's having a stroke!" she said sounding choked.

"Stay with us Marshall," she said kneeling down in front of him, but he was losing consciousness.

"I can't see, I can't see," he spoke incoherently.

"Hold tight, the ambulance is on its way and will be here soon."

Mama tried to stay calm for his sake. It took about fifteen minutes for the ambulance to come and by that time he was no longer awake. Mama said she'd meet them at the hospital. I grabbed Ronnie and we rushed to get in the car but couldn't follow them because they put their sirens on to get him there faster.

By the time they'd made it to the hospital, they said he'd stopped breathing. He was rushed into a back room where we couldn't see him. About ten minutes after being taken from the ambulance, a doctor came out and took off his scrub hat.

"Mrs. Clark?"

"Yes?" Mama said, standing up and taking a step toward him.

"I'm sorry. Your husband had a stroke and he didn't make it." All the blood depleted from her delicate face.

"Didn't make it as in he's dead?" Her voice was desperate and scared.

"Yes ma'am, unfortunately, he has passed away." She fell to her knees with her hands over her face.

"No!" she sobbed. "No!" I ran to her side and got down on the ground with her. I was thankful I had come home for this moment, as unknowing as I was.

"I'm so sorry Mama," I started to cry too. I tried to re-gather myself though to remain strong for her.

"My Marshall. Are you sure he's gone?" She looked up at the doctor from her kneeling stance.

"Yes miss, I'm certain. I'm very sorry for your loss."

"How could this be happening? We were just barbequing?" she wailed.

"What am I going to do without him?" I didn't have an answer.

"You still have me and Ronnie and Gen," I offered.

"I know, but he was my love. You understand what it's like to lose your love." And I did, all too well.

"I sure do Mama; it breaks your heart. But we'll get through this together just like you helped me get through Ronnie. It's going to be okay." She slowly got up and went to a chair.

"Oh Marshall, why now? Why today?" she spoke aloud.

The doctor approached, "Would you like to see him to say goodbye?"

"Yes," Mama said, and we followed him to his room. He looked at peace. Mama bent over and hugged him.

"My sweetheart. Why did you have to leave us? I need you," she continued to sob. I just let her have her time with him. She held his hand.

"What am I going to do without you?" she asked rubbing it.

"You're going to make it," I answered trying to instill power in her. I left the room so she could have some alone time with him, and she came out about ten minutes later. She took my hand and gave me the keys.

"I need you to drive."

"Yes, of course."

"Do you want to stop at the diner and pick up some dinner? You two really should eat. I'll try but I don't know how much I'll get down."

"Sure, we can do that."

"I'll just stay in the car though," she said.

"Of course."

So, we swung by the restaurant and I ordered us burgers and fries to go, explaining the situation. They took her off the schedule for the next week, understanding there would be need for funeral arrangements to be made and had, not to mention her grief. Knowing Mama though, she wouldn't want to be gone for too long, she'd need the distraction.

The next morning, I headed back to the commune to fetch Gen—it was certainly an inconvenience not having a phone at times like these. She was working, so I told her to pack her things as soon as she was done and tell them that she needed a few days off.

Luckily, 'Bell's' was a pretty flexible place from the restaurant to the motel, and they were fine with Gen needing to come home. I did the same with 'The Del Mar' and they were equally as accommodating.

June 31st 1973

Gen and I took the reins planning the funeral as Mama was too distraught. She didn't even want to get out of bed. We had to borrow Henry back more hours from Mrs. Knight to oversee the farm until it was sold, which she was fine with, feeling for our loss. The funeral was a large one, as Marshall was beloved in our town, with both farm hands and the wealthier of individuals.

The church was packed to the brim, and everyone wanted to offer Mama their condolences. She just wanted to be left alone but accepted them graciously. Pies and casseroles came rolling in, so we didn't have to cook anything, that's for sure.

She had to meet with an estate lawyer, because she couldn't stay in the house and attend to the farm. It was difficult for her having people trapsing through her matrimonial home to see if they wanted to buy it. She said she felt like she was betraying Marshall by giving it up.

"He worked so hard for this place, now to have to sell it right from under him…"

"No Mama," I reassured, "he would understand, it's the only thing you can do. He wouldn't expect you to be able to tend to the crops and keep the business going. That would be near impossible."

"I suppose," she finally succumbed, and poured herself tea out of the pot Ronnie had given her.

"Rubin seems nice, though I'm a little skeptical with this being his first big sale."

"Well, you've got to start somewhere, and he might as well start with us. He's eager to do well, I think it's a good thing."

The next day, he brought a kind young couple through who seemed aware of Mama's situation. They toured the house and spent an extensive amount of time in the fields.

I went outside to eavesdrop and heard him say, "It comes with the equipment."

"Yes, he took excellent care of it, it's in tip-top shape," and "the barn's only about twelve years old, as is the house."

I saw them shake hands and then they came back inside, and the woman said, "Miss? Thank you so much for welcoming us into your home to look around, especially at such a terrible time for you like this. We are most impressed—with the farm and the house."

The man added, "Your husband did an immaculate job keeping it up. We've been looking to upgrade, and this place checks all the boxes."

"I'm glad," Mama said half sad and half relieved to have someone interested.

"If you're okay with it, we'd like to sit down with your agent and put in an offer."

"Of course, if it suits you to," she replied. She took a sip of tea and partially smiled.

"Let's go back to my office and draw up some papers," Rubin said to them.

"Alright soldier, we'll follow you there," the somewhat boisterous man replied.

And that was the end of that. The house was sold to the nice young couple only a few days after being on the market without hassle. Mama asked for a thirty-day closing date so she could find herself a new place and they were fine with that. Henry's more consistent presence would remain until then.

After the mortgage was paid off, and the funeral costs, with the money from the house and Marshall's stocks Mama was left with sixty-three thousand dollars. More than enough to find a homey place of her own and have extra money left over. She said she wanted a small place, but one big enough for me, Gen, and Ronnie, to be able to stay in when we visited.

Gen and I had been back and forth from the commune to Andrews, and I promised we'd be back again in a few days, that I'd get more time off of work, and we'd make an adventure out of finding a new place. This seemed to cheer her a bit.

"An adventure…We're good at adventures, aren't we?" she said.

"The best," I said kissing her cheek.

After being back at the commune for about a week, I asked for another week off, and both restaurants were understanding and moved the schedule around, granting me the time. Ronnie and I drove back to Andrews to find Mama in her housecoat mid-day, completely out of character for her.

"So, does Rubin have some houses lined up for us to look at?"

"I don't know, you'll have to give him a ring. I've been sleeping and might have missed his call."

"Let me draw you a bath first, sound good?"

"Sure," she said complacently. I ran the water trying to make it just the right temperature and put some bubbles in just to make it fun.

"All ready!" I shouted.

She came sauntering down the hallway in a zombie like fashion. I was feeling guilty for having left her alone for a week in this state.

"Here you go, now I'm going to go contact Rubin."

He said he had two properties lined up to show us and was just waiting to hear back from Mama. I apologized on her behalf, explaining how she was just struggling with the death. He was very compassionate about it, and set up the showings for the next day, which was a Saturday.

I barbequed us hotdogs for dinner that night and trying to get Mama to engage had her cut up Ronnie's into little pieces so he wouldn't choke. The only happiness I saw in her was when she was interacting with him, so I tried to encourage it. We both slept in her bed that night, hoping the extra bodies might bring her comfort.

I wrapped my arms around her, and she put my hand over her heart. It was beating slowly, as though every pump was an effort.

"I'm excited for our adventures tomorrow," I whispered. "We'll make it fun," she said—which was a better response than I'd expected.

The next day, Mama put on one of her church dresses and I drove her to meet Rubin at his office.

"I tried to pick a variety for you ma'am best I could. There's not too many for sale in Andrews right now that fit the criteria you're looking for, but I found you an older one and a newer one. Let's hop in our cars and you can follow me to the first one; it's a three bedroom."

It was built in '65 but smelled of must. It had lots of built-ins, which unbeknownst to me, Mama 'hated' and green carpeting throughout of which she was 'not a fan'. She liked its distance to town, and its front porch, but that was about it. Strike one. About a five-minute drive across the main road of Morgan Avenue was Carberry Street.

"This one," Rubin announced, "was just built last year."

It was a little light brown brick ranch with a car port on it's right and shutters painted red. It had four distinct white columns across a small front porch, which I knew was an attraction to Mama as she loved the columns on Marshall's house.

"They just make any home look regal," she said.

Inside, there was wood paneled walls, and a stately mottled light brick fireplace and mantle from floor to ceiling. There was a formal living room and dining room as well as a den. There were two spacious bedrooms and bathrooms, and laundry was located off the carport.

The carpet was a peachy pink cream color which gave the room a certain glow when the sunlight poured in onto it. After spending most of the tour in dead silence, (unlike the last place where she was complaining at every turn), I didn't know what to expect.

She paused in the middle of the living room, let out one of her famous deep sighs, and said, "I love it. I want it yesterday," and laughed at her own joke which brought me pleasure.

Rubin was equally as pleased.

"You want this one? I'll head back to the office and contact the sellers immediately. Now, they're asking twenty-one thousand for it, how much would you like to offer?"

"Well, twenty-one thousand if that's what they're asking for. I certainly hope you didn't stoop like that while selling our farm!"

175

"No, no ma'am, of course not. You got asking price. Don't you worry your pretty little head about that," he said condescendingly, though not meaning to be. Mama put in her offer and got the house with the long driveway and peachy pink carpets. Its lawn was a fair size too, so it was actually quite a good deal.

When word got back to the commune about Mama moving, Tim immediately volunteered, "We'll do it. Doug has his truck, and with another car or two we can get the job done."

And so he went about arranging for member's to get the day off to help Mama transfer her belongings from the big farmhouse to her new little abode on Carberry Street.

August 1st 1973

The commune rallied, Doug drove his truck, Tim, Gen, and Charla drove their cars and everybody but Nancy who stayed behind to look after the kids (except for Ronnie, he was in tow) came together to move Mama. We laid out sheets on the carpet so it wouldn't get dirty, and Bobbsey and Sal watched curiously from their cages off to the side.

"The rest from that room is going to storage in Georgetown," she directed.

Since the new house was only a two-bedroom, Gen and my room's needed to be condensed into one. Mama decided not to move the couch in favor of buying a new pullout couch in case Gen and I were staying over at the same time. We were going to pick it out tomorrow, so she didn't have to go without one, though she did have Marshall's favorite armchair.

It took seven full hours to complete the move—from ten until five. Mama got everyone burgers, fries and coke from the diner which was much appreciated because we were all famished.

Once the hot August sun began it's decent in the clear sky, Tim said, "Well, looks like our job here is done miss. I hope you're happy with our work."

"Oh, I'm more than satisfied!" Mama said.

"I'm so grateful for your help. Thank you all very much."

"Glad to be of service," Johanna responded with a sympathetic smile, patting Mama's back in a soothing manner.

"I'm going to stay back and help Mama pick out the couch and get settled in. I'll be back the day after tomorrow. I have to work," I said.

"I have to work tomorrow, or I'd stay too," said Gen. "There's no room for you anyways, so best you aren't!"

I laughed.

"Very true!" Gen jokingly agreed, "See you in a couple days."

And with that they piled into the truck and their cars, sticking their hands from the windows waving, and with a few celebratory beeps they were gone.

"What a great group of kids they are," Mama said half to me, half to herself.

"Hey—let's let Bobbsey and Sal out to explore now!" I excitedly opened their cages. They both stepped out quickly, but then proceeded with caution. I picked up Bobbsey, holding him on his back like a giant baby.

"Let me show you around," I said, taking him from room to room, Sal following at my feet. I hoped Mama wouldn't be lonely here. That was my biggest fear. As though, as often happened, she could hear my thoughts, she came up behind me and put her chin on my shoulder.

"I'm going to be just fine here," she said. "Especially when I get that new couch!" she emphasized with more excitement than I'd heard in her voice recently.

I smiled and turned and kissed her cheek.

"Do you think Lucy will be okay with Henry?" I asked.

"Henry loved Marshall, so he'll love the dog like she was his own. I think she'll be alright."

"Good. Sal and Bobbsey won't mind life without the big lug I'm sure," I laughed.

"True, they'll be king and queen of the house again," Mama agreed.

"Let's make up the beds my dear. I had them put the sheets in the bedrooms."

And we did, resulting in me sleeping soundly with Ronnie and Bobbsey curled up next to me in the new house. The next day I arose with the promise of picking out the new couch with Mama. We headed to the furniture store and soon found out what we were looking for was called a "Simmons Hide-A-Bed."

There was one in a taupe plush finish with a dimpled back which matched the décor of the house well enough, so she bought it. It was quite the miraculous contraption, the way it folded out into a full-sized mattress!

It was to be delivered the next day, which suited Mama just fine. When it was, it looked lovely in the living room. The perfect addition to Mama's new forced beginning.

Chapter 27

February 1974

That's when Bennie and the Jets came on the radio; Ronnie loved it because they said his name. I used to sing to him "Oh Mommy and Ronnie have you seen them yet?" and he'd giggle and giggle. It was also the month of the 'Little Miss and Mister Pageant' in Eutawville at the community center.

Everyone at the commune wanted me to enter Ronnie because he could sing so well around the campfire, so how could I resist? There was a costume portion, a formal portion, and a talent portion. Mama was all about it. She wanted to dress him as a little cowboy, and she went to town. She got him a tiny pair of cowboy boots that fit perfectly into his Levis.

She sewed him a suede vest to wear over his red plaid shirt and at the same store in Georgetown where she got him the boots, she got him a child-sized cowboy hat to top it all off. He certainly looked the part. For the formal portion, she got him a pair of beige slacks, a light blue button up shirt, a pair of pink suspenders, a pink pocket square and a little pink bowtie with some white shoes.

As for the talent part, thankfully he was fluid linguistically for his age, and Gen came up with the idea that he sing L-O-V-E by Nat King Cole. He already knew the song because I'd sing it to him all the time. So, we practiced and practiced—much like my driver's test—first singing it with the recording, then with just me, then alone. It was priceless.

He just couldn't get his mouth around 'extraordinary'; it always came out 'ectornary' and I mean, what more could you expect from a three-and-a-half-year-old? Before the big day, I knew I needed to cut his long baby hair, I'd just let it grow, unable to part with the soft dark strawberry locks. But it was time for them to go.

I cried while I did it, but boy, did he ever look even more like my Ronnie when I was done. Admittedly, he looked even cuter than before.

On the night of the talent show, Mama came into town. Gen said she could spend the night in her cabin, and she'd stay the night in the van. We just figured it might be more comfortable for her. Charla offered me her bed, so essentially, we just switched sleeping arrangements for the night. But before all that—the pageant. The age range for it was two to ten, so Ronnie was on the lower end.

There was a piano accompanist there, bald as a billiard with thick gray curls sticking out the sides. I snuck off before the show started to ask if he knew how to play 'L-O-V-E' because I didn't have the sheet music, and against all odds, he did! I told him who Ronnie was and asked him if he could play along when it was his turn and he agreed.

"No problem."

"Just be prepared to play along a little slower than normal, he's only three and a half," I warned.

"I'll play lightly and let him set the pace," he politely agreed.

"Thank you, you're an angel. Hopefully we do your playing some justice," I praised.

"Don't worry, you'll be fine honey. I'm sure he'll do just great," he said.

"I'm aiming low, just that the experience doesn't traumatize him. Anything but that and I'll be satisfied," I said.

"I think it's good to expose kids to this kind of thing. Lights, camera, action, crowds, earlier in life. It gives them confidence. You're giving him a gift." His words really touched my heart.

"Thank you for easing my anxiety, you truly are a lifesaver."

"Good luck," he said as I left to go backstage to find Ronnie, poor little guy, who'd been patiently waiting for me where I'd asked him to stand.

Everything was all abuzz—mothers left and right, kids underfoot. There were five girls and four boys who were in the competition, and they were put into a lineup to walk out in their costumes to be introduced. 'Tie a Yellow Ribbon' was being played in the background as the kids were being marched out.

Ronnie walked on stage like he owned the world, and the whole commune stood up and cheered for him, whistling and cheering, causing a bit of a scene, albeit a supportive one.

"What's your name little fella?"

Ronnie pulled the microphone close to his mouth, "My name is Ronald Eugene Owens, but you can just call me Ronnie."

The crowd went wild for this, and you could tell by his face he was confused why.

"How old are you?"

"I'm three and a half."

"And what's something you like to do Ronnie?" putting the microphone back up to his mouth.

"Nursy!" he said with excitement.

"Okay, I'm not really sure what that is, but, I'll take your word for it!" He moved onto the next contestant.

"Now, what's your name pretty lady…"

"Oh my God. I can't believe he just said he liked to breastfeed in front of an auditorium of people." Maybe this was my wakeup call!

"Alright, now if you two want to just strut yourselves to the one side of the stage, and then the other, so everyone can get a good look at your sharp outfits, that'd be just dandy."

Ronnie did what we talked about and when he got to the end of the stage, he popped his thumbs through his belt loops and propped up his boot heel. The crowd reacted positively to this too. As soon as he got backstage, I scooped him up in my arms and hugged him.

"How'd I do, Mama?"

"You did perfectly, my love. Now, we've got to change into your fancy clothes for you to sing."

As I was in the middle of clipping one of his suspenders, one of the other mothers, chomping away on what appeared to be a massive piece of gum, came over and asked me, "What's nursy anyways?"

"Hospital. It's when we play hospital." She thought it over for a millisecond and the answer was satisfactory to her.

"Ya, that makes sense. Cute."

And walked away.

"Mama, we don't play hospital though—"

"I know Ronnie, but our nursy time is private, kind of like a secret. People don't understand it, so Mama fibbed. You shouldn't tell a fib but sometimes you just have to, so I did."

I said adjusting his bowtie and pocket square just so.

"Do you feel nervous?" I asked trying to redirect his train of thought.

"No. Why?" Fear had not even entered his peripheral.

I had made a mistake. "Oh, sometimes I just like to check in on ya," I said tickling his belly.

"He's onto the next," the woman coordinating the acts said to me. So far, a boy had blown bubbles, told jokes, recited the alphabet backward and did a walking handstand. Ronnie took the stage, and they handed him the microphone.

"This song is called LOVE," he said and started singing along with the piano, he looked back at me after saying 'ectornary' and smiled because he knew he'd gotten past the worst of it. He powered through the rest of the tune, hitting all the notes with the voice of an angel, seriously, and then in an impromptu move spun in a circle at the end of the song and went on one knee.

He got a standing ovation from the whole place. As I peeked around the corner the piano player caught my eye and mouthed "I told you so," and I just smiled and did a little wave back before opening my arms for Ronnie to run into.

"I did it Mama, I did it!"

"You sure did! I'm so proud of you!"

Since Ronnie was the last to go, it was time for the judges to do their deliberating. Finally, they gave their signal that they had made their decision. First, they announced the girls. Getting to the winner, she did her lap across the stage with her tierra and trophy. Then came the boys.

"First runner up goes to Tyler Hicks," he's the one who had recited the alphabet backward.

"Second runner up goes to Michael Fairfield," he's the one who had done the walking handstand.

"And the winner of Little Mister Eutawville 1974 goes to Ronnie Owens!" I ran on stage to help him carry the trophy as it was quite large.

"A reminder that our winners will receive twenty dollars in cash and a ten-dollar voucher to Bell's Restaurant."

I laughed. But that's how we'd found out about the idea, so it was fateful. Ronnie did his lap, with me carrying the trophy, and the commune members, again, making quite a fuss. I took us backstage to gather our things, and get our prizes, and then to meet Mama and Gen out front.

"Congratulations buddy!" Gen said upon sight as he jumped onto her.

"You did such a good job singing!"

"Ya?"

"Ya!"

Suddenly a man approached from behind.

"I don't mean to interrupt, but you've got quite a talented boy here."

"Yes, he's my son," I said instinctively taking his hand.

"Well, my name is Bill Barnes and I'm from DeJardins Talent Agency run out of Atlanta. We scour the South for fresh talent like your little Ronnie there. We do modeling, acting, recording, you name it. If you're interested in doing something with your son's natural gifts, give my office a ring. If I'm not there, don't despair, I'm in and out. Leave a message with my secretary and I'll get back to you. Sound like a plan?"

"I mean…" I stuttered; I'd never thought of Ronnie taking that path before. "I'll have to think about it."

"Of course, of course. Just know with a mug like that, he'd get hired for modeling straight off the bat. Singing is really just the cherry on top. The sky's the limit."

"You've certainly given us some food for thought—what was your name again?" Mama chimed in.

"Bill Barnes."

"We'll be in touch if we're so inclined. Thank you for the offer, it's flattering indeed."

"No problem, hope to hear from you soon. You ladies have a good night," handing me his card.

"What a whirlwind of an evening!" I said hugging Ronnie on my lap in the car. "Is the ice cream place where Charla works still open?"

"I think so," Gen answered from the front seat. "Why, you having a hankering?"

"A little, and I just think our star of the hour deserves a treat. How would you like that baby? Some ice cream?"

"Ice cream!" he shouted, "Yes please!"

"You can get anything you want. It's your reward for being such a brave boy tonight."

"I'd like a banana split please."

"Okay, well those are pretty big, so how about we split on a split," and made a chopping motion with my hand. He thought this was funny and dismissed my qualms about having to share. Mama got a strawberry cone, Gen a chocolate.

"I hope you sleep alright tonight in Gen's bed Mama," I said.

"I'm sure I will, but if I don't it won't kill me. It was worth it to come see my precious grandson croon the county away!"

"Did you get scared when you were out on stage, and you knew you had to start singing?" I could ask him now that his performance wasn't at jeopardy.

"No mommy, I felt excited."

"That's so good baby boy! You're a born entertainer. Maybe all our campfire singing has given you a nice singing voice."

"Or maybe God gave it to me." How profound!

"Yes, you're very right. Right. I think God did." We all laughed at his precociousness, but at the same time pondered his words' validity.

Mama said she slept like a log, and when she got up, Tim ran across the street to 'Bell's' and got a twelve pack of pastries for breakfast.

"So hospitable you are. Why thank you," Mama said as she selected her butter tart, and I nabbed a couple of donuts for me and Ronnie.

Tim lit the fire just for Mama to sit by it and have her tart, and draped his woolen sweater coat over her as she ate. He was always taking care of people.

When most were gathered by the fire he said, "Let's give a round of applause to the commune's superstar, Ronnie Owens!" Ronnie hopped up and took a bow without prompting. What a ham!

"You did a stellar job last night my man. Maybe you want to give an encore performance right now? Except we don't have a piano?"

"Okay sure, I don't need a piano," he said confidently. And so, he belted out L-O-V-E once more, much to the amusement of the onlookers. He even did the twirl onto one knee thing he'd invented last night at the end—which meant a change of clothes because it was muddy as it had rained overnight.

"Man, when I was his age, I was barely talking," Doug said.

"Ya, there's no way Adelaide, bless her heart, could have done that at age three-and-a-half. Heck she's eight now and she'd still not be able to."

"Is he some sort of savant?" asked Paul. I laughed and smacked his arm.

"No, I'm serious, it's abnormal talent, that's all I mean."

"Well, this guy did approach us after the show—"

"What guy?" Johanna interjected. "This talent scout from Atlanta, saying he wanted to sign Ronnie. I told him I'd have to think about it."

"Think about it! You're going to do it though, right? You could have the world's next Donny Osmond on your hands here."

"Well, he's a modeling agent with singing and acting on the side from what I could understand. I suppose there's no harm in inquiring a bit more, right?"

"No harm? I think it would be a gain. You don't want to deprive Ronnie of experiences that could change his life for the better. I mean, even modeling. How exciting!"

"If they invite me to Atlanta, would you come with me?"

"You bet your bottom dollar I will. I'll make sure this dude is legitimate too, and it's not some sort of scam. Oh Gina, this is so breathtaking! In the meantime, we should teach Ronnie a new song. Speaking of the Osmonds, what about 'One Bad Apple?' That would be so adorable! Oh my God, Oh my God! I'm so excited for us. Let me know when you've talked to his office."

She squeezed my hands and ran off. I went back over to Mama who was sitting with Ronnie on her knee. He was perched forward with her arms wrapped around him. She was wearing jeans, loafers, and a white collared shirt—slightly popped—a necklace and now had her carcoat overtop.

"Mama!" Ronnie said reaching out his arms for me. I went and hugged him.

"Two hugs, I like it," pointing to the fact that Mama still had her arms around him as we embraced. We both leaned in and held him extra tight.

"You're so sweet my boy." He thought about this for a moment.

"Sweet like chocolate?" he finally came out with.

"Yes, like yummy candy," I said. This made him kick his feet up in the air and smile.

"Well, my dear, it's been lovely, but I think I'm going to head home in a few minutes."

"I have next weekend off, so we'll be down to Andrews, if you don't mind having us that is."

"Never do I mind my love," she replied. And that was the end of Mama's trip to the commune.

Everyone hugged her goodbye and told her they wished she's come back, how she's always welcome, how it was a pleasure having her there. I felt proud of my people and of my mama. It had been an altogether successful twenty-four hours.

On Monday before work, I thumbed Bill Barnes' card around in my hand before putting my coin in the slot to make the call. Finally, I dropped it in and dialed.

"Hello, DeJardins Talent and Modeling Agency, how may I help you?"

"Oh hi, my name is Gina Owens, I was given this number by Bill Barnes this past weekend and told to call and book an appointment with him if I decided I was interested in moving ahead with him investing in my little boy, and well, I guess I decided I was," I said, fumbling my words and feeling ridiculous for it.

"Hello Miss Owens, Bill mentioned you to me that he was hoping for your call."

Hoping for my call! I thought. Maybe Ronnie did make an impression.

"The next available appointment I have is for about three and a half weeks down the line, on March thirteenth at 1pm. Does that work for you?"

"Yes, that works just fine for me," I said, scribbling it down on my work notepad (I was already in uniform). She proceeded to give me the address and detailed directions on how to get there once in the city, which I also wrote.

"I'm looking forward to making your acquaintance, we will see you on Friday March 13th—oh Friday the 13th, hopefully no bad luck, knock on wood," she laughed.

"Anyhow, see you then. Have a pleasant rest of your day."

"You too," I said.

Well, I thought, *at least the agency is successful enough to afford a secretary,* and went to go find Johanna so she could be sure to book the day off.

"Are you going to go into town and get that single so you can start teaching it to him?" She was really hung up on that song! But I thought she was right.

"I'll go after work today, I'm off at three."

"Great idea. Oh my God this is so amazing. I feel like Bahá'u'lláh is working for us. What if he becomes a celebrity, Gina?" I laughed.

"Johanna, I think you're getting a bit ahead of yourself. All he's done is sing one song at a community center. We've got a long way to for celebrity status."

"Ya, but he was scouted, that's a big deal. He's going to make it big. I can feel it in my bones."

This reminded me of my old Ronnie, it was a phrase he'd use often. When it was called for that is. My poor Ronnie. Oh, how I still missed him so.

Chapter 28

So, just like before the talent show, we practiced. We went home to visit Mama and practiced some more. There were a lot of verses for him to learn and big words like 'guaranteed.' Which were hard for him to get his little tongue around. But we did it!

Mama gave me a blank check, "There will be a fee you know," she said, "so take this, as long as it's within reason. And use your intuition. If you feel like you're getting scammed, get out."

"I will Mama, trust me. I won't be taken for any rides. I'll have to use the house as my contact number by the way, so I guess that makes you Ronnie's agent and secretary!" We both chuckled.

"Happy to be of service. You know, I always knew he was special, from the moment you brought him home from your Nana's. He just had that extra little twinkle in his eye. I'm not surprised that someone with clout picked up on it."

"Well, I am!" I said, "I wasn't even expecting him to win, though in hindsight I should have been. We'll see where this goes. It's a bit thrilling, isn't it Mama? My boy's got star power."

"It is exciting honey. You deserve it though. You're such a great mom and he's such a special kid. You're a special pair, actually. One in a million. And the world is yours baby girl."

"Thanks, Mama, for being my cheerleader."

"Always," she said; and we turned on the TV to watch Ed Sullivan.

March 13th 1974

March 13th came around quickly and me, Ronnie and Johanna were off to Atlanta in the Cortez.

"I'm in the lap of luxury for this ride!" Johanna said from the back.

"Welcome to van life," I retorted.

It was an extremely simple drive, thank God, I just took #20 all the way west until I was in the city and then followed the instructions Mr. Barnes secretary had given me.

Their office was on floor six of a ten floor golden brick building with big, long windows that looked like they'd be difficult to clean. We walked in to be greeted by the woman I'd spoken to on the phone. She had graying hair, pulled back in a neat bun and was dressed rather sophisticatedly.

"This must be Ronnie."

"Hi, yes I am," he said in response.

"Adorable," she said folding her hands together with bent elbows.

"And I'm Gina Owens, his mother," I extended my hand in greeting.

"It's nice to meet you dear. Alice Albright."

"This is my friend Johanna. She wanted to come along and see what everything was all about, and I appreciated the support, so she'll be joining us today."

"Oh, that's wonderful. How nice to have a friend who's taken a keen interest in your child."

"I love him like he was my own," Johanna interjected.

"How sweet," said the lady.

"Now if you don't mind taking a seat in the waiting area just off to your left, I'll call into Mr. Barnes and let him know you've arrived."

"Hello Mr. Barnes. Gina Owens is here now with her son Ronnie. You're ready now? Okay I'll send her right in."

"Astonishingly, Mr. Barnes is actually on time today and is ready to see you!" She led us around a corner and knocked on the first door on the left. "Come on in," he bellowed from the other side, and with that, we were ushered in, and the secretary departed.

"I see we have a beautiful third party here! And who do I have the pleasure of making their acquaintance?"

"My name's Johanna."

"Lovely name for a lovely girl. And Gina, just as pretty as the first time I laid eyes on you last month. Little Ronnie got his good genes from you."

I guess it was his job to be focused on outward appearances, but it was a lot to take in.

"Welcome, are you ready to sign some papers?"

"Do you mean Ronnie doesn't need to audition?" Bill cackled, drawing up the sides of his blonde mustache into a wide smile.

"Nah, I saw what I needed to at the pageant. I mean, unless you have something prepared, I'd be more than happy to watch the little tyke put on a show."

"We did actually prepare a song for you."

"A song for me?" he said, looking at Ronnie.

"Yes sir, I worked really hard."

"Well then," he said with a smack of his desk, "I guess I better be hearing it. I don't want your efforts to go to waste my boy!"

"Thank you, sir." I had prepped Ronnie to refer to Bill as 'sir' and he was taking my advice to a tee. So, with Johanna and I seated off to the right, Ronnie took 'center stage' in the office and jumped right in.

"I can tell you've been hurt by that look on your face girl…" and proceeded to sing the song in its entirety with a flawless voice.

When he was finished Bill clapped and said, "That's my little fella', well done, well done! You've certainly got a talented young lad on your hands Gina. Let's see what the world's going to do with him." He took out the papers for me to sign and added.

"There's a thirty-dollar finder's fee, and that covers the headshots too. Plus, our company gets fifteen percent of whatever Ronnie makes in the business. Sound fair?" I didn't know whether it did or not, but it didn't sound outlandish, so I agreed.

"Yes Mr. Barnes," I said and signed the papers, and handed over the check.

"Now, the photographer is just down the hallway. I told him to hopefully expect you. I'll walk you there and introduce you. He'll do the headshots I'll send out. Then I'll give you a call if I get any bites. And we'll get bites, trust me, with his cute little face, I'd give it a week and we'll have a call back."

"Wow!" Johanna exclaimed. "That's fabulous!" I echoed. "Now let's go down the hall and get these photos going. Can't get anywhere without 'em."

Bill got up from his chair, and we followed him down the hallway to the photo studio.

"Floyd, this is Ronnie Owens, he's your subject here this afternoon."

"What a handsome young man you are," said Floyd. He was tall and slender with a rather feminine flair about him.

"Come over here and we'll get started," leading Ronnie over to an area with a blue backdrop. He had him do a few poses, then changed the background, then got him to pose some more, changed the background again and repeated.

"That should do it," he finally said. "Thank you for being so cooperative Ronnie, you were a delight to work with."

"No problem," he responded, and we all laughed as Ronnie stuck out his hand to be shook. He was so beyond his years!

"I think somebody deserves McDonalds!"

"Me?" said Ronnie as we walked out of the building.

"Yes you! You were such a good boy today, I'm very proud of you."

"Thanks Mama."

So, we stopped at McDonalds for burgers and fries on our way out of Atlanta. We didn't get back to Eutawville until just after dark.

And as Johanna put it, "Well, that was an adventure."

"Thanks for coming with us," I said, "the moral support was helpful even if it wasn't obvious."

"Of course! I was more than happy to tag along. I'll be able to say I did when he makes it big someday."

"We'll see about that. For the time being, we've done all we can do. Now, we just have to let it lie, and in the words of Mr. Barnes, see who, if anyone, bites."

March 23rd 1974

And bite they did! About a week and a half later, Mama received a call from Bill Barnes' secretary saying the Sears Wishbook wanted to cast Ronnie in their toy section. She wanted us to come on the thirtieth of March to a different studio altogether, not Floyd's, to which she gave directions. I was elated that we got such a quick callback, and for something as big as the Sears Wishbook!

To make sure I wasn't scheduled to work that day I had to explain the situation to get keep the day off. At first, I think they thought I was lying, as it does sound a little far-fetched, but I secured it, nonetheless. I decided I ought to take Ronnie into town to the barber to get his hair trimmed nicely for the occasion, instead of just my makeshift cut.

How I loved his deep auburn hair—like autumn incarnate—it was so soft and smelled so sweet. It was darker than Ronnie's, yes, but that's because he came from me and I have deep chestnut hair, but still had that strawberry hue to it.

So off to the barber we went, where he got a lollipop after being done. I guess some children needed a bribe to get their hair cut, but not Ronnie, if anything, he enjoyed the attention of the situation! He looked so handsome when they were finished with him.

Mama said she'd come to Atlanta this time, so she drove down to Eutawville early that morning and arrived with the sun. We decided to take her car, as it was less cumbersome than the van. We stopped for lunch at the same McDonalds we'd been to on our trip before and made it to the studio for one o'clock.

There were other children around, and they ushered Ronnie into a room with a long vinyl tunnel with Winnie the Pooh on it. There was another little girl there in pigtails and a striped shirt around the same age. The photographer directed them to "play in the tunnel and look at the camera." I had dressed Ronnie in a blue turtleneck and navy-blue corduroys, and this must have been acceptable as they didn't ask him to change.

Mama and I were allowed to stand off to the side, and Ronnie was a regular ham, smiling away, darting in and out of the tube. I think the little girl had a crush on him, but who wouldn't? He was so cute. At the end of the shoot, Ronnie and the girl were each given a tunnel to take home which Ronnie was very excited about.

"I get to keep it for good?" he asked jumping up and down.

"It's all yours," the photographer said laughing at Ronnie's delight. He took it gingerly from his hands—I'd taught him not to grab—and he ran over to me and Mama.

"Look at what I got! One of those tunnels to keep!"

"Wow, that's amazing buddy, you'll have lots of fun outside in that. Does it have Winnie the Pooh on it?"

"Ya it does."

"Who's your favorite from Winnie the Pooh?" I asked, already knowing the answer.

"Tigger!" he responded.

"How come?"

190

"Because he bounces!" and he started hopping around.

I grabbed him mid-hop and picked him up and hugged him.

"I'm so proud you're mine," I said to him kissing his cheek.

He wrapped his arms around my neck and said, "And I'm so happy you're my mommy," kissing my cheek back.

My heart hadn't felt so full since I was with my old love, Ronnie. They ignited the same feeling of wholeness in me.

"Let's blow this pop stand and head home, what'd say sweetie? Ready to go?"

"I'm ready."

Even though it was a bit early, we decided since it was enroute to stop at Sambo's for dinner on our way home. We all got shrimp and Ronnie was over the moon for being able to have it as it was one of his favorites. He fell asleep shortly after it got dark until when we got home. Tuckered himself out climbing through that tunnel, I guess!

I'm only joking around, it was an extremely taxing day for a three-and-a-half-year-old and I was blessed he nodded off, rather than acting out like some children. He really was the perfect child. So obedient and loving with a naturally cheerful demeanor. It creeped into my mind from time to time that his father was really missing out on a wonderful kid, but I'd push it away immediately.

I couldn't imagine having to send him off with a virtual stranger for visitation time any point from birth forward. He was mine. Watching him grow only reinforced this fact.

I knew one day he would want to know about his father, and the last thing I wanted was for him to think that he didn't want him. I didn't want him to feel unlovable. Then two days after being back from Atlanta the news came. Charla called me over to her cabin.

"Hey, you know that guy you slept with who's Ronnie's dad?" I got uncomfortable immediately.

"Yes, I remember him rather vaguely," I answered.

"Well, he just died in 'Nam. I'm sorry. I mean, I know he wasn't in Ronnie's life, but I don't know if you were ever planning on changing that or whatever. So ya, I'm sorry. Just thought you'd want to know."

"I'm glad you told me, thank you so much Charla I really appreciate it," I said putting my hand on her shoulder trying to feign some sense of disappointment.

Obviously, I wasn't happy he was dead; I didn't have any real feelings of sadness though because I wasn't emotionally attached to him in anyway. Truthfully, what I felt was relief. Now I could tell Ronnie his dad died in the war and that's why he wasn't in his life. The onus was off of me and onto natural—well unnatural natural—causes. When it came time, I had a reason.

The next call we got from Bill Barnes was about a talent competition for kids between the ages of two and ten in Atlanta on April 21st where there was a cash prize of a whopping five hundred dollars. This was a huge event, much bigger than Eutawville he warned, so he should be prepared for a large audience.

I told Johanna and she came up with the idea of him singing 'Georgia On My Mind' which I thought was quite fitting. But could I get him to learn it in three weeks? I think I could. Maybe with Gen's help. Same routine. Bought the record. Played it for him over and over.

Got him to sing along. Then with me, then piece by piece, alone. I called ahead to Mr. Barnes' office trying to sound very official and that my request was very ordinary—though I had no idea if it was or not.

"Hi, this is Gina Owens calling from South Carolina. I was wondering if Mr. Barnes could please get the sheet music for 'Georgia On My Mind' sent over to the pianist at the talent competition as early as possible, as that's what Ronnie will be performing night of."

I hoped I sounded authoritative but not demanding.

"Yes, certainly my dear. I can arrange for it to get sent to the Alliance. That was the sheet music for "Georgia On My Mind," correct?"

"Yes, that's correct." "Not a problem. Is there anything else I can help you with today, Miss Owens?"

"No, not that's I can think of. Thank you for your help, it's much appreciated."

"It's my job, I try to do the best I can."

"Okay. Well, have a great day!"

"You too. Goodbye."

That was a success! I felt a weight off my shoulders not having to deal with that snag anymore. No more last-minute scrambling like at the 'Little Mister' show, all was set, and my stress alleviated.

April 21st 1974

Mama went all out again on the clothing front and had bought Ronnie a tiny pastel tuxedo. Boy, did he ever look sharp! We lay it out flat in the trunk, so he didn't have to wear it until we got there. Sue-Ellen, Adelaide, Tim, Johanna, and Kory were also making the trip to see us which I was so grateful for. How lucky I was to have such devoted friends!

They really were like family though after living with them and raising Ronnie with them for over three years. When we arrived, I was amazed at the capacity of the theater, being about 1800. I was certain the event wouldn't fill it, but even partially it would be daunting. I learned last time though, not to ask Ronnie if he was feeling scared, only to ask him how he was feeling.

We were escorted into the backstage area where everyone was prepping to perform. There were seventeen children, mixed genders and ages, as mentioned before, between the ages of two to ten. Ronnie was given the #8 ticket to perform, so about halfway through.

Not the best placement I thought—not so early that you're catching people's attention right away and setting the stage, and not near the end to be remembered unless you really made an impact. Oh, have faith! I told myself.

The little girl who went before him did a ballet dance; she was alright but nothing mind blowing in any sense of the word. All I knew was Ronnie had to really bring it home with his routine. The host did the usual chit-chat with him beforehand, but at least this time I had prepared him. It was like a repeat of Eutawville.

"What's your name young man?"

"Ronnie Owens."

"And how old are you?"

"Three and a half."

"Well, you're getting up there." The crowd laughed, as he was the youngest contestant to be spoken to yet.

"What do you like to do for fun?"

"Play pretend with my Mama."

"Oh, that sounds like fun! What kind of pretend?"

"Doctor."

"Is that what you want to be when you grow up?"

"No, I want to be a singer."

"Oh, well then! That's what you're going to do for us tonight, isn't it?"

"Yes sir."

"Let's get to it then! Here is young Ronnie Owens singing 'Georgia On My Mind'."

The lights dimmed and the spotlight went on him.

'Georgia, Georgia. The whole day through…' his voice was pure and clear and rang out through the hall.

My heart swelled with pride as he sang on. I didn't care if he won, he was already a winner to me. Such a brave boy to get up there and sing in front of all these people.

"…Just an old sweet song, keeps Georgia on my mind." He nailed it. Hit every note. He got another standing ovation from everyone.

The commune hollered and whistled above the crowd, "That's our boy! Atta' boy Ronnie, show 'em what you're made of!"

He hustled to me off the stage. "Did I do good Mama?"

"You did so well sweetheart! Didn't you see all those people standing up for you? That means you did a great job!"

There were two other kids that sang, a six-year-old and ten-year-old, and neither of them got a standing ovation so I wasn't concerned. Once all the contestants had had their turns, the three judges deliberated, and handed the host their card. All the children lined up on the stage, in order of appearance.

"You all did an excellent job and we thank you for entertaining us this evening. But, there's prizes up for grabs, so there must be winners, and I have them here in my hand. The $50 second runner up winner is Madeline Alright," who had done an Irish dance. She came forward and took her small trophy and check.

"First runner up and winner of the one-hundred-dollar prize is Stuart Brown,"—he'd played the piano, and I had been quite worried he was going to win as he was very adept.

"And now, the winner of this stately trophy and grand $500 dollar prize is, no surprise here ladies and gentlemen, little Ronnie Owens!"

The audience let out a big cheer. The commune went wild. I let him go by himself this time, hoping he could handle it. He walked over, shook the host's hand and took the check and trophy, which was half the size of him, and waved at the applauding crowd. Thank you, Bill Barnes, for the recommendation! Well, I guess he got 15% of the five hundred dollars so that was his thanks.

"What are you going to do with all that money Ronnie?" the host asked. "Buy a trike!" I had promised him a trike, even if he hadn't won, so the answer made sense. "Wow, that's a pretty big purchase, don't be spending it all in one place," everyone laughed.

"Well, that's all folks. On behalf of the state of Georgia, I hope ya'll had a good night here with us. Please travel safe for those of you from out of town. We'll be seeing you."

And with that the lights went on and I ran on the stage to take the trophy from his little arms.

"Look what I got mommy!"

"I know! You won baby!"

"What does it mean that I won?"

"It means that your performance was the judges' favorite of all the performances they saw tonight."

"Out of everybody?"

"Yes everybody."

"Wow." He said, contemplating this idea, then seemingly shrugging it off.

Various people came up to us and congratulated him. He was very sweet and gracious; I don't think he understood the gravity of what he'd achieved.

He certainly didn't understand the amount of money we'd received. I was still in grateful awe that my baby had earned in one night what took me months and months of laborious work at the restaurants.

Mama, Ronnie and I headed to the hotel—we were staying overnight in town as it was too late to drive back. The air conditioning in the theater had been freezing so I had a hot shower once we got up to our room, and Ronnie watched TV for a little while. He was pretty wound up and it was going to take him a bit to calm down and sleep.

Ronnie wanted pizza, so room service it was! It tasted good after a long day. Even Mama had some. The next morning we checked out and drove home, stopping at a Walmart along the way so Ronnie could get his trike. It was blue and gold with a little bell on it. He picked it out from a lineup of them. I was more than pleased to be able to reward him in any way that I could.

"This is for being brave, right Mama?"

"Right honey." He showed it off to everyone at the commune who all acted impressed.

"This is my bravery bike," he said.

I displayed the trophy proudly by the sink in the van. There wasn't very much room for it, but I wanted it to be seen. Tim gave Ronnie a red bandanna as a 'prize,' and he tied it around his neck and it would fly behind him as he peddled around the commune like a small cape in the wind. I called him my 'little bandit'.

We had the most fun singing *Bennie and the Jets* by the campfire, with Ronnie dancing away to it. I swear he thought they wrote it just for him. I would hum it as I worked and catch myself daydreaming about my sweet little boy. I felt so lucky the universe picked me to be his mother. Another few weeks went by, and we got another call from Bill. Ronnie was wanted to be in a K-Mart Flyer.

May 13th 1974

This time we made the trip alone. It was the same photography studio as the Sears Wishbook, so it was easy for me to find. I dressed him in a red, blue, and white striped shirt and blue jeans. They said 'very Americana' about his outfit and seemed pleased. Ronnie got to keep the Lego set he was playing with for the ad, which made him happier than words.

Forget the tunnel! This was where it was at for him. It brought me joy that that he liked what he was doing, if not I would feel guilty about it. But he seemed to love the camera, though I think it loved him more. He got paid a whopping two hundred dollars for this particular shoot. Bill Barnes was certainly getting his money's worth!

May 16th 1974

Today was the day I tried LSD for the first time. Tim got it and promised it was safe. We all took it, except for Sue-Ellen, just in case we were to become incapacitated we needed someone to be responsible for the kids and she volunteered. I put it on my tongue and waited.

At first, I didn't think it was working, but then slowly, things started to change. I looked up in the sky and it seemed the clouds were made of plasticine. I had this intense urge to listen to music, so I put on '*Sleepwalk*', and I could literally see the music coming out of the player in colors. The notes were like a stream of rainbows.

It looked like the walls of the van were actually breathing, which made me claustrophobic, so I grabbed Ronnie and went outside. I kept seeing little red foxes and wanted to run up and pet them. I picked up Ronnie and sat with him on my knee on a lawn chair.

"How come you're squeezing me so tight Mama?"

"Sorry baby, I didn't mean to." I just felt so much love for him in that moment I wanted to merge with him. Become one.

Tim got out his guitar and played *Dancing in the Moonlight*, *The Locomotion*, and *I Want You Back*,—one of Ronnie's favorite songs, which he sang along to at the top of his tiny lungs.

He amazed me and not just because I was under the influence of LSD. As I watched him though, there was a white glowing halo around his head, like an angel. *My angel*, I thought. His face started morphing into my other Ronnie's right in front of my own eyes—I was really tripping out.

The petals of the daisies on the ground were all different colors and when I plucked them, they hit different musical notes. When the night sky came it seemed so close that I could reach up and pick the stars from the sky. The craters of the moon seemed so vivid.

How could I have missed them before? I lay on my back on the grass with Ronnie beside me just marveling at the evening sky. I wondered, for the very first time in a very long time, if I would ever find love again. I knew I would never find a love like Ronnie's—he was my perfect complement. My other half as I always knew him. There's only one of those. At least that's how it felt. But was I destined to find love ever again?

Did I want to? Or was that my only chance and it was lost? I had to stop myself from going down that rabbit hole of self-blame. Being under the influence of LSD was not the time to be reflecting on that situation. The campfire's neon glow was a million different colors; a spectacular light show that I could hardly look away from.

The only thing that got to me was knowing I was going back to the van to cuddle with my special boy. I loved the way it felt when he was in my arms. When we returned, he quickly put on his pajamas as I got the bed set up.

He jumped in and said, "Come here Mama," with his arms open wide.

"I'm coming sweetheart," I said as I slipped into one of my Ronnie's old t-shirts and came over.

He embraced me and nuzzled into my breasts, falling asleep immediately. I stroked his velvety hair that was pulsating with that halo which had earlier appeared and I peeked outside. I could still see the foxes, who though were cute, unnerved me a bit, so I decided to just try and go to sleep.

When I closed my eyes, however, it took hours. I kept thinking about Ronnie, and Greg and everything from that incident that caused me to lose him. It was so odd; my thoughts were playing back in a black and white movie that I couldn't stop from reeling.

The lack of color made it all the more eerie. I became paranoid Greg was going to break into the van and I got up to check that it was indeed locked. I felt the pain come back, in my body and heart. Thankfully, I had my new Ronnie with me, if not the experience would have been more terrifying.

After that, I decided I would never do LSD again, it wasn't worth the nightmarish experience I was going through, despite the positive effects it had had at first.

Chapter 29

May 27ᵗʰ 1974

It was my birthday, and I woke up to my van being decorated all outside with streamers and twenty-three balloons being tied between my front and back doors. They sure did know how to make me feel special!

"Mommy, Mommy! Balloons, look!" Ronnie said, looking out the window, both hands flat on the glass.

"It's my birthday today, that's why."

"Happy birthday Mama," he exclaimed, running toward me and giving me a big hug.

"Thank you honey, that'll be my favorite present of the day. Sit down now and finish your orange juice before you go anywhere else Mr. Man."

"Yes Mama."

"Are you excited to see Nana today?"

"Yes!"

"And Bobbsey and Sal?"

"Double yes!"

"Me too. We'll leave by eleven and get there around lunchtime. Sound good?" "Sounds good."

It was sunny out then, but I could see clouds moving in.

"Hopefully we'll beat the rain," I said.

We got out to say goodbye and thank you to everyone for the decorations before they headed off to work.

"Here, we've got a present for you, open it now since you're heading off this morning."

I did and it was an authentic Adidas track suit in the color red.

"For your morning runs," Tim said.

"Thank you all so much, it's gorgeous. I'm going to go try it on right now." I did and came back and showed everybody.

"It fits perfectly!"

"That's Vee's doing," Tim offered the credit.

"What can I say, I know my sister," said Gen. I gave Gen a hug, and then Tim.

"Ya'll spoil me. I love it. Please tell the others I haven't seen thank you from me until I get back."

"Of course, we'll pass it along. When will you be getting back?"

"I'm staying two nights in Andrews, so probably later on Wednesday."

"I suppose we can do without you for that long," Tim joked.

"I don't think the restaurants were too pleased with me asking for more time off, but hey, it's my birthday! I didn't tell them that's why though," I laughed.

"We won't rat you out then," Gen said.

"It's too bad you can't come too Vee."

"I know, but my work's not as flexible as yours, and I don't want to risk pushing it with them. I've got a pretty good gig there."

"I understand," I replied with an edge of disappointment in my voice, trying to curb it. I did understand though, there were multiple waitresses and just Gen and one other girl who manned the front desk at the motel in the daytime, so it wasn't easy for her to get vacation.

"Anyhow, I won't disrupt your morning routines any longer. Thank you again for the lovely decorations and gift. It's more than I ever could have asked for. You guys are the best."

"No problem birthday girl," Tim said putting his arm around my shoulder and giving me a quick squeeze.

"I'll see you on Wednesday when you get back. We're planning on going to a rally next week. I'll have more details by the time you return, so you have that to look forward to. And that suit's fire on you by the way."

"Agreed," said Gen. "And ya, I'll see you when you get back. Tell Mama I say hi and I'm sorry I couldn't come along."

"That's great about the rally, I'm ready for it! And will do Vee, she already knows how you have to stick by your post."

And with that we made off back to the van. I got changed out of my new suit and did up the breakfast dishes while Ronnie played with his Lego set. The clouds had rolled in more by this point, looming dark low and menacing in the sky.

"Doesn't look like we're going to beat the rain bud. Oh well. A few drops never hurt us before." Ronnie was so immersed in his playing I don't think he even heard me.

"Ok sir, time to pack up and get on the road."

"Aww, do I have to?"

"Yes, the Legos go away while we drive. You can try and save what you built if you want though."

"Nah, I'll just build it again at Nana's," he said breaking it up and putting it back in the box defeatedly.

"Do you want to pack your trike? It will be fun to use on Nana's driveway."

"Ya!" This brightened him right up. I went and fetched it from outside. There wasn't much room for it so I set it in the 'hall' on its side so it wouldn't roll around while we were driving.

We took off just short of eleven as planned and made it about forty-five minutes before the rain hit, and it hit hard. I couldn't see an inch in front of the windowpane, and I started to feel jittery. I couldn't even see to pull off the road. In the background *Heartbeat, It's a Lovebeat* played on the radio, being drowned out by the angry strafing of the rain. And then it happened. The van lurched forward and fell into something.

With the jolt I hit my head on the steering wheel and blacked out. When I came to, I was up to my neck in water and Ronnie, who'd been beside me in the passenger seat, was nowhere to be found. The van was on a downward angle in a sinkhole in the road with water rushing in at us by the second. I managed to undo my belt under water but my space to breathe was getting more and more limited.

I had to get Ronnie was my only thought. I dove under the rushing muddy waters and groped around for him. I couldn't find him. I wouldn't leave without him. I dove down again, frantically feeling around. Nothing. Where was he? My baby! I was swallowing water as my space to breathe diminished. My heart was pounding. I was dying and I knew it. And there was nothing I could do about it.

I went down a third time trying to find Ronnie. The mud burned my eyes. Where was his little body? I couldn't find him! Finally, there was no room for me to come up and breathe. Who knew this struggle for air would be my demise? I tried to open the van door, but the water pressure against it was too strong for me to be able to push it.

I held my breathe until it felt like my lungs were going to explode, then I inhaled the dirt and water. The sensation of knives in my lungs. I choked. Then light. Then I saw the light. The pain ceased. It started out as a pinprick, and then grew to be all-encompassing. I saw Ronnie.

"I'm waiting for you Mommy," he said.

I was dead. I had drowned and so had Ronnie. Inherently I knew this. How could it be? I took his hand, and we went into the tunnel of light together. We ended up in a room of iridescent light. There was no panic or fear, oddly, only feelings of joy.

"We're home now Mommy," Ronnie said. "And I've got a surprise for you. Wait here." He gave me a big hug and kiss on the lips.

There was a door on the other side of the shimmering room that Ronnie walked over to, opened, and went behind and shut. When he came out, it was not my little boy anymore, but my old Ronnie who came through the opening.

"Ronnie!" I shouted flying into his arms, "It's me, it's been me all along Kim."

"I've missed you so much," I said kissing his face, and him kissing me back.

"I can't say I've missed you too, cause I've been with you. I was given the option of reincarnating as your son as a way of, well, atoning my suicide. I jumped at the idea of getting to be with you. I knew I'd temporarily lose my memories, but I still wanted to do it. To be close to you. I knew our path ended here when I came back. But again, I wanted to do it anyways."

"So, we were supposed to die just now?"

"That's the way it's written in the stars. It was our time to come home and be with God. It's more complicated than that…I can't explain everything right now, you'll see though. When I killed myself, it wasn't really my time, and that's why I was given the unique option of coming back briefly as your son. You see, everyone has a divine complement, another half to their soul that they long to be with like Adam and Eve.

"You're my other half, so when I separated myself from you with the suicide, it was very painful. My soul longed to be back with your soul but couldn't be, it had to wait for the opportunity to come around reincarnate, which God helped orchestrate. When I got here, our true home, and saw that the officer had lied to me, my heart broke into pieces.

"Why had I believed him? I was so angry with myself. But anger doesn't get you very far, so when I was presented with the reincarnation plan from God, I was elated, but had to wait. Time flows different here, still, those were a long three years."

"You knew I was going to have a baby when you died?"

"Sure did. To soothe my tortured soul, God allowed me to see into the future. I was able to see my life as Ronnie the second and that's how I knew we were destined to die when we did just now. Though if I had lived as Ronnie the first, we would have died just the same. It was our time." He paused for a moment and gazed into my eyes.

"There's so much to tell you my love. I don't know where to start. I guess the next thing is you'll get to have a life review shortly, where you go over your life from birth to death in great detail. You get to see how other people were feeling and thinking throughout—it really sheds some light on things. For example, when I died before, I got to see what the officer was thinking when he lied to me about not contacting you.

"How he actually thought he was helping. Not that that made it any better. But it's interesting to understand things from everyone's perspectives. I'll be having one as little Ronnie, too; it'll be a short one, but I'll have one just the same. They have guides that help out with that. I'm guessing they should be here any minute."

I then embraced Ronnie for what felt like the first time in a million years. I kissed his sweet lips like I never had before, savoring every second of it.

"They call us twin flames," he said.

"We're a perfect match on a cosmic level. Everyone has one, they just don't always find them. We were lucky enough to find and have each other, both romantically and as mother and son. Both bonds were equally as strong. We've developed good karma over our lifetimes which allowed us these opportunities to be together, even as we are now, here on the other side.

"When we're done our life reviews we can begin the process of healing from our last lives together. God will lead the way with that. But one step at a time, I'm getting ahead of myself. Life reviews are the priority at this point. Look! Someone's coming right now."

I gripped his hand tightly as a woman walked through the same door Ronnie had come out of. She had long dark hair to her waist and eyes that were slightly downturned at the sides. She emanated love and respect.

"Welcome Kimberlie, and Ronnie, you made it."

"Terrifyingly so," I said.

"I'm sorry your experience was so traumatic. Many deaths are. We have 'activities' for lack of better words that will help you work through those feelings after your life review if you so choose to engage in them. That's why I have been sent, to set up your reviews for you and Ronnie."

"Well, I guess that's my cue to change back," Ronnie said.

The lady continued, "Once your life review is completed, you'll be returned to your "ideal states," which I have been told for you two is sixteen. Does that sound about right?"

I supposed sixteen was the ideal age if I got to pick any, so I agreed. Then it started coming back to me that this was always our age when we were here. Since the beginning of time.

I wondered if the fact that I lost Ronnie on earth when we were in our 'prime' so-to-say had a an even deeper impact on us. Just a thought. I hadn't noticed, but Ronnie was already in his ideal state because that's what he had been when he had died in '67, except I knew he had to revert to little Ronnie for his review.

"Kim, come with me."

"Bye baby, see you soon," I said to him.

"See you in a jiffy. It will be paradise after this babe," he said to me. The lady, who had introduced herself as "Amelia," led me down an equally light filled hallway to another room. Here, there was a large comfy looking armchair and a giant screen.

"This is your life review," she prefaced.

"It is intended to give you insight into events in your life that you previously only understood from your perspective. If you have any questions, please feel free to ask me, or of course, God. If you need me, just think of me and I'll be summoned telepathically. Do you understand?" she asked gently.

"Yes, I understand. Except, how do I ask God a question?"

"Oh, you simply ask and they will hear. You need not even speak it out loud, if you do not wish. It's all telepathically, like with me."

"Wow, okay, thank you. I think I get it now. Wait, won't this take a long time?"

"Time is a non-factor here. To put it in layman terms, one day can pass like one second when necessary. You're always free to take a break from your review, though only on the rarest of occasions have I seen anybody choose to do so.

"The option is always there, however. When you're done, you'll be reunited with Ronnie once again and you'll go into the second layer of the light. That's where all the fun is," she added.

"Again, if you need me for support in any capacity, I'm just a mere thought away. Don't hesitate. Life reviews can be very emotional, and you might decide you don't want to be alone. On the other hand, you might prefer it to be in solidarity for the experience as many do. There is no right or wrong."

"That makes sense," I responded.

I wanted to get this show on the road so I could get back with Ronnie—either of my Ronnies!—so I snuggled in the big comfy chair and set my eyes on the colossal screen before me. It began with my birth and how happy Mama was to have another girl to be a playmate for Gen. I was able to feel her lack of attraction to my father, but her sense of duty as his wife.

I was able to be inside her mind as she grappled with wanting to return to work and her decision to hire Henrietta. I felt the inherent trust between them that set Mama at ease leaving us alone with her. I was also able to see Henrietta's perspective, working for a white family and coming to love them as her own. I experienced the horrible sting when my father let her go, and her worry for me and Gen.

I saw that she had suspicions about my father, she just couldn't put her finger on what. I saw my father's evil, distorted thoughts. How he felt he had the right to our bodies because he provided for them.

"The devil worked through him," God interjected. This is the first time God had spoken to me. Their voice seemed neither male nor female, soft and booming all at once.

"Why God did you let this happen to me?" I asked.

"Free will, my child. I can't control those I have created. I set them on their paths and hope for the best. Some go wayward like your father, but they suffer for it in the afterlife. He will not go to the same place as you and Ronnie, unless he recognizes and repents his sins.

"Unfortunately, most in his position choose stubborn ignorance, and not to take responsibility, and they are stuck with the dark forces they have aligned themselves with. If we take a pause from your review and check in on your father now, we find a bitter, angry man who blames you, your sister and mother for leaving him in an embarrassing position, not one who regrets his actions and sees what drove you away.

"So right now, he is on the side of the devil, and it is difficult to disentangle oneself from him when it comes to being here. Imagine him having his review and having to hear you and your sister's thoughts and feelings while he was assaulting you?

"He will likely refuse it. If he does, the dark side is where he will stay. You don't have to worry about ever encountering him, even if he were to choose the light, you would never be forced to see him. Unless, of course, you feel this would be therapeutic, we could set up a meeting."

"No thank you. I don't wish to see that man ever again. Especially if he's not sorry."

"Wise decision my dear one. Now let's continue with your review."

It was fun watching the part when Ronnie and I met, and how his feelings mirrored mine.

God interjected again, "Your feelings reflected each other's because you are, what Ronnie already briefly explained, divine complements. Two peas from the same pod, so it was only natural you were feeling the same things."

I got to re-experience making love for the first time, and see how it felt from Ronnie's viewpoint, which, again, was much the same as mine. It was validating experiencing his love for me. If I ever had any doubts, then they were expelled. I was even able to see how my drive tester was jealous of me and that's why she didn't pass me, not because of my parallel parking!

When it came to the rape scene, I felt Ronnie's helplessness which was painful. I saw how Greg had planned it out in his mind during the civil rights meeting when he's offered us the ride. Most importantly, I was able to observe the conversation the police had with Ronnie that pushed him to the brink that caused his suicide.

I saw how the cops genuinely thought they were helping by keeping him away from me. I felt the utter abandonment rush through Ronnie's body, and how he felt there was no point in living without me, how there was no way out. I understood how it echoed his abandonment of his mother, and how this played into why he made the assumptions he did.

I experienced Mrs. Knight's perspective of having lost her husband and then her grandson which was very sad. But I felt the happiness little Ronnie brought her when he came around. I was able to feel little Ronnie's instant bond with me, which matched mine with him. His joy nursing, the comfort and calm it brought him. The interconnectedness of the souls at the commune was highlighted, how we were all karmically meant to be together.

How Tim was really Kory's "Soul Father," and actually his other half, and it was meant to be that custody would end up in his hands. It was healing to see how much my little Ronnie loved me in return, which, not to be redundant, emulated my love for him.

"This goes back to you being twin flames," God commented. "Your love for each other was always equal."

Importantly, I got to see that there was little fear that came with my baby Ronnie's death. He inhaled the water quickly and drowned almost immediately. He was gone by the time I had become conscious. This brought me some relief, that I couldn't have saved him if I had wanted to.

God reminded me, "You were trapped in the van, even if you did find him, there was no getting out. It was your destiny to come home to me, and that could not be derailed."

"Why did you want us to come home now?"

"I wanted you to have time to play and heal before Ronnie sets out on his next assignment. Don't worry, it's a bit down the road from now. And you will be his guide."

"But I don't want to be separated from him ever again though."

"When you're his guide you're intimately involved in your charge's life, so you're not technically separated from them. It's a crucial project that Ronnie is needed for and non-negotiable, that has been centuries in the making. Try not to focus on that now.

"Focus on the time you have in front of you to be free from the restraints of the world. That's what I wanted for you. A space to love endlessly as you so deserve, and have the capacity to do. Let me bring in your little boy one last time."

"Mommy!" Ronnie came bursting in from the doorway.

"I just got to watch a movie of my whole life. I got to see your feelings. It was really cool!"

"Come sit with me my baby." He came over and I took him on my lap and I held him for a long while.

"It's pretty nice over here, huh?" he said.

"Yes, it's very nice," I replied.

"I got to talk to God. They told me I was special and that I achieved my mission."

"That's excellent sweetheart. You are special. Never forget that."

"We're going to stay here, aren't we?"

"Yes honey, we're not going back right now."

"That's okay, I like it here. And God said there's lots to discover. Whole universes," he struggled with pronouncing the word.

"That's amazing my sweetness."

"God said that we will explore them together, you and me."

"That sounds amazing."

"I'm going to be bigger Ronnie though, if that's okay with you. I can always change back to little me if you want me to though."

"I love big Ronnie, so that's alright with me."

"I'm going to do it now if that's okay with you Mama."

"One more kiss from my little boy." He gave me a big kiss on the lips with his tiny mouth and wrapped his arms around my neck.

"I'm always me, no matter what size I am. Remember that Mama. It's not goodbye it's goodnight. I'm always right here if you want me."

He said repeating the phrase I'd passed down from my Mama to him.

"Thank you, baby."

I kissed his cheeks and his forehead, and he walked out of the room. Thankfully, I was not alone for long. Big Ronnie, in his ideal form, poked his head in.

"I'm back!"

"Oh thank God, I missed you already."

"Well, there'll be no more missing me needed, we're together now. Time to heal and play and be free. God's orders. First, Let's get you into your ideal self."

He ushered me into a room down the light hall. It was bright blue like the sky on the clearest day you can imagine, but all-encompassing and surrounding me from head to toe.

"Just let it wash over you, it'll be done in just a second."

And it was. I was sixteen again, and it felt wonderful. We were both ourselves, back before our trauma. I felt cleansed.

"This is the way we always are on this side. Sixteen is our standard selves, it just so happened that we were in an ideal place in our last life when we were sixteen too. Everyone chooses their own age, sixteen is on the younger side. Our mental capacity is fully developed though."

"I love it, it feels right."

Chapter 30

However, no sooner was I feeling comfortable in my own skin, did I start having concerns about the people left on earth.

"What about the people down there Ronnie? What are they going to do? Are they going to look for us?"

"Yes, they'll look and come to the conclusion of your demise. Your Mama's probably already done it. We can look down and see if you want?"

So, we checked in; saw Mama waiting and waiting. Finally, she got in her car and drove the route I would have come and came across the terrible crevasse in the road and could go no further. We saw her wondering if I, Kim, had fallen in it.

At first, she thought the chances were slim but possible. At least that's what she told herself. She drove home and waited another hour before taking the alternate route to the commune. When she arrived, everyone was surprised. No, she had left at eleven this morning they told her, and her heart sunk.

"She never made it to Andrews," she said, and the whole commune went into a panic.

"What do you think could have happened to her?"

"Well, there was this big sink hole enroute to where she normally drove. I'm worried she fell into it. It was huge. It could have swallowed her up and we'll never know. I'm scared guys, really scared. I think she's gone."

Gen had come home from the motel upon hearing of Mama's arrival.

"Don't say that Mama," she swallowed tightly, knowing it was true.

"Maybe she just got washed downstream and is caught somewhere. Let's go guys. Get in your cars."

Tim and Doug, who were luckily home, jumped in their trucks and Johanna got in her car. Mama led the pack.

"You know the way she always takes, keep an eye out for her along the ditches in case she went into one because of the poor visibility."

And so, Ronnie and I watched as they paraded toward the spot of my death, where my van had long been washed away by the torrid currents. I could feel the fear and nausea of all five of them when they saw the gaping hole in the road, as they all imagined what might have happened to me and Ronnie.

It had stopped raining by this point, but the air was still heavy with moisture leaving a slick layer on everyone's skin. There were woods on either side of the road with the wide creek overflow of water running onto it, with barely visible slippery banks, making investigating nearly impossible without putting oneself in peril.

Mama walked up and down the upper embankment shouting "Gina! Gina!" whereas Tim got closer to the water looking for signs of the van.

There was no hope for either though. The water flowed so rapidly and was so murky you had no chance to see what was going on below its surface. It soon became obvious it was a fruitless mission, though nobody wanted to stop.

"Do you think this is where she ended up?" Mama asked with tears streaming down her distraught face.

"Miss. Oh, I don't know what else could have happened to her, unless she was abducted along the way, which I suppose is possible, though quite unlikely." The rain today was blinding, I looked out and couldn't see but an inch past my window, and I was just in my cabin.

"Gina was always a nervous driver, she expressed that after they failed her that one time, she lacked confidence. That's why I always worried about her driving to Atlanta. But to think, just driving home to Andrews, something like this could happen, I can't believe it. On her birthday of all days."

Mama broke down sobbing, and Tim reached over and hugged her, "I don't know what to say to make this better," he said as the wind rustled through the trees behind them and the sun tried to make an appearance.

"There's nothing you can say," she responded. Gen came over and took over the embrace.

"We'll find them Mama, don't give up yet," but the tone in her voice implied that she herself didn't believe they would.

"I'll come home with you Mama, how about that?"

Thank God, I thought watching from above. Once home, she collapsed again into Gen's arms.

"She's gone, they're gone," she started crying again, Gen held her, wanting to tell her different, but knowing that she couldn't.

"I'm sorry Mama," was all she could conjure, and all that could really be said.

I felt sad, but a strange sense of detachment, "You're not supposed to feel attached to it," Ronnie said, reading my thoughts.

"If you were, it'd be too hard to cross over. I, on the other hand, in '67 didn't have that luxury because mine was a suicide, I was stuck feeling all your pain and grief, and my own regret. It was beyond horrendous. Your Mama's going to be okay and so is Gen.

"They have each other to lean on during this tragedy. I know it's hard for them, because they're not just losing you, they're losing me too. The one person who would remind them of you is gone as well. It's unfortunate it had to end this way, but you and I needed our free time here unrestrained by the sins of the world. Besides, it's only a matter of years before they both come home.

"Gen comes home in '79 and your Mama in '81. I know it was scary to die. It was scary for me too. But those few minutes of fear have brought you to an unabashed place of happiness. It was worth it Kim, trust me; you'll see what's beyond that door is more beauty than you can comprehend in life.

"And it's all ours for the taking. There are a thousand creeks for us to choose from to make our special spot that make our creek back at home on earth look like a dingy mudhole. Let me know when you're ready to go exploring."

"Oh, I'm ready," I said, getting up promptly from the big plush chair.

"We can check in again on Mama and Gen later if I want to?"

"Anytime you like," which was a great comfort to me.

"Now then, let's get outta this room then," Ronnie said, taking my hand and leading me to a door in the far-left corner.

I felt like Dorothy in the Wizard of Oz stepping into Munchkin Land. Everything was so vivid! The trees were the most beautiful specimen of their sort, the flowery kinds—magnolias, wisterias, almond trees—and lined a walkway down to the water. The water was a river and so clear you could see to the very bottom of it where there were beautiful stones of a myriad of colors.

I dipped my toe in and it was so temperate, it was tempting not to strip down and go in. I looked across and down and saw a rope tied to a tree.

"Look at that! Too bad we didn't have our suits."

"But we do! That's the magic of being here. Just think it and you make it, watch." Ronnie closed his eyes and in a whirling dervish swim trunks appeared.

"You try."

So, I closed my eyes and thought of my red polka-dot bikini and I opened my eyes and there it was. With no one around we changed and made our way to the rope and Ronnie pushed me off the embankment making me scream in delight. The water felt so good on my body. So warm and soothing.

I realized I wasn't afraid, even having just drowned in it. I could actually breathe underneath it! It was bizarre and beautiful. This must be part of the healing they were talking about. Ronnie jumped in right after me, making a huge splash.

"Ha! Gotcha!" he said.

"You're silly, I was already wet it doesn't matter."

"Look at those!" I pointed to the bottom of the water, and noticed how some of the stones were actually gems.

"Nothing is worth money here, so those type of things are plentiful. Around us were fruit trees: orange trees, apple trees, cherry trees all in bloom. It was the most spectacular sight to see.

"There are no seasons changing here either, so everything just regenerates. There's a place to find the different seasons though, different realms. If you want snow, we can find snow."

"Oh snow! I haven't seen snow in years! Let's go there next!" I said from the bathing pool of the creek.

"We can build a snowman together Ronnie!"

"Well, I've never built one before, not in any of my lives, so you'll have to teach me."

"I've only made one before myself after a freak snowstorm in Virginia. It's fun! We just make three giant balls, one each a little smaller than the other, and then we find accessories to add to it to make the face."

"Far out! Sounds like a blast! Can't wait to make my first snowman with you."

We dove down and kissed under the translucent water; our hands chained together as we did. I momentarily forgot all about Mama and Gen and was simply wrapped up in my new found paradise. When I woke up this morning, who knew I'd be finding Ronnie again? Who knew I'd be dying? Life is so unpredictable.

Do you remember what I said about not being able to untangle your blessings from your curses? It turns out it's very true. Would I have met Ronnie if my father hadn't raped me? No.

That's just one obvious example. Still there are a million woven into the fabric of our everyday lives that we don't come to notice. Not just blessings and curses, but how each action, each word can change the trajectory of a situation.

And that plays into the whole 'free will' thing. It was all so complicated but so crystal-clear at the same time. Thinking here, on the other side, was different—it flowed smoother, more quickly; information came to you as you wondered it so that you barely got the chance to ponder!

There were warm towels and a soft blanket for us to lie on awaiting at the side of the creek. We got out and made sweet love and in God's name, it was indescribable. Here you aren't just on a physical plane, your souls merge into one because we are twin souls, and it was pure and utter ecstasy.

When we were done, Ronnie asked, "Ready to visit the snow now?"

"You bet I am," he took my hand and we were immediately transported to what looked like to be a cabin in the snowy mountains beside a roaring fire. And we were both in appropriate attire of cozy sweaters, no longer in our bathing suits.

"The fire smells so good!" I exclaimed, but before I could think much more Ronnie interrupted, "Wanna makes smores before we build our snowman?"

"Why not?" So of course, at our fingertips were graham wafers, chocolate, and marshmallows.

"Let me do it. I'm kind of an expert. I made them when I was here, on the other side, before."

I took a bite into his masterpiece as it gushed out all sides, and all my tastebuds were singing. It literally tasted like the best thing that had ever touched my tongue. Perhaps it was because our senses were heightened here, or maybe it was just because it was that good. Or both. Either way, I was living the dream.

"Thank you, Ronnie, it's absolutely delicious!"

"I knew you'd like them," he said casually, but proudly. I took notice that off to the side were two snow suits and two pairs of snowshoes.

214

"Have you ever used those before?" I asked gesturing toward them, mouth half full.

"Nope, but I'm not worried about it. Here, you just instinctively learn and know. Time to get dressed and build that snowman you've been dreaming of?"

"Sure, let's do it."

We got into our snow garb and headed outside into what was the beginning of a beautiful sunset. We rolled and rolled, and when it came to the face, Ronnie conjured up some buttons for his eyes, a carrot for his nose, and some coal to form a smile. We decided he needed a scarf as a finishing touch, so on went a red plaid one of those.

"He's great, just the way I envisioned him. Wait." He stopped, then popped a corn cobbed pipe into his mouth.

"Now he's complete."

"Gee, our very own Frosty. Whoever thought we'd be building one of those when we were together in Carolina." Ronnie laughed.

"Very true. Now let's go inside. I want to kiss you some more."

The feeling was mutual. It was like being re-fueled. We'd been empty for seven years, so we had a lot of catching up to do.

"I don't know about you, but I'm exhausted. Are you up to catching a little shut eye with me? After some more kissing of course?"

He winked that wink I saw the very first time I saw him at the stand. But he was visibly exhausted.

"Of course, my love, do you think there's a bed?"

"I know there's a bed, God always provides, we just gotta find it."

We poked our heads into a room and there was the most luxurious looking bed I'd ever seen. It had four wooden posts, all carved intricately, and the fluffiest looking pillows, they could only belong to heaven. When we lay on it, it's soft, downy like mattress contoured into our bodies like a gentle hug and the sheets of silk were both cool and warm all at once.

"It's like lying on a cloud," I said.

"We can always test that theory out some time," Ronnie said half-jokingly. He kissed me as we intertwined our bodies under the satin like sheets. *This is what 'bliss' is*, I thought to myself.

As we untangled each other Ronnie asked, "Do you want some hot cocoa?"

"Yes, please!"

"Me too."

"We'll see how this holds up against my grandma's," he said returning from the kitchen with two full mugs. It was the richest, most voluptuous hot chocolate I had ever had. Baby marshmallows bobbed on the top.

"I think this puts Grandma's to shame, no offense to her of course. Couldn't be any better, huh?" Ronnie said in a satisfied tone.

"Nope, it certainly couldn't."

We drifted off and the next thing I knew, I opened my eyes and the sun was rising. It was blazing hues of yellow, red, orange and candied pink. We started up the fire and cuddled up by it, still in our pajamas, eating blueberry muffins that had been left out for us. He wrapped his arms around me.

"We're together again—can you believe it?"

"No!" I exclaimed truthfully. Just one day before I had been receiving the track suit and getting ready to head out on the road. If only I'd known what laid ahead. Form terror to paradise, all in twenty-four hours. I did have a nagging question for God, I hoped they could answer.

"I can answer, ask away my child," was the response I got while 'wondering.'

"I know I already asked this, but why now, why not let little Ronnie and I live on?"

"My answer is the same. Your soul needs time to heal, and in another twelve years, Ronald has a new assignment where you shall be his guide."

"So, you really mean we'll be separated again? My heart can't take it."

"It depends on your definition of separated. But yes, there will be a distance, but only for a time. Your love is so strong, you will find each other again. I promise you that. Not even the boundaries between human and Spirit will stop you."

"What kind of assignment is it?" I asked through growing tears, anticipating this leave-taking down the road.

"He's going to be a little girl, and be born to an evil father, much like yours Kim. The karma between this man and you and Ronnie scores deep, many lives of torment. Unlike your father however, this man has run out of chances to reincarnate if he does not conduct himself properly in this lifetime, and if Ronnie is able to remain strong and defeat him, he will no longer be able to come back and torture anybody else.

216

"It is his/her and your destiny to bring justice around to this man. It will not be an easy battle, but this girl will have the opportunity and it will be your job to make sure she takes it."

"Will I be able to successfully get them away from the abuse? Does she have a fighting chance if I do?"

"That comes down to your collaboration with other guides, of other people in her life, your ability to connect with her and steer her always toward the light despite the dark surrounding her, and of course, the ever-overwriting menace of free will. However, I have full confidence you will be able to free her of the abuse, and beat the challenges that will follow, which are, indeed many. An eating disorder for example.

"You can't let his evil eat her alive. It will be up to you to keep her on earth. It is part of why I chose you two for the mission to take out this particular evil. He's a tricky one. You and Ronnie have been dealing with him across multiple lifetimes. He's targeted him before, and will again, but with you by his side, I am confident even-handedness will prevail.

"It's heavy work my dearest one, but it's our job. To fight evil. To love. It interferes in our ability to love, that's why it must be fought. Think about how evil caused the death of Ronnie Tisdale? The evil rape spiraled into the rest of the situation, the misunderstanding, the death. It all roots back to evil. You will be able to channel your story, the story of Ronnie and Kim, to her when she grows up and share it with the world.

"Your relationship will be as close with her as it is with Ronnie right now. How Ronnie faces and overcomes his trauma is how he ends up rediscovering you, post-childhood relationship."

"You can't tell me how?"

"No, I'm afraid I can't. I don't want to subconsciously effect your decisions that could ultimately derail it from happening, plus it is part of the gift of your relationship, earning that communication. So no, I won't say anymore on that subject. You will be an excellent guide as you have been before. I have complete faith in you, have faith in yourself."

"Thank you," was all I could think to say. I felt disappointed.

"Did you know this, Ronnie?" I asked, assuming he's been listening in, which he had.

"Ya, I knew about it before I came back as your son. It's part of why I wanted to get as much time in with you as I could. Don't stress about it yet.

We still have time to play and learn and heal. That's why we were brought home, remember? Like I said, time flows differently here. Twelve years will feel like a full lifetime because we want it to, I promise. But it will pass, so we've got to make the best of the time we have together now and live in the present, while honoring our past and not fearing our future.

"Like I said when I was little Ronnie. We have universes to explore together like this one, literally. But we also have school—we always want to be bettering our souls through education, but not the kind you're used to. They've got classes on things, like synchronicities for example. I took a class on singing, that's how I was so good as little Ronnie. There are classes on mother child relationships, or one I'm particularly interested in, courage. Just a few off the top of my head.

"Basically, if there's something you're interested in, or your soul needs some help in the development of a certain area, there's a class for it. There're taught by our peers. Sidenote, soon you'll be ready for your second review— the review of your lives before Kim. This is where you see the magic happen. You get to see who came back as who in your other lives and how those relationships have evolved over time.

"Maybe, if we ask God, we can stay with each other and watch each other's together. I had this when I died after the hanging, but it's all been erased. Part and parcel with the rebirth; you gotta go through the same routine when you come back."

"I give you permission to watch each other's past lives reviews together as a bonding experience. Make the most of it kids."

God had obviously been eavesdropping on our conversation, as they seemed to always be. How convenient! We didn't even have to ask. We watched the sunrise melting into a vivid magenta before finding it's place in the sky. It was so breathtaking it was almost shocking to the senses, reflecting off the crystal white snow.

"Feeling ready for your review?" Ronnie asked.

"Yes, I'm excited," I responded.

"Who's do you want to watch first?"

"I'm ready for mine."

"Sounds good to me." We made love again, then got dressed. I noticed a fox outside in the snow.

"That's our spirit animal," Ronnie said.

"Everyone has one, ours is the fox. We each have an individual one that represents us, but they live in a separate realm. This little buddy must have just come to remind us. We'll go visit them after our reviews. They're so cute. They usually have baby foxes running around."

"That's adorable, I can't wait. So, everyone has one?"

"Yes, everyone has a spirit animal that represents them that remains here on the other side. For example, your Mama's is a swan."

"How elegant!"

"And your Mama's elegant. Traits of the animal are reflected in the person. We're playful like foxes, among other things of course," he said.

"I'm looking forward to going to see them, let's get these reviews on the go."

And with that we were back in the room with the comfy chair—this time a couch. There were some lives spent apart, though very few, in between our lives together, but I will just detail the ones where we were in each other's.

It began with our life before Ronnie and Kim where Ronnie was a fighter pilot in WWII from New Jersey named Bobby Morgan Dorsett. I was an actress and we met when I toured his base in Arizona in April of '44. We ended up having a secret romantic affair, as both of us were technically married at the time; though I was separated. It was a whirlwind that only lasted 9 months; much of it spent apart he was stationed, eventually in Hawaii, and I did a tour of the Pacific.

Our love was expressed through letters though in between our meetings. He crashed in the South China Sea after being sent out on a mission in poor visibility and was taken POW by the Japanese. The man who was to become his father in his next life was one of the prison guards who tortured him and ordered his death.

I assumed he had just changed his mind and abandoned me, and it broke my heart. I didn't know until we met at the light in 1948 when I committed suicide that he had died before me.

In the life before that we were sisters. He was a girl named Sarah, younger than me by eight years, and I was Eliza, better known as Lilly. She wrote a diary in that life that ended up getting published posthumously, about their experience during the civil war.

In this life, she was raped by the man who would become Ronnie's father. Where she wrote about it in the journal, the pages were torn out so it was not part of the publication. I thought it to be quite admirable that Ronnie was an official author.

In our previous life together, we were brother and sister, and his name was Pip. Again, there was an eight-year age difference. We lived in Ohio Virginia—or what is now West Virginia—and our last name was Stuart. We were a family of six children; Pip was the youngest.

The Revolutionary War came and in 1777, and he and our other brother were taken for ransom at ages twelve and thirteen and ultimately killed by the Red Coats, a mission led by the man who would be Ronnie's father in his next life. Though tragic, I found it all so fascinating how the karma was evidently linked to his future life.

One life that varied quite from the others was one we had in the late 1600's, which was altogether different, as we were African, and we did not usually incarnate into a different skin color, and even more odd, I was a boy. We were captured at ages six and nine and taken from our homeland in Africa on a slave ship over to Haiti.

We were two of about two thousand on the island at the time. Our Masters were the man and woman who were about to become Ronnie's parents in his next life. He was a particularly cruel slave owner, often depriving us of our basic needs of living, so after three long years, we decided to run away.

He ended up finding us, and chasing us into the water, which was fruitless for him labor wise, because not knowing how to swim, we could not navigate the choppy waters and drowned. Our last thoughts were of love for each other, as we had lived like brothers through the trauma of our excavation.

Another life together was again, in the 1600's, in England, where the man to be Ronnie's father was my dad. Ronnie wanted to marry me but my father wouldn't let him. He had betrothed me to the son of a man he was having a gay affair with. So, we ran away, with help of the monastery.

We were married and had a child but three years later, my father had Ronnie traced, and hunted down and murdered, alongside our landlord who tried to step in. Myself and the child were spared. I, however, died a year later of illness, as my soul could not bear to be away from him.

In the 1500s we had a glorious life together, betrothed from childhood forward and married at fifteen. We spent much of our lives together in relative opulence, riding horses, reading to each other, conversing. We had a child in

220

this life as well, a son, who was Gen. When I was twenty-four, I fell off my horse and hurt my back, and Ronnie had to tend to me.

The review showed my guilt for feeling like a burden, but also how genuine his compassion was toward me which I felt was very sweet. When I was twenty-six, I fell sick and succumbed to my fever.

His soul tried to stay strong for our son, and made it another two years, without me, before he died of what we now know to be cancer. Gen, known in that life as Stephen, went to live with his grandmother.

Our life before this one together was in the 1400's where Ronnie was a horse trainer born into a decently well to do family. I started our quite poor and became a prostitute at age fourteen. We met by other means, on the street, and he vowed to get me away from that lifestyle and married me. We were both quite talented in art.

His Uncle, was a relatively famous artist Bonifacio Bembo, and was commissioned by the Viscontio-Sfroza family to create a tarot card deck for them, but he was too busy and disinterested, so he passed the project onto us, unbeknownst to the family of course. I did the art, and Ronnie did the male modeling for it.

He was very proud of me for my work and Bembo was more than satisfied to present it to the family, after contributing three cards himself, so he felt like he had done something. Ronnie and I were deeply in love and our shared interests—of art and animals—only served to bring us closer.

We lived into our fifties in that life, I fifty-one, and he fifty-three, but he was two years my senior. We both died of the same illness within eight days of one another. We were grateful for this, not having to be separated for long.

Our second last life together was in the mid-1200s wherein Ronnie died in a duel over me. I died of a broken heart five days later. Literally. I was so in love with him, I died of a broken heart. I think today it's called 'broken heart syndrome' or 'takotsubo cardiomyopathy.'

That truly shows the power of the twin flame connection. I mean, it is shown in all of our lives—we are always miserable without each other—but especially in this one. I had been betrothed from a young age to a boy, the man who was to be Ronnie's father in his next life, who I had no feelings for. I tried everything I could to get out of the marriage, but couldn't manage.

I wanted to marry Ronnie, a mere stable boy, that is who had my heart. So finally, it was decided that a duel would make the decision, which was completely unfair, because his opponent was rich and could afford protection far more advanced than his primitive outfit.

It was doomed from the outset. The jousting stick went right through his heart and right through mine. So, yet again, he had taken Ronnie's life.

Our first life together was in 1101 in an area now known as Crimea. When I was eighteen my village was taken over by a bunch of soldiers from a rival 'tribe' and I was basically taken POW and forced into marriage. The man was brutal and disgusting, and it turns out that man was Greg. He would beat me for nothing, and forced sex upon me often.

It's not surprising then that my first child came at age nineteen, it was Ronnie, except he was a little red headed girl. I started standing up to my husband more when the baby was born to protect her. He didn't know how to take my new found assertiveness and actually backed down a little. I went on to have three more children.

When Ronnie was eleven, they came down with an illness that ultimately took their life, which destroyed me as they were secretly my favorite and being the oldest, did many things alongside me that I would miss. We had basically grown up together with me being such a young mother in a strange place with strange people, she had been my life preserver.

What I clung to when I felt like I was dying in a sea of unhappiness. I died at age 35, so five years after Ronnie. I just couldn't make it long without him, consciously or subconsciously, so the stars aligned. Our village was pillaged and myself, along with my three remaining children, were murdered. It was not much of a loss though. That life was going nowhere for any of us.

"I hope it was helpful going through and seeing each other's thoughts, feelings and intentions along the way. I expect it brought you closer. Are you up for round two? Ronnie's experiences?"

"Oh yes," I said. "I'm so excited to see the lives I didn't get to be a part of. Thank you, God again for this opportunity."

"You're very welcome. Ronald. Did you learn anything about Kimberlie through her past life reviews?"

"I learned she's even sweeter, smarter, more sensitive, stronger, creative, and more emotionally intelligent than I already knew she was."

"Aw, thank you sweetheart, that's very kind."

"And Kim, did you learn anything about yourself?" "I learned why it was so hard losing Ronnie—because it's happened so many times in so many traumatic ways."

"But did you learn anything about yourself?" I thought about it for a minute. "I learned that I'm brave."

"That's what I was looking to hear. Watch Ronnie's, then you are free to go and play."

Going backward again, I got to bear raw witness to Ronnie's panic and true belief that I had abandoned him again as I had in my review, and it was awful. I came to even better understand how it linked to his mother constantly forsaking him, by choosing the men in her life over him on a constant basis wore down his self-worth, how the deaths of his grandfather and Jeb left him feeling abandoned, and how this all played into the conclusions he drew that night.

It was heartbreaking but also healing to see how when he was POW he was warned that I was going to think he'd abandoned me—which I did—and I could see how I was a motivating force in him wanting to get out of there, and his attempts to run away which ended in torture. How his last thoughts after being hog tied and thrown in the water were of me.

These lessons went on throughout the lives and I learned of Ronnie's resilience, his faith, his capacity to love, his talents and general compassion. I felt blessed to have such a wonderful twin flame. He was everything I could want and more.

Chapter 31

Now, with our reviews behind us, we were off to see the foxes in their den. We passed into a different realm, which felt like you would imagine passing through a bubble would feel like. The area was densely forested but we had been brought right to their den so we didn't have to search.

There were three sets of baby foxes suckling their mama. When I say three sets, I mean three sets of twin flames, so there were six. As they began fumbling away from her, I asked Ronnie if I could pick one up.

"They're our foxes, our scent won't do anything to them, go ahead, grab one." I picked up a roly-poly little guy with white on his nose and he smuggled into my breast.

"See, he loves you, you're of him and he's of you. They're the babies of our representative foxes, so they're kind of like our offspring," he laughed.

I was in my glory watching the little fox tykes bumble about, picking them up and caressing them. Who I really needed to be concerned with though was their mother, my counterpart. I approached her slowly and she set her intent eyes upon me.

I made it to sitting down beside her and reached my hand over to pet her. Her fur was coarse but smooth; I started on the back, just small strokes. When I eventually made it up to her head, she nudged into my hand, much the way a cat does when they are enjoying the attention they are receiving.

Telepathically, she told me to take in the beauty of my surroundings. They were quite stunning; to my left were bleached cliffs with paths that led down to clear blue water. In front of me were woods that fed into a grassy plateau leading down to a white temple on a pale pink sandy beach.

"You are beautiful too," I told her. She batted her eyes at the compliment.

"I am merely a reflection of you in animal form," she responded.

"Your unity with Ronnie creates babies for us. Your connection causes reproduction, whether you are on the earth plane or this plane. Needless to say, we have lots of little ones."

Ronnie was play tussling with his fox, and it was a sight to see as their hair and fur matched.

"Merlin lives down there," she motioned with her head to the left, just above the cliffs, "oh that's exciting, he's a legend!"

"He's our friend, so he is yours. Take the time to sit down and talk to him. He's an expert in twin flame relationships and you might be able to glean some wisdom from him."

"What's that?" I said, gesturing toward the pavilion.

"Oh, it's a lot of things," replied the fox.

"It's a portal for spirits, but also for earth spirits on shamanic journeys. This is the universe they visit when channeling."

"So, when Ronnie and I are done here we can go down there and it will port us to somewhere else?"

"Yes," said the fox, preening herself. Ronnie came over, "you about ready to continue our adventure?"

"I certainly am. My fox mentioned Merlin—the Merlin—lives down there and is an expert on twin flames. Do you want to pay him a visit before we leave this place?"

"Sure, why not? We'll see what he has to say about us," he chuckled.

I bent down and hugged my fox which she responded to by pushing her body back into mine.

"It's been so nice seeing you. I'm privileged to have such a gorgeous, sweet fox representation of me."

Ronnie said goodbye to his fox with a head rub and a back scratch and we set off down the hill behind and to the left of the den to go find Merlin. We discovered him in a perfectly quaint cottage with azalea, rose of Sharon, roses and peonies all in bloom in front of it. It was sheltered by the woodland trees and almost glowed with a luminescent halo around it.

It reminded me of the halo I'd seen around Ronnie when I was on LSD. The well-lit front porch was held up by four beams of medium darkness (like the wood on rest of the house) and as I put my hand up to knock the door suddenly whipped open and there he was.

"My children! I have been expecting you. Do come in!"

He opened the door wide for us to step inside. Merlin looked to be about the age of forty, which must have been his chosen age; he had a well-tended to white beard and short white hair. Ronnie was by no means a giant at 5'10, but he seemed to tower over Merlin, who must have only been about 5'7 with a very delicate build.

"So, you want to talk to me about twin flames, eh?"

"Yes sir, I mean, how did you know sir?" Ronnie stuttered.

"Oh, there's been lots of rumblings about your return. You're a power couple, did you know that? Whenever something significant goes on in the world of twin flames, I get notice, and I got notice about you two. You're here to heal, play, and learn before Ronnie's next time on earth. Am I up to speed?" he asked.

"Sounds to be as much as we know," Ronnie spoke up.

"Well, I'm here to tell you, your relationship is exceptional. Your heart strings are tied tighter to each other's more than most pairs. You probably don't recognize it, because you're in it and have no one to compare it to. You should see the carelessness of twin flame couples these days. It's enough to make me ill. I'm not talking about what happened with you Ronnie, the suicide, that was born out of heartbreak and passion and due to your attachment to your twin.

"I mean the couples out there treating opportunities with indifference, nonchalance. Wake up! Seize the day! The other half of your soul is right in front of you! I don't understand it. But you two, you are a model couple. Always searching for the other on a subconscious level because you are so attached.

"I must confess, I was a scallywag and cheated on my twin flame during an incarnation. I can see that that's never crossed either of your minds when you're together. You are a special couple indeed. I see, I see."

His eyes fluttered shut and he looked as though he were downloading information.

"Interesting indeed!" he exclaimed.

"So, it seems you occupy a unique space in the circle of humanity's soul existence. You see, as you know, Adam and Eve were the first two human souls created. God went on to produce the rest of the human race in pairs during his "seven days," and you two, were the last two to be created. The end of the chain. The babies of the family dare I say," he chortled to himself.

"To be honest with you, I don't really know what that means in the bigger picture of things, but I'm being told it made the capacity for love in your relationship, how shall I put this, a little extra. And with that love you have the power to raise your frequency, and therefore your level, rapidly. I'm talking at a sky rocketing pace in the next life that Ronnie incarnates into, if you can make it past a few roadblocks."

"Are you able to tell me anything about how Ronnie and I connect in that lifetime? I know there were things that God said we couldn't know but any information would help ease my anxiety."

"My girl's looking ahead," said Ronnie.

"I just want to hit the ground running so we can be back connected on as conscious a level as soon as possible. I won't go a whole lifetime being without you, I won't do it."

I started to cry. Ronnie moved closer to me and held me.

"Don't worry sweetheart. We've got lots of time before I have to go, and I do, I know we'll find a way. You'll just have to be patient and persistent. Keep your eyes on the prize and you'll get through this thick skull of mine somehow."

Merlin interjected, "There will be two periods of connection, I'll tell you that. One in early childhood in the midst of severe trauma, and one in adulthood, when this trauma is being addressed. Was I supposed to tell you this? Who knows, seems harmless to me."

Merlin went on with grand hand gestures.

"When you make this deep connection in adulthood, you start skipping through and over soul levels like it was nobody's business. Has anyone explained to you the soul level system to you since you've been back?"

"No," we both said in unison, our voices melded together in an eerie but saccharine way.

"Okay, so we use an alpha-numeric system. It can be adjusted and readjusted to different frameworks, but this one is the most popular because it's the easiest to explain and understand. In your first life, born there on earth, you are a level A. You climb the levels—B, C, D etc., by achieving certain things.

"Like you can gain a level for a good deed, for example, having an elderly grandparent come live with you. Or, something like acquiring spiritual insight.

227

When Ronnie discovers his past lives with you this with you, this will bring him up—you up—many levels. You also get them for acts of bravery.

"A woman leaving her abusive husband. Ronnie, in his next life, charging his father for the abuse."

"So, when we left Virginia did we gain levels?" God poked their voice in.

"Yes, you all gained a level by leaving, but Kim you also gained a level by being in tune with your intuition when you met Ronnie. You felt something before even getting out of the car. That's worth a level to me. But I don't set the parameters.

"You do it in your pre-life planning. You observe your challenges and see how you're going to face them, giving yourself milestones to pass or fail. Kim, in your case, your challenge was, will my intuition be strong enough to tell me there's something special about Ronnie? Am I in tune with our twin flame connection? The answer was yes, so you were moved from a Z to a Z1."

Merlin stepped back in, "Z1-Z10 is the next part of the level system. Here things are more intense and you usually only gain means of climbing levels via dramatic things happening. Once you have completed Z1-Z10 you become a "Master." People come to you from different soul groups for advice and guidance, you have an area you specialize in, which I know you do, following in my footsteps. There are again, ten Master levels. Always very powerful. Like Z1-10 squared. Then comes the coveted Ascended Master status, and the alpha-numeric code for that one is through infinity. We will never stop learning and should never want to.

"But you might say 'Ascended Master' is like a graduation of sorts. It's lovely to live in leisure as I do. Free of karmic chains, here to help. Though I do wish my twin flame were with me. She's having a relatively jolly time without me though, so I can't fault her! Our relationship, despite our status, isn't even as strong as yours. I envy your bond, you little rascals."

"What levels are we now?" I asked.

"Kim, you're a Z2 and Ronnie, you're a Y. You've got some catching up to do my friend."

"It's because of the suicide I'm behind. It set back my progress and took away years we could have been growing and advancing levels together. I'll do my best in my next life to get where you are."

"Can you gain levels as a guide?" I then inquired.

"Oh yes!" Merlin answered, "but Ronnie will likely do some lateral movement before you gain more levels to even things out. It is most ideal that twin flames are at the same level together. Now do you have any other questions?"

"Can we gain levels here, the two of us together?" Ronnie chimed in.

"Excellent query! No, you cannot. Either one or both of you need to be incarnated. You don't have to be together, just there, on earth. Earth is the play yard. Anything else?"

"Not that I can think of," I said.

"Me neither," added Ronnie.

"Well, I'm glad we cleared all that up then. Now, how would you like to go somewhere romantic?"

"We'd love it!" Ronnie exclaimed.

"Go down to the portal and ask to go to the "emerald lagoon." You'll love it there. At least I do and I can't imagine how an in-love couple like you wouldn't."

"Thank you for your hospitality and wisdom sir," Ronnie stuck out his hand in gratitude. Merlin took it with both hands and pulled him closer for a hug.

"You've got a good girl here. You keep treating her right, and you'll be among the stars my boy. And you my lady," he came in for a two-armed embrace.

"I'm, so glad you stopped by. Please don't be strangers. Your story is dear to my heart, and I want you to succeed. I'm invested!"

"We're pleased to have you on our team," Ronnie said as we were passing through the door.

We followed our path, back up the hill, past the dens, through the woods, through the grassy clearing, down to the white pavilion by the pale pink beach. It really was quite a breathtaking structure, with many pillars and a domed top.

We entered and stood at its center and said, "We wish to be transported to emerald beach," and the next thing we knew we were beside a white sandy lagoon with the most sparkling, opulent, emerald waters your mind could summon.

We were encapsulated by weeping willows and Spanish moss draping itself over trees like a scarf over a woman going to a fashionable dinner. It was alight with fireflies, making it look nothing short of magical. There was a paddle boat pulled up to the small shore under the drapery of the trees.

"Wanna take a ride?" Ronnie proposed.

"I'd be honored," I replied as I moved to help him drag it into the water. And to think last night we were building a snowman!

We climbed in the boat and Ronnie took my hand. The ever-familiar grasp, no less comforting over time. I remembered the occasion he came over for Ed Sullivan. Now, having had our life reviews, I knew that he had been extremely nervous about taking my hand, especially in front of Mama and Gen, but he felt so compelled to do it he didn't want to wait until we were alone.

The air smelled like a thousand flowers mixed into one. I grazed one of the hanging willow spindles with my hand and dipped it into the calm emerald pool below us.

"So, what did you think of Merlin?" I asked.

"Eccentric guy. Very knowledgeable and good at explaining things. Seems like the type of guy who is friends with everybody, do you know what I mean?"

"Ya totally, I agree," I said, seeing his point.

"We're more exclusive," I said.

"Exactly. We're of a different sort, that's for sure. Like I'd never want to live where anyone could just pop in on me like we did on him. No thanks. Hopefully that doesn't come with being an Ascended Master. If so, less incentive to climb the ladder." Ronnie said, half-jokingly.

"It's not," God's voice resounded, which made us burst out laughing. How unexpected that the almighty was listening in on our conversation! I guess it must be true that God can be everywhere all at once.

"So do you want to sign up for the same classes?" Ronnie asked rather shyly.

"Of course!" I answered. "I wouldn't want it any other way. I'm sure we'll agree on, how many is it we have to take, two?"

"Ya, two."

"Easy peasy, it'll be fun! I'm looking forward to it. We haven't had a class together for almost ten years, can you imagine that? Back in Andrews."

"That really puts things into perspective. Doesn't it seem like yesterday to you though? Cause even though I've lived a whole other life since, it doesn't seem very long ago I was walking you down the hall to our first class together, or that I was passing you that note in study hall."

During the life reviews I got to feel Ronnie's heart nearly beating out of his chest in fear I'd say no (like I ever would have). I got to feel his hand trying to steady the pen so his nervousness didn't show in his handwriting. Ronnie was embarrassed that I was seeing and experiencing it, but it just endeared me to him further. I also got to feel his jubilation and relief when he read that I said yes.

"When you passed me that note back in study hall, I felt like I had won the lottery," he reflected.

"You know now—I'd been hoping that you'd felt that way—but you can never be too sure," I said.

"I think you would have been sure if you loved yourself a little more, because I'd given you the signs. Don't you think?"

I pondered this for a moment.

"Yes, I suppose you're right. You just seemed too good to be true to me. You were so handsome and kind—I loved you from the moment I set eyes on you from the car truthfully. You radiated an almost saintliness. I know you're not aware of it, but you did and you do. It just made me anxious I'd come up short."

"But we're two sides of the same coin, you radiate that same saintliness to me too. The first time I saw you I swear you were glowing. I felt like, on a superficial level, God had designed my perfect girl and she was standing right in front of me. Then you spoke and the sweetness came out and that sealed the deal."

As we were speaking, we left the enclave into a small lake of iridescent emerald waters that glistened rainbow when the moon hit it in just the right way. There were houses on the shore—great mansions of unique designs, each one quite different form the next.

"I guess we better be finding our home soon huh?"

"We get to design it. That'll be fun! I'm guessing tomorrow we'll sit down and figure out the layout. Now, sometimes people in the same soul group room together, so we could tack ourselves onto some of the others if they have room, or we could build our own, just you and me."

"I think you know the answer to that," I said with a laugh.

"Now what are soul groups?" God stepped in again. Always welcome of course.

"When I was creating the pairs Merlin was talking about, I was doing them in groups, or families, of different sizes. This connects you karmically to one another. With soul groups, you have to wait until every member has reached Ascended Master status to fully ascend and be one with me. Also, it is these group members who serve as your spirit guides when you're on earth. To be one's spirit guide, you have to be in their soul family.

"We tend to reincarnate with each other also, forge singular paths and connections to other groups, which is crucial. Amelia, who you met, is in your soul group. You call yourselves the "Nuts," as in actual nuts, and you each have a nut assigned to you. You and Ronnie are acorns. There are four pods in your group. I created one pair from each pod then cycled onto the next then back etc. Each group has a varying number of pods.

"However, there are nine pairs in each of your pods, and four pods, making it so there are thirty-six pairs in your group, and seventy-two individuals. It sounds like a lot, but compared to some other groups it is relatively close-knit.

"When you're trying to balance guides with who's reincarnating it's difficult because each person who is born needs to have at least two guides, so the fewer the Spirits we have over here, the heavier their case loads are."

"Are we going to get assigned?" I asked.

"Yes, I'm assuming! It's a fun thing though, because you automatically unconditionally love the person you're in charge of. You'll be starting with Ronnie, for instance, from birth which is kind of nice because you'll basically be raising him. Currently, you'll be coming into the middle of people's lives now which is a bit different."

I was a bit overwhelmed at this prospect, but I assumed I'd done it before, so I could do it again.

"Who are we going to be assigned to?"

"Kim, don't fear, you'll both be assigned to guide your mother. You are also assigned to Johanna as well."

"When do the assignments start? After you have secured an abode for yourselves, and settled into your courses, which I urge you to pick out tomorrow. Review your options tonight."

"Well, we better be getting back to the beach then," Ronnie said, paddling away. When we returned we found an encampment set up for us for the rest of the night. A big sleeping bag, a tent, pillows.

"I guess we're supposed to stay here for tonight," Ronnie surmised drawing me close and kissing my head.

When we went in the tent there was a big book at the foot of the 'bed' labeled 'courses' for us to look through and choose from. They seemed endless. After browsing for hours, we decided upon one ran by Merlin on twin flames and one ran by Betty Grable of all people—she was in our soul group—on the topic of courage.

The two Ronnie had had his eyes on. Don't forget these teachers are drawing on from a vast wealth of knowledge that supersedes their own, plus all of their lives on earth, and their time as a guide.

So, to think "what does Betty Grable know about courage?" is to think narrowly.

Plus, there was a little affidavit at the end that said we were required, as well, to take a short course on Canada since that's where Ronnie would be incarnating to. We both agreed it would likely be boring, but you had to do what you had to do.

Chapter 32

The next day was a busy one. First, we were ported to a room to sign up for our courses. It looked much like a library, with books on tall walls on all sides and sliding ladders to reach them.

We were handed documents to fill-in our choices and sign and told we would join the following day, intermittently, one course one day one the other, then a break, then so on. Twin flames course first.

"I didn't know if we'd ever see that Merlin dude ever again when we left his place," said Ronnie "now we're stuck with him for the next twelve years," he chuckled.

"He's a good man, so I'm not worried about it. If you remember, Betty Grable was in my life before Kim and we weren't the best of friends. I don't know if I should try and meet with her before the course or what I should do. Try and clear the air?"

"I think that's a great idea," God suddenly appeared in the conversation. "I'll arrange for it."

How nerve-wracking!

"Can I have Ronnie with me God?"

"Yes, of course." That took my anxiety down a bit. I had felt bullied by her in that life, so I needed the extra support.

"Now, onto designing your home. You'll be with the rest of the Nuts, your soul family, over Moonstone Isle. Lovely universe. You'll love it. You've been settling, and resettling there since the beginning of time, so you'll feel right at home. It's your 'natural habitat' so-to-say. Every life you rebuild, give yourself a fresh start, though your homes often come out looking the same as before," God laughed.

"You know what you like! So go ahead, work with your architect, design your dream home."

We agreed we wanted something 'cozy'—a one bedroom—cottage like feel to it. We wanted it to be on the water. Ronnie basically made me in charge of it because he trusted my "feminine intuition." So, I made it an all-white house with two pillars on the front porch which had two steps leading up to it. In addition to the one bedroom, I gave us a den, a living room, kitchen, and a bathroom—but no toilet since you didn't have to worry about that here.

In the backyard, I put a deck and a gazebo as it was a fairly large lot with lots of gardens for many flowers of all kinds. Inside was painted a very faint pastel pink. The ceilings were high and vaulted and there were crown moldings around their edge. We had French doors leading from the kitchen to the dining room, but it was open concept from there. We had a white four posted bed with a canopy and the comfiest white couch.

When we moved in the fridge and the cupboards were stocked with all our favorite foods and then some, though eating was just for pleasure, not for sustainability. The closets were filled to the brim with brilliant clothes, perfectly tailored to our tastes. This truly was heaven! But oh, how quickly I've forgotten my meeting with Betty Grable. I stepped back and looked at the outside sources that caused the tension between us, mainly the men behind the scenes of the movie industry pitting us against each other, like puppets on strings.

I tried to draw upon our other lifetimes where we had had positive relationships. Like in our life before that one, she was one of the Morgan sisters as well. She was closest to my age so we had 'grown up' together and got along fantastically.

God, ever intuiting my thoughts, said, "Get dressed, and you shall meet with her now." I picked out a light purple crocheted dress to wear.

"You look stunning," Ronnie encouraged. "I'll be right there with you I promise I won't let her be mean to you."

"Thanks baby," I said. "Let's just get this over with."

"It will turn out well. Trust in me," God's voice came through clear.

"Now go to your portal point. It is in your bedroom. You will find a small circle of stones between the bed and the window. Please step in it."

We stepped in and were immediately transported to a white garden bench, draped with flowers, near a clear stream running by within eye and earshot. After sitting for about two minutes, I felt someone tickle my shoulder.

"You're actually here!" I stood up and turned around.

There was Betty Grable, around the age of twenty-three.

"Come here," she motioned for me to come around the bench. I was sensing no animosity. I went around and she gave me a big long hug.

"I can't believe you made it! I'd heard you were coming and I just couldn't believe it," she kept repeating.

"Well, it's true, we're here," I said as my segway to introduce Ronnie.

"This is Ronnie, he's my twin flame. He was my son in my last life and died with me in the sink hole."

"What a scary way to have to go. I'm sorry guys. Ronnie! We of course have met many times before, but it's nice to re-meet you and see you again," She went in for a hug.

"I've missed ya, good to see you," he said. I tried to derive comfort from the comradery but was unsure.

"Kim, that's the name you're going by now right?"

"Yes," I said.

"I'm so sorry about our life as Carole and Betty. I was a petty fool. That man Darryl Zanuck set us against each other and I took the bait. I'm sincerely sorry and hope you will accept my apology. We've had so many good times together. Don't let that one life ruin them. We can be the best of friends again if you give me another chance?"

She seemed so sincere in her apology; it would have been hard and cruel to do anything other than accept.

"Of course, Sis (what I had called her in previous lives). She hugged me again, even longer and harder, and I felt the negative karma melt away.

"I heard you're thinking of taking my course on 'courage' and I'd be lying if I were to say I wasn't absolutely delighted and honored!"

"Yes, we are, we've signed up for it," I said.

"You'll love it. I think it will come in handy for Ronnie's next life. I really feel it's a perfect fit."

"We start our classes tomorrow," Ronnie said.

"I'll be looking forward to your presences' in the classroom, I think it will really shake up the dynamic! I'm so glad I got to say sorry to you Sis, I feel a huge weight off my shoulders. When I heard you'd killed yourself in forty-eight I felt guilty for the way I'd treated you, and then after my life review it was unbearable. Ahhh, what a relief! Friends again! And Ronnie, we're still good of course?"

"Yes ma'am."

"One big happy family," she gathered us for a group hug.

"I'll see you two, not tomorrow, but the next day." And with that, she was gone.

"Wow, that went well!" Ronnie exclaimed.

"Yes, it did," I said, relieved it was over.

"Was she what you were expecting?"

"No, not at all. But when I saw her, the old memories started coming back, like the pre-Betty memory feelings so it made it easier. It felt like I'd just been in a tiff with my sister, so it was easy to forgive."

"Forgiveness is a powerful thing; it frees up your karma. Not that I really know what that means," he said.

"We could have taken a course on forgiveness!" I offered.

"Nah, I think we're actually pretty good at that. That class is for people who hold grudges and can't let things go."

"True," I said, "I think we made the right choices. I want to learn everything I can about twin flames, and it can never hurt to learn about courage."

"Now what do you want to do for the rest of the day? That creek looks awful nice for swimming in if I don't say so myself."

"Are you saying you want to go swimming?" I teased.

"Just an idea I'm floating around. Get it. Floating."

He laughed. I looked and there were two blow up tires by the creek waiting for us with bathing suits on them. They were the same as before, a red polka-dot bikini and a pair of bright pink swim trunks.

"Ready to go for a ride?" Ronnie asked.

"Sure am," I said changing into my suit.

This water was crystal-clear, and at the bottom was white sand, its temperature was perfect to the body, coolly refreshing against the heat of the sun. It was a winding river through a tropical rainforest, yet the trees were parted enough where the sun could still come shining through. I wondered if it was the same sun as on earth.

"Yes, it is," God said, "We share the same suns and moons."

I wasn't sure wasn't sure what they meant by the plural usage but I let my mind pass it by. I didn't want to bothered by complicated things. I wanted to enjoy my surroundings. I mean there were monkeys in trees and leopards and panthers in the bush! But there was no threat.

Since there was no hunger here, there was no inter-species danger. All lived in harmony. I could get out of my tube, approach a leopard, and it would roll on its back for me to rub its belly—which I did! It was a royal experience.

When I started coming near it, I received the telepathic message, "You may approach," so I did.

Its fur was luxuriously soft and thick between my fingers, and made me think of Bobbsey. My big boy seemed so small in comparison to this giant creature! It yawned revealing a mouth of huge overbearing teeth, but I did not fear them. I knew he had no intention of using them on me.

"Hold on I'm coming back," I yelled to Ronnie.

"Thank you," I said to the leopard, rubbing its head. It nudged into my hand powerfully.

"My pleasure," it said in return. It got up, walked in a circle, and flounced down in a comfortable position as I walked away.

"Ronnie! It was so soft and kind. Like a giant Bobbsey—he made me miss him."

"Why don't we go visit Bobbsey, Sal and your Mama tonight? Do a little something to make her think of you?"

"Oh yes, that's a good idea. I've been wondering how Mama's been doing. It's so easy to get caught up in this wonderfulness, I can't forget about her."

"She would want you to be having the time of your life, just remember that. This is what she would want for you. Not sadness and pain. She's coming home in '81, but that's two years after Gen, so she does have some lonesome times ahead."

"You know for sure when Gen and Mama are coming home?"

"You do too, one hundred percent, you just have to concentrate on it."

"Do you know how?"

"I sure do, but you try. Try and concentrate on Gen and her future."

"Okay," I said and tried to focus on Gen.

I saw the commune deciding to move west in July of '76 to California where there was also a big Bahai community. I saw that in early, maybe March of '79, Nancy, Johanna, and Gen are driving together to Oregon with the rest of the commune. They're making another move.

They stop up in the mountains to camp out, in a remote spot, and they shoot up some heroin, but it's a bad batch. All three cross over. But Gen comes back as a boy in 1981 to the sister of Ronnie's mother. She is diabetic and not destined to live a long life, but is coming back nonetheless.

"I did it!" I said, and reiterated what I had just witnessed.

"What do you see for your Mama?"

"I see she comes home after a swift battle with lung cancer in '81. She's already starting to get sick but doesn't know it. She doesn't come back until around 2050. That seems like such a long wait to see my Mama, but at least I'll be here to greet her and will have lots of time to spend with her when she's back."

"That's very true. Let's focus on tonight though. What do you want to do?"

"Maybe have her turn on the radio to the 'and Ronnie' part of Bennie and the Jets?"

"Perfect! So, we need to work on influencing her to turn the radio on to the correct station at the correct time. Sounds harder than it is. Let's look into the future of these DJ lists. Alright, perfect. This one, WGEO, is going to be playing that part at 7:43 and 54 seconds. Next step is we've got to subtly encourage your Mama to turn on the radio at that moment. That's the plan. Til' then, how's about getting out of this tropical paradise and going home?"

We were instantly dry and our hair, instantly back in style—one of the many conveniences of the afterlife—and we got changed to leave. We ported back to the little circle in our room.

"We'll want to get there in good enough time to really get on her wavelength so I'd say about 7:15 her time."

As it rolled around, back to the circle we went to go to Mama's house. It worked like a charm! There we were in the living room by the TV, perhaps because of the antennae, I'm not sure. Then we got to following mama around. Fusing your energy is kind of like making a smore. There's a lot of melding going on. Melding without intruding. Intruding burns.

You don't want to intrude on a person's energy field and effect their autonomy. That would be going against the clause of freewill. You just want to direct their attention. Think of how when you rub a balloon on the carpet it makes the hair on your arm stand up when brought near.

The connection between the hair and the balloon are like the energy fields of the spirit and the living person. Getting that particular distance—to make the hair stand up—between the balloon and the hair isn't as easy as one might think.

It was a good thing we came at 7:15 because 7:42 came quickly and I wasn't sure if I'd mastered connecting our fields properly or not. Then came the intent. You had to get her to think of you, then pass on the intent of going over to the radio and setting it to 252.1. It was a task. So, I hovered. She started thinking of us at 7:35, and was crying at 7:36.

"God, what did you do with my kids?" she said aloud.

It was extremely hard to there and bear witness to her pain without being able to physically or verbally comfort her. The moment was coming so I battened down and focused: "go to the radio, dial in 252.1," and sure enough she wandered over and turned it on and stared tuning.

"Oh, Candy and Ronnie have you seen them yet? Oh, but they're so spaced out." She let out a noise that was half laugh half sob. She'd gotten the clue! Success! She remembered how much we loved the song, and how it came on just when he was about to sing Ronnie's name.

"We'll learn more tricks," Ronnie said, seeing how pleased I was with our achievement.

"I'll take this as a sign that you and baby boy are alright in heaven because that's the only place I can think you to be," again, she spoke out loud.

I wanted to let her know I heard her. I quickly went for the radio and used all my core power touching it with all my intention of increasing its volume. I could feel energy draining out of me like sap from a tree on a spring day. But then it came, the surge. The volume blasted and Mama nearly jumped out of her skin.

"You heard me did you pretty girl? I know that was you and that was your way of telling me you're okay like I said I hoped you were."

I started to cry because I was so happy Mama knew we had communicated. It helped me remember we are in a "goodnight" not "goodbye" phase and that I'll be waiting to greet her as soon as she comes through the light.

"We did what we came here to do," Ronnie said.

"Yes, we did," I agreed.

"I want to see Bobbsey," I said.

I moved into my old room, to find him on my bed. He was all curled up in a touching and innocent way. I stroked him and he stretched in his sleep.

"He can feel you," Ronnie informed me.

"Animals have that extra sense that humans don't. Especially cats."

"Bobbsey, you're my special man. I love my handsome boy," I said, and he curled his toes. He was adorable. I wished it were as easy with Mama. At least I got through to her somehow.

"I rushed back to the living room to be in her presence, but she was starting her evening routine now to get ready for bed. Still, I just wanted to be around her for it. She washed her face, got changed into some lounge clothes, and went and put on the TV. Suddenly Ronnie said, "my mom's not coming home until 2017, and I'll be reincarnated by then."

"Maybe, you'll find her as Morgan?"

"Well, first off, I'm not sure if I care to, and second of all, how'd you propose that I do that?" "I don't know...If you and I are connected, I could feed you information that would lead you to her?"

"It's so totally different than with your Mama. I don't even know what I'd be looking for with the interaction, if there ever were one. There was never that foundation of unconditional love like you and your mother have, so it's not the same."

"Pamela is in your soul group, Sybil is not," God suddenly interjected.

"You're dealing with two different brands of karma. Interfamilial and extrafamilial."

"God sure is funny, you never know when they're going to stop in," I said. But they weren't finished yet.

"Before starting your courses, you will learn about you're your soul families, and meet some of yours. Nothing better than a union of souls cut from the same cloth. It will be a joyful experience. Pencil it in for your morning. Goodnight for now."

"Goodnight God," Ronnie and I both said at the same time and again burst out laughing.

"Like, what is this?" I said.

"What is happening? One day I'm sleeping in a van with my little boy, the next I'm back with my old Ronnie conversing with God? What is happening here? Absurdity!" (That was a word I'd picked up from Mama). He couldn't stop laughing either.

"I know. This shit's crazy. I mean a week ago, I was a three-year-old bombing around the commune on a trike. Now I'm sixteen again and we're invisible in your Mama's house. It's absolutely unreal. Unreal, crazy ass stuff.

But most of it's good. I get to be with you. So long as I get to be with you, it's good."

"I mean, I pet and conversed with a leopard today! Who can say they've done that."

"Well, no one on this side for sure," he said, referring to the earthly plane.

Mama was now sitting down with some tea to watch TV before bed.

"Are you just about ready to leave?" Ronnie asked looking weary.

"Yes, I'm ready. I'm suddenly extremely tired. Maybe we should get going."

"I guess we should go back to where we came from, over by the TV," I gave Mama a hug and kiss, knowing she couldn't feel it, and went over with Ronnie to where the antenna was sort of in our way.

He said, "We want to go home," and just like that, we were back in our room in the circle of crystals.

"At least the transportation is quick and painless," he commented.

"Do you want a glass of wine before bed?"

"Sure!"

"Any particular kind?"

"No, surprise me." I heard Ronnie uncork it as I came from the bedroom.

"How about strawberry?" he offered.

"Oh, that sounds lovely. Let's have it on the back deck."

So, we did. All the sounds of summertime were in the air, but none of the pests. The slight breeze smelled of honey. I couldn't have been any more comfortable. When we were finished, we raced to bed but Ronnie won. We slept with nothing on and it felt so wonderful to have his body up against mine.

When he held me, I always felt like I belonged in that moment. We were sixteen in body, but adult in mind, so I was mature enough to appreciate the perfection of my reality.

"Rise and shine. It's time to get ready to meet your soul family. Some background information before you do. Just like people are either sun (male), like you Ronnie and moon (female) like you Kim, and the two of you constitute one whole twin flame relationship, your group as a whole also has a soulmate group.

"Your group is the moon, so you bring the female energy into the dynamic. A majority of your members are female gendered, as in body, as a result. This is not to be confused with energy. You can have a female sun, the masculine energy, and of those you have plenty, naturally, as a result of having a higher number of female gendered members.

"Gender is the outward expression of the soul. In short, it's whether you come across as a boy or a girl—man or woman. Energy is the soul's makeup: it's strengths and weaknesses, it's general aura. Your group, the Nuts, is made up of two types of twin flames, and so is your sister group. I say sister group because it's an example of a female sun, as they are gendered female.

"Both groups have mixed gendered pairs: male/female, and female/female however. Other soul groups may have mixed with all male/male, or like you and your sister group, female/female, though never male/male *and* female/female within the same group as they are either gendered one way or the other.

"Regardless of gender, suns and moons are properly balanced within. Each group varies in size and number of pods, though you are always the same as your twin flame group. When I created you and you were gathered into your soul families, I asked you to group yourselves together for organizational purposes. Very unspecific instructions, I know. I intended it to be so."

God chuckled at themselves.

"Some chose thirteen pods—the highest number—one group chose not to divide at all! Defiant little toads. The Nuts and the Notes, you and your sister group, chose four. I believe you already know this, from Merlin, but your soul group has seventy-two members, or, thirty-six pairs. Of those seventy-two, thirty-two are currently here on the other side and responsible for guiding those incarnated in their day-to-day lives.

"To make this possible, each Nut is assigned two to four incarnated individuals. They may play a stronger role in the life of some they are accountable for than others, but since the number of incarnated outnumber the un-incarnated, this is the way it has to be. How does all that sound? Any questions?"

"So there are no groups with male/male *and* female/female pairs in it?" I double checked.

"That is correct."

"I think I understand."

"Me too," said Ronnie, giving the first indication that he was awake and listening.

"Our group is the moon half of a female/female pair, is that right God?"

"Yes Ronnie, you've caught on quickly."

"And because of this, we have a lot more girls in our group—not moons, I mean female gendered spirits because there are exactly thirty-six moons and thirty-six suns?"

"Also right! Atta boy!"

"Gender and energy aren't technically connected, which might confuse some people, but I picked up on it," Ronnie said proudly.

"There's going to be a little bit of changing of the guards in about a decade to two decades. Around when you return Ronnie. Many who you will be meeting at the party will be reincarnating and others on the earthly plane will be trickling back. Kim, you will be a constant during all this change. Keep that in mind."

"Okay God, I will."

"Keep that in mind,"—I didn't really know exactly what they meant by that, but I would be aware of it.

I got up and changed into a light blue dress of lace that came right above the kneecap. It had a tapered waist and thin straps. There was a pair of white moccasins in the closet that matched perfectly and I believe they were intended to go with the outfit which I slipped into.

Ronnie put on a pair of gray shorts and a pale pink button down short sleeved shirt. He added a pink tie that had a darker shade in it and that matched his shirt.

"How do I look?" he asked, "be honest."

"Adorable!"

"What about me?"

"Like a fairy princess."

"Well, it sounds like we're ready to rock and roll then."

"The party is ready when you are," God announced.

"Perfect timing, let's get this show on the road then," Ronnie said. And we stepped into our circle.

Chapter 33

When we opened our eyes, we were in a lovely hilly garden landscape, with trees and flowers and shrubbery abound.

"Will you take my hand? I'm nervous," I asked Ronnie.

"Of course, baby girl. Don't be scared though, these people love you. Not just like, love. They are you. We are them. Since the beginning of time. This is a happy space, trust me."

The first person I saw was my old friend Sasha from my life in the 1500s. She had been my very best companion, and good to Ronnie too. She had been around as we grew up together. The memories came flooding back upon sight.

"Sasha, Sasha!" I flagged her down. She came bounding over. Looking to be about twenty-four, she had shoulder length brunette hair, curled perfectly, and the most attractive face that resembled Mama's.

"You're back I can't believe it! I've been here for just over a decade now and I'm still adjusting to the loveliness of it. I've missed you. And you James! Or Ronnie is it now. You're looking well my boy. It's so refreshing to see you together again.

"I guess the last time was when I was born as Vivien. I came home in '68. That was a life full of highs and lows. I found fame and glory, but I also suffered mentally, from manic-depression. But I'm sure you two can learn all about that if you care to."

And I did. Because I cared to, all the information came at me like a wave, and I downloaded her life in one fell swoop. I was able to see and feel her struggles, like a life review in fast forward.

"We sure do," Ronnie said, who'd obviously just had the same experience, kissing her cheek.

"Let me take you to meet some of the others. You'll remember them as you see them," she offered. "I'm nervous Sasha, what if they don't like me?"

I asked, heart lightly thudding.

"Who wouldn't like you? You're a sweetheart. Look, here's Tara right now. She was your sister when Ronnie was Pip and you were Mary during the Revolutionary War. Tara! Over here!"

With the snap of a finger, Tara was beside us. She was around thirty, had long brown hair down her back, dark brown eyes and a face full of wonder.

"Mary, Pip, you're back!" She embraced me and then Ronnie.

"I've missed you both so much. We've not been able to coordinate in-between lives for quite a few now. I'm so happy to see you. I'm sorry to see how you had to go—that must have been scary—but hey, you made it! You're home with us now. Do you know when you're leaving next?"

"I'm not leaving until 2078," I said.

"But I'm leaving in 1986," Ronnie added.

"Oh, that's why you had to come home. At least God's giving you a break between. I'm going back as a girl in November. One of my endings is really bad. I hope things don't end up in that direction."

Suddenly, I saw a despicable murder play out in front of me like a haunting pantomime. Georgia: a kidnap, a rape, a gunshot, a fire, an almond grove. A man she was dating on and off coordinating it all to get rid of her. I tried to shake the image off and focus on the conversation.

Still, I wondered at the horrors of the earth, and God's voice weighed in, "Free will my child. People get drunk with power and do unthinkable things, like your father. Evil gets its tentacles around them, and they act in ways that are insane to the good at heart. You have never lost your purity so you will never be able to comprehend these heinous acts. Consider that a blessing."

"What classes are you two taking?" Tara asked, putting on a brave face to her potential fate.

"Twin Flames and courage," I said.

"No way! I'm in the courage class. You're going to love it, it's great. Oh, I'm so excited you both are joining. I only wish we had more time together in it. I probably should be in the twin flames course, but it's not as fun doing it alone, and as you know Ronnie, my twin is your sister Glenda. My other class is one on empathy. I didn't need it really, I just thought it would be interesting.

"Courage is my favorite though, and it's going to be even better with you two there. Right now, there's only seven of us, about half the size of my other course. It's nice though having the smaller class; makes for a more intimate setting. Grable's a pretty good teacher. I like her at least. Not to switch topics, but Pip, can I give you one more hug?"

"Of course," Ronnie said. "It's so good to see you. When they took you from the house, I thought it was the last."

"Well, you wouldn't see me again in that life, you were right insofar as that."

"I saw in my life review what happened to you and Elton,"—when she said 'Elton' it immediately flashed in my mind from my review that Elton was Gen—it broke my heart.

She was referring to when we lived in Ohio Virginia, raised as a family of six children. Pip and Elton, my brothers, were the youngest and all the rest of us were girls. I was the eldest. Pip and Elton were taken by the Redcoats for ransom while Pa was away on war business. Things ended up going awry and the two of them were taken out into the woods and shot execution style.

They were only twelve and thirteen. Pip looked almost identical to Ronnie, my baby, and at his death was like a projection of what my boy would have looked like if he'd lived another nine years.

"Mary, and I couldn't eat or sleep for the longest time we were so worried about you."

Tara was still living at home with Ronnie/Pip at the time, but I lived just down the road since I was eight years older and was already married. Therefore, I wasn't there to witness the abduction that Tara had.

"I'll just never forget them dragging you out, and you crying—oh God it was treacherous. You let out this wail that's ingrained in my soul I swear. My baby brother."

She had been five years older.

"I just can't believe we're back together again. Albeit for a short time."

Her eyes welled up with tears; she blinked and they fell.

"Aw, well I've missed you too, and we can do lots of hanging out between now and November to make up for lost time."

"Okay it's a deal. Now don't let me monopolize your time, you've got lots of other members to see."

I thought it was interesting that she used the word 'members' like our family were a club. We were meeting our soul blood.

As the discussions went on, it became clear that being one of us was an exclusive thing. We were proud of our status as Nuts. As previously mentioned, each pair in each pod had a nut that correlated to them. There were nine different types of nuts and nine pairs per pod, so no repeats. For example, we are acorns in pod A and there is a pair in B, C and D that are also acorns. Same with beechnut, hazelnut, pecans, etc.

What did it all mean? Nothing really. God just told us to get organized in the best way we knew how, so it was a means to identify ourselves. I was a Pod A, acorn, senior moon, fox. Oh, that's right, I haven't explained what 'senior' means to you. It is very important, in my eyes at least. God created the population in two waves.

Just like Adam and Eve, though I know it's a parable. It gets at the idea of how creation went down. So, God created his first wave of human beings, which would include Adam, who I'm naming the "seniors," and one by one, they took us aside and questioned us on our ideal mate while getting a spiritual blueprint of us so that our partner could be the complete complement to us. Now there are different ways to be complementary.

You can be the exact same, or you can be opposite and balance each other out. Indeed, it is most often an admixture of the two that creates the perfect match. This process is the taking of Adam's rib so-to-say from him; it is the creation of the twin flame. They are the juniors, made of their seniors. So that automatically makes Ronnie a Pod A, acorn, *junior*, *sun*, fox. The juniors were the second wave of God's creation.

The junior may incarnate as older than the senior, there's no rule against that, though for Ronnie and me, that was never more than a few years, like two to three, during our lives. We could have had it where he was my grandfather! But that would have just felt unnatural for our dynamic. However, some more flexible pairs make these broad moves, as they find them to be valuable learning experiences.

It's all in preference. Learn your lessons in a way that feels authentic to you and your twin. Now, where were we before I went all didactic on you? (You guessed it, Mama's word). Oh yes, I had just met Tara and was proceeding with the others. As we met them, one on one, a deluge of memories came back to me. Every moment I'd spent with that person came rushing at me as they hugged me, or more formally, shook my hand.

I downloaded my entire relationship with them in a matter of seconds, settling on a cumulative feeling about them in the end. None of them were bad. I had loving relationships with everyone in my group, but I was closer to some.

We'd had more lives together, we'd worked side by side as guides more intensely, or were simply more compatible.

All were very welcoming, all warm familiar faces. It's a strange feeling remembering someone all at once, but exhilarating in a sense as you are making that connection. Humans were made to be social creatures so these connections were positive things. Their involvement is often instrumental in one gaining a level.

We went home and went to bed, preparing to start class the next day. Merlin's class had sixteen people in it including us, surprisingly, not all were twin flame pairs. Some were there independently. This made me fearful for their relationship, but I didn't want to say so. When we arrived the first thing Merlin had us do was write down our happiest memory and lowest point.

What a difficult question! There were so many to choose from. For my lowest point I chose being raped in front of Ronnie by Greg. As twin flames I felt like we were ripped apart, or we were being attempted to be ripped apart. It didn't work in the way he planned, but it worked in Greg's favor nonetheless.

For my highest point, I picked our wedding day in 1552, for it made official what was already a union of the hearts. It was a beautiful ceremony outside in the gardens in the sunshine. Magnolia all in bloom. The air was fragrant with them. There were about forty people attending, all of our closest friends and family and I was so happy I was going to get to share the joy of our special day with them.

My dress was perfect. It had short sleeves attached to the bodice that had lace and fine bead work on it if you looked up closely. The rest of it was simple with some lace around the neckline which fell just above my breasts. In the front, the first layer of the bottom was cinched up with a faux white flower off to my left side. My father in that life was a kind and gentle man, and he walked me down the aisle.

I'll never forget seeing Ronnie with the biggest smile on his face I'd ever seen. We repeated back the minister's request that we love, honor and obey the other partner in sickness and in health. As I did, I remember it as being as though in a dream I was so elated to be promising myself to someone I considered so noble and handsome, so humble and faithful.

I'd been in love with him for so many years—since we were introduced as children—I knew no different, but I knew there was different, knew enough that I would love, cherish, honor and obey effortlessly and he I. I'd heard of marriages just for business purposes, and I suppose mine was to an extent, to keep the family rank up, but these other marriages I'd heard of were void of even friendship.

I suppose that was the most amazing part of it all—I got to marry my very best friend in the world. They'd been bringing us together since we were three, and we had our first kiss in the snow at age eleven. Now at fifteen, our affection for each other was impenetrable and overflowing. I couldn't believe after today I'd get to spend all my time with him in the same home.

How glorious! He looked just like Ronnie except with a little more sand and a little less strawberry in the hair. Both of our families had money, but mine had a little more, so technically, he was marrying up. He was a baron and his family owned two estates, one of which they gave to us. It was northwest of where we were from and with similar proximity to the ocean for riding distance that I was used to.

I would ride my horse Marvel there who Ronnie/James gave me for my fifteenth birthday, (also a very happy moment), who, with the insight I had now, I was able to see was Bobbsey! How funny that history really does repeat itself. I know he didn't give me Bobbsey for my birthday, but on both occasions, he provided me with my special animal companion.

Whenever there was a storm, I'd go down to the stable to be with him, as he got upset at the thunder. Just like Bobbsey would go under the bed, except there was no bed to run under. Poor fellow—he got so spooked. But my presence calmed him so I stayed the duration. James/Ronnie was always supportive when I did things like this; such as getting myself soaked and muddy in the middle of the night.

He always validated my feelings, and never made me feel stupid over any decision I made. Ronnie, to this day, has never made me feel inadequate, which I think has been key to our relationship's success. I hope he could and would say the same thing about me. Within the first year we had a baby boy. We were a picturesque family.

We didn't have to worry about money, the only people who came around us were friends, and we had plenty of good ones, for example, Sasha. She was my childhood friend who around the same time married her betrothed. They were lucky to be in love too, in fact they were twin flames as well, so the energy when the four of us together was high because of all the compatibility in the air—with us all being from the same soul group and being two sets.

When our son got old enough, we'd go out chasing fireflies, and feed the ducks at the back pond. Those were joyful days. We had a nanny, though she didn't do much, so when I wanted to go out riding, I'd fetch her and ask her to take over our duties. Or if James/Ronnie and I wanted a romantic dinner alone, she would handle them.

Otherwise, it was all me raising Stephen, with James/Ronnie to help; and a good father he was. He was so attentive to their safety and in tuned to their needs I never felt insecure leaving him in his charge. On certain occasions we'd get all dressed up and throw ourselves a country ball, and people would flock to us. There would be music and dancing and kissing in our not so humble home.

I enjoyed being hostess to such merriment. When Stephen was nine, I was out traversing the countryside and someone let their mad hunting dog off their lead and it began to try to attack Marvel. He kicked back on his haunches and knocked me off. There was an immediate searing pain in my lower back. I was able to move my legs, thank God, but the pain was excruciating.

The hunter came along grabbing the snarling dog, mumbling a half apology and dragged it away. As Marvel finally came back around, I found that the pain shot down through both my legs, despite their mobility. I managed to get back on him and ride home, whereupon my arrival I threw up from the pain.

James/Ronnie laid me out, got some extra blankets to support under my back, and sat with me stroking my forehead. I remember him saying, "when you hurt, I hurt," which now makes sense understanding how twin flames are connected.

I was never able to ride again, which left me depressed as it was my favorite pastime, and I missed being able to bond with Marvel in that way. I made sure James/Ronnie rode him though so he didn't feel like a lost cause. Things got more difficult to enjoy after that, as the pain turned chronic.

I even called the witch doctor who gave me a plaster and a tea to drink. It just burned my pale skin an angry red and made me violently ill. I felt like I was letting James/Ronnie down, though he assured me I wasn't. So, I tried my best to keep going on as though I weren't in pain. Directly after one of our country summer soirees I fell ill—high fever, hard to breathe, vomiting, diarrhea.

I couldn't keep anything in me and my temperature soared. I knew I was dying and all I wanted was to be held by my one true love. And I was. As I faded out of consciousness I was in his arms. It was a sad life to lose, although the last part of it was spent in pain. Our wedding day, though, was truly the happiest day of all my lives. That I could think of at least. And there were many happy times, don't get me wrong. Everything just seemed to align then.

When it came to sharing, I couldn't believe Ronnie picked the same two times as I did! When asked why it was our lowest point, we agreed it was the helplessness involved in the situation that made it so awful.

"You were helpless in the life Ronnie's future father had him murdered, why was that not your lowest point?" Merlin pushed.

"Innocence lost," I offered. "It was the combination of our helplessness and our innocence being lost that made it so terrible."

"Very good," Merlin praised.

"Excellent insight, that's what I was looking for." None of the other pairs that were in the course picked the same experiences like Ronnie and I did, so I felt proud of our "oneness."

After class Merlin pulled us aside, "You know it's magical that you picked the same experiences. Your connection is extra special, I see it, God has big plans for you. Don't take for granted the divine nature of your relationship; God fused you together a little extra. Yes, I do think so. And it shows."

"We know there's something special about us Mr. Merlin, we won't squander it," Ronnie responded.

"Yes, I agree," I said.

"I knew it when were alive, and now I just know it for sure."

"Ah, so you sensed it on the earthly plane as well."

"Yes sir. We never argued, it was always too good to be true. I know it's not like that for all twin flames, but I think we are always putting ourselves in each other's shoes and that empathy helped shape us. We vowed to always consider the others' position before incarnating the first time and it worked pretty well for us. Except in the life of Ronnie Tisdale, it wasn't effective enough to prevent the suicide because of all the crossed wires, but other than that it has proven helpful."

"You have a naturally easy compatibility, but you've also worked hard at maintaining your relationship. You've put the effort into resolving things between lives, never letting any negative karma build up. You will be rewarded for the meticulous maintenance of your union. It won't be until the life after Ronnie's next—Kim, you'll be born in 2078 and you will give birth to Ronnie in 2099. You will live a blissful life together as mother and son, able to focus on earthly joys instead of trials and tribulations that so often come along with incarnation.

"Your names will be Mia and Jimmy Stuart—no relation to the actor who will always be remembered at Christmastime. Mia, you will be born on Staten Island to the same mother you had in your last life. Both your parents are doctors. Your father is a neurologist and your mother is a psychiatrist. Your father is a Nut too; he's currently incarnated. Feel free to take a peek at him whenever. We call him "Doc".

"Anyhow, when you're fourteen, your parents' divorce, and you and your sister—who is also a Nut and currently incarnated—move to Toronto with your mother for her to take a job there. When your sister gets pregnant, it makes you want to have a baby too, and you stop taking your birth control. This is successful and within three months you are with child. The end of 2098. You end up having the baby one year after your sister, Virginia (who you call "Gin").

"Flash forward two and a half years, and Gin takes a job in Nova Scotia— she's in the environmental field—and Mia, you decide to follow her. Around this same time, Ronnie, little Jimmy, starts talking about being a fighter pilot in Japan and living in a van with "Mama." As a left-wing psychiatrist, your mother is into past life research with her practice, as is your father, so naturally they explore these conversations as memories with Jim.

"He reveals much, and is considered a hero in his grandfather's old neurology department, and others bothering to study past lives as a valid facet of existence. By three, Mia, you have Jimmy playing the piano, and by four, the drums! You've immersed the boy! And it pays off. He becomes a gifted and soulful piano player, and a unique beat keeping accompanist because you put these tools in front of him.

"And sing, boy can he sing! Just like little Ronnie, Jim can hit the notes long and hard. He becomes a local celebrity of sorts, but you don't want it to go any further. When he is, in 2106, you have another child via insemination with your gay friend. He is another redhead, and his soul is the mother of Ronnie from his next life (or the life before the one I am discussing).

"His name is Morgan and he's a frustrated tot, and you both work with him to help him keep his cool. Jimmy is homeschooled with Max, his cousin, and Mia, you do the teaching.

"They both attend music school; Max plays the guitar. Thankfully your parents are able to support your lifestyle. You do some hair and voiceovers on the side, but not enough to sustain yourself to the extent of the lifestyle you prefer. In 2108 you get pregnant again, a third time, via insemination through a different, anonymous donor father.

"This child is dark and looks nothing in coloring like you or their brothers. Jimmy is like a little father and husband, attending to your every need and need of the little ones. In 2108 the music school puts on a show and Jimmy is given a solo song where he plays 'Easy Like Sunday Morning' on the piano and sings it while Max accompanies him on the guitar.

"Before he begins, he says 'I dedicate this song to my mama, Mia Stuart' and he changes the lyrics in the middle to say 'I want to be free, just me'—(adding) 'me and my mama'—and gets a standing ovation. It's very reflective of his performance as little Ronnie, except he's slightly older of course.

"Because of this, he ends up singing the national anthem at an international curling tournament and some jingles on the radio via Mia's work. In 2112, Gin's job transfers her down to Maine, and there's no way they can split up your boys, they're closer than brothers, so you follow her again. Since you and Gin have dual citizenship already, it makes the move a bit easier than it would if not.

"I forgot to mention, Jimmy is a gifted pitcher in baseball. He has his eyes set on a competitive team right before you announce you're moving so he takes it a bit hard. You explain to him how many more opportunities there are for ball players in the US compared to Canada, so he comes around.

"Some people judge your relationship with Jimmy, saying it's too close, that it's 'odd' for a boy his age to be so attached to his mother, but that bothers neither of you any. Jimmy makes new friends with his new homeschool group and his new music school easily, but his little friends end up teasing him about his relationship with you.

"One time Morgan overhears one of Jimmy's friends calling him a 'Mama's boy' and like a bat out of hell comes to beat him up—despite his tender age! It is comical, but also a tipping point to where you know you have to channel his energies somewhere productive.

"He is goalie already for the local hockey team, but you sign him up for kickboxing to help direct his anger. Patrick is a docile baby, sleeping through

254

the nights—not refusing to nurse like Morgan or obsessive like Jimmy—it is almost easy to forget about him.

"You, Mia, are bisexual, leaning actually to prefer women over men and by age thirty-five you still haven't been in a long-term relationship. Then along comes Rosy Agelhed. You start dating and it is the beginning of a twelve year on again off again 'thing'.

"She's a fellow hairstylist you meet at a convention in Kennebunk Port. Mia's beauty is untouchable, flawless. Rosy has beauty too, but in a raw sense. You have to take two glances to see her beauty, whereas with Mia, for your eyes merely graze past her is enough to catch her exquisiteness. Jim is a writer and gets his first book published at age twenty-three.

"As soon as he is done college—which he gets into full scholarship with his baseball skills—he writes, and it turns into a bestseller. Morgan goes on to be a police officer, and then is promoted to detective, and Patrick, a high school physical education teacher and football coach. Jimmy just writes. He has a mastery in English, and that is good enough for him.

"He writes of past lives; their adventures and misadventures. People love his writing! He is so eloquent but to the point. A talented communicator indeed. Basically, Jim and Mia live out their lives together until Jimmy gets sick in 2154. The cancer prognosis turns out to be terminal and Mia, you have to be by his side to help him transition into the light.

"You live another ten years without him, which feel excruciatingly long. When you get the news that you have breast cancer, you almost celebrate because you have faith that you'll be seeing Jimmy soon. You die a peaceful death, knowing the two boys have each other. And that's how your story ends. It's full of rewards though, do you see?"

"Yes, I see, thank God for those. How can you see what's going to happen so far away?" I asked.

"It was one of your lives set in stone, rather than one on a whim, like little Ronnie, so I was able to glean more information on it than some. Gifts were built into it though, due to Karma deserved from your last life."

"What do you mean 'set in stone'?"

"Well, since this is a reward life, you set it up many lives ago as a goal life for yourself and your twin. It means that other lives must work around it."

"Wow, I can't believe I don't come back until 2078! Things will be so different by then."

"Time will fly my sweet child. When you are a guide for Ronnie, you'll be totally enveloped in helping him and time will lose all meaning."

"I hope so, because a whole lifetime is a long time to be away from him."

"Yes, his exit point is not yet determined. But you won't be apart while he is there. Remember, you will connect in unforeseen ways, trust me. You'll be in love with each other, although in Spirit and embodied. That will be your biggest struggle relationship wise.

"You will make it work though, you dynamic duo you! It will be a love story in and of itself. Also, once you are Ascended Master, you have no obligation to continue to reincarnate, and if things stay on track, you'll be one by the time he is thirty-two. Going back as Jim and Mia is just a treat. So, you can stay with me indefinitely on this side if you so choose after that life. How exciting!"

"I wish that were now," I said. "You can't skip the hard parts, that's what brings the good. It will be worth it. You two have been chosen to fight this particular brand of evil because God thinks you're up for the task. It's not easy, but if you beat it, you'll be rewarded bountifully, I promise. That's what Jim and Mia are. Rewards for a life of fighting evil."

"I'm up for the task," Ronnie spoke, giving the first indication he'd been listening.

"I know you are. However, remember that feeling you had when Kim was being raped by Greg?"

"How could I ever forget," Ronnie replied.

"Kim is going to experience this tenfold when it comes to your next life with your father. She will see, hear, feel your pain, but be able to stop nothing. It will take great strength to continue to guide you through the deviance and violence and not just cower away."

"I will never abandon my twin," I declared, and meant it. "I believe you," God said.

"I second that," Ronnie said. "And I believe you too," God reassured.

"You two are quite the pair, and when I created you last, I created an extra special bond. The runts of the litter would need each other."

They mused.

"Merlin does twin flame work, but there's plenty to be done in the universes and that seems to be the mission of your souls, perhaps to teach others to be as you are: so in synch, so in love."

"Hey—if we can pass it on, consider it done. There's nothing that gets me more excited than sharing my love with the world."

"Well, that's your destiny, so your future jives with you!"

God was funny. I liked their sense of humor. It made me giggle. Anyways, sharing our love with the world being our destiny was a pretty sweet one.

"I, for one, couldn't be more thrilled that that one of our soul's missions," I said.

"Couldn't be better," agreed Ronnie.

"Now, take the next twelve years and absorb as much as you can from your courses, and play and have fun together. That's what I brought you back to do! Play, have fun, be merry and bright together."

God prompted.

"We will be. I can't help it around her," Ronnie elbowed me, and at once I knew he meant it. Here you had a radar for sincerity. It was, in a sense, a bit of a nuisance, but most of the time interesting and helpful.

"Your guide orientation will be on your next day without classes," God changed the subject briefly.

"For now, explore. Explore the world around you, explore each other. Do what you wanted to do on earth but never got to. I love you both, goodbye for now."

"Well, I was always wanting to go to the coast to see the ocean but it was always so close but so far; except for that time with Nana. And I was always wanting to horseback ride."

"I was always wanting to go to the coast too. I should have taken you myself, it's my fault for letting other things get in the way."

"No faults here babe, we have the opportunity to make up for lost time so we have no time or space for regrets. I love you so much and I'm so happy I get to experience this with you."

I took his face in my hands and kissed it.

"I am too. I literally couldn't ask for anything more. Hey, off topic but do you want to visit our neighbors on the way home?" he asked.

In our vicinity were other Nuts' houses, many of them living together.

"To be honest, I just want to go home and be with you right now if that's okay. I'm a little overloaded and just need some Ronnie time to unwind."

"Of course, no pressure here. We've got plenty of time for visits so no worries there."

"Ed Sullivan is on tonight."

"Great, we can hunker down and watch the show and relax."

"Just like old times."

"Just like old times," he repeated back to me and kissed my forehead.

Courage class was the next day, and despite our loving reunion, I was intimidated by Betty, our teacher. I got dressed into a burgundy sweater and gray pleated skirt with knee socks to match.

Ronnie went more causal, with a magnificently tie-dyed pink sweatshirt and jean shorts. We uncomfortably were the last two to arrive so there was no time to adjust to the attention being put on us.

"There they are! Our new classmates. Why don't you introduce yourselves. Tell us how and where you passed in your last life and how old you were."

"Okay," Ronnie spoke up, "my name is Ronnie, I died by drowning when our vehicle fell into a sinkhole in the road in South Carolina. I was three and a half."

Then came my turn. Oh, how I felt self-conscious speaking in front of such an intimate group of people. I almost would have preferred a giant crowd!

"My story is the same as his, just that I was twenty-three. Or rather, I was twenty-three that day. It was my birthday."

"How tragic!" exclaimed Betty.

"But now you're here with us and you're going to learn. Today I'm going to read to you a quote on courage. It lists courage as having three components. I want you to pair up with someone who's not familiar with your last life, and I want you to take them through examples of when you exercised courage in these three ways at some point in your previous life.

"I'll give you a few minutes to mull it over, then pair up. I saw Tara from across the room and gestured for her to come over. Here is the quote she wrote on the big black board at the front of the class:

"Have the courage to say no. Have the courage to face the truth. Do the right thing because it is the right thing."

"For my 'no' example, I showed her my Seven Minutes in Heaven fiasco. For facing the truth, I showed her my various stages of grieving that Ronnie was gone. For doing the right thing I decided to show her me helping out Ronnie's grandma on the farm.

"I just did it because it was the right thing to do after losing her husband and grandson. It was difficult revisiting these moments, as they were so fresh.

It made me feel nostalgic for earth in a way, even for instances when courage was needed."

After class Ronnie reported, "I've been asking around for our ocean day, and apparently 'Magenta Cove' is a nice place to visit. The other spirits in our class said that we'd even be able to ride horses on it if we wanted to. What do you think for tomorrow?"

"I think that sounds like a fine plan!"

"Oh shit, aren't we supposed to meet with someone for our guide orientation?"

"That's okay, we can go after the training. Good thinking, I almost forgot about it."

The next morning about 7:45, we were awoken to a rap, rap, rapping on the front door. We both looked at each other.

"No, not this early," I said.

I could see in my mind's eye (I was getting better at using it), that it was indeed her—our trainer—and we needed to get up ASAP. Ronnie threw on the closest pair of trousers to him and a white t-shirt, and made a dash to the door.

"Hi there, it's just me, Mandy. Well, it's a good thing you're so handsome, I'll forgive you for having me wait."

I could hear her talking from the other room. I emerged from the bedroom to make my presence known.

"And look at you, even more radiant than when I saw you the other day. Just beautiful. You two make quite the lovely couple."

"Thanks," Ronnie replied drawing me close.

"We pride ourselves in that."

"God made my job easy by assigning you the same two from our group. This is good though. It will allow me to be thorough with both of them. First, we will watch a review of Pam's life, then Johanna's.

"You'll gain insight into them by seeing how they were feeling and seeing and what they were really thinking in various situations, good and bad. Similar to your personal life reviews. If you have any questions as you go along, I'll be right here."

Mandy looked about twenty-three but presented much older. Her hair was red, but real red, not of the natural sort, with big eyes and a disarming smile. She told me she'd been my guide when I was Carole, which, she said, was a challenging assignment.

She explained how after Bobby's (1922-45) and Carole's (1919-1948) lives, we didn't have anything set in stone until 1986, so to atone for my suicide as Carole, I decided to come back as Kim and learn things a little differently, though I knew my life would be short. I thought that to be rather thought-provoking. Anyhow, we got to watching Mama's study, and then Johanna's.

Then we learned how to subtly effect their thoughts from afar—like what we were doing the other night with the radio, except not having to be in their vicinity—on a small and grander scale. We learned about working with other guides—the guides of other people—to coordinate the goals of our charges that they had set out before incarnating, which was quite complicated I must say.

All in all, it felt like a mighty task, especially having to deal with Gen and Johanna's deaths in '79 since they're not from natural causes like Mama's from lung cancer.

Chapter 34

And believe it or not, those deaths came around rather quickly. I was very excited to see Gen—though obviously the circumstances were poor. Ronnie and I, along with Gen's, Nancy's and Johanna's other guides managed to maneuver them attaining bunk heroine which was step one. Then we just needed it to be only these three that used it.

They were on their way to Oregon to set up camp there in a new state. Tim had grown tired of California and figured a move north might help. Plus, it was a fresh opportunity to spread the Bahai word. When they were choosing car-pooling for the trek, this is when our true intervention was needed. We knew Johanna had purchased the heroine and would cut it with whomever she shared the ride with.

We managed to sway their thinking in the direction of Johanna and Nancy going in Gen's car, since Johanna had sold hers. So, now that that was set up, we were as good as gold. The heroine they were taking was far stronger than what they understood it to be, hence the bad batch. They stopped about thirty miles south of Oregon, in the mountains, to shoot up. Johanna went first, Nancy second, Gen third.

It was a painless death, though a bit confusing for them. Unlike when I drowned, and knew I was going to die, the three of them were not expecting to see the light and had to be coaxed into it. Gen came first, then Johanna and Nancy.

I was standing there at the end of the tunnel waiting with balloons. In their case, they came out at the pavilion, near the foxes' den by the crystal-clear water. Gen ran to me and gave me a long hard hug.

"I've missed you so much!" she exclaimed.

"I've missed you too," I said back.

"Was it that hole in the road?"

"Yes, that's what did us in."

"What I figured. I guess it's better than you having been kidnapped, but still, an awful way to go."

Johanna and Nancy were talking to Ronnie.

"Mama's going to be devastated."

"I know," Gen said, ashamed.

"She comes home in '81 from lung cancer, so just in time for you to see her before you go back. You go back in '81."

"I do? For how long?"

"Just 21 years."

"Okay, good. Another short life. What takes me then?"

"Diabetes."

"Oh, interesting. I guess we'll see how that all goes in a couple years. For now, I just want to relish in being back here."

"Do you remember it?"

"I do!" said Gen, closing her eyes and taking in a deep breath through her nose.

"I didn't really remember it," I said honestly.

"Each of us is different I guess."

"No," God interjected.

"Gen is just farther along on her path and the higher the level you are the easier such things as remembering home are."

"Very fascinating," said Gen.

"You know what God is talking about in regards to levels?" I asked.

"Yes, I vaguely remember."

"Oh wow, I hope it's like that next time for me. Having to relearn everything is frustrating, knowing you've been shown or told it multiple times before."

"I don't remember all of it, like my past lives or anything, but most of its coming back to me."

Gen. Always a step ahead!

"Well, I guess you can show me around then!" I said. She laughed.

"It's not quite like that."

"Your house! Where are you going to live?"

"I usually live with a few other Nuts, in my own separate apartment of course. Just around the corner from you. With Jackie and Amelia. That's who I room with since my twin isn't here."

"That's a pleasant pair. I'm sure you girls will have lots of fun. Ronnie and I are comfy in our little cottage. Well, I shouldn't speak for anyone but myself. I'm content. Hopefully Ronnie is too."

"You bet I am," he interjected.

"Living the dream with my lady—couldn't be happier."

"You two are always off in your own little world it makes sense you live separately. Just don't be strangers, come visit time to time. We've only got two years before I embark on my next mission."

"We'll make the most of every moment I swear. Hey, have you haven't signed up for your courses yet. Take the courage course with us," I encouraged.

"You'll love it. And it totally applies to your next life with the diabetes and all."

"Alright, I'll join that one," she conceded.

Gen was in our Canada class too, which was about as exciting as watching paint dry. She was just in time for our partner project coming up—lucky her! I mean I am grateful for the healthcare system Ronnie was incarnating into, especially considering the eating disorder he is set to battle, but the history of the place it flat out boring.

I didn't really see how me learning about Canada's past would improve my guide skills, but I rolled with the punches as it was compulsory. For the project, we got assigned 'The Edmund Fitzgerald' as our presentation, which apparently was a shipwreck. Naturally, we sought out one of the sailors to interview and asked if he'd come to speak on our day, in an attempt to make it somewhat interesting.

I'd never met a character like him. He presented at about the age 37, and was rough around the edges. He spoke funny, seemingly having retained his seaman's accent, and liked to spit a lot. He'd died that night and reveled in telling the tale. Unfortunately, when he was giving his speech, which involved a little sea ditty, Ronnie had to remove himself from the room because I can laugh silently but he can't.

He came back composed for the question period. Our teacher was a dull woman, and I could tell she was impatient with Ronnie's antics. Her clap was slow and brief at our conclusion, and I could tell we weren't going to get a very good grade, despite our innovative collaboration. Oh well! As long as we passed. I didn't think I could spend another minute in that class. Boring epitomized.

1981 came around, which mean many things. First it meant for Mama to come home. When it was time for Mama to arrive, I lingered with bated breath. I couldn't wait to see her and for her to finally know what happened to me and Ronnie.

Sadly, her demise was not swift like mine or Gen's, it was drawn out and painful from lung cancer, so death was a long-awaited reprieve although she feared it, regardless of her religious convictions. It was a sweet reunion to have Gen, myself, Bobbsey and Sal all together again in the same space, with them having come home in 78' and 80'. It was almost unreal.

"My babies, you're here. I was afraid I'd never see you again. I knew you died in that hole, I just knew it," she said to me kissing my face.

"You must have been so scared my brave girl. I always felt partially responsible for whatever happened to you because it was me you were driving home to see. I carried that burden with me until now. I can see, finally, that it was your time no matter what, and if it hadn't been that way, it would have been another, so I feel as though there was a weight lifted from my chest.

"God wanted you home and no one can interfere with their plans. Sadly, I had to suffer without you and Ronnie and my heart was broken. But hey, I need not think of that now as we stand here together, finally, again. Ronnie—you're such a handsome young man.

"A reflection of what my grandson would have grown into no doubt. And Gen. I'm glad your passing was peaceful though the pain of living without you was indeed unbearable. However, all my babies in one place now. Finally. I feel complete again," she said tearing up in the best of ways.

"It's unfortunate that Gen, that you have to go so soon. At least God coordinated it so we were able to see each other again before you embarked so I need not complain."

She embraced her in an emotion ridden hug which was returned whole heartedly by Gen whom I know felt the same way.

I was assigned to show her the ropes, as I was one of her guides. I helped her design the portion of her house she's be living in. She was sharing it with some of the fellow Nuts she met at her meet and greet, similar to mine and Ronnie's. She certainly was well loved! Everyone was so pleased to see her. She wasn't in either of our classes, and instead enrolled in ones on 'trust' and the one on 'synchronicities.'

In her life review she was able to see the signs we'd given her over time, this made her feel validated and inspired her to want to sharpen her abilities to do so in the future for others. Her Spirit animal was the swan, and I took great delight in accompanying her to their pond. I had never visited there, though it was just adjacent to the foxes' den; Ronnie came along and we made a day's adventure out of it.

As Mama bonded, we watched the sunset. It was gorgeous from the vantagepoint of where we were, with hues of pink and red, yellow and orange, fusing together like a professional work of art. As always, however, it was a comfort to return to return home to our little abode, and cuddle together as one under our sheets of silk.

The four of us (well, six if you count the cats) got much quality time in together before it was time for Gen to reincarnate that July. We had many memorable adventures below and among the stars. This time she was to be a boy, as I already have mentioned, the cousin to Ronnie—or "Morgan" as he'd be known—in his next life in 1986.

Her name was to be Matthew, or Matt, and was predestined to come home again at the age of twenty-one, and to facilitate this, would be afflicted with diabetes at the age of one and a half, like a detonator. Gen would be needed back here on the other side to help with Morgan and her father; keeping her alive long enough to be able to bring justice around—protecting her and guiding her decisions when it came time to come forward about the abuse.

Gen knew the father from their other lives in 1777 when the father was a Redcoat and he took them both hostage and killed them execution style in the woods, as well as in 1945 when he was a Japanese prison guard and they were POWs and he killed them both. It was difficult saying goodbye to her again, but knowing it wouldn't be that long until I saw her again made it easier.

"Watch out for me kid," she said, before heading out the door of our cottage, having come by to say goodbye. "Always," I called after her, and meant it. I would perpetually have her back, even if I wasn't her guide, technically speaking.

The next five years were those of sheer ecstasy. We hiked through majestic mountains and spent nights touching stars. We swam in crystal water until we were exhausted and all we could do was collapse on the white sand under the golden sun. We rode horses through enchanted forests and encountered animals of all kinds, making new friends.

Though time passed differently, it still went too fast for my liking. As 1986 came around, I was not ready to lose Ronnie, even though if everything went according to plan, I wouldn't be losing him all together for long. At age three, his father would start injecting him with needles in his sleep, in order to sexually assault him, and to protect his brain from the trauma, his spirit would dissociate and come to me.

It petrified me to think I was sending my baby—my heart, my soul—into a life to be abandoned and tortured. God assured me we were the chosen ones to defeat this pathetic evil, and there was no other way to get it done. They said if we were able to bring him to be accountable for his actions he would no longer be allowed to reincarnate as he had digressed so far from the light over a multitude of lifetimes.

The only positive Ronnie would inherit from his father would be his psychicness—though, because of his evil, his father would only see the dark, whereas Ronnie would be able to communicate with me. Poor Ronnie was equally as scared and did not want to go. What a jolt to the soul it would be separating from me into the presence of a man who had harmed him life after life.

He pleaded with God not to go, but they said he must, it was part of the karmic circle that could not be avoided. He was to be a little blonde girl with gray eyes with little brown freckles in the middle. Such a cute little thing. It was impossible for me to think of anyone being able to inflict pain on such a precious being. My being. My tot, my junior, my sun. How was I to let him go?

We'd done it so many times before, but this was the hardest by far. Thankfully, we had our next life planned after this one, where I was to be his mother. I would atone the pain. I had to cling to that. Time passes, no matter how much you want to slow it down or speed it up. It passes just the same, and our time would come.

We would be Mia and Jimmy Stuart one day on earth again and our life would be a blessed one for all the struggles we'd gone through. In the end, it would be worth it. God promised us this, and God does not break promises.

In the few days leading up to Ronnie's incarnation, we made love endlessly. We didn't let each other go, not even for a second. Both our courage class and our twin flame classes threw parties for us, which was encouraging.

They were certain that we could and would complete our mission with flying colors.

The courses had been helpful, and we did feel as though we had some tools in our belt. Nothing could tear us apart. Especially this evil man, in spite of the subconscious efforts he would put forth. I knew I had to be strong, because there would be more than one time where keeping Ronnie alive long enough to hold his father accountable was crucial.

The first would be an overdose of the drugs; a short lived but very serious scare. The next, however, was far more complicated and was going to take all my energy. It was part of why Gen had to come home. At age twelve he would develop a serious eating disorder.

Within two months he would be afraid to ingest even water for fear of gaining weight, and when he/she put anything in his body, they would feel 'dirty'—a feeling which reflected the sensation they would have after being molested by their father.

It was my job, along with Ronnie's other guides (including Gen who would join the taskforce when Ronnie/Morgan is sixteen), to navigate them away from these demons. But it would not be easy. Feeding tubes, hospitals, treatment centers. The chances of Morgan dying was 8/10. But we could do it. I know we could.

Once he/she survived and recovered from this disease and flourished into adulthood, then he/she would confront their father legally. This, again, would open up new doors to safety concerns as they would be stalked by the father and their life would again be in danger, so our vigilance would once more be required.

But by then, we would be intimately connected again. That's what I could see at least.

Our love was stronger than evil and I would dedicate my entire being to keeping them on earth to defeat his/her father. We would not let God down. If they had faith in us, we must have faith in ourselves. We would beat the odds. Our love was more than capable of it.

We did not sleep the whole night before, and the day came around like a dark menacing cloud over the sun. We lay in bed with Ronnie clinging onto me, shaking from head to toe. I stroked his head, holding him tight, and continuously showering him with kisses. But nothing could dissipate the fear of what was to come.

"What am I going to do without you?" he asked sounding like a helpless child, tears streaming down his reddened cheeks.

"You're going to make me proud, that's what you're going to do. And you're not without me. I'll be with you all along. As close as we are now, even if you don't know it, I'll still be there. You're going to survive, like I did after you died and before you were born again. I know it's going to hurt.

"It's going to be gritty and unnatural and lonely and like there's a hole in your heart that you don't understand. But you're going to make it. We're going to beat that man and you're going to come back to me again before we embark on a beautiful life together. This is a blip and you're a soldier. My soldier. We can do this baby. It's going to be okay."

"I believe you," he said, trying to gather himself.

"I just love you so much, I can't imagine a lifetime without you."

"That's why we took the twin flames class though, so you wouldn't be without me. We will connect. We will communicate, and I'll be right there by your side."

"Do you think I'll fail? We've never beaten him before."

"Ah, that's why we took our class on courage. It's going to take a lot of bravery, but no, I absolutely believe we will succeed. All the lessons with him from our other lives have come down to this one. He may have won before, but it's our destiny for you to win this time. Don't you feel it in your heart baby?"

"I do," he said with a solemn sense of hope.

"I'll do it for you. For us. For God. Because God gave me you." He kissed my hand.

We went one last time to see our foxes so Ronnie could say goodbye. He hugged his boy who promised to guide him with his animal wisdom. They nudged forehead to forehead and parted ways. We made divine love one last time on the crystal sand of the beach, and I cradled him like a baby in my arms when we were done.

It was time for us to make our way to the tower of reincarnation. It was an archaic looking building that was both tall and sprawling made of white stone and ivory. When we entered, we were greeted by a tall thin man with a kind smile and white beard.

"Welcome on this world-altering day," he said.

"You're expected in room number four. I'll be your attendant today. Let me show you the way."

The room was filled with a familiar iridescent light and had a visible blazing opening to earth on the one wall.

"How are you feeling?" he asked Ronnie.

"Scared," he replied simply.

"Understandable. I'm aware of some of the challenges that await you in this life ahead. But I'm also privy to the blessings that may come from it. God has great faith in you and even in your darkest hours will be by your side. I'm hopeful you will be able to sense that, my friend.

"You will never be alone, no matter how lonely you may feel. Only special souls are chosen to beat the odds, you should feel honored my boy," he said patting him on the back.

"I do," Ronnie responded, taking a deep breath. "I'm sorry to say it, but you're expected at 11:42, so it's time to say goodbye. Please just remember as you leave—God never wastes your pain," the man said with a heartfelt sigh.

Ronnie was crying so extensively he started hyperventilating.

"Baby, it's okay. We've been apart before, and we'll be together again. This is just a blip in time. Think of it that way. I know I keep saying that word but that's all it is. Just a blip.

"I love you so much, my darling, I'll be with you every second. I'll never let you go. Even if you can't feel me, I'll be holding you, as I am now. As we kissed our tears melded together as one holy stream.

"Okay, I'm ready to be Morgan," he said, with all the bravery he could conjure. I held his hand and lead him to the light wall.

"You won't forget about me?" he asked forlornly, looking me straight in the eye, wet with tears.

"I'm devoted solely to you,"—which was true. God had taken me off my other guide cases in order for me to be able to focus exclusively on Ronnie, or 'Morgan'."

"How could I forget about you? You're my sun, my junior, my everything. Like Mama used to always remind me: this isn't goodbye, it's goodnight."

"Alright," he said.

"This is for you, my moon."

Holding hands, he took one step into the brightness and tried to muster a smile.

"I adore you," he said, looking toward me.

"I adore you more," I whispered back; I was losing my voice from grief. As he took his second and final step, our arms were outstretched and fingers lingered until the very last moment.

"Goodnight, my love," he mouthed to me.

Our grip on each other slipped away like hurried sand in an hourglass as he dissolved into the earthly light. And with that, our new chapter began.